Praise

"[Wheeler] is among the top living writers
of Western historical novels—if not the best."
—*Tulsa World*

"The kind of writing that leaves you feeling much
smarter than a mere mortal."
—*Kirkus Reviews*

"A master of character and plot."
—*Publishers Weekly*

"A master storyteller whose many tales of
the Westward Movement . . . weave fact, fiction,
and folklore into pure entertainment."
—*Library Journal*

"No one does it better than Wheeler . . .
an extraordinary writer."
—*The Roundup Quarterly*

Yours to Keep
Withdrawn/ABCL

By Richard S. Wheeler
from Tom Doherty Associates

Aftershocks

Anything Goes

Badlands

The Buffalo Commons

Cashbox

Eclipse

The Exile

The Fields of Eden

Fool's Coach

Goldfield

Masterson

Montana Hitch

An Obituary for Major Reno

The Richest Hill on Earth

Second Lives

Sierra

Snowbound

Sun Mountain: A Comstock
Novel

Where the River Runs

SKYE'S WEST

Sun River

Bannack

The Far Tribes

Yellowstone

Bitterroot

Sundance

Wind River

Santa Fe

Rendezvous

Dark Passage

Going Home

Downriver

The Deliverance

The Fire Arrow

The Canyon of Bones

Virgin River

North Star

The Owl Hunt

The First Dance

SAM FLINT

Flint's Gift

Flint's Truth

Flint's Honor

RENDEZVOUS

A BARNABY SKYE NOVEL

Richard S. Wheeler

3 9075 05483163 8

FORGE®

A Tom Doherty Associates Book / New York

NOTE: If you purchased this book without a cover, you should be aware that this book is stolen property. It was reported as "unsold and destroyed" to the publisher, and neither the author nor the publisher has received any payment for this "stripped book."

This is a work of fiction. All of the characters, organizations, and events portrayed in this novel are either products of the author's imagination or are used fictitiously.

RENDEZVOUS

Copyright © 1997 by Richard S. Wheeler

All rights reserved.

A Forge Book
Published by Tom Doherty Associates
175 Fifth Avenue
New York, NY 10010

www.tor-forge.com

Forge® is a registered trademark of Macmillan Publishing Group, LLC.

ISBN 978-1-250-30508-4

Our books may be purchased in bulk for promotional, educational, or business use. Please contact your local bookseller or the Macmillan Corporate and Premium Sales Department at 1-800-221-7945, extension 5442, or by email at MacmillanSpecialMarkets@macmillan.com.

First Edition: December 1997
Second Mass Market Edition: February 2019

Printed in the United States of America

0 9 8 7 6 5 4 3 2 1

For Frederic Bean,
treasured friend and fine novelist

Chapter 1

The moment had come. For this moment the jack-tar Barnaby Skye had waited seven brutal years. For this moment he would risk being hanged from the nearest yardarm or being hauled back to London in irons to a life in a cage.

All that had kept him alive was the dream of this moment. Night and day, on the high seas, or anchored near a shore, he had nurtured this dream until it roared in his head. The Royal Navy knew it and had set a watch over him whenever His Majesty's Ship *Jaguar* raised land. It was so this time. They had thwarted him in the past; this time they would not.

The Royal Navy had been his warden ever since a press-gang had "recruited" him at the age of fourteen, not far from the Thames and his father's redbrick warehouse. They had snatched a lad off the cobbles of London and stuffed him into a frigate of war. They had made him a powder monkey, his task to haul casks of gunpowder from the powder safe deep in the bowels of the warship to the gunners on the decks above. And they had turned him into a bloody slave of the Crown, howling curses at his powdered and periwigged captors.

He never saw his parents or his brother or sisters again. Neither did the Royal Navy admit to his existence, or grant him a seaman's rights, or give him a hearing. He became a whisper, a rumor, an amusing secret as the lordly captains rotated command, one after another. He also became a legend, a storied villain who schemed, who defied, who spent much of his short miserable life locked in irons, who scarcely ever set foot on land—the one exception being the Kaffir wars in Africa—and would never again set foot on land if the admiralty had its say.

Now the moment had come. He needed a moonless night or deep fog and had neither, but he would take his chances. The torrents of yearning, the need for freedom overwhelmed him but did not this time erode his caution. The *Jaguar* lay alongside Fort Vancouver on the Columbia River of the Oregon country, at the farthest reach of Empire. This was simply a courtesy call, a visit to the newest outpost of the Hudson's Bay Company, and another proof of British domination of Oregon. Even now, late in the evening, the commodore and most of his officers were feasting at the board of the hospitable Dr. John McLoughlin, the post's factor, no doubt toasting not one, but two empires, one of them mercantile, both of them predatory.

The watch had been doubled and Skye had been confined to the fo'c'sle as usual. Two sharp-eyed men roamed the deck of the frigate, waiting for such as Barnaby Skye to alter the light and shadow on the moon-washed teak. They patrolled the midships, rounded the taffrail, expecting a deserter to go over the side or off the stern. But that was not where Skye waited on this moon-clad night. He lay on the bowsprit, wrapped in canvas, looking like a fat sail. Just under him, suspended from the bowsprit, was his kit, his few possessions stuffed in a waterproofed bag.

The watch circled close—this time the bloody bosun McGivers—his gaze raking everything that was in or out of order. But it wasn't his fate to see anything unusual about the bowsprit, and he passed by with a weary clop of his clogs.

The gates of the distant fort opened, spilling yellow light. The commodore was returning. Skye judged this to be the moment, now or never—go now or lie in seagoing hulks another lifetime. The watch stood fore and aft, observing the oncoming shore party, McGivers not far away. Skye edged out from under canvas, dropped onto the rigging under the bowsprit, untied his kit, and stared at the inky water that gurgled past in the night, glinting moon back at him. He heard clipped English voices. The shore party was clambering into the jolly boat.

A beautiful spirit flooded through him, something akin to ecstasy. He eased into the furious cold of the river, his bare feet first, and felt the icy blast crawl up his legs and belly and thick chest. The shock stunned him. He let himself drift downstream, treading just enough to keep his head above the surface, feeling the cold suck the strength out of him. He knew he must not swim until he was lost in the night, a hundred yards at least from those watching eyes and keen ears. His young body could barely endure the murderous cold but his spirit soared like a soul rising to heaven. He could see the officers settle in the jolly boat, see oars probe the glinting water, and then he could neither see nor hear them. He dog-paddled urgently toward the bank until he could stand, and then staggered up a mucky grade, his body numb and his soul afire, water sluicing out of his heavy winter blouse and trousers. He shook violently, unable to stay the convulsions of his body. But that was God's good earth under his naked feet, clay and grass in his toes.

He intended to penetrate deep into the interior of mysterious North America, into a wilderness scarcely known to white men, inhabited by wild savages, wild animals, and governed by wild weather. And after that, who could say? But now he walked north, because an eastbound vector would take him to the fort and under the surveillance of the watch. Shivering, he raced across croplands where the powerful Hudson's Bay Company grew its post provisions, stubbing his toes on stalks and weeds. He wanted a horse but saw none. Slowly he arced his way around the great fort, which now lay dark and silent in the night, a mausoleum of empire, and headed eastward well back from the river. After another mile or so, he paused to pull dry clothing from his kit, pleased that the oiled and waxed bag had turned the water. He wrung out his jack-tar woolens, donned his spares, and slid his wet feet into his boots. When he laced them up, he felt a surge of power: he was on land, he could walk, he was free. He pulled a sailcloth poncho over him, and trotted swiftly into the night, rejoicing, his heart tumultuous in his chest.

An odd feeling engulfed him. This was a sacred moment. Here in the deeps of a moonlit night, he tarried a moment to perform an act of emancipation. He tugged at some dead grasses, marveling at the feel of the brittle stems, and then he scooped up some of the soft soil and let it filter through his hands. This was the soil of a great continent: his soil, his grasses, his wilderness. He claimed the land, prayerfully and joyously. Henceforth he would be more than Skye, a last name spoken with contempt by the officers over him; he would be *Mister* Skye, a title the Yanks bestowed on any man here, even a commoner like himself, a mark of each person's innate dignity and worth. *Mister* Skye he would be ever more. This wilderness was his, he claimed it for the empire of his heart, and no force on earth would take it from him while he lived. The Royal Navy or Hudson's Bay might yet capture him but they would not take him alive.

They would come, of course. The Royal Navy would hunt him down, and soon. Hudson's Bay would come for him, too, and put word out among all its allied tribes. McLoughlin would hear of a wild man and felon, and not of a boy pressed off the banks of the Thames and treated as a slave. McLoughlin and all his traders would join the hunt and think of themselves as rendering a valuable service to the Crown. The prospect was daunting. So was the vast interior of this continent. So was the loneliness he faced.

Skye trotted eastward along a river road, hoping the dry clay would not record his passage. For now, distance was his sole objective. He wanted a dozen, nay a hundred, miles between himself and his pursuers. But he knew that ere long he would face new ordeals, feeding himself with nothing more than two hooks and a line, two ancient knives, and his hickory belaying pin. He had given much thought to his kit and now it would have to do: navy pea jacket and skullcap, raincoat-bedroll improvised from purloined sailcloth, a flint and striker pilfered from the galley, his razor and shaving mug, a large tin cup, some ship biscuits, tea, an awl, shoe leather, thong, fishing gear, and a small coil of manila. That was all. And even that had been hard to gather and hide in His Majesty's frigate.

He fled eastward, trotting, running, stumbling, barely pausing for breath. With the first gray of dawn he ascended massive bluffs until he was far back from the well-traveled river road, and continued onward, never stopping, his body responding to liberty even as his feet responded to the good earth. As the sun ascended on that April morning of 1826, he found himself in a vast land. An enormous snow-capped mountain vaulted upward from the south side of the river, and green slopes, mostly forested, rose from both sides of the river. He had scarcely remembered that land is rarely level. But again his limbs responded, as if they hadn't been punished by the hard night or the icy bath. Such was the rejoicing of his spirit that his stocky body knew no weariness. He danced on a ridge. He was free.

From time to time he eased back to some promontory where he could survey the shimmering river far below, and saw nothing on its banks. He was tempted to rest but

refused to do so. He toiled eastward again, aware that his
tortured passage along the bluffs would be much slower
than passage along the river road below, and that his pursuers would gain on him this day. He wished he had
stayed on the road, counting on speed to keep him hidden. But it was too late for that. He struggled through
brush and forest, up and down giant shoulders, until at
last he could go no further. He found a pine-clad promontory overlooking the Columbia and made a camp there
where he could see for miles. He gnawed some ship biscuits and then he dozed.

They came in the afternoon, a well-armed party of seamen and officers along with some leather-clad men, no
doubt Hudson's Bay guides and scouts. He couldn't make
out which of the officers were commanding this little
expedition or which of his shipmates were hunting him.
But they marched by, pausing at every ravine to probe it.
They were thorough and relentless, and no doubt cared
little whether they brought Skye back alive or dead. Even
from his aerie, he sensed their contempt for him, saw it in
their thorough, studied manhunt. Then they passed
upriver and vanished.

Something had altered. Now, once again, the Royal
Navy stood between him and his liberty, and he didn't
know which way to turn. His only weapons were his
belaying pin and his wits.

Chapter 2

Skye waited restlessly until the jury of his peers vanished upriver. Thirst deviled him but he chose to ignore it. As a last resort he could descend some cleft to the river, drink and retreat. Instead he continued eastward along the ridge, so effervescent with joy that he scarcely noticed the protests of his body. Never in his life had he felt such ecstasy. The very earth was his father and mother and brother and sister and friend. His protector, too, hiding him in its rocky fastnesses.

He hiked warily, wondering whether he would run into some jack nastyface, perhaps a salt he knew, probing the ravines or studying the bluffs for signs of passage. He crawled out on promontories and saw nothing below but the glinting river hurrying its burden to the sea. He paused, letting the majesty of the place seep through him. This was better than seeing the horizon from a swaying crow's nest.

Thirst savaged him, and he knew he would have to descend and take his chances. He turned into a pine-shot ravine, sliding downward to a grove of new-leafed trees, yews he guessed, but he knew so little of those things. And there he discovered a seep dribbling clear water down a rocky facade and into the grove. He cupped his hands and drank, learning something valuable from the moment: a burst of emerald foliage might be a sign of water. He would see the wilderness with wiser eyes henceforth. He had no doubt passed dozens of such springs.

He gnawed on hardtack, knowing it wouldn't last long or subdue the howl of his belly, and resumed his eastward journey. Eventually he reached a saddle divided by a tumbling creek that raced toward the Columbia far below. At the confluence of the creek and the Columbia stood a native village with some sort of fishing apparatus projecting into the river. From his vantage point he could make out brown natives wearing little more than loincloths—and the Royal Navy in blues among them, roasting what would no doubt be a salmon feast.

There they were, his shipmates, old hands, wolfishly hunting him down because they feared the lash. They were less than half a mile below, and all his leagues of walking had not freed him from the clutches of the King's avengers who wanted to make an example of him. He could not cross that arid saddle without being seen, and someone among them would raise the alarm. He pitied them. They wished him no harm but the Royal Navy knew how to bend humble men to its imperial will. Lads who had holystoned the teak deck beside him would be in that party below, balancing the harsh powers of royal officers against their rough sympathies. He studied them, discovering the unmistakable bulk of Smitty and the bent-over form of Hauk. Men he knew, set against him.

He peered about, looking for a way around. He discovered animals grazing above, and with them the possibility of village herders. To the north and east stretched treeless plains, offering little shelter.

He could not circle around by day. He could only wait

or retreat. He edged back a hundred yards, making sure not to leave bootprints, and found an area of shelf rock veiled by brush where he could hide unless someone stumbled on the very spot. There he spent the rest of the afternoon, making occasional reconnoiters to a point where he could peer down upon the fishing village. The Royal Navy didn't budge. His shipmates had eaten, smoked, and were enjoying the sight of bare-breasted native women. Maybe that was all for the good, Skye thought. Their minds were on a different sort of chase.

He weighed his chances. He needed to eat and find a way past the tars. But what good could come from hastening upstream with the search party hot on his heels, guided by scouts who knew the country? He studied the fishery, a trap of poles that steered the salmon into seine nets. Beached on a gentle bank were several pirogues, dugout canoes, their paddles lying in them. With one, he could escape to the far shore—if he had the courage to walk through the village at night and take it. His instinct was to cross and then shove the dugout into the river so his passage would not be remarked.

He needed darkness. Moonlight would betray him. Give him the north star and he would navigate the inky river. He studied the village some more, noting a rack where salmon were being smoked. He waited impatiently for dusk—the itch to run, run, run mounting in him. But at twilight he was rewarded with information he needed: his erstwhile shipmates were settling down west of the fishery. The native huts clustered to the east. He spotted dogs, many of them gorging on the offal of the catch, and they shot fear through him. He didn't quite know when the moon would rise, only that in this phase it rose an hour or so later each night, and he would have to act early and fast after true darkness settled.

Restlessly, he bided time until he could no longer see the last band of blue in the west. The cookfires had dimmed. Midshipman Cornwall Carp—Skye recognized the choleric officer commanding this detail—would post a watch and the village mutts would form another sort of watch. Skye wondered what he would do if the mutts howled. Run for the pirogues, he supposed. But would he be strong enough to drag a heavy dugout into the river and escape?

He weighed, one last time, the alternative: hike around the village by night and continue up the Columbia on its right bank, a fox running ahead of the hounds. That made sense, too. And yet . . . the crossing appealed to him. The thought of some smoked salmon did, too. He wrestled back his terror and set out, retracing his way to the saddle and then cautiously working down it in taut darkness, his senses raw. The flutter of a night bird startled him. The scurry of an animal froze him. He reached the edge of the village, wary of the dogs, and studied the gloom for the Royal Navy's watch, but he saw nothing. His pulse lifted. The place was redolent of fish and smoke. He waited a long while, his gaze seeking the glow in the east that would signal the rising moon. He listened to the rhythms of the night, eyed the hulking native huts and fish trap, his senses filtering the shifting darkness that would tell him of the approach of a man.

Nothing.

It was time. He edged out onto the flat scarcely twenty yards from the bivouac, discerned the fish processing area but could make out no fish. He finally found some on a wooden rack, lifted two, and eased toward the river. It reflected pinpoints of starlight off its ebony surface. He chose the nearest pirogue, carefully lowered his kit and the fish into it, felt about until he grasped a paddle and another and another. He lifted the stern of the vessel, found it heavy, and pushed hard. It slid a few inches, scraping loudly. His pulse catapulted. He tried again, and it slid some more. He peered about him, ducked behind the pirogue when he thought he saw a shadow emerge. But the shadow was only in his fevered imagination. He pushed and tugged some more, wild to break free, and at last eased the craft into the sucking water and hopped in just before losing it to the swift current, which caught it and drew it west. He settled himself, staying low, looking for signs of alarm and finding none. Then, safely away, he slid a paddle into the river and began his crossing, keeping the north star at his back.

He found the opposite bank too sheer to land, so he paddled upstream, fighting the muscle of the giant river, looking for a place to beach the canoe. A while later a beach hove into view, and he dragged the pirogue well up the gravel and out of harm's way. Once again, he felt ecstasy as he stood on dry land, his chances better now. And there to light his path was the lamp of the moon peeking over the mountaintops. He hiked eastward again, confident that he had given his pursuers the dodge, his kit slung over his back, and fifteen or twenty pounds of smoked salmon strung over his kit—enough to feed him for a while.

His body felt light and supple, his legs springy, his muscles fueled by his wild joy. Could any mortal experience such exultation as this? He laughed, a big, booming eruption of delight that billowed out of his frame, and trotted upstream on a well-defined trace. At dawn he found himself in much more open country, the arid bluffs farther back and lower, the barren hills beyond them not much higher than the river. He paused to study this new world, look for signs of pursuit on land and water. But the gray light revealed nothing amiss. He needed rest, so he turned up a gully that descended out of the south and found a grove of evergreens a half mile in. The generous pungence of pines filtered through the quiet air. Here he would eat and rest. Here he would take stock.

He found a small ell of rock and decided to build a fire there. He had trouble with the flint and striker, having barely used the device before, but in time he set some tinder smoldering, and with a few gentle breaths he brought a tiny flame to life. He had chosen the site well. The fire could not be seen from any angle. The smoke would dissipate in the surrounding pines. He kept the fire small and let it burn hot while he filleted a salmon and ran the flesh onto a wooden spit that he held over the hot coals.

The half-smoked fish didn't taste good, but he devoured it as if it were a palace delicacy. Henceforth he would live on salmon. He wouldn't have much else. He lacked the weapons to kill game, and April wasn't the time to find wild fruits and berries. But he had hooks and a line and a river full of a legendary fish that fed whole tribes.

He lay back in the grass, satisfied for the moment. He needed sleep. But he needed something else, intangible but insistent in his mind: a future. Where would he go, and what would he do, and what did he want to be? He scraped dirt over the remaining coals, packed his kit in readiness for a hasty retreat if he had to, and then let his mind wander like a homeless ghost in the cemetery of his life.

Long ago, he had been destined for Cambridge, where his father had been schooled in political economy before turning to the overseas trade. The boy, Barnaby Skye, had a lively interest in English literature and poetry and in his family's Anglican religion. He had entertained the thought of becoming a dominie if he didn't choose his father's profession. Then, in one dark moment on an overcast day in London, all his dreams were shattered and he no longer owned his own life.

Now he would fulfill his dream. He intended to cross this wild American continent, find his way to a comparable university on the Atlantic seaboard—Harvard came to mind— and achieve what had been his original goal. He knew little about the American college, except that it was respected and that it was located in Cambridge, Massachusetts, nearby Boston. The thought appealed to him. He had planned to go to Cambridge, England, but would settle for Cambridge, Massachusetts. He could pick up where he had left off seven years ago, work through college somehow, settle in Boston, and start a business. He had sustained himself with that dream, and now it was becoming reality.

But the thought left him restless. He was no longer that boy and wasn't so sure what he wanted now that he had, in a fashion, seen the world, if only from 'tween decks. The newly pressed seaman, Barnaby Skye, had fought bitterly in the bowels of the frigate just to survive, just to wolf his ration of gruel each day, just to win a little purchase on life. The boy had learnt well, fought the bullies, learned to give more than he took. But it had cost him a broken nose and numerous scars, the punishment meted out by harder, crueller, older men who built ruthless jacktar empires 'tween decks, out of sight of bosuns and midshipmen.

He didn't know what he would do. Freedom bewildered him. For the first time in his life, he had no one over him, no one telling him how to spend his every hour. He ached with the burden of choice, ached to find someone he could share his dream with, anyone who might help him decide what to do with his life.

He dozed well into the morning, bolting awake with every shift of the breeze or catcall of a crow, and then settling back into the benevolent grass again while his heart steadied. No one came. He possessed the earth—and himself. That was it: for the first time in his young life, he owned himself.

He was troubled by a sadness that lay just below his wild delight in being free. He didn't know what he would do, or be, but he supposed the next months would teach him. He had never imagined that liberty could be such a burden.

Chapter 3

Dr. John McLoughlin had had more than his fill of his demanding guest, Commodore Sir Josiah Priestley, but there wasn't much he could do except wait out the visit.

Priestley had all the hallmarks of his class: a fine wit, a scorn for commoners, a loyalty to the Crown that was more rhetorical than real, a smidgeon of learning in most of the branches of knowledge, and an assumption that all the world should treat him with the deference demanded by his station.

The commodore, in command of a small Pacific squadron consisting of three twenty-four-gun frigates, relics of the Napoleonic Wars, was paying a courtesy call to the new Hudson's Bay post, Fort Vancouver. There McLoughlin presided over a fur trading empire that stretched from Mexican possessions in California northward, and from the Pacific to the Continental Divide at the apex of the Rocky Mountains. Priestley had sailed up the treacherous Columbia with only his flagship, the *Jaguar*, leaving the two remaining frigates to display the war muscle of King George IV to the dissolute Mexicans farther south and then meet him in the bay of San Francisco.

The giant McLoughlin, born of Irish and French parents in Quebec, could be an accommodating host, and indeed had at first welcomed the visitors, sharing whatever luxuries and wines he had in his yet-unfinished fort on a flat north of the Columbia. He had more urgent things to do, chief among them putting the new Hudson's Bay Company division on a profitable footing. He presided over an area so vast it defied the imagination; an area largely unexplored, although his best brigade leader, Peter Skene Ogden, was swiftly mastering the country and locating the prime beaver-trapping areas.

On a less lofty level, McLoughlin was overseeing the planting of crops that would supply the post with its grain and vegetables, and was building the corner bastions of his fort along with comfortable residences for his chief men within it. He was also overseeing the post store and its profitable trade in peltries, all the while dealing as diplomatically as possible with his bullheaded and demanding superior, Sir George Simpson.

McLoughlin, a commoner and licensed physician who had spent years in the fur trade, mostly with the North West Company, had little use for titled nobles with all their conceits and blindnesses, but they governed his world and he had no help for it. And if he was a cynical adherent of the Crown, he nonetheless did his duty whenever called upon.

But now his sense of obligation grew thin. Priestley had intended to sail earlier. McLoughlin listened impatiently as Priestley explained in detail, with that nasal and shrill Hampshire voice of his, why his departure had been delayed.

"I should have hanged that wretch long ago. Pity I didn't. He's costing the Royal Navy a pretty penny, I say. Straight out of Billingsgate and with a coarseness to match. Troublemaker from the start, this Skye. Pressed in seven years ago, and refused to serve the Crown. Skulking brute with the mind of an ape and the habits of a pit bull. He's been the joke of squadron, you know. 'Oh,' they say, 'you get Skye this tour, Priestley. If he acts up, quarter him and feed him to the sharks.' Good advice, but out of the kindness of my heart I spared the devil his due. And now how am I repaid? He went over the rail! Over the rail! And I'm shorthanded. I'll give that watch a whipping when we're at sea. That Bosun McGivers! Right before the man's sleepy eyes Skye gave me the slip."

McLoughlin was hearing this the tenth or eleventh time. "I presume the navy'll fetch him back 'ere long," he replied, as he already had.

"Of course we will. That brute's scarcely set foot on land since we pressed him and doesn't know a thing. He won't get far."

"You were saying that some days ago. The party you sent downriver hasn't returned."

"McLoughlin, where can a man go? Up the river, that's where. Or out to sea, that's where."

McLoughlin disagreed. A deserter could go anywhere and lose himself in an unexplored wilderness. "He might strike overland—up the Willamette to the Mexican country, my lord. If I were in Skye's shoes, I'd make it my first business to escape the Crown's territories."

"Skye wouldn't be so smart. He hasn't the slightest knowledge of the local terrain. He's been below decks. How would he even know of the Willamette? Don't give him credit, McLoughlin. The man's an ape. And besides, he speaks only English, and barely that. Why would he go to Mexico? He couldn't even ask them for a cup of grog."

"Perhaps because you wouldn't expect him to go there, my lord."

"Ah, you mock me, McLoughlin. Insolence, insolence. But I'll let it pass. I wish to enlist you against this free-booter, this traitor to the crown. He's no ordinary deserter; he's arguably the worst man in the Royal Navy, incorrigible, reluctant to perform his duties, given to brawling, sullen and contemptuous of his betters. I want him back. On the small chance that my search parties don't haul him in, I'm charging Hudson's Bay with the responsibility of catching him, putting him in irons, and sending him to London for his hanging."

"We'll do our best, my lord."

"Of course you will. Anything less than your best will result in a report to the Admiralty and the Colonial Office. Catch him. I'm putting a ten-pound price on his head, dead or alive. It's to your advantage, of course. You don't want this murderous, ruthless brute loose in your country."

"He's murderous?"

"Why, I imagine he'd murder a thousand if he could. We prevent it by keeping him behind iron strap when he provocates."

"But he's killed no man?"

"What difference does it make? He has the penchant. He has that low brow, the mean cunning of the criminal class."

McLoughlin smiled. "Very well. I'll post the award. You'll give me a description, of course. If you don't catch Skye, he'll show up eventually at one of our posts. We have our ways, in HBC. I can enlist a dozen tribes, for starters. I can alert every factor at every trading post."

"That's not enough. I want more. I want an expedition to go after him if the navy fails."

McLoughlin poured some more darjeeling and arched a brow. "And who'll pay?"

"You will, of course. It's your duty to the Crown."

"I see," said McLoughlin. "You'll need to put this in writing, and I'll send it along to George Simpson for approval. I don't have the authority—"

"Tut tut, McLoughlin. Just do it."

"—to spend resources that are not included in company objectives. But we'll catch the devil if we can."

Commodore Sir Josiah Priestley's response was

thwarted by the appearance of McLoughlin's clerk. "Excuse me, sirs, but Mr. Carp requests the commodore's attention."

"Ah, McLoughlin, news at last. I'll wager they have the bugger, or at least his head. Send him in directly."

A smooth-cheeked youth barely in his majority stepped in, saluted smartly, and addressed the commodore. "With permission, sir—"

"Yes, yes, have you got the devil?"

"No, he gave us the slip. Not a trace. We penetrated several leagues upriver, as far as a native village. No luck. But one small clue, sir. The villagers lost a pirogue that night—maybe a mishap, maybe not."

"And you failed to follow up."

"Your pardon, sir, we looked up and down the river. It moves right along, you know."

"So you failed, Carp. I seem to have misplaced my trust. Or perhaps I overestimated your abilities."

The young man, holding the juniormost officer's rank in the Royal Navy, stood silently.

"It's all politics, McLoughlin. These useless sons of knights and barons get preferred over men of ability. Go, my boy. Tell Lieutenant Wickham we'll sail at dawn before we're fighting a headwind and rowing our way out."

"Very good, sir. I—I'm sorry. It's a huge country, sir—"

"Excuses."

The youth fled.

"So, my crew couldn't round up a common oaf. If the Admiralty'd give me a few good men, I'd have strung up the blackguard long since. Now, thanks to them, I'll look bad. Very well, McLoughlin. I'm expressly placing this matter in your hands. Hudson's Bay will pursue this Skye by all available means and report to the Admiralty."

"What does Skye look like, my lord?"

"Why, you can't possibly mistake him—the low cunning, the criminal brow, the wildness of eye—"

"Ah, my lord, is his hair brown or blond or black?"

"How should I know?"

"His age, then?"

"He's been in service forever. I inherited him. Three commanders before me inherited him. Who knows?"

"His eyes—are they blue or brown or gray?"

"I never examine commoners closely."

"His build, then."

"A brute, McLoughlin, an ape. And yes, there is something. Skye has a battered nose, broken a dozen times in his brawls. Look for a man who's all nose. That's all you need."

"Like me, I wager," McLoughlin said, aware that he had a royal nose, a nose that dominated his face like a hogback.

"No, McLoughlin, twice your nose; grotesque, I'd say. The monster of degenerate parents. Look for a physical degenerate and you'll have your man."

"What is he wearing?"

"Sailcloth. I've learnt that much."

"The charges, sir? Murder, theft, disobedience? Attacking an officer?"

"Worse than that. A habitual criminal, as devoid of civilization as the Arctic. A lone wolf. And desertion of course."

McLoughlin had a sneaking suspicion he might like Skye. Or at least admire him. But he set that aside. "I'll put out word. We'll have scores of men looking for the man or his bones."

"See to it," Priestley said, rising. "You have your company on the wharf at dawn to see us off. I'm going to press one of your trappers. When you give us Skye, you'll get your man back."

"My trappers? But—"

"No buts. HBC owes me a man."

"We owe you nothing of the sort."

"McLoughlin, I'm an officer of the Crown. I'd press you if I had to. Thanks to HBC's laxity, the ship's company is even shorter. We lost four men to scurvy."

McLoughlin knew better than to argue. He stood suddenly, stretching his six-foot, seven-inch frame, filling the primitive office with his presence.

"I will see you off in the morning," he said in a way that brooked no further discussion.

Then he escorted the commodore to the gate and had his men bar it. If they wanted to press an HBC man, they would have to resort to the ship's battery to do it, and then answer to the Admiralty and Home Office. Let that titled fool try.

Chapter 4

Rain, cold, starvation, and fear dogged Skye, sometimes all at once. A Pacific storm dropped snow on the mountains and a cruel drizzle on the Columbia, numbing him in spite of his woollen skullcap, pea jacket, and sailcloth cape. He lacked the skill to build a fire in wetness, and wished he had pocketed some dry tinder while he could. He regarded his ordeal as a lesson in wilderness survival, and would remember.

The thought of pursuit tormented him: time and again, he climbed an outcrop or low rise to study his backtrail. If not the navy, then surely some HBC man, a veteran of the wilds, would pursue and capture him. He saw nothing, but that didn't allay the imaginings of his fevered mind.

But worst of all was the hunger, which maddened him, reduced him to weakness. At times he even considered backtracking and turning himself in at Fort Vancouver. Anything for a belly full of hot food.

One desperate morning he whittled off a willow limb

with his knife, grubbed about for worms, and rigged a fishing pole, using a navy hook he had pilfered from ship's stores. But the salmon ignored his bait. Then he tried one of the navy's ocean lures, thinking maybe salmon didn't eat worms or bugs. Over and over he drew the bobbing wooden lure through the water, but he caught nothing. That day he trudged eastward on an empty belly, dizzy from the want of food and fearful he would starve. What did he know about catching fish or killing game? What good were these big hooks and lures, intended for ocean fish?

He tried again that warm evening, hoping a fish would strike at dusk. He baited his iron hook with a caterpillar, tossed it as far out as he could, and let it bob on the river supported by a stick he used as a float. Moments later a silvery fish struck, almost yanking his crude willow pole from his grasp. He dragged in a salmon that weighed several pounds. Madly, he gutted and filleted it, tempted to wolf it down raw, but instead he spitted the fillets and set them to cooking. That evening he filled his complaining belly and cooked enough more to sustain him for a while. But he was unable to catch another fish although he tried until night overtook him.

He hiked eastward into dryer country, the river running through gloomy flats that oppressed his spirit. But here he enjoyed some spring sun. He knew the vagaries of fishing would leave him hungry more often than full, so he began a systematic hunt for other foods, scarcely knowing what was edible and what was foul. He could only sample roots and bulbs and wait to see if they sickened him. His best discovery was cattail roots, thick, foul-tasting, but starchy. He found them more edible if he mashed them between stones. In this fashion he managed to supplement his diet. But he longed for meat; any kind of fresh meat would have quelled his ravenous needs.

He scarcely saw game, only one or two distant does and a goatlike animal he thought might be an antelope. He found plenty of ducks and geese but lacked the means to kill them. He dug up plants, hunting for bulbs, but found nothing edible. Then one evening he stumbled upon a deer carcass, scaring off the predators feasting on it. Belly and haunches had been eaten out, but there was meat around the chest and forelegs. He built a fire from deadfall and set to work with his knife, slowly cutting strips and setting them over the fire on spits. This was a bonanza, a starving man's gold. He ate greedily and then cut more meat, intending to cook it and take with him what he could.

He was wildly lonely. The frigate had offered rough companionship. Here he knew only solitude, and it oppressed him more than he had expected. Even his days of confinement in the ship's brig had been marked by exchanges with his warders, the drift of conversation outside of his iron cage, the knowledge that he was never really alone, and he had friends 'tween decks.

At first he thought he could do nothing about his loneliness other than to dredge up memories. But as he walked eastward, he found himself enjoying the solitary life. To pass time as he hiked, he became an acute observer of his world and discovered that it was brimming with living things, and they spoke to him in their own way. The crows cawed his passage to each other. Ducks burst from cover when he approached and flapped into the skies. The birds became his scouts and sentries. If they burst from a tree, he paused to find out why. If they warned each other of his passage and followed along, hopping from bush to bush around him, he knew that probably nothing else was troubling them. The ears that no longer registered human voices began to register nature's subtle changes, and Skye knew such knowledge would help him survive.

One morning his newfound awareness of nature's rhythms kept him from discovery. He was walking through unusual silence, and felt it. He rounded a gentle hill and spotted Indians ahead cooking a meal, their three heavy log pirogues beached on a gravelly shore. There were at least twenty, all stocky bronze males, enjoying a breakfast drawn from the river. Their spears and bows and quivers lay about. He ducked out of sight, wondering whether he had been discovered. He retreated to a swale and hiked up it until he was well off the river road, and there he waited. He could afford to wait. He was a lone man going nowhere, on no schedule at all. But that didn't make it easier, and he knew he would need to learn patience if he hoped to survive.

He waited for what seemed an hour and tried again. They had left. He had not seen them going downriver, so he knew they were ahead of him and would continue to pose a menace. Maybe they might be friendly, but he suspected that Hudson's Bay would have a say in that. He scavenged their campsite, looking for anything useful, and found nothing except fishheads and tails. They tempted him. He had lost weight and his clothing bagged about his shrinking frame. He needed food and lots of it, much more than roots and bulbs and the occasional fish. He had exhausted the tea and hardtack and now had nothing at all to preserve him. He dreamed of bread and butter and beef and even burgoo, the oatmeal gruel that had been the jack-tar staple in the navy. His boots and clothing were showing signs of serious wear. Sooner or later he would have to stop dodging these people, walk into a village, and get help if he could.

But he didn't rue his escape. Indeed, with each passing day he rejoiced more. These days tested his mettle, tried his courage. He was a freeman, master of his destiny, even if his destiny was to starve to death. He wished he had counted the days since his escape, but he hadn't, and his mind stumbled when he tried to think back on his flight. But he knew a fortnight had passed, and he had made good his escape from the navy. His impulse to run, run, run had ebbed these last days, and now he intended to learn how to wrest food and perhaps clothing from this silent wilderness.

That warm spring day he set up his fishing rig and then

whittled a thick sapling into a lance, pleased with its weight and heft. He sharpened its point, and practiced throwing it, not unhappy with the result, but aware of how much he had to learn about the weapon. He fire-hardened the wooden point and threw his lance at targets until his arms hurt. Then he checked his fishline and found nothing on it. He would go hungry again that evening, save for whatever roots he could choke down.

He collected his gear and hiked a few miles more across dreary plains until he came to a slough with fat geese swimming on it. Without a bow and arrow, or sling, or firearm, he would not be able to kill one. But perhaps if he sat bankside as quietly as he could for an hour, one might drift close enough to club. He settled on moist earth, close to thick cattails, and waited. The distant geese eyed him but never approached, and after an hour or so he knew patience and quietness wouldn't fill his belly. He was feeling miserable and at the end of his wits.

But he calmed himself. He had won the gift of liberty; he would subdue his body. Dusk settled without visitations from unwary geese, and he gave up. He had gnawed on cattail roots before, and would again. This time, though, he would do more. He pulled up quantities of the plant, cut off the gnarly roots, scoured the slimy surfaces, cut the roots into small pieces, and then patiently ground them into a fibrous pulp. He acquired two or three pounds of roots this time: real food if he could stomach it. He built a fire, boiled a few pulped roots in his large tin mess cup, and then set aside the mushy material to cool while he boiled more. He made a satisfying meal of the mash, and learned that patient preparation could yield edible food. This wasn't Eden, and nature's bounty could not be plucked off trees—but he had filled his stomach.

That evening he pulverized and cooked more of the starchy root, making enough mush of it to last a day or two if he should need it. A small reserve in his kit would lift his spirits and strengthen him. In the last light he doffed his boots and waded the slough, intending to camp on its far side and start off in the morning with dry clothing. He found a much-used campsite there, probably because of the geese and ducks in the slough, and rolled up in his sailcloth. Sleep came hard; he had never gotten used to sleeping on the earth.

A cold drizzle awakened him in the night. Miserably, he sat up, donned his skullcap and pea jacket, pulled the sailcloth cape over his head, and waited for better times. Sharp gusts of wind drove rain into his tiny shelter. In that brutal cold, his spirits slid to their lowest ebb. He was alone in a black and bitter night, wincing at every volley of icy rain, without a friend in the world, without anyone to love, without the ordinary comforts. He rummaged about in his mind, looking for succor against this bitter moment and finding none—except the long-remembered, half-blurred prayers recited from a church pew in his youth. He stumbled through these fragments, feeling hollow, and then enduring the numbing night.

Something came to him then, something important that he had ignored from the beginning. He didn't know how to survive alone. He could not live long on his own, without help. He could not count upon a stray carcass or the occasional catch of a fish whose habits he didn't know, or a diet of roots. He could survive only if he approached other people, trusted them, made friends, sought their help, learned their ways, and gave something in return. In short, he could not live a hermit's life. If he did not starve to death, he would go mad with loneliness. Only these tribesmen could show him how to garner food, or supply the companionship he craved, or shelter him from the elements. His God was telling him he wasn't alone in the world, and he should not be afraid.

Chapter 5

At first light Dr. John McLoughlin walked through the great gate of Fort Vancouver and instructed his men to bar it after him and defend the post if they must. He walked majestically down to the riverfront, where the *Jaguar* lay anchored in navigable waters twenty yards off. The crew was unfurling sail to take advantage of a freshening southeasterly breeze. Sailing a three-masted, fully rigged frigate down the Columbia against prevailing westerly winds would be a tricky business.

He stood silently on the bank, waiting for Commodore Priestley to notice him, but for the moment the ship's master was overseeing his junior officers. Then at last Priestley observed the white-haired Hudson's Bay factor.

"Where are your men?" he shouted across the turbid water.

"Defending my post."

Unfurling sail high above caught the eddying breeze and flapped. The ship strained against its leash.

Priestly laughed. The commodore's threat to press an

HBC man had dissolved in the night, as McLoughlin knew it would if he resisted.

"Not much of a hail and farewell," Priestley said. "The Royal Navy has a long memory."

The factor stood like a rock, silent and unbudging.

"Bring us Skye, McLoughlin."

"Permission to weigh anchor, sir," bawled a junior officer.

Priestley nodded. A crew turned the squeaking capstan, water dripped from the rising anchor cable, and suddenly the ship sprang free, heeling away from the wind and sliding down the half-mile-wide river, running like its namesake. In minutes it rounded a bend and disappeared.

McLoughlin returned to his gloomy office and lit a lamp. The *Jaguar* had reprovisioned at Fort Vancouver, taking on firewood, sugar, flour, tea, dried apples and vegetables, tobacco, whiskey, and sundries. Priestley had expressed outrage at the prices, never pausing to consider the pounds and pence of bringing such goods to a wilderness post. McLoughlin totted up the charges, drafted an invoice, and set it aside for the next express to his superiors. It would be a long time, if ever, before HBC collected from the Admiralty.

He turned to his post journal, and entered the departure of the Royal Navy, not failing to include the commodore's threat to press a man, the factor himself if necessary. Then he added a final sentence to his entry:

"Have decided to conduct intensive search for the deserter, Skye, apparently a man of criminal nature. Will direct that the tribes be notified, a reward posted, and my brigades and posts informed as fast as feasible."

He set down his quill pen. A favor to the Crown would not hurt HBC. And cleaning a criminal out of his district would be desirable. If the man survived, he would eventually show up. All this he would discuss further in a letter to George Simpson, governor of Hudson's Bay, up at York Factory headquarters.

He spent the next hour penning identical messages,

instructing his factors to be on the lookout for a deserting seaman named Skye, stocky, big-nosed, powerfully built, probably in seaman's attire. If possible, they were to capture the man alive. The man would be tried, perhaps in London. They were also to post a five-pound reward and offer it to any tribe that brought Skye in alive—definitely alive and well. There would be no reward for a dead man. John McLoughlin did not intend to encourage the killing of a white man, or to give such a license to the various tribes that HBC traded with. He penned an additional letter to his gifted brigade leader in the Snake country, Peter Skene Ogden, saying much the same thing.

He summoned two of his senior French Canadian engagés, Pierre Trintignon and Antoine Marie Le Duc, to his office and addressed them in his fluent French, the tongue of his mother. "I have decided to catch that deserter if possible," he said. "Which means sending expresses to the posts where the brute's likely to show up. Antoine, I suspect that Skye's heading up the Columbia—his other choice is Mexico—and you'll have the more urgent task. Take these expresses to Nez Perces House and Flathead House, and look for Ogden south of the Snake, delivering this express to him en route.

"Pierre, you take this express to Spokane House and continue onward to York Factory with an express for Simpson. You'll each take a mount and remount, and draw whatever provisions you need. The sooner the better."

"Ah, *oui!* And what does this Skye look like that the lord commodore wants so badly?" asked Le Duc.

"Priestley was rather vague. Odd how some men don't see what's before their eyes. Look for a man of powerful build, medium height, with a formidable nose—probably in seaman's clothing."

"Ah, *le nez formidable!* Such a man will identify himself without a word."

"This nose, I gather, rivals or exceeds my own nose," McLoughlin said, "and that makes it a nose unlike any other you have ever examined."

"It is so. I shall study *le nez.*"

"All right, then. If you run into Skye, bring him in. He probably isn't armed. He may be starving unless he's a canny woodsman. I want him alive. He'll have his trial, but I also want his story."

"This Skye, he makes the trouble, *oui?*"

"If Priestley is to be believed, yes."

"But you don't believe the commodore."

McLoughlin stared out the wavery glass window, one of the few glass windows in his post—or all the far west. "The commodore is a faithful officer of the Crown, but he sees commoners through the lens of his class. Skye is probably just as bad as Priestley makes him out. But I reserve judgment. I did learn that Skye was pressed into service as a youth and fought it. When you pull a man off the streets and make him the Crown's sailor, the man has a grievance." He smiled wryly. "Some men regard their lives as their own. It's a novel thought to feudal lords, even now."

"They pressed this Skye. *Mon Dieu!* Let the Crown press me, and there would be blood spilled."

McLoughlin thought the conversation had gone far enough in that direction. "Skye is no doubt exactly the blackguard he is made out to be. Pressed or not, he deserted."

"Maybe we should help him," Trintignon said.

McLoughlin didn't reply for a moment. "Bring him in and let Simpson and me decide that. Pierre, you take the north bank, which is your route anyway; Antoine, you ride the south bank. Have Gervais sail you across."

"I'll be gone before the sun reaches noon," Le Duc said. "This man Skye, he will walk into my snare. I will scatter bait and catch him like a goose."

"See to your safety. He's a brawler."

The burly Canadian laughed cynically.

His engagés took the expresses and vanished. Riding good mounts, they were likely to overtake Skye in days, or at least reach the posts well ahead of the deserter. HBC might preside over a vast wilderness, but it had its ways, and the veteran factor McLoughlin knew them all.

He debated sending a man up the Willamette to check for Skye's passage, and decided not to waste the precious manpower. If Skye was making his way into Mexican California, HBC would be well rid of him. But that was unlikely. The deserter would try to find refuge among the Yanks.

If any HBC man were to capture Skye, McLoughlin hoped it would be Ogden. Peter Skene Ogden would be a match for a dozen Skyes. The brigade leader had single-handedly rescued the faltering Columbia Department, and before that the faltering Nor'west Company, from certain ruin, using a combination of toughness and good humor while dealing with the company's free trappers, harsh discipline, an eye on the purse, and sheer strength of character. Ogden might even transform the deserter into a valuable HBC man. There were other valued employees with worse records behind them than deserting and brawling, and Ogden had nurtured industry and loyalty in them.

McLoughlin wondered how Ogden's brigade had done this season. The man's mission had been both hard and delicate: to trap out the Snake country so thoroughly that the slim pickings would discourage the Yanks, who were flooding into the jointly held Oregon country. The course of empire, both HBC's and Great Britain's, required that the Yanks be shut out until a boundary could be agreed upon. The Yanks were truculently insisting on the 49th parallel; Great Britain, with just as much determination, was holding out for the Columbia River as the boundary, which was why Fort Vancouver was built on its north bank.

If Skye ended up with an American fur brigade, it would be just one more problem for HBC. Ogden would know what to do: the man had a genius for cheering up sour engagés and winning the loyalty of bitter men. If Skye was not utterly incorrigible, HBC might have a new man. That was a thought McLoughlin would not share with Simpson, whose blind loyalty to the Crown sometimes overrode good judgment.

But all that was speculation, McLoughlin thought. Ogden was due to return after the spring hunt south of the Snake, travelling right along Skye's probable escape route. And with any luck, he'd have Skye with him, the sailor glad to have some food in his belly. And if Skye slipped by Ogden, he'd run into the equally formidable McTavish at Fort Nez Perces, located at the confluence of the Snake and Columbia.

McLoughlin laughed softly. What was a poor hungry seaman to do against men like that?

Chapter 6

Antoine Le Duc rode up the left bank of the Columbia, finding nothing. The spring rains had washed the trail clean, but this seaman, Skye, would be easy to find. What would such a one know about wilderness? Le Duc rode easily, enjoying the fresh April weather, glad to escape the post, always happiest when he was prowling alone, unfettered by the will of others.

He led a rawboned pack horse and a spare riding mount. The three beasts of burden would give him speed and enable him to catch up with the sailor, if indeed the man had wandered up this bank. Perhaps the honor of capture would befall Pierre Trintignon, himself a wily French-Canadian like Antoine.

For two cheerful days Le Duc hastened eastward, and then, suddenly, he came upon a beached pirogue lying on a bank above a Klikikat fishery. It had been drawn up a gravel beach and its paddles rested in its belly. Ah! It all came clear to Antoine Le Duc. The sailor was either a fool or excessively scrupulous. The man should have pushed the dugout into the river after the crossing, and thus make his passage invisible. That made him a fool. Or else the fugitive had beached the boat so that it might be recovered by the Klikikats, and thus salve his conscience. That made him a fool also, but a fool with honor. Le Duc decided he liked his quarry. A pressed seaman who would desert the Royal Navy and plunge unarmed into the wilderness was a man after Le Duc's heart.

After that, Le Duc rode leisurely eastward through the deep canyon of the Cascades, where the Columbia breached a mighty mountain range. He saw no sign of his quarry on the rainwashed and sun-dried trail, but that didn't matter. Would such a man suddenly abandon his sustenance from the river and head over the mountains? Anyone experienced in the wilderness, like himself, knew that mortals, like any other animal, would go where passage would be easy and life could be sustained.

Soon, he found ample evidence of Skye's journey. The ashes of cookfires, a fishhead—so the man had hook and line—and a place where the sailor had hacked off a tree limb and whittled it into something. And bootprints, too. He was getting close. The man was eating cattail roots, leaving the fronds in heaps. *Alors,* a clever one. Le Duc knew that the Indians used the roots as an emergency food, and it was clear the sailor was answering the rumble of his belly in just such a way. It was worthy of respect.

Then one dusk Le Duc passed Skye. The man's boot-prints vanished up a coulee and did not return. So, the sailor was up there, well off the trail, imagining himself well concealed from pursuers. Le Duc smiled and continued onward. Let Skye discover him ahead, a lone voyageur roasting meat, the smoke of the burning fat drifting with the evening breezes. Skye's belly would lead him straight to the cookfire and then the fun would begin.

Le Duc wished to leave no hoofprints, so he led his horses well off the river road, an easy thing to do now that the river rolled through prairies, and headed upstream all that day. He found an antelope, shot it with one ball, and took the carcass with him. Antelope steaks would whet the appetite of a starving man.

He returned to the river road and made camp at an amiable place he knew, where a copse of trees supplied firewood, the prairie grasses would sustain his horses, and an arrangement of rock would keep the wind off the cookfire. An admirable place, where one could observe river traffic. He settled himself comfortably, hobbled the horses and put them on grass, hung the antelope, gutted it expertly, and hacked off some good flank steaks. Ah, the smell of meat. What the deserter would give for a bellyful.

He built a cheerful fire and let it burn low and hot before he spitted the meat and roasted it. The shadows were long and the sun was dropping, but Skye did not appear. Very well, then. The man would come at dusk, as cautious as a ferret. But Skye did not appear at dusk, either. Uneasily, Le Duc gathered the horses and tied them in camp where the desperado could not steal them. At full dark, Skye had not come in, but Le Duc sensed he was being observed, a sense well known to any voyageur. Ah, this Skye, an admirable rogue.

"Monsieur, I am a child of the wilderness, and I know you are out there, whoever you may be. One feels these things," he said conversationally. "I will take your silence for a hostile act, and prepare myself. If you mean no harm, come share the meat—I have more than enough—and smoke a pipe. I'm Antoine Le Duc, a Canadian trapper."

Le Duc listened intently. He heard movement but no one responded. No doubt Skye was taking a closer look. "Very well, you are as silent as an owl. That means you are no *ami, oui*? It is time for me to put out the fire and then you will not have the advantage."

"I'll smoke the pipe." The voice rose from the east. Skye had circled clear around the camp. Le Duc's respect increased.

"Alors, come have *le tabac,"* he said. "And an antelope hangs. Meat is plentiful."

The man emerging from the darkness was exactly as McLoughlin described him: medium height, stocky, powerful—and with a nose. Mon Dieu! *Le nez magnifique!* Never had Le Duc seen a nose so noble.

"Bien, bien, I am Le Duc. And you?"

The man hesitated. "I'm Skye. If you're looking for me, say so. If not, I'll share the camp."

"Why would I be looking for you, monsieur?"

"I thought you might be. I was a pressed seaman with the Royal Navy until I jumped ship a fortnight ago. If you intend to capture me, be about it. I've put everything on the table, and that's the way I deal with people. Well?"

"Formidable!" Le Duc said. "Let me start some meat. We'll need some more wood."

"No, you answer the question first. The meat can wait. Are you looking for me?"

"I am always looking for friends."

The seaman stared. "You've dodged my question. You're looking for me. I won't be taken alive. If you doubt it, try it." He turned away and walked back into the night.

"Mon ami, wait."

But Skye didn't. He vanished into blackness. Le Duc had to admire the hungry man's will. He could have feasted, but he treasured his liberty more. Surprised, Le Duc admitted he had lost the first round. This Skye was a *man.*

Le Duc sprang up and trotted into the darkness, in Skye's general direction. "Monsieur Skye. You are a discerning man. *Oui,* I am from Fort Vancouver. I was sent to find you. McLoughlin, the factor, sent me. Now come share the meat. You are starving. We will talk, *oui?"*

This met with such a silence that Le Duc wondered whether he had been heard. But at last Skye responded in that booming voice of his. "That's better. Now say the rest—that you intend to take me in."

"It is so."

"Now I'll repeat what I said. You won't succeed unless you kill me first. My freedom is worth my life. Go ahead and put it to the test."

He reappeared out of the gloom, squinted at Le Duc in the faint light of the distant fire, and walked to the camp. The man deliberately, carelessly turned his back and set a seabag or some sort of kit on the ground. The act tempted Le Duc to draw his dragoon pistol from his belt, but he didn't. Let him eat and talk, and then he would decide. Skye divested himself of his gear, including a hand-hewn lance, but he kept a single item at hand, a hardwood club with an odd flare in its middle.

"That's a belaying pin," Skye said. "Hardwood. Used to belay ship's lines. Anchor the lines. It's a weapon you'll be testing shortly, I suppose. But I'll eat first."

Le Duc sawed meat from the hanging antelope and set it cooking, and then, gauging his man, cut more. Skye looked ready for two or three servings. Le Duc added some wrinkled potatoes he had collected from the post's root cellar.

Skye didn't devour the food as Le Duc expected, but ate slowly, savoring it all. Le Duc studied his man all the while. Skye had strong, bony features, big hands, and an unexpected youthfulness. Le Duc had expected an older man, but this one was barely into his twenties, with a somber, silent nature that probably concealed a great deal of passion.

Le Duc pulled out his clay pipe and filled it, tamped it, lit it, drew and exhaled an aromatic smoke, and asked Skye if he wanted a pipeful. Skye shook his head.

"What are they saying about me?" Skye asked abruptly.

"I will tell you that after you tell me your story."

Skye hesitated. He seemed to hesitate in all his decisions, something that Le Duc filed away as valuable information. Then Skye described a life, in terms so stark and simple that it took only minutes. A fourteen-year-old boy destined to enter his father's mercantile business, pressed into the Royal Navy off the streets of London. A sullen powder monkey who never surrendered, fought his superiors, tried to regain his liberty, suffered years in iron cages, all the while trapped in vessels of war that took him to Africa and the Kaffir wars, and the Bay of Bengal and the uprisings on the Irrawaddy. A rebel who was watched, who rarely put his feet on land, and whose hope of freedom withered—until now.

"Now tell me what they say about me," Skye said.

"Incorrigible, a criminal, a degenerate. Catch Skye and return him to London for court martial. There is a reward for you. Five pounds—alive, nothing dead."

"Then no one will claim it," Skye said.

"I could shoot you."

"Go ahead and try. I'm going to walk away. You'll have your chance."

"Ah, monsieur, it's simpler to wound, simpler to wrestle you into submission."

"If you can," Skye said. "I expect you'll try." He stood suddenly, the belaying pin in hand.

The challenge had to be met. Le Duc's pride was at stake. Not for nothing had Le Duc made himself king of the voyageurs, the right-hand man of the factor, the brawler who could bring anyone in HBC to his knees. Grinning, he sprang up and circled Skye.

"Monsieur, my soul awaits this moment of truth. Now we shall see. Now I'll pound you into dust and carry you back upon my spare horse."

Le Duc sprang joyously, intending to plant a boot in Skye's groin and end the matter in an instant. Instead, Skye's club hit his chest like a ramrod, staggering him and driving breath out of him. When the voyageur tried to yank the belaying pin from Skye's hands, the slippery hardwood offered no grip. He barged into Skye, but the club caught his knee, sending howling pain up his leg. Le Duc gasped. He had never experienced such agony. Next the club rapped his head until his ears rang and slammed into his right arm, rendering it useless. A beast!

It had taken only a moment. Skye stood unscathed, Le Duc's body howled pain. Not a drop of blood had been spilled.

"Take me if you can," said Skye, who was scarcely even breathing hard. "I'm not going back alive."

"Mon Dieu," Le Duc muttered, massaging his useless arm, rubbing his hurting kneecap, and wondering whether his aching ribs had been broken. His breath returned in gusts. *"C'est magnifique. Sacrebleu!* A thing to remember. A story for the campfires. You are one of us. A man of the wilderness. A grizzly bear. Come to the fire and we shall pour some spirits I took the precaution of carrying with me for medicinal purposes, and I will tell you what fate awaits you."

Chapter 7

Skye lifted the flask, swallowed some awful concoction that burned his gullet, and spit it out, gasping for air.

"What is that?" he cried, his eyes leaking.

"Ah, Monsieur Skye, it is the elixir that lubricates the fur trade. Indian whiskey."

"It's the bloodiest vile stuff I've ever tasted. Have you some rum?"

"Ah, *non,* no one but John McLoughlin possesses any grog worthy of the name. But this is a noble drink, *oui? Formidable.* Pure grain spirits, with a dash of the Columbia River and a plug of tobacco for taste. Ah . . . one little drink and my right arm will work again, my headache will vanish, my ribs will repair themselves, and my knee will stop letting me know its displeasure. Two little drinks and I am the master of men."

Skye sipped again, wiped away the tears, and tackled another dose while a second meal of antelope haunch sizzled over the cheerful fire.

"All right, Le Duc, what's my fate?" he asked.

"Your commodore wishes for your safe return, and has persuaded our factor, the White Eagle, as the giant is called—the resemblance is pronounced—to reel you in like a fat salmon. Little did he know you can't be reeled, monsieur. In my saddlebags are letters to the factors at the posts—McTavish at Fort Nez Perces, Ross at Flathead House on the Clark fork of the Columbia, and another to Peter Ogden, who's leading a trapping brigade south of the Snake—which is on your route if you choose to escape His Royal Majesty's empire."

"I didn't know this was settled country."

"It is not. A few trading posts to get furs from the Indians, nothing more. A few brigades cleaning off beaver before the Yanks flood in. You'll reach Fort Nez Perces in a week or so. It's at the confluence of the Columbia and Snake. A formidable man, McTavish. He will shoot you if it pleases him. He is a cold, mean Scot, without the warmth and humanity of a Frenchman. Me, I would spare your life; a man deserves his liberty if he wants it more than life. But McTavish, he is a political animal, and will make meat of you if it pleases the company."

"I'll dodge the post."

"*Mais oui,* go around it. He will have the express I am delivering and will be looking for you. And so will all the Indians he trades with."

Skye sipped the fiery brew and contemplated that. "I knew Hudson's Bay would throw out a net."

He pulled the sizzling meat off the spit, let it cool, and then began gnawing on it while Le Duc drank and coughed and drank more.

"I'm getting my courage back, Skye. Whiskey courage. Soon I will try you again. *Voila!* I can move my right arm again. Next time, it won't be so easy for you. I shall be wary of the belaying pin. And you'll be sotted on this poison, an easy target."

"If you whip me, you still won't take me back alive," Skye said, gnawing meat.

"I will whip you. No man defeats Antoine Le Duc more than once or for long. I will show you what a man is."

Skye said nothing. He hadn't escaped a brutal life just to get into a contest of manhood with this voyageur. The more Le Duc drank, the more he was nerving himself to try Skye again—maybe with fatal results for either of them. Skye swallowed back the instinct to prove he was a match for any Hudson's Bay man—his pride was at stake—and considered.

He knew, somehow, that this was a defining moment in his life. He could guzzle more of that noxious brew, keeping pace with the voyageur, and then find out which of them ruled the roost. Or he could reach for better things. He had his liberty—if he could keep it.

He was still young, and probably much more serious than most his age. Years of oppression had left their mark on his moods. In all his years in the navy, he had fought when forced to fight, just to assert his right to a life, or to get food, or to stop the harassment of some petty lord of the 'tween decks. But not because he enjoyed hurting others, or lording over them, or playing cock of the walk. He would have preferred to read a book.

Quietly he arose, ignored Le Duc's taunts, and sawed more meat from the hanging carcass. He didn't stop at one serving, but cut all he could—enough to last two or three days if possible. Le Duc drank, swore gallic oaths, and gathered his courage to provoke another brawl, but it didn't matter. Skye loaded the meat into his seabag, stowed his cape and other gear, gathered up his rude lance, and walked into the darkness.

"Skye, *merde!* Halt or I'll shoot."

Skye ignored the man and hastened into the blackness, veering to the right. He had told the voyageur his freedom meant more than life, and now he was being put to the test. Live free or die. He walked quietly, awaiting his fate.

"*Va t'en au diable,*" the man cried.

The crack of the musket didn't startle Skye, nor did its

ball strike him. The shot was bravado, fired into the air. He slid into the void of night and circled back, keeping an eye on the distant pinprick of fire until he was well west of the campsite, and then he rolled up in his sailcloth. Let Le Duc sober up and ride ahead in the morning. There would probably be meat left over to cook and eat, and Skye was in no hurry.

It began to rain in the night, and Skye spent the last miserable hours before a gloomy dawn huddled under his sailcloth and feeling cold. He thought he was about half a mile inland from the river, but this was open prairie and if he rose and walked he would be visible. So he waited while the gray day brightened slightly. He could not see Le Duc or his horses, but still he waited. Let the man go ahead and warn the HBC. Skye would bide his time.

At last, he trudged down to the campsite and found no one there. The carcass was gone. Le Duc, with his wilderness instincts, knew exactly what Skye would do. The meat was probably feeding the fish in the river. Skye sighed. He liked the Canadian and knew the Canadian liked him, and knew Le Duc would redouble his efforts to bring the deserter to his knees.

Skye edged back from the river and hiked eastward once again, solitary but safe, his energies focused on preserving his freedom and renewing his life. The prints of horses preceded him. If they veered off the trace, he would be watchful. But he suspected that Le Duc would hurry to Fort Nez Perces and elsewhere, delivering his expresses, and never say a word about encountering the fugitive himself.

The evening with Le Duc had been rewarding. He now knew that HBC was looking for him, and he knew what lay ahead. He knew there was a reward for anyone who brought him in alive. That was all important, potentially lifesaving knowledge.

He hiked through a silent land and came late in the afternoon to a cold river rushing out of the south. He knew he would have to swim it. Unhappily, he doffed his clothing, stuffed it into his seabag along with his belaying pin, and wobbled into the water, feeling it stab his feet and ankles and then suddenly his thighs. The thunderous cold smacked him but there was no help for it. He swam furiously, feeling the icy water sap his energy and swirl him toward the Columbia, but at last, exhausted, he crawled up the far side, stubbing toes on rock, and dressed. He was chilled to the marrow and needed a fire.

He trotted eastward, trying to warm his numb body, and largely succeeded. But late that afternoon he rounded a bend and came upon an Indian fishery and village. Short, golden-fleshed people swarmed around him, looking him over, their countenances cheerful. Skye eyed them uneasily, wondering if they were measuring him for a reward from Hudson's Bay. But the men of the village didn't seem hostile. They crowded about, eyeing his warbag, his crude lance, and his clothing. The women smiled and studied him when they thought he wasn't aware. The naked children stared politely.

Wasn't this what he wanted? Wasn't this the succor that he knew he needed? Skye heartened at his reception, and tried some English on them. "Well, mates, do ye speak my tongue? Can we talk?"

They smiled blankly. One tried some hand signals that Skye took to be a means of communicating, but he could not make out the meaning. He thought he ought to give them something, anything, as a signal of his esteem. But he needed everything he possessed: he could not spare his awl or shoe leather or flint and striker or fishhook and line, or any of his ragged clothes. But yes, there was something he needed a little less than the rest: his coil of rope. This he extracted from his kit and offered to an older, wire-haired man whose bearing and dignity suggested he was the headman.

The muscular older man hefted the line, uncoiled it, found it a worthy gift, and grinned. This, in turn, evoked a flood of gifts in return, much to Skye's astonishment. The women hastened to their bark huts and returned bearing all sorts of things: a fine, tanned deerskin, a fringed leather shirt with dyed geometric designs on it, smoked salmon, and baked cakes made of some sort of meal. A bonanza. Skye bowed, expressed his thanks in English, and found himself being escorted to the center of the place where meals were cooking in big iron kettles that must have been gotten from Hudson's Bay traders.

That evening Skye feasted on all the fresh pink salmon he could eat, along with some sort of greens and meal-cakes. The women vied to please him, and he acknowledged each gift, each delicacy. A little boy edged close and finally ran a finger down Skye's giant nose, and Skye knew what it was about him that fascinated these people. They had never seen a formidable nose before. Perhaps they thought big noses signified power or importance. That dusk the headmen shared a pipe with him and he was ushered into a bark-walled lodge and to a pallet. Luxury, he thought, a respite from starvation and loneliness. He did not even know the name of this river tribe, or their personal names, but they had welcomed him generously. A dozen people, grandparents, parents, large and small children, called that hut home but Skye didn't feel crowded. Instead, he felt safe. He had not been in the bosom of a family since he was a boy, and now he lay in the close dark, aware of all those people, knowing he must never spin out his life alone.

Chapter 8

Skye pulled the elkskin shirt over his navy blouse and found that it fit well enough to use without alteration. It had a curious design, with leather fringes dangling from the arms. The skins had not been trimmed below the waist, and the fringes there hung unevenly, making an odd hemline around his thighs. It was well-used and soft, and permeated with tallow that would turn the rain. Bold zigzag designs in red and blue decorated the chest and back. He appreciated its warmth and knew a good leather shirt would be comfortable in the wilds, subduing the wind.

The headman's family stood around him, enjoying the spectacle. He prepared to leave but they insisted he breakfast with them, and once again he filled his belly, this time with some sort of fish cake that had berries in it.

Even that early in the morning, many of the village's young men were perched out on a rickety catwalk over the river, slender spears in hand, stabbing the occasional salmon that swam by. Skye watched, fascinated, believing he could fashion a spear out of his spare knife and a pole. If he found an abandoned fishery poking into the river, he would tarry there and try to spear salmon.

Several of the village men carried bows and quivers full of arrows, and Skye ached to possess the weapon. He had never shot an arrow in his life but he didn't doubt that necessity would teach him swiftly. He would learn well enough to kill game—or starve. Inspired to trade, he dug into his warbag and pulled out a treasured possession that he could nonetheless do without. He used his folding straight-edged razor now and then to keep his whiskers at bay. But now he needed a bow and arrows far more than a shaven face. He approached one of those who carried a bow, gestured toward it and the quiver, and then laid his shaving kit before him on the ground. He opened the razor and handed it to the man. The man gingerly ran a thumb over the blade and grinned. Skye's shaving gear included a battered white mug, some soap, and a shaving brush, and with all these and some river water he shaved himself while the villagers crowded about.

The man took the razor and handed Skye the quiver and bow. Skye rejoiced. With luck and some hunting skills, he might feed himself. He counted eleven arrows: enough to keep him fed.

He turned to his host, wondering what to give the man for his hospitality, and finally decided he could surrender his woolen skullcap. He handed it to the headman, who grinned and put it on. A swift command sent his wife hurrying into the bark hut, and she returned with a beaver-felt top hat, a trade item from Hudson's Bay. Much to Skye's delight, it fit, perhaps too snugly but it would stretch with use. The brim would shade his chapped face and keep the rain off his neck.

He ached to do more trading, especially for a horse, but he saw none. He doubted these fishing people had any. He knew what he would offer for one: his pea jacket. The new leather shirt would do for warmth, and summer was coming. After thanking his hosts with gestures he hoped would be understood, Skye departed eastward, enjoying his new wealth. He had a little antelope meat and some fresh fish—and a bow and arrows.

He examined the arrows, curious about their manufacture. They had been made from reeds and had sheet-iron points bound to the shaft with sinew. The points were trade items from Hudson's Bay. The bow had been fashioned of a blond wood that reminded him of yew, and was strung with animal gut. He would have to be careful with it because he lacked a spare string. As he walked, he nocked arrows and shot them ahead, getting the feel of the weapon. He collected the arrows as he passed by. He knew he had much to learn, and his efforts had been awkward. He didn't even know how to hold the bow and arrow. But by the nooning, he was getting better.

The country turned rugged again, and the river boiled between dark rock cliffs. The road veered sharply away from the Columbia and ascended a steep and much-used trail. Plainly these narrows blocked passage along the river and one had to detour around them. He could hear a faint roar as the Columbia bored through the gorge. When at last the trail took him back to water, he found himself in a land largely devoid of trees.

That evening he counted the day a good one. He baited his hook and line, and then practiced with his bow and arrows, gaining skill through the dusk. No longer was he helpless. But skill with a bow wasn't the same as being a hunter. He rarely even saw an animal. But as he penetrated these steppes day by day, he spotted distant herds of antelope, and once he saw wild horses. His first success with the bow was a humble one: he shot a raccoon. Greedily, he dressed the animal and then built a fire to cook it. The result was abominable, but the mouthfuls of soft meat helped sustain him. He counted it a milestone.

He had better luck with his fishhook and line, occasionally netting a salmon that kept him fed for two days. The weather warmed, and his passage would have seemed idyllic but for his constant hunger. He was plagued by loneliness, too, and ached to talk with some-one, anyone. How far to Fort Nez Perces? How far to the edge of the Oregon country? How far to the American settlements? North America was a vast continent, but he had hiked eastward for weeks on end. Surely he would arrive at the Atlantic side soon. Or would he?

He was traversing a vast plain, broken by outcrops of dark volcanic rock and populated by horses that galloped madly away as he approached. He ached to capture one, but he knew little about them. He had never sat a horse.

His boots fell apart, and he repaired them with his awl and some thong. His trousers wore to pieces, and he sewed the rents and patched them with sailcloth. All this time he saw no one, and his loneliness ate at his spirits. Was this all there was? Would he die some lonely death in these empty wilds? What good was freedom if it came to nothing? He talked to himself, talked to the prickly pear cactus, talked to the crows that gossiped about his passage. Some evenings caught him in places without firewood, but he had learned to cook all of any salmon he caught and could make a meal of cold fish if he had to.

Then one day he lost a hook and line. It snagged on something and his line snapped. Skye found himself holding a pole with a foot of string dangling from it. With no more line, he might well starve.

He felt more and more oppressed as he considered the loss. He stood on the riverbank, drawn bow in hand, knowing the wealth of food that lay in those waters, mad-dened that he could capture none of it. He would have to turn himself into a hunter or starve. Immediately he hiked far away from the river, looking for game and finding none. When he returned at dusk, a terrible pessimism stole through him.

Standing there beside the mighty Columbia River with all its unreachable food, he asked himself why he had been set on earth. He had suffered in the navy, and now he suffered more. Did some people's lives simply take a wrong turn, never to be redeemed? Would he wander this wilderness until he died an early death? Would he be better off turning around, tracing his way back to Fort Vancouver, and turn himself over to John McLoughlin? It was tempting, if only because he would have companionship.

In the past he had occasionally fallen into bouts of despair, especially when he was locked in ships' brigs for weeks on end. He knew that there was only one cure for it: he had to drive the demon out of himself. He must never surrender to despair. He might now be in grave trouble, but he was not defeated. He reminded himself that he was alive and free. He had to help himself because no one else would. It was bootless to question the meaning of his existence, or why his had been a hard lot, or whether there was justice in the world. Such speculations never solved anything. He would keep on. He would suffer and starve if he must, but he would not quit and he would not surrender the liberty he had won at such terrible cost. With that resolve, and with a half-muttered prayer to the mysterious God who let him suffer so much, he started east once again.

The next day he shot an antelope. He could not explain it. The handsome animal stood on a slight rise, watching him approach, probably a sentinel for the nearby herd. It should have fled, but it didn't. Itchily, he nocked an arrow and eased closer, to perhaps thirty yards. A long shot for a novice with a bow. The antelope didn't present much target, facing him almost squarely. But he drew, aimed, and loosed his fingers. The arrow whipped true and buried itself in the animal's chest. The antelope took a few steps and collapsed.

Exultantly, Skye raced to it and found it was dying. He retrieved his arrow, pulling gently until it came free. He was a long way from the river a longer way to firewood. In fact, he didn't see a tree anywhere, but he knew a few grew near the water, often hidden from the prairies. The antelope was too heavy to carry and cumbersome to drag. Skye decided to lighten the load by gutting it, which took a while in hot sun. He didn't really know what he was doing, and doubted that his kitchen knife was the ideal tool. The carcass was still too heavy, so Skye slowly cut off its head, having trouble with bone and cartilage. Now at last he felt he could hoist the carcass to one shoulder, his warbag over the other, and stagger back to the river.

The half-mile trek exhausted him, but he reached the stony bank, washed the carcass and himself, and hunted for wood. He saw none. He stumbled a mile more along the river before he came to a crease in the land full of stumpy trees and brush, enough of it dead to give him what he needed. He exulted, and set to work at once, building a hot fire, butchering meat, and preparing for a feast.

He ate a bellyful of the tender meat, and toiled relentlessly at butchering the rest of the animal. He meant to cut it into thin strips and dry it if he could. The sheer toil amazed him. He lacked so much as a hatchet and had to break dry limbs off trees with brute strength to keep the fire going. He had to saw the meat patiently, being careful not to cut himself. And then he had to rig a grid of green sticks upon which to dry and smoke the meat.

Dusk arrived but he was scarcely aware of it because this bonanza of meat inspired unceasing labor. When he did look up at last, he discovered he wasn't alone. Half a dozen white men in buckskin stared down at him, and even as he reacted, he saw dozens more, including Indian women, join them. They multiplied, more and more of them crowding the hilltop along with pack horses and mules.

He had run into a fur brigade, but knew not whether it was British or Yank.

He paused, wiped the sweat from his brow, lifted his top hat, and waited.

Chapter 9

Peter Skene Ogden saw at once that this was the fugitive sailor, Skye, although the man was wearing a fringed buckskin shirt and a battered topper. McLoughlin's express, which Le Duc had delivered a few days before, warned that the Royal Navy considered this man a dangerous and incorrigible criminal.

Ogden had kept the information to himself. He had a cynical streak, and nothing aroused his amused skepticism more than the posturing of the servants of the Crown, especially the dread lords of the Admiralty. Ogden also had his own designs, and perhaps Skye would fit into them. Nonetheless, the man bore watching.

He hurried his trapping brigade down the long slope while Skye waited in the dusk, wary and silent. The man certainly fit McLoughlin's sketchy description. The nose—my God, what a nose—identified him.

"Ogden here. I don't believe we've met," he said.

Skye paused, his gaze searching, and then seemed to

come to some conclusion. "I'm Barnaby Skye, sir. Call
me Mister Skye."

"Mister Skye it is, then."

The brigade swarmed around Skye, eyeing him curi-
ously. Ogden had taken these thirty trappers and camp
tenders, plus their Indian wives, out last fall, and now was
returning to Fort Vancouver with the winter's harvest of
beaver pelts. They had trapped the Snake River country,
garnering somewhat fewer than the three thousand pelts
Hudson's Bay needed to turn a profit.

"I've some meat here," Skye said. "Just cooking it up.
Help yourself."

"That's mighty kind. Fact is, we haven't seen a four-
footed beast in two days. We're subsisting ourselves on
salmon. All right, gents, divide it up."

An antelope wouldn't go far among thirty-seven men
and women, but the whole brigade would get a serving.
Ogden examined Skye's gear, finding only a bow and
arrows. Offering that meat had meant sacrifice, which
only heightened Ogden's curiosity about this notorious
man.

"A man grows weary of salmon," Skye said.

"You heading somewhere, Skye? Any way I can help?"

"It's Mister Skye, sir. That title gives a common man
dignity here in the New World. Any man can claim it, and
I do. I've been known only by my last name since I was
a lad of fourteen. I heard not even Barnaby, my Christian
name, sir. Only Skye, as if a freeborn Englishman
deserved nothing more."

"I share the sentiment. Call me Mr. Ogden," the
brigade leader said, enjoying himself and Skye. "You're
an Englishman. I'm a Canadian. We're bound by the
Crown, then."

Skye said nothing, his face hiding some interior world
from Ogden. It wouldn't do to push the man, Ogden
thought. "We'll make camp here, if you don't mind.
You've found the only firewood in miles, and there's

plenty of grass for these half-starved mounts. I'm taking a lot of beaver back to Fort Vancouver. We've been in the Snake River country. You heading that way or heading west?"

"East, sir. Perhaps you can give me directions."

"Ah, directions to where?"

"Boston, Mr. Ogden."

"Boston?"

"It has a college I wish to attend, sir. Harvard. In a place called Cambridge. My schooling was interrupted long ago, and I wish to continue with it."

"But Boston's on the Atlantic coast."

"It's where I'm headed."

"Do you have any idea—no, obviously you don't. We have some tea I've been hoarding. I'll break it out. We'll have a cup and talk, eh?"

Skye smiled for the first time. "Tea. It's been a long time since I've sipped it."

Ogden could hardly believe his ears. In the space of a minute or two, Skye had demolished the reputation that preceded him. College. Boston. Sharing the antelope. Politeness and courtesy. Insistence on a dignified title. Either Skye wasn't the man the navy represented to McLoughlin, or else Skye was a master dissembler, capable of impressing people with the appearance of transparent honesty.

The man wandered the camp, looking itchy and uneasy while Ogden's brigade settled down for the night. He seemed a loner, unwilling to make friends with the voyageurs. But maybe that should be ascribed to his fugitive status.

Ogden let Skye wander while he set some tea to brewing in a fire-blackened pot. His Creole free trappers required constant attention. If he wasn't on hand to make sure the horses were hobbled and put out to graze, they might not be. If he wasn't around to set a guard, no guard would be posted. He had learned to command his trapping brigade with good humor, some jawboning, and an occasional show of strength. He wasn't a large man but he could mete out more than he took from any of them. HBC had entrusted him with its most important trapping brigade precisely because he was good with the men.

The embarrassment of last season still aggrieved him. That was when the Americans had set up their rendezvous system and lured away twenty-three of Ogden's trappers by offering much higher prices—eight times the HBC price—for beaver pelts, while selling them supplies at moderate cost right in the mountains, so that the trappers didn't have to head back to a Hudson's Bay post for equipment. It had been an ugly season that had come close to bloodshed. Ogden despised his deserters, abominated the shifty Americans, coldly refused to leave the territory the Yanks were calling their own, and met threat with threat. At the same time, he had swiftly informed his superiors that many more of HBC's trappers would desert unless they were paid decent prices for their plews, as beaver pelts were called. The Creoles rightly protested that HBC had deliberately kept its trappers in bondage, working to pay off trading post debts that could never be repaid.

The company had reformed itself, more or less, and now Ogden led a brigade that had remained loyal and reasonably content—in a tentative sort of way. His mission had been to sweep the entire Snake country of its beaver, to keep the Americans out. He had done just that, ruthlessly cleaning beaver out of the country south of the Snake. But he was still shorthanded, and reliable men were a rare commodity in the wilderness. Maybe there'd be a place for Skye—if McLoughlin and HBC's governor, George Simpson, agreed. Which was a big if.

"Mister Skye, the tea's steeped," he said.

He handed the fugitive a cup. Skye settled on the ground, near Ogden's own small fire. They sipped contentedly, while Ogden wondered how to broach the various topics that came to mind. The trappers were all busy making camp, so they were more or less alone.

"I wonder if you know how far Boston is, sir. And what lies between."

"It doesn't matter, Mr. Ogden."

That answer, too, astonished the brigade's bourgeois, as the Creoles called him. Ogden tried another tack. "You're ill-equipped to cross the continent. It's nearly two thousand miles to the Mississippi River, and another thousand to Boston. Cold, heat, starvation, savages, disease, clothing falling off your body. Don't try it. If you'll hire on with HBC, you'll soon have enough to go east in safety and a chance of keeping yourself fed. I'll supply you right now, and you can work off the debt."

"That's a kind offer, Mr. Ogden. But I will go my way with what I have."

"It's suicide."

"Death, sir, can be the lesser of two evils."

"I see you're serious," Ogden said, impressed. It was mountain etiquette not to inquire too closely into a man's past. His brigades had been populated by wanted men, scoundrels, dodgers of all sorts. But by some sort of unspoken agreement, they all had a chance to redeem themselves here. What counted was what a man could do, the contribution he could make, and not what he had been. In any case, the harsh and dangerous life weeded out the malcontents and worthless men. Weak men didn't last long. They died or fled.

"This life can be so terrible that one is forced to put his hope on the next one. The lowest and darkest corner of paradise, Mr. Ogden, is the dream of a man whose every hope has been crushed." Skye stared at Ogden somberly. "I am a free man. This wilderness is paradise itself. Every hour of my journey, my heart leaps and my soul rejoices and I sing my own hymns to our Creator."

Ogden, for once in his life, was speechless.

"I believe you already know much about me, and all this dissembling evades the issue," Skye continued.

"Why—"

"I am called a deserter by the Royal Navy and the company is offering five pounds to anyone who'll deliver me to Fort Vancouver alive. My capture will please the Admiralty."

Ogden laughed. "Somehow, you've met and impressed Le Duc, our express runner. The rogue never confessed to meeting you, but I know he did. He acted oddly. I met him ten days ago on the Snake River. He was on his way to Flathead Post, bearing the same express he gave me."

"No one will collect the five pounds, Mr. Ogden. Because I won't be taken alive. Try it and you'll find out soon enough."

Ogden shook his head, intrigued with this man. "I have no designs, Mister Skye. The fact is, I was hoping to make a trapper of you. I need every man I can get."

"That won't be possible, sir. I won't work for Hudson's Bay or any of the Crown's men, and I won't stay in British territory."

Skye's assertion certainly had a finality about it, Ogden thought.

"Well, sir, would you honor me with your story? If you want my opinion, the official version of events is usually concocted by men protecting their backsides. In your case, by a titled fool who commands His Majesty's ships more by politics and connections than merit. They all get along all right—except in war, and then they serve the kingdom badly."

Skye ladled more tea from the pot and sipped it. "I'm the son of a London merchant," he began, "intending to join my family's import-export firm after a good schooling at Cambridge, Jesus College, my father's alma mater. It never happened . . ."

For the next half hour Ogden listened to a story of desperation, obstinate courage, official malfeasance, despair, and sheer determination. This unfortunate might have won his freedom in time had he smoothed things over and done a lengthy stint as a seaman without further blemish, but he had stubbornly resisted until he could escape. Maybe that had been poor judgment on Skye's part, but he had been a fourteen-, fifteen-, seventeen-year-old boy through the worst of it. Ogden wasn't sure but he would have fought just as hard, had he been that boy.

Skye finished his story and stood up, gazing into a cloudless night. "There's the north star and dipper, sir. For the rest of my life, no man will ever keep these eyes from seeing those stars. If I cannot leave my house or shelter and see those stars at will, I will cast my life away as a useless thing."

"You could have that life as a free trapper for us. I'll arrange it. I can set things right with the company. If by any chance it puts you in danger, I'll be the first to let you know. You impress me. That's all I can say."

"Thank you, Mr. Ogden. I'm an Englishman and always will be. But I'm a man without a country now."

That sufficed for an answer, and Ogden knew his options had reduced to two: let him go, or watch him die because the man would not be taken alive.

Chapter 10

Skye liked Peter Ogden but didn't trust him. He would know in the morning what Ogden's intentions were. At that time, the fur brigade would load its horses and head toward Fort Vancouver. And Skye, if he were left alone, would continue east.

Would they seize him at the last minute? He had no way of knowing. He had done what he could: told Ogden, with utmost seriousness, that they would never take him back alive. And he meant it. He would keep his liberty or perish.

He dozed restlessly that night, awakening with a start at the slightest shift of the rhythms of the night. He kept his larger kitchen knife at hand and would use it if he had to. But the night passed quietly, and even before dawn the camp tenders and the country wives, as the trappers called their Indian mates, were building cookfires.

It seemed a good time to go. Most of the trappers still lay in their bedrolls, although some were collecting horses in the gray dawn and throwing packframes over them. Skye rolled up his sailcloth and stuffed it in his warbag, gathered his bow and arrows, and returned his kitchen knife to a crude sheath at his belt. He would miss breakfast, but liberty was worth more than food.

"Mister Skye."

He whirled to find Ogden standing behind him, grinning.

"Stay and eat. You're a free man and you'll stay a free man. Shake on it."

Reluctantly, his mind swarming with suspicions, he shook Ogden's outstretched hand.

"I'm going to repay you for the meat. We've some jerky. I'll give you the rest of our tea. The Creoles don't care about it. They aren't Englishmen."

Skye nodded. "Obliged," he said. "I'm looking for some other things. I have one thing to trade—a heavy wool pea jacket—and don't know what it'll bring. I need a rifle or musket and powder and balls, a trap, fishing lures and line, hatchet or ax, a fishing net, blankets, horse . . ."

Ogden considered. "There's things the company can't do, such as take a contraband jacket in trade. And we're desperately short of arms. Five trappers lack firearms. Lost, broken, stolen. Then again, there's things the company can do. It can lose a trap. I've a Nez Perce fishnet I traded for some gunpowder. The company's short of horses, but most of the Creoles have their own. Maybe one or another will decide a warm coat's worth a plug horse."

The prospect gladdened Skye. He followed Ogden over to the cookfires, where two camp tenders were hustling up some grub. Ogden raided some panniers and supplied Skye with a canister of tea and several pounds of jerky. Then he headed toward another pile of gear and rummaged through panniers.

"Trade stuff. Most of it gone. Here." He handed Skye an iron hatchet blade, oddly made.

"War hatchet, the kind they like. You'll have to whittle a haft and wedge it in. That's about as much as I can get away with, Mister Skye. It's a trade for the meat."

Skye hefted the iron hatchet head as if it were gold, and then examined the trap.

"Here, let me explain a few things," Ogden said. "This is an American trap we picked up on the Malade. It's not even in my HBC inventory. It'll catch beaver, but you can use it for small animals as well. If you're going for beaver, you'll need castorum for bait, and you'll need to learn a few things."

Skye listened quietly while Ogden demonstrated how to set the trap, how to chain it in place, how to bait it, how to look for beaver grounds, how to check the trap. Ogden described how to cook and eat beaver tail, how to gut the beaver, flesh the hide, stretch it on a hoop and let it dry that way into a presentable plew. It all seemed too much to master, but Skye absorbed all he could, listening carefully. Ogden gave Skye a small, stoppered bone flask of castorum as a final gesture, and then led Skye to the cookfires. The fare that morning was salmon. The brigade, at the end of its trapping season, had little else.

The sun was rising by the time the cookfires were extinguished, and Skye knew he had only minutes to strike a trade. He pulled out his pea jacket and approached a Creole.

"Ah, you are Monsieur Skye," the man said. "I have the great honor. You gave us meat. I am your humble servant, Bordeau."

"I'm interested in a trade, Mr. Bordeau. How about this wool coat? Does it interest you?"

"Ah, such a warm coat always interests Bordeau."

"Try it on. It looks about right."

"Ah, but what is it that you wish to trade for? I am only a trapper, owing HBC all that I make."

"A horse and bridle and saddle."

"Ah, *non*, that is not possible. My two horses must

carry me and my equipage, and I have none to spare. A pity. I would give two wives and a daughter for such a fine coat. Too much do I freeze my bones in these wilds."

Skye approached the other free trappers, one by one, with the same result. They all had their reasons, but it came clear to Skye that none of them considered the coat worth a horse and bridle, and so they had politely declined to trade. Skye caught Ogden grinning. Skye's efforts had become this morning's spectacle.

Skye considered trading for other things. A good warm coat should fetch him all sorts of items: moccasins, knives, things to trade to the Indians, gloves, leggings, spoons, forks, a frying pan. But time had run out. Ogden was putting his brigade on the road. The beaver packs were back on the gaunt, hard-wintered horses, the camp gear stowed, the trappers standing about, scratching under their buckskins for greybacks, or off in the bushes.

Ogden approached. "No luck, eh?"

"Mr. Ogden, I'm a lucky man. I'm free, and I'm outfitted, and I have you to thank."

Ogden smiled, mischief dancing in his eyes. "See that log? You sit on one side and I'll sit on the other. We'll arm wrestle. You lose, and I take you with me. I lose, and you get a horse."

Skye darkened swiftly. "Mr. Ogden, I'll arm wrestle, but not on those terms. No bet. Nothing, no one, takes me back—alive."

Ogden gestured Skye toward the log and sat himself on the far side of it. The trappers congregated. *Très bien,* what a morning! Skye settled himself on the other side, and dug his boots into the clay. The bourgeois looked to be slightly shorter but powerfully built.

Skye had done this before with many seamen, and he knew the tricks. So he was ready when Ogden clasped his hand and went for a victory with one violent lurch. Skye had intended to do the same, and the result was a brutal standoff. Skye felt his sweat rise and the muscles of his arm strain and hurt. He dug in and threw his weight into a victory plunge, only to lose ground. Much to his astonishment he found himself twisted the wrong way, his hand only six inches from defeat.

He felt the tremors as he twisted his arm upward an inch, then two. Now it was Ogden's turn to sweat. The dance in Ogden's eyes told Skye the bourgeois was enjoying himself. Two more sallies yielded nothing to either man. Then Ogden laughed, gathered his resolve, slammed Skye's hand onto the log, and kept it there long enough for the trappers to hoot. Then he let go.

Ogden danced to his feet, saying nothing, his face alive with delight. Men hoorahed and slapped his back. He shrugged them off and helped Skye to his feet.

"I let you go," he said.

"No," said Skye, "you let me live."

Ogden slapped Skye on the back, found a stick, and led Skye to some sandy soil, where he drew a map. "You'll follow the Columbia another forty or fifty miles pretty much east. Then the Columbia swings north, like this. Near there you'll reach the Walla Walla River and Fort Nez Perces at the confluence. Visit it or not, as you choose. You can follow the Walla Walla into the Blue Mountains and over to the drainage of the Snake, like this. But most of the country south of the Snake's unexplored. Or you can go up the Columbia until you reach the Snake, and follow it east, like this. It loops north and then dips south in a big arc. It's rough country and the trail will take you miles south of the river where it cuts through a long canyon. I don't recommend that route.

"You'll likely run into two tribes—Nez Perces and then the Snakes, or Shoshones. I can't say what they'll do to a lone man. They're friendly enough to a fur brigade with things to trade, but they're likely to steal anything they can get from you, so be on your guard. Watch out for Blackfeet—plains Indians, well dressed in gaudy clothes, good horses. They'll butcher any lone white man they can find."

"Is there a way to befriend the Snakes and Nez Perces?"

"A white man never knows. They live by their own rules. But they're likely to be friendly, especially if you give 'em a gift or two and smoke the pipe with the elders. If they ask you to smoke, do it. Just follow their routine exactly. It's a peace ceremony."

"Where'll the Snake River take me?"

"To the Americans. They're all scoundrels and black-guards, and I shouldn't send you to them, but they'll get you to Boston and maybe outfit you. They rendezvous in July down in Cache Valley—that's Snake country, and the Snakes'll take you there. They go to trade."

"Rendezvous?"

"A mountain fair. They—Ashley and his partners—send a pack-mule supply outfit from St. Louis and trade with the trappers for beaver pelts, which they take back. Long journey, over a thousand miles. It's your ticket to Boston. Your only ticket. You've got six weeks to get to Cache Valley."

"How do I tell the Snakes I want to go there? I can't speak their tongue."

"You won't have to. If you reach 'em before they leave, you'll be taken right along. They'll think that's where you're going anyway." He stood up. "Write me from Harvard, Mister Skye."

"I will, Mr. Ogden."

"And don't linger in British territory. HBC is an arm of the Crown. John McLoughlin's a bulldog. If he wants you, he'll get you sooner or later. Maybe next year, maybe in three or five years. Mark my words. Stay out of any place claimed by Great Britain. And if you stay in the mountains with the Yanks, watch out anyway. HBC has its ways, and if they want you they'll take you—dead or alive, right in front of a crowd."

"I won't forget."

Odgen clapped him on the back. "Good. Don't forget." The brigade left immediately, and suddenly Skye found himself back in an aching wilderness, more silent and lonely than before. He watched the outfit climb the slope and vanish on the far side. He wanted to run after them.

He was alone again. Nothing stirred, not even so much as a crow. He felt desolated. Once again he realized how badly he needed company. Ogden had helped him. It was the first help he had ever received from anyone during his adult life. No one in the navy had helped him—or cared.

He wondered why Ogden had helped, and no good explanation came to mind. Skye had never thought much about getting along with people or what it took. Maybe that was because he was never free. But in Ogden he had found a friend.

Joyously he examined his new gear. The number four trap was heavy, and so was its chain. His hatchet head was heavy, and so was the small seine net, which had lead weights at the bottom and loops at the top for floats or a long supporting pole. The jerky, wrapped in an ancient piece of oilcloth, was heavy, too. He loaded all these things into his warbag, slipped his bow and quiver over his shoulder, and started east, toward Boston.

Chapter 11

Dourly, Skye examined Fort Nez Perces from across the Walla Walla River, wondering whether to go on in and risk trouble. It was walled by a stockade of upright logs planted in the sandy earth, and bastions loomed at opposite corners. A crimson flag bearing the cross of St. George in an upper corner flapped lazily on a staff. Skye supposed it was the Hudson's Bay ensign. It looked British.

The post stood on the Columbia's shore just above the confluence of the Walla Walla River. The country was so bleak it gave Skye a chill. For miles he had followed the river through arid, rough, treeless country unfit for habitation. Just why the post had been planted in such a locale he couldn't imagine—unless the Walla Walla was a thoroughfare into more bountiful lands. He thought he saw distant mountains in the eastern haze and wondered what they were.

He decided to go in. He needed instructions. He was dressed as a trapper now and his brown beard had sprouted luxuriantly since he had traded his razor. In addition to what he had started with, he was carrying a beaver trap and bow and arrows—hardly the equipment of a seaman. His heroic nose might give him away; it already had. But he would take that risk.

For days he had toiled upriver alone, carrying a heavy duffel now: the trap, seine net, and the rest. The bleakness of this empty land tormented him, awakened a hunger in him for companionship, the sound of voices. He forded the Walla Walla, which ran cold and hard with spring runoff, and climbed the sandy soil to the post, which slumbered in midday sun. He saw not a soul about the fort, although he could see someone hoeing in a distant garden plot that probably provided the post with its vegetables.

He plunged through the open gates and found himself in a yard, with what appeared to be the trading area immediately on his left. There he entered a low, dark, rough-made room with a counter and shelves lined with bolts of bright fabric, gray iron traps, casks and sacks of sugar and coffee and beans, and sundries. The scents of burlap and leather were pleasant in his nostrils.

"I've been watching ye through the glass for nigh twenty minutes," said an angular, red-haired, fierce-looking man with a voice that grated like sand under a horseshoe. "No living creature passes Fort Nez Perces unknown. Not even an ant."

"Then there must not be much else to do," Skye said.

"It's our protection, ye well know that or ye don't know the country."

"I don't know it."

"I'm Ross McTavish, factor here, and ye speak an Englishman's tongue."

Skye shrugged. "And you a Canadian's, I suppose."

"You're not giving me a name."

"Mr. Ogden told me Ronald Mackenzie would be here."

"He's not. Ye have it wrong. Mackenzie founded it,

eighteen and eighteen, when he was still a Nor' Wester. Then it was run by Alexander Ross. And now I'm the man. This is mine, all mine."

"A Scots post, then."

"And what is the matter with that? Ye be a bloody roundhead Englishman and think ye rule the world?"

"No, I rule only my own life."

"Ye haven't given me a name, and I'll give ye no more time to think on it. If ye be not the deserter Skye, then prove it. It's the nose. McLoughlin said the sniffer would tell the hull story. And it does."

McTavish reached under the counter and whipped a dragoon pistol up at Skye. "Now then, set down the pack and walk ahead o' me."

"No."

"What do ye mean, no? Do ye think I won't shoot? Put down the pack!"

Skye stared into the huge bore of that weapon and wished he hadn't surrendered to the impulse to stop here. This fierce Scotsman was going to try him. He didn't answer. Instead, he deliberately turned to leave, and took two steps toward the door when a deafening blast erupted behind him and his topper sailed off his head.

"Stop or I'll be on ye, Skye. That was a warnin'."

He headed toward the door, heard McTavish leap the counter and plunge after him. Skye whirled, belaying pin in hand, and jabbed it hard as McTavish leapt at him. McTavish howled, pulled himself up, and rammed into Skye's torso. Skye rapped McTavish on the head and arms as he tumbled backward, not really wanting to hurt the HBC man, just to teach him a little respect. But the ferocious redhead wouldn't quit and used all four limbs, his skull, and his teeth, sometimes all at once. He tried to wrestle Skye's club out of his hand while not neglecting to knee Skye and bite Skye's arm.

Skye was losing his advantage, with McTavish staying

well inside the swing of the club and twisting Skye's arms as they rolled over the earthen floor.

"You'll not have my name, not ever," Skye roared between gulps of air.

McTavish was giving him a fair beating. Skye had rarely been set upon by such a fighter as this one. His mountainous nose bled, and his right hand was numb. The belaying pin dropped out of it. McTavish was on him, twisting his arm back, back, back until it threatened to snap.

"All right," Skye muttered.

McTavish jammed all the harder. "Tell me you're Skye, ye bloody coward. Or lie to me if ye will."

"I'll say nothing to you." Skye peered up at the man through a haze of blood. His heart raced wildly.

"What does it matter? I've got ye. You're whipped and good. I'll ship ye to McLoughlin at Vancouver, that's what." McTavish eased off Skye and wiped blood from his face with his cuff. "Get up now."

Skye sat up shakily, uncertain which of his parts worked. His chest ached. His ears rang. The numb hand wouldn't hold a twig, much less his belaying pin.

"Ah, see here, this is a belaying pin. I've seen a thousand. Stolen from the Royal Navy. Deny that, will ye, Skye?"

McTavish picked up the pin and waved it menacingly. "What kind of lies did ye tell Ogden, eh? Try me and see if I believe a word." He picked up Skye's warbag. "Where'd you get this truck? Stole it, I imagine. Stole the bow and arrers, stole the trap. I've got ye red-handed, ye thief."

Skye's pulse settled and he recovered enough of his wind to talk a little. "I'm on my way to the rendezvous of the Americans. Ogden told me I could get directions here at the post."

"He hates the Yanks, and he'd tell ye no such thing. What do ye take me for?"

"Man who comes to conclusions before he get the facts."

"Well, are ye are aren't ye Skye?"

"Call me Mister Skye. I don't answer to Skye."

"I'll call ye deserter. Get going now. I'm locking ye up until I decide whether to hang ye or slit your throat."

It dawned on Skye that McTavish lacked the means to take him under guard back to Fort Vancouver. He doubted that the post had more than half a dozen men. He'd seen none within it, and only one out in the fields.

"A shot would be faster, McTavish."

"I dinna waste good powder and lead on a swine."

"I'm hungry."

"Then starve."

"Water, then."

"Help ye'self." He motioned toward an earthen pot with a metal cup next to it. Skye drank, left-handed.

While Skye poured water down his parched throat, McTavish pawed through Skye's possessions. "See here, a pea jacket. Now I have ye. And a fine buckskin hide— that'll help pay for your keep. And an awl—good for one beaver from the Indians. And a seine. Hatchet, two knives, cup. Good enough. It'll repay HBC for the cost of dealing with ye." McTavish carted every last item Skye possessed into a storeroom, closed the door, and turned the iron key.

Skye was tempted to bolt but knew he wouldn't get twenty yards in his condition, and wouldn't have so much as a knife to keep him alive even if he did outrun the factor.

"Write me a receipt, Mr. McTavish. A receipt for my possessions, if you will. Write that HBC confiscated these goods. Mr. McLoughlin would want that."

"Ah, ye live in a fantasy, Skye."

"Call me mister."

McTavish cackled nastily. "I'll call ye whatsoever I set my mind to. All right. Walk ahead of me now."

"Where?"

"That beaver press in the yard. I'll tie ye down good to the posts."

So they had no way to lock him up, no way to take him back under guard. That interested Skye. "I want my hat, Mr. McTavish."

For an answer he got a sharp crack of his own belaying pin across his arm. Pain shot through his shoulder and clear down his torso. Skye stumbled into one of the posts of the fur press and sagged there.

"Put your back to it and your hands behind," McTavish said. "I've cord here to bale the plews, and it'll bale deserters just as fine. I wonder what deserters fetch by the pound."

Skye hurt all over and was too tired to resist. But he had learned never to give up. He had spent weeks and months in ships' brigs, and now he would endure some more. "I'd like to sit down," he said.

"Stand up or I'll poke you up."

Skye felt rough hands wind cord tightly around his wrists behind him. Then McTavish tied Skye's ankles, too. Skye knew that in minutes his arms would hurt almost beyond endurance, and his tight-bound hands would prickle and go numb.

"Now, ye miserable deserter, I'll be taking your boots for insurance," McTavish said. He knelt before Skye and unlaced a worn boot, yanking one and then the other off Skye's feet.

"What are you going to do, Mr. McTavish?"

"I'll think of something unpleasant, Skye."

"Call me Mister Skye."

McTavish laughed, and left him there to bake in the fierce sun.

Chapter 12

Skye didn't know how he could endure more pain. His arms felt as if they had been ripped from their sockets and his hands had gone numb. The day waned and at least he no longer suffered its heat, but he doubted he could stand much longer. If he slumped into his bonds, he would hurt all the more.

Then, near dusk, a paunchy Creole appeared in the yard and cut him loose. Skye fell to the clay, unable to make his limbs function at first.

"Come, eat, *mangeur du lard*," the man said.

Skye struggled to his feet, staggered, and then followed the man into a kitchen area with a hand-hewn trestle table and chairs fashioned from poles and leather. McTavish sat at the head of it, looking like a choleric country squire just this side of apoplexy, while one other Creole sat halfway down, well below the salt. The Creole who brought in Skye sat down across from the other. Two young and pretty Indian women were serving.

"There you are, you craven Royal Navy scum,"

McTavish said. "Sit down there at the bottom of the table where you belong. That's your gruel. Eat and don't complain. It's more than a deserter deserves."

Skye beheld a skimpy bowl of oatmeal and a wooden spoon. He set about eating as well as his numb hands and shaking arms would let him. McTavish and the Creoles devoured their plentiful roast beef, squash, bread, dried-apple pudding, and garden greens, all washed down with red wine.

Skye glanced furtively at the women, both of them dressed in patterned calico gowns rather than native clothing. Each wore a ribbon in her hair, and both were uncommonly beautiful, with strong cheekbones, glowing amber flesh, and shiny jet hair. He wondered whose mates they were, if anybody's.

McTavish seemed even more sour than he had that afternoon, and he ate furiously, sawing and torturing the beef as if to humiliate it, glaring at Skye, belching and muttering. It took the man scarcely two minutes to down an enormous helping, but the Creoles dawdled with their food, more intent on enjoying it.

Skye wondered whether the women would join the men at table, but they simply hovered about, serving seconds to all but Skye. He caught them glancing shyly at him, their gazes alive with curiosity.

"No wonder the Royal Navy suffers. If it's manned by the degenerate dregs of England like you, the King's foreign affairs are doomed. I could've whipped you with one arm tied behind my back, Skye. I ended up beating you with your stolen belaying pin. The King's navy's rotten to the core, a paper tiger, and you're the proof of it. Where'd they pick ye up? Out of some bloody penal colony?"

Skye saw where this was heading and kept his silence.

"Ah, I'm right, then! They took you out of some stinking gaol where they keep all incorrigibles. It was that or Botany Bay, no doubt."

Skye finished his oatmeal gruel, well satisfied with the plain dish.

"That's where they got you, then. Ye deserve to hang. Ye don't even speak back to me because ye know it's so, Skye."

"It's Mister Skye, sir."

"It's what I bloody well choose to call ye. Now, then, I'm putting you out."

"I don't understand."

"Of course you don't. Ye can't get ahold of the simplest idears because you're a degenerate with a brain the size of a pea. I'm putting ye outside the gates and I'll keep everything—your stolen goods and your boots. How's that for a verdict? Go, and don't come back."

Skye sat stock still.

"I can't take you down to Vancouver, blast it. If ye'd skulked in a week ago, I'd have sent ye down the river with the pelts. I sent Pambrun and Vincennes with the spring returns. And Pryor's taking trade goods up to Spokane House. There's but three men here—Gris, there, Souvanne, there, and me—and I can't spare a man and I won't be feeding you and guarding you and dirtying my post for a bloody month while I wait for relief. So get ye out, ye filthy deserter."

"That's murder."

"Of course it's murder. You won't last a week. Any good Creole or HBC man'd make it, but not some dross from a London lockup."

"Are you judge, jury, and executioner?"

"I am all of that, Skye. I'm also king. This is my bailiwick. My word is law and my fists enforce it."

"It's Hudson's Bay's bailiwick."

"I'll do what I please, and it pleases me to put you out. You're done? Go!"

Skye refused to move.

"I said go. Gris, open the gates and throw 'im out." The factor bolted up from his rude chair and loomed over Skye with cocked fists.

"If you're going to murder me, Mr. McTavish, you'll do it here, not outside your gates."

Skye's pulse leapt. He would fight here and die, then. But they would not throw him out in the cold, barefoot and without a kit. Without a flint and steel.

The Creoles stood reluctantly.

"Return my kit and I'll walk out. Otherwise, I'll fight to the death."

"*Sacrebleu,* McTavish!" Gris exclaimed. "I will get his kit and put him out. It is *assassinat.*"

But the factor didn't wait. Grinning, he closed on Skye, delight firing his burning blue eyes. "Teach you another wee lesson, eh, Skye? Show the Royal Navy's scum what a Hudson's Bay man is?" McTavish's voice rose high and crackled.

"It's Mister Skye, sir." Skye rose quietly from his chair. "And you'll have to kill me."

The Creoles were holding back, wanting no part of this. He ached from the afternoon's ordeal, from sunburn, and from his previous set-to with this vicious Scot. Anger percolated through him, softly at first, and then with resonance. Some obdurate courage rooted Skye to his spot in that dining hall. He knew that he would not leave that hall conscious—or alive. It came down to life or death, and so he waited.

McTavish paused, glaring at Skye, comfortable with his belly full of meat. The women watched silently. Skye could not say what sort of mood or menace or courage he conveyed in that taut moment, but McTavish paused.

"You mean it. I'd have to kill you."

"If I don't kill you first."

"Maybe I will."

"Try me. I've nothing to lose."

This was the moment, the hinge of fate. Skye waited. He would die here or not. But he would not die helpless and barefoot in the wilderness. He stood ready to kill McTavish with his bare hands.

McTavish glared unhappily, muttered something, his face reddening. "All right. I dinna want an inquiry. Mind ye, I'd as soon bash your skull in and throw you in the river, but I don't want to report it. Damn ye. Go to the Americans. You're not a worthy subject of the Crown."

"That's it exactly, sir. I'm not a subject."

"They're scum, like you."

"I take that as a recommendation."

"Deserter. Thief. Come along. I'll give you some of it back. I'm charging you for your stay. You'll not get a free feed on the company."

He walked to the store with an oil lamp in hand, Skye following. The redolence of fabric and good leather struck Skye, and he eyed those precious goods on the shelves with yearning while the factor opened the storeroom door with the iron key and pulled out Skye's kit.

"I'll keep that buckskin pelt. That's the price of the meal."

"How much is a good tanned deerskin worth, and how much is a meal worth?"

"What difference does it make? That's what ye'll pay because I say so. Don't tempt me."

"How much is the skin worth, and what's my meal worth?"

"By God, I'll not bargain with a deserter and degenerate."

"What do you pay the Indians for such a skin?"

"As little as I can, ye scoundrel."

"How much was a bowl of gruel worth?"

"To a starving man, plenty."

"What do you charge trappers for a bowl?"

"As many pence as I can milk out of 'em, Skye."

"It's Mister—"

"Get out before I shoot you. I've a loaded piece at hand."

Skye smiled. "Thanks for the hospitality. I'll remember Hudson's Bay. You have beautiful women."

McTavish snarled, but Skye took up his kit and checking it, threw the seine over his shoulder, hefted his belaying pin, and then remembered.

"Where are my boots, McTavish?"

"Where you can't get them, Skye."

"Then I'll take what's at hand to replace them."

"I'll kill you cold."

"Do that."

Skye set down his burdens and headed for the shelves, looking for something for his feet. He found no ready-made boots, and knew that he would not find any, half a world away from English cobblers. But there were hard-soled moccasins, perhaps made by French-Canadians. He reached for a likely pair.

"I'll kill you, thief." McTavish held his dragoon pistol in hand.

Skye paused, smiling. "Odd how I had just the same thought." He picked up the knee-high moccasins and found they were fur-lined.

The deafening shot grazed his hair and made his ears ring. Skye sprang forward, his belaying pin in hand, and knocked the empty pistol out of McTavish's grip. They circled each other.

"Try me," said Skye.

McTavish seemed to deflate. "I'll get your boots, and then get out."

He went after Skye's boots while Skye tried the moccasins, found them small, tried another pair that fit, and bound them tight. They had thick soles, maybe buffalo-hide.

McTavish returned with Skye's ancient boots.

"I think we'll trade, McTavish."

The Scot turned cunning. "Trade, will ye? Boots for moccasins?" He examined Skye's footwear and smiled suddenly. "You get the worst of it. Good navy boots. Ye be a fool."

"I came here to ask directions. How do I get to the rendezvous of the Americans?"

"It'll be good riddance putting you out of Crown lands, Skye. Go up the Walla Walla, cross the Blue Mountains at any pass you find, go down any drainage to the Snake, find the Shoshones before they go to the rendezvous, and let them take ye. And may the devil or some wild tribe destroy ye on the way."

"Thank you."

The factor walked Skye to the front gates and opened them. The night yawned ahead. "If I had my way, you'd be bound in irons and on the river to Fort Vancouver. Don't ever set foot in Crown lands or I'll come after ye. I'll tell you something: it isn't over. If you linger around the mountains, we'll catch you and ship ye back to London. HBC sits like a spider in the web, the sovereign over an empire. John McLoughlin's a great patriot, and he'd like na' better'n to put a deserter in irons. Some time, when you least expect it, we'll catch ye, Skye. So go to the Yanks to save your miserable life."

"I plan to, Mr. McTavish. I'm going to Boston and start college."

"You fooled Ogden, but you don't fool me," McTavish snapped.

Chapter 13

Skye found himself in a bountiful land as he hiked up the Walla Walla River, and his spirits matched the country. He had passed through fire and brimstone and had emerged from it alive and free. For the first time in memory, he lived each hour with sheer joy. This well-watered and mild country cried out to him.

The land! In his flight and hunger he had scarcely noticed the land. A childhood in London and a life in the prison of the sea had blinded him. But now, as he passed through a verdant and sweet country bursting with new life, the land bewitched him. Everything he beheld was a sweet mystery. He paused frequently, enchanted by the world about him. He marveled that he could name most of the plants and the creatures, and wondered where the knowledge came from. Poetry, perhaps. English poets had never ignored the land, and he had read them all.

Everything caught his eye and ear. The trill of a red-winged blackbird delighted him, and the whirring flight of a meadowlark. He paused to examine the fronds of weeping willows, and bent to inhale the acrid smell of a juniper. He lay for an hour on the grassy bank of the river, watching minnows dart, tadpoles swim, and a great humped turtle sun himself. He plucked the silvery sagebrush and rubbed its aromatic leaves upon his flesh. He watched squirrels, robins, raccoons, ants, red foxes, with eyes that had never beheld such wonders. He discovered that each creature had its own habits, and he could ferret them out. One dawn he discovered a doe with a newborn fawn at the river. The little creature wore white spots and stood on wobbly legs so thin he wondered how it could support itself. The doe picked up his scent and hurried her baby into red willow brush. Barnaby Skye smiled.

He absorbed this new world and loved it. Again and again he stopped to examine some new wonder, things as ordinary as a bee or a bright butterfly or a dragonfly. This was the good earth, and it awakened a new awareness in him. He wanted to walk this entire land, know it, possess it, nurture it even as it nurtured him. It dawned on him that he had been stunted and shriveled and warped by his sea-prison. The mortal soul needed the good earth and all upon it, just as much as any plant needed the good earth. He might have loved the ever-changing sea if he had not been a prisoner, and if it had not been a monstrous barrier against his liberty. But he could not put down roots into the sea. Here on this vast continent he could—and would.

Ever mindful that he needed to find the Americans in July, he continued eastward, but not in a rush, and always taking time to learn how to live upon the breast of the world. Bit by bit, he was becoming the master of his fate.

He experimented with various types of tinder for his fire steel, finding merit in the fibrous inner bark of dead cottonwoods. He learned to make his beds more comfortable by plucking away the smallest sticks and stones, and even to make a hollow for his hip bone. He practiced with his bow and arrows as he walked, knowing his skills were barely adequate. But one day he bagged a wild turkey, and several times he shot mallards, much to his astonishment. And he didn't neglect the sparkling Walla Walla River and its salmon.

If this was a paradise, it was also a land of unknown tribes, some of which might be dangerous. He found ample evidence of them: hoof and moccasin prints, and campsites. His Creole moccasins blended with these signs of passage and concealed his journey from knowing eyes. One day he found a discarded moccasin and put it in his kit as a pattern. He learned what he could of the ways the Indians fed themselves, noting what roots and bulbs they dug up, what trees and bushes showed signs of being disturbed, and what firewoods they used. Just by being observant, he learned the lore of the natives. The Indians had collected a tall herb with a cluster of half-inch-thick roots that he found edible. And they had dug up a low plant with bright white blossoms. This plant had a root that tasted bitter raw, but when he sliced and boiled the root in his tin cup, the white root tasted better. He discovered wild onions, and a small lily with purplish white blossoms that offered up a valuable root.

But the plant obviously prized by the local Indians grew everywhere and had blue blossoms on foot-high stalks. Its bulbous root, the size of a small onion, proved to be without taste but filling and edible raw as well as cooked. Skye collected the bulbs and stuffed them in his kit. Nature was providing a bounty as the warm season progressed, and he stopped worrying about feeding himself. He didn't know the name of any of these foodstuffs, and vowed he would find out when he reached the Yanks. Names were important. He wanted to know the name of everything around him.

An occasional cold, rainy day taught him to study the land for shelter as he passed through, and to thatch brush huts from boughs cut with his hatchet. He learned to build a fire near a rock escarpment that caught the heat and radiated it back upon him. Windy days he had simply to endure, because there was little refuge in nature from the blasts of air that plucked at his flesh.

He experimented with his trap, chaining it down, baiting it with meat, and setting it two or three hundred yards from his campsites. He caught nothing, and wondered why. Perhaps it was his scent. He scrubbed the trap in the river, using a root that yielded a frothy substance like soap. The next morning a foul odor permeated the entire area, and he found a dead skunk in the jaws. He wondered if he could endure its flesh, decided he could not, washed the trap in the river, and fled the area.

He walked up the broad valley through golden days, seeing not a soul and glad of it. He wanted to be alone. His ordeal at Fort Nez Perces had scarred his soul, left a rancid memory of a fur company's arrogance, and deepened his hunger to reach the Americans. The river swung south through mounting slopes and east again, into foothill canyons. He was nearing the Blue Mountains.

He followed the diminished river ever upward through private canyons and hidden glens. The river turned into a tumbling torrent, icy with snowmelt, sometimes hidden from the surrounding slopes by its log-choked canyons. He came upon large swampy plateaus chocked with wildlife, moose and elk as well as deer. One day a huge brown bear with a cub scared him witless, and he backed away from the creek while she stood on her hind legs and snorted. After that, he habitually noted trees he could climb and lines of retreat. He had not won his liberty only to let himself be butchered by a wild animal.

He arrived at the headwaters of the Walla Walla, a mass of springs and soggy turf. From now on he would travel without a reliable source of water, and it worried him. He would need to keep his eye peeled for springs and seeps. He hiked the rest of that day through chill mountain air, finding no sign of a spring, and feared he might have to retreat to the headwaters. Some unknown distance ahead he would reach a summit and enter the Snake River drainage.

The pungence of pines intoxicated his senses; he had never smelled anything like it. But his quest for water preoccupied him, and he feared he would make a dry camp that night and hope his body would endure the drought. Then, as he wound his way around a steep north slope, he found the rotted remains of a snowbank, mottled with dirt and bark on its glistening surface. Meltwater leaked from its lowest point and he drank it, gasping at its cold. After that he hacked out several pounds of the dripping snow and packed it into his poncho.

He camped that night high in the Blue Mountains, warding off an icy breeze with a crackling fire of knotty pine, and satisfying his thirst with the decaying snow. That night he slept cold even though it was the end of May, and finally built up his dying fire and sat in the pine-scented night, waiting for the sun.

The next dawn he swallowed some of his hoarded jerky and boiled some of his carefully husbanded bulbs in his little cup, using the last of his snow, and then set out again. He topped a saddle midmorning and descended a dry watercourse, wondering whether he had reached the Snake drainage. That day he hiked across a broad alpine meadow berserk with flowers. That evening he set up camp beside a foot-wide rill, and swiftly drove an arrow into a small deer, which ran, shuddered, stopped, and sagged to the ground a hundred yards away. He had never killed a creature that large, and felt a certain sadness he could not explain. It was odd, he thought, that a man who had fought the bloody Kaffirs would feel despondent about taking the life of a deer. It was as if the deer were innocent and undeserving of its fate, while the two-footed demons deserved what they got.

He dragged the limp yearling buck toward his camp, then thought better of it. He would leave it well away from his campsite. He attacked the carcass clumsily, eventually gutting it, up to his elbows in blood and gore. After two hours of sawing with his dull knives, he quit. He took ten or fifteen pounds of venison back to his camp, built a fire, spitted some of the meat on green twigs, and roasted it. It had taken an amazing amount of bloody work to make meat. Thinking back, he realized he had used too light a hand: next time, he would take his hatchet to a carcass and make quicker work of it. But that experience, like so many others these sweet days, had taught him much.

That night an unearthly howling awakened him, and he knew at once he was hearing wolves. He crawled uneasily to the fire and found a few live coals, which he soon fed into a hot yellow flame. Out in the blackness orange eyes stared back at him, one pair, two, then five pair in all, some holding steady, others bobbing, catching and losing the firelight. The sight raised the hair on the nape of his neck. He had no idea whether wolves would attack a man—no doubt the scent of meat had drawn them—but he took no chances. He put on his moccasins, grabbed his hatchet in one hand and his belaying pin in the other, and ran toward one of those pairs of orange eyes, roaring like a mad bull. The eyes vanished.

When he returned to camp he discovered that the wolves had pilfered the leftover meat he had cut. Unthinkingly, he had stored it near the fire—and not far from his head. Some bold wolf had come within ten feet of him. That ruined his sleep for the night, and he sat at the fire, feeding dry wood into it now and then, his mind filled with images of wolf packs hamstringing their prey, clamping their long jaws over vulnerable throats, and ripping open bellies.

He stirred with the first grays of dawn, much more aware that wilderness was no Eden. He hiked to the place where his deer carcass lay—and found no sign of it. When at last he found the remains fifty yards distant— nothing but well-gnawed bones now—he knew a large animal had been at work, most likely a bear.

Skye had gotten only one meal out of an entire deer. That was something to think about. He glared into the surrounding brush, and discovered he wasn't alone, even in the dawn light. A wolf stood watching, shaggy and feral, waiting to attack the well-gnawed carcass for whatever last bit of meat remained. It edged silently into shadow, sat on its haunches, and watched him. Skye had enough of wolves. He strung his bow, nocked an arrow, aimed, and let fly. The wolf exploded into the air, howled, and ran away with an arrow poking from its side. Skye followed the trail of blood but never saw the animal again. He had lost an arrow. He wanted a good warm wolf skin, and the next wolf to cross his path would donate it. He hated the wolves for reasons he couldn't explain. The wolves had done nothing but be themselves and yet they prompted a dread and rage in him. The bear had been bad enough, the wolves worse.

The next two days he descended the east flanks of the Blue Mountains, following a cheerful creek that rushed down awesome canyons that boxed him into their bottoms. He was plunging into arid country again, filled with broken volcanic rock. Then one morning he reached a grassy flat and discovered it was where the creek debouched into a larger river. And it was also the site of a large Indian village consisting of conical lodges of animal skins, such as he had never before seen. He didn't know who these people were or what his fate might be, but he had been discovered by bold half-naked children, and there would be no escape.

Chapter 14

Skye set down his heavy burden and waited. Children swarmed him, excited and curious, the boys slim and naked, the girls in leather skirts. Then men ran up, the women holding back. The men carried lances, bows, and arrows. He saw no firearms. These people were short, stocky, golden-fleshed, and had coarse black hair worn long. They stood erect and alert and conveyed a certain dignity. They studied Skye with obvious curiosity. He yearned to greet them but felt helpless. He could not speak to them, nor even let them know his intentions were peaceful. He held out a hand, but no one took it. They seemed to be waiting, and sure enough, emerging from the village was a gray-haired elder wearing ceremonial robes. A headman or chief of some sort.

The village lay alongside the Snake River on a grassy flat, in a mountain bowl. Out on the pasture oddly marked horses grazed, their rumps spotted, as if their maker had splattered white paint over them. But some lighter-tinted horses carried black or brown spots, and sometimes the spots covered the whole torso. Hundreds of these strange creatures dotted this basin, giving Skye the idea that this tribe knew horses well.

The headman wore a bonnet of eagle feathers that stood vertically, and also a white-man's shirt cinched at the waist. He surveyed Skye with eyes that revealed neither hostility nor friendship, but did convey a profound authority. Skye desperately wished he knew the protocols for this sort of thing. All he could do was talk.

"I happened upon your village," he said. "I don't know who you are. I'm heading east, toward the rendezvous of the Americans, and hope you can tell me how to get there."

No one understood. Skye stared at blank faces.

Maybe a gift. Skye swiftly considered the few items in his warbag, wondering which one he could do without, and finally settled on the canister of tea that Ogden had given him—something he treasured, but something not essential for his survival. He dug into his kit, found the enameled canister, and presented it to the headman, who accepted it without quite knowing what it was. He opened the canister, saw the tea, sniffed it, puzzled.

"I'll show you how to make tea," Skye said.

"Hudson Bayee," the headman said.

"No, just a man passing through."

Skye's shake of the head was understood, if not his words.

"Americeen?"

"Rendezvous."

"Ah." The headman had some inkling of something, and so did Skye.

The village men crowded around, examining the canister, admiring it more than what it contained. Women edged in now, peeking shyly at Skye, studying his gift to the headman. The ladies wore soft doeskin dresses, although a few were decked out in traders' calico, their dresses crudely cut but finely sewn.

The headman beckoned, and Skye picked up his kit

and followed him into the village, which consisted of thirty or forty skin lodges, some brightly dyed with animal figures, all of them smoke-blackened at their apex. The village was redolent of salmon and meat and offal. The chief's lodge loomed larger than the others, and seemed to have more poles supporting it. Several handsome young women, apparently the headman's wives or daughters, stood about shyly. The headman spoke briefly to one, and she trotted away, vanishing among the lodges.

There they waited for what seemed a long time. Skye relaxed a little; no one had manhandled him or threatened his life. His gift had cemented his status as a guest—for the moment. The headman's woman reappeared, this time with an ancient white man in tow. The man seemed to be all or mostly blind, and stared out upon the world from milky eyes.

"Eh? *Bonjour*," he muttered.

"Do you speak English?" Skye asked.

"Eh?"

Skye realized the old Creole was both blind and deaf. "English? Do you speak English?" he bellowed.

"Pierre Gallard, Nor' West," the man said, and slid into French again.

"Hudson's Bay?" Skye bawled into the man's ear.

"Eh? *Non, non, Nord Ouest Compagnie.*"

Skye understood: the North West Company, once a bitter and violent rival of Hudson's Bay and now absorbed by it. A lovely young woman appeared beside the old man, and Skye realized she was his mate. She, it turned out, could communicate better than he.

"Nez Percés," she said. "You Hudson's Bay."

"No, madam, I'm alone. I want to go to the rendezvous."

"Ah, *les Americains.*"

"Yes."

Swiftly she translated all this to the headman and villagers. It took effort, but in time she and he had exchanged information. He was in a Nez Percé village that had come here to fish. She was the wife of the honored white man, Gallard, from Montreal, and cared for him now that he was old and helpless. Gallard despised the English, and Hudson's Bay Company, but not Americans. Last year's rendezvous, the first, was the talk of all the tribes.

Skye asked for directions, and after much consultation, she told him not to follow the Snake because it ran through a terrible canyon, but to go around to the south of it for many days, and then pick up the Snake again where it came out of the canyon and ran through plains. The more she murmured, the better Skye understood her French. He dredged up words and phrases from his childhood, and from his occasional shipboard reading.

The headman thrust the tea canister at her. She examined its contents, smiled. *"Thé,"* she said, and explained what it was to him. He nodded and spoke to her at length.

"You guest," she said. *"Allez."* He followed her to the chief's portal and started to leave.

"Wait. What is his name? Will he trade for horses?"

She stared blankly.

He pointed to himself. "I'm Skye. Skye." Then he pointed at the chief.

"Ah! Skyeskye." She smiled and pointed. "Hemene Moxmox." Then she pointed at other leaders and village men: "Eapalekthiloom, Ealaot Wadass, Hematute Hikaith, Chelooyeen, Alikkees." Skye couldn't even pronounce the names, much less repeat them.

Skye remembered the word for horse, and yelled it into the old man's ear. *"Cheval?"*

Gallard nodded and said something to his wife. Skye dug into his warbag and produced his pea jacket, which he hoped to trade. She understood, and addressed her auditors at length. The headman took the blue woolen coat, examined it, tried it on—it was too long in the arms, but otherwise serviceable—and smiled. It would keep him warm next winter. And no one else in the village would have anything so magical. He talked at length with the Frenchman's woman, and then with his friends, and at last nodded. A nod, at least, seemed to be a universal sign that Skye took for a yes. He waited impatiently, hoping he had been understood, afraid that he had just given away his coat as another gift.

But the iron-haired headman spoke gently to two young men, and these trotted off toward the fields where the herd grazed. Then he nodded Skye into his lodge. Skye discovered surprising comfort within. Its skin sides had been rolled upward a foot or so from the ground so that the spring zephyrs might percolate through and up the smoke vent at the top. Decorated parfleches held this family's possessions. Pallets lined the periphery. A stone-lined firepit occupied the center, but the fire was out this warm day.

Skye's dignified host walked around the firepit and placed himself opposite the lodge door. He beckoned Skye to follow and seat himself next to the host. Others in the village followed, seating themselves in a preordained order.

The headman withdrew an ornate pipe with a red stone bowl and a long stem from a leather bag, tamped what appeared to be tobacco in it, and waited. A young man appeared at the lodge door, bearing a hot coal wrapped in a leaf. It was passed to the headman, and in due course he lifted it with bare fingers, lit his pipe, and sucked until the tobacco was fairly ablaze. Then he lifted the pipe with both hands, chanting something as he did, in each direction of the compass and to heaven and earth. Skye knew this was some sort of important ceremony, perhaps a blessing of his presence in this village, and waited quietly. These people were in no hurry, unlike Skye, who itched to look at horses and select one.

The headman drew smoke, exhaled, and passed the pipe to Skye, who assumed he should do the same. Skye completed the ritual and passed the pipe along. The pipe went the full circle, no Nez Percé saying anything, then went another round, as a great peace descended on this group. Skye felt the peace, felt himself relax, and joined the quietness of spirit that seemed to occupy the lodge. He knew that this, too, was a lesson. Perhaps this smoking of the pipe meant something to all these American tribes. He would find out. Hundreds of questions had arisen in the last weeks, and he yearned to find the answers to them. For now, he had only his wits, his powers of observation, and perhaps whatever could be conveyed to him by an old deaf Creole and his younger Nez Percé woman.

These tribesmen had stopped time. Until this moment, Skye's focus had been escape, survival, and the future. Now, in this breezy lodge, among these elders, he experienced only the moment, without thought of his bitter past or uncertain future. The headman talked a while, sometimes addressing Skyeskye, who grasped not a word, and then suddenly dismissed his guests with a gesture. One by one, the men stood and ducked out into the blazing sun. Skye followed. There, tied to a picket stake, stood two handsome ponies, each with the peculiar markings these people cherished, one white with black markings, the other brown with white splotches across its rump.

This was a critical moment in many ways. Skye had never before ridden a horse. He had seen horses, the big British kind, chestnut or bay or black, often in harness.

The headman was eyeing him, waiting for something. Skye looked desperately for the old Creole or his woman, and could not spot either of them in the quiet throng. He studied the animals, looking for flaws, but he could scarcely tell a bad horse from a good one, and wouldn't know a horse that misbehaved from an obedient and eager one. Each wore a leather bridle of Indian manufacture. Skye realized they had no iron bits, and surprised himself by understanding that these devices were hackamores, and they could be used to start, stop, and turn a horse as well as an English bit and bridle.

He turned to his host. "These are fine animals. I don't know a thing about them. I don't even know whether you mean for me to pick one, or keep both. I lack a saddle, and will learn to ride them as you do."

The headman raised two fingers. "Skyeskye," he said.

Skye nodded, the universal gesture of affirmation. "Thank you, Hemene Moxmox," he said.

The chief nodded gravely. A small wave of his hand set one of the youths to demonstrate. The boy climbed easily over the back of the lighter pony, took the loop rein, and rode it in a loop. Skye watched intently. Then the youth rode the other in the same manner, and handed the reins of both to Skye. He took them as one would take the keys to a kingdom.

Chapter 15

Skye spent that night in the lodge of Hemene Moxmox. He didn't sleep well. Everything was so strange, not least of which was the intimate presence of the headman's wife and daughters, all of them crowded close. He heard movement in the night, breathing, snoring, people turning about. Someone left, and for a moment starlight appeared at the lodge door. Not even the crowded forecastle of the *Jaguar* was as packed and intimate as this.

But it was the presence of the women that troubled him. How did these people manage certain things? How could they all live through the nights without experiencing the stirrings that plagued Skye? A certain shyness tormented him as he lay there. He had suffered a living death in ships of war, and all the heat and need of youth had been ruthlessly suppressed. But now he lay within reach of several women, and his thoughts troubled and maddened him. He ached to leave the lodge.

Dawn crept in, but no one arose. He had already learned that these people weren't in a hurry and didn't count hours. They would arise whenever the spirit moved them. But Skye, restless and eager to be off, couldn't endure his buffalo robe pallet any longer, and slipped into the hushed morning. He wanted to be on his way; if he missed the rendezvous of the Americans, he didn't know how he might survive.

His horses had been returned to pasture by the headman's youngest son so they could graze and water through the night. A few horses stood beside the lodges of their masters, ever ready for trouble or use. Skye settled quietly in the brown grass beside the lodge, absorbing the village. He felt at peace there even though it was as strange a place as he'd ever visited.

He wasn't entirely alone. Here and there an old woman stirred, or someone headed to a brushy area. He supposed a village would have to move frequently to keep from fouling itself. But here there was land in such plenitude that moving from one locale to another offered infinite possibilities. A few dogs prowled, but these seemed to be the only night guard the village had. Most of the skin lodges had been erected in a large ring with a commons in the center. But here and there were other lodges situated without rhyme or reason.

He explored quietly, not wanting to disturb the dogs or the sleeping villagers. One lodge was empty, its door flap open. Smaller lodges, well back from the main circle, seemed to be occupied by single young men or the very old. Another, almost a hut, set well back from the village, puzzled him. Was it a place of banishment or taboo?

He studied everything around him, marveling at the uses of wood and bone and leather. Some of the ponies were hobbled, and he studied these devices, shaped like a figure eight, which caught the forelegs of the animals and prevented them from all but the smallest steps. He would need two, and if he couldn't trade for them he would have to manufacture them. Most of the horses were tied with braided leather cord—something he could weave himself. He had braided a lot of rope for the Royal Navy.

Most of the horses were ridden bareback, but he saw numerous saddles, too, ranging from simple pads to elaborate seats with high cantles and pommels. Where could he get one for himself? And a packsaddle for his spare?

The curs sniffed him and growled, threatening to awaken the village, so he returned to the lodge of Hemene Moxmox and waited outside its door, absorbing the redolence of an Indian village. The sun was well up before anyone stirred, and then almost by unspoken command they all were up and bustling about. The headman's daughters appeared one by one and headed for the river and their morning ablutions.

Bit by bit, blue smoke layered the village as one woman after another stirred up coals and added firewood. They were taking their time about all this, too, and Skye realized it would be midmorning before he could leave. He decided to put the time to good use, and wandered freely, studying the manufacture of everything: saddles and tack, backrests, woven reed mats, buffalo robes, fish and meat drying racks, rawhide pouches used to carry goods, a packsaddle that looked rather like a sawbuck. A partly butchered deer hung high above the reach of dogs, but the birds—especially a bold iridescent black-and-white type—were feasting.

The headman's women fed him some sort of fish cakes, no doubt salmon, on smooth slabs of bark, something to eat with his fingers. The cakes had an odd, nutty flavor, and he guessed the flour in them had been made from some pulverized root or another. Hemene Moxmox stirred about, occasionally eyeing Skye, but not trying to breach the barrier of tongue that kept them from conveying their thoughts to each other. It seemed best to Skye just to wait; events would take their course, and meanwhile he was studying everything in the village and learning swiftly.

When the time came, Hemene Moxmox's son brought Skye's ponies to him, and now a moment of truth arrived. He packed his warbag, gathered up his belaying pin and seine and sailcloth, and stared helplessly at the animals. A crowd had gathered, and while they were outwardly impassive, there were glints of amusement on those brown faces.

Skye approached Hemene Moxmox. "Though you can't understand me, I want to thank you for your hospitality. I hope it's understood just by this talk."

The headman nodded solemnly.

Inspiration struck Skye. He had one more thing to give the headman—his big, bulky seine net. He hadn't used it for a while, and with a horse to help him go after game, he could well part with it. He handed it to the headman, after rolling it open a way. It had been made of traders' cord, patiently tied together by one of the fishing tribes, and had small lead weights along its bottom edge. "This is for you, sir," he said.

The chief received the gift happily, his eyes alive with delight. He unrolled it, found it to be a majestic length and height, and spoke rapidly to several youths around him, who scattered into the crowd. The whole village, it seemed, had come to see Skye off.

Earlier, Skye had observed the youth swing gracefully over the bare back of the brown pony and ride him. The boy had done it in two stages, first up on the back in precarious balance, and then a leg over the croup. Skye set down his truck and gathered the rein. Then he leapt. The horse sidled away and Skye crashed into the earth. The crowd stared politely. Skye picked himself up and tried again. This time he catapulted clear over the pony's back, and tumbled to the earth again. No one laughed, and Skye fathomed that would be impolite—at least until the village guest was safely out of sight.

Ruefully, Skye eyed the crowd, knowing what they thought of his riding abilities. But then Moxmox clapped his hands. The youths appeared at once, each bearing things, which they laid before Skye. One was a small pad saddle with bentwood stirrups and a leather cinch. Another brought some sort of saddle blanket made of soft hide. Another brought hobbles and braided halters and lead ropes to Skye. And the last gift was a packsaddle and an ancient pelt for it. Swiftly the youths saddled the two ponies. Skye stuffed the hobbles and spare line in his warbag and tied it on the packsaddle.

Then they helped Skye up on the brown horse. It skittered sideways, almost toppling him, but he managed to stay aboard. Now at last the villagers grinned, some making odd clucking sounds while others simply cheered.

"Thank you, friends," he said, lifting his topper to them.

"Skyeskye," they replied.

The horse alarmed him with every step, but he resolutely steered it away from the village and onto a trail they pointed out to him, and in minutes he was riding alone, wondering how to manage horses, fearing a runaway, fearing they would stop dead or bolt back. But they didn't. They plodded steadily in a direction that took him away from the Snake. He realized he now had not only his own life and water and provender to worry about, but also those of his creatures. It would be entirely up to him to find grass and water, to rest them and keep them from injury, to examine their hooves and brush their backs. It was up to him to keep them from wandering or being stolen. To stay on board when they became excited or began to pitch him off. To track them down when they ran off. To catch them when they didn't wish to be caught. He vowed he would learn.

Every day was going to give him forced lessons in horsemanship, and he wondered if he would be up to the test. He rode quietly that sunny morning through a brown land of vast slopes and isolated green oases, always pausing at water. He soon ached in the saddle, and knew that these first days were going to be lived out in hellish pain.

But he was free. And he now had a mobility he never dreamed he might possess. He no longer struggled with his heavy kit, which rode easily on the animal behind him. Hesitantly, he kicked his pony into a trot. It danced along easily, jarring him with every step until he jerked the hackamore hard, and the horse settled into a lazy walk again. Next time, when he got his nerve up, he would try a canter. But for now he was more than content just to get to know his animals and master something about staying on a horse. He *had* to stay on; he doubted he would ever catch them again if he fell off. He studied his low rawhide saddle and found he could grip it if he had to, and vowed then and there to cling to it with an iron hand if he must.

He endured the pain until he could sit no more, and then slid off and walked, leading the animals and working the knots out of his legs and thighs. He marveled. Here he was, a British sailor who'd scarcely set foot on land since boyhood, leading two obedient horses as if he knew what he was doing.

He spent the rest of that day walking and riding, and in spite of his clumsiness he traveled many miles into dryer and harsher country. He had seen no one all day, but that didn't mean he was safe. A lone man with horses would be an invitation to trouble. But he would give trouble as well as get it if it came to that. He was learning, and the more he learned, the safer Barnaby Skye, formerly of the Royal Navy, would be.

Chapter 16

Skye pondered his fate as he made his solitary way eastward along a trail he hoped would take him back to the Snake River. He knew what he had been; he didn't know what he would become. He was still young, but unsure of himself. Why was Barnaby Skye set upon this earth? He could have answered that not long ago, but now he didn't know.

His solitude troubled him. For years he had been stripped of his own will. The presence of other mortals around him had largely meant slavery, with only glimmerings of friendship from a few sympathetic shipmates. Now he was alone, free, sovereign, untroubled by the will of others—and desperately lonely. He needed friends, but had none.

The wilderness he saw about him, the vaulting slopes, the hot sun, a land scarred with angry black rock, made him pensive. Mostly it seemed benign but he knew that was an illusion, and every little while something happened to confirm it. Once his horse bolted, almost unseating him, when a rattlesnake coiled upward. On another occasion he ran into a bull moose with humped shoulders, and whirled his horses away when it lowered its great rack and pawed the earth.

He could not afford mistakes, and when they did happen, he knew he must learn from them and never need another lesson. Once, when he failed to hobble a horse properly, it dodged him until he walked it down. On another occasion the brown horse yanked a picket pin loose and drifted away. He learned from those episodes that the horses stuck together. He could ride one and the other would follow, helter-skelter. But he knew that if both horses got loose, he would be in trouble.

He learned watchfulness from his horses. When they stopped suddenly, their ears perked, their gaze focused on something, he knew he should be looking that way, too. Once they halted in brushy cover, and he was just about to urge them out of it when he spotted an Indian party in the distance. A dozen males, armed for war and painted in grotesque fashion, topped a distant rise and continued at an oblique angle. Skye's spotted horses had kept him from being discovered.

He had little difficulty feeding himself. He continued to harvest the bulbs of the blue flower and reduce them to starchy food. Each evening he staked and baited his trap a quarter of a mile from his camp, and often he caught something in it, a mink or weasel or chuck or raccoon. He butchered these into tasteless meat, and tried to preserve and flesh the better furs, especially the mink. He spent his evenings at that task, clumsily scraping with his dull knives, and then with a sharp piece of glassy volcanic rock.

He shot bobbing mallards or canvasbacks regularly, but they took a long time to clean and gut and cook. A pot of boiling water would have helped him pull the feathers, but he had only his large tin cup for a pot. Still, he occupied himself during the long spring twilights by preparing bits of food while he watched his horses graze.

The horses fascinated him. He needed to know all there was to know about them. They were shy, easily frightened animals, whose instinct was to flee rather than fight because they had few weapons other than teeth and hooves. One was sullen and did not like to carry him. That one became the packhorse, but he determined to ride it now and then because there would be times when he would have to. The other one, the brown mare, accepted him without sulking, but wasn't obedient or didn't understand what he wanted. He didn't know how to discipline her and decided just to be patient until he knew.

One day he struck a great river that had to be the Snake. It ran in a trench cut in volcanic rock, across a dreary plain with distant peaks in sight. A well-used trace ran along its south bank. He rode eastward through vast silences, acutely aware of his loneliness but not melancholic about it. He had too much to celebrate. He was free!

May passed into June. He was sure of that, though he had lost track of the days. He had a month or so to find the Americans, and not the faintest idea how to do it. If he did not find them, he would push ahead anyway. Somewhere, far to the east and across a continent, the Americans had forged a civilization out of the wilderness. He would find it.

He added an otter pelt to his growing collection of furs. If worse came to worse, he would have enough pelts to fashion into winter gear with the coming of the cold.

Twice he forded formidable streams flowing out of the south. There were well-beaten trails on both sides of each river. The Snake itself ran through an astonishing black canyon with walls so vertical that they denied him access to its water. From then on, he took every opportunity to work his way down to the river with his horses. Eventually the canyon played out and the river returned to the level of the plains. And still he saw no Shoshones—or anyone else.

The river swept to the northeast, and Skye sensed it

would lead him away from the rendezvous. All he knew was that the trapper's fair would be well south of the Snake country. And then one day he did find a whole congregation of Indians on the move, perhaps even a village. He drew up his horses and waited while the vanguard approached. Then he lifted his hand in what he hoped was a friendly manner.

These were a less handsome people than the Nez Percé, plainly adorned, the women mostly stocky or fat, and the men lean and hawkish.

"Are you Snakes?" Skye asked.

A headman lifted a finger and described a wavy line with it. Skye suspected it meant snake or people of the snake. Ogden had told him that was their sign.

"I'm looking for the rendezvous," he said, relieved.

"Ah, rendezvous," said the headman, his face lighting up. "Rendezvous." He consulted with other headmen, and then motioned for Skye to wait.

Had he found the right people? Skye and the village leaders gazed at one another some more, while the rest of the long procession crowded in. Skye thought there were two or three hundred here, innumerable horses drawing poles that carried the tribe's possessions. Many of the horses dragged the skin lodges he had first seen among the Nez Perce. These were not salmon-fishing Indians, such as he had seen on the Columbia, but a tribe that depended on the bison as well as the abundant fish. The men were well armed, some with muskets, the rest with bows, arrows, shields, lances tipped with iron points, and various war clubs.

"You Yank?" the headman asked, drawing his pony beside Skye's.

"British, mate. I am Skye." He waved a hand in a gesture he hoped would convey a sense of the heavens. "Skye," he said.

"Skye," the headman returned, duplicating his gesture. "Rendezvous." The headman summoned a gray man forward, an elderly Indian, but taller and gaunter than these stocky people.

"Perrault. I'm an Iroquois. I speak de Englees. What you want, huh?"

"What's Iroquois?"

The old man wheezed cheerfully. "Where you from?"

"London."

"You Hudson's Bay, eh?"

"No. I'm alone. I want to go to the Americans' rendezvous."

"Ah, dat's where we go. You come. What's you name?"

"Barnaby Skye. And what's Iroquois?"

The old man cackled again. "Eastern tribe. Big civilized tribe. Me, I ain't civilized no how. I'm a trapper before I got sick and old. Canada and United States, that's where the Iroquois are from. New York, Quebec. I don't want nothing to do with Hudson's Bay. Them'd starve you to death. You HBC, I'd shoot you."

"These are Snakes?"

"You betcha. Mean bastards but I got a woman takes care of me. How come you here? You all alone."

Skye debated whether to tell Perrault, and finally decided to. "I was with the Royal Navy. I jumped ship at Fort Vancouver."

"Ah! You make a good free trapper then. Hate them damn British. You come with us and we make friends. Ah, Skye. I'll tell 'em you a big-water man. They don't know 'navy.' We holding up the parade now. Tonight, we talk. You got some whiskey?"

"I haven't anything."

"It don't matter. Soon comes rendezvous and then we drink whiskey until we get sick." He laughed.

Perrault talked at length with the Snake elders, who eyed Skye now and then. Skye had no idea what was being said or how much trouble he was getting into. But eventually they nodded at him to join them and the lengthy procession began again, retracing country Skye had passed through until they reached a river that flowed out of the south. The great caravan swung into that mountain-hemmed valley and made its stately way another five miles until dusk.

The village headmen left Skye to his own devices. He watched the women build cookfires while the youths took the horses to the thin grasses on the slopes. No one was erecting a lodge. He hunted for Perrault, and found him with three women, one older, the other two stamped in their mother's image.

"Ah, Skye, you got food, eh?"

"I have some otter—not very tasty but it's food."

"Good, we eat it."

"And these bulbs. I found they make a paste I can eat."

"Camas. Big food for Snakes. Taste like no damn good. I don't want none of that stuff. You get me meat and you make old Perrault and his women happy. Me, I got big belly. I got some French blood. French and Iroquois know how to eat meat and make love. Tonight, Skye, we eat big, then we all make love. I got some damn good women. You take your pick, eh?"

Chapter 17

Skye's blood ran hot but his memories ran bitter. He stared at Perrault's younger women and found them comely. They were stocky, golden-fleshed, cheerful, with bright black-cherry eyes and heavy cheekbones. One wore her straight blue-black hair loose; the other's jet hair had been done in braids that she tied with ribbons. He watched them, burning with sudden heat as they cooked a supper. Sometimes they gazed at him with broad smiles, almost coquettish.

Skye's life had suddenly plunged into a vortex of hunger, hope, need, and excitement. Women were a mystery to him. He could remember his sisters and his mother, but they were ghostly presences lost in the mists of time. He remembered the starchy girls he knew as a youth, in their pinafores and frocks, with all their politenesses and reserve. They had been fair-skinned, brown-haired or sandy-haired, their girlish figures buried in ruffles and layers of petticoats. About the time he was pressed into the navy, some of them were budding into women, giving him flirtatious glances, foolish and giddy girls suddenly shy around boys because they knew of things they hadn't known about as children. One of them, Molly, he had been drawn to, and she had filled the thirteen-year-old Skye with joy and terror and intense curiosity. What was this mystery? He had kissed her once and told her he would marry her someday. She had whickered and kissed him back, and they had held hands, happy and content.

Then ruffians had manhandled him into a cart, and he had scarcely seen a woman again. At sea he had the run of the ship, but when they approached port, the lord officers always managed to find some infraction and throw him into the bilge, where he spent days and weeks in irons, tormented beyond anything he could put into words, a young man with volcanic needs and rages and deepening bitterness. It wasn't misconduct that put him in the brig at every port; his masters knew his soul, his rage, his history—and what would happen if the boy got loose. It amused them to torment him.

So he rarely saw a woman in his seven years with the Royal Navy. Once in a while, though, Lady This or Dame That or Princess So and So came aboard, always on the arm of Admiral Lord Such and Such, and then Skye would glimpse a female at last. They all looked indescribably beautiful to him, and their smiles set his heart to fluttering. Then they would go away, and another year or two would pass without his even seeing a woman in pastel silk or crinoline or linen, and all the while his young body howled.

His shipmates knew his torment and enjoyed torturing him. They came back after shore leave and told him lurid stories of easy women, seamen's conquests, bordellos and bagnios and easy times, women who cheerfully did this and that and ten times a night. Of Burmese beauties and Singapore sweethearts and Marseilles bawds, of bare-breasted South Sea islanders who wore only grass skirts, and gorgeous Chinese, and Greek harlots, and icy

Spanish ladies who exploded like a canister of grapes, and uninhibited Filipinas and midnight black Kaffirs.

Skye heard it all, and these things hurt, as his boastful shipmates knew they would. Danny Boggs and Harry Peck loved to torment him. Even the bosuns and lieutenants loved to torture him.

"You missed it again, eh, Skye? Well, it's all your fault, laddie boy. Make yourself into a good seaman, and you'll taste the sweets," they would say.

But Barnaby Skye knew that no force on earth would reconcile him to his slavery. So he endured, hated, hurt, yearned, and tried to remember his sisters, his aunt Clarice, his mother, the sweet pigtailed girls he had met at tea parties and May fairs. These women were different from sailors' women. These women went to church, took communion, and got married and had families. Or were they so different? Maybe they enjoyed the mating, too. How could he know? Miserably, Skye pushed all his confused thoughts, his ignorance of females, his yearnings, aside when he could. But no young man in the prime of his life could put such things aside. The hungers returned again and again, brutal in their power.

Now he watched Perrault's women cook, watched their heavy breasts shift under their dresses, watched them talk and laugh among themselves. These were Shoshones, Snakes, savage women, wild and uninhibited.

He watched eagerly, alive with anticipation, wild to find out what this ultimate mystery was about. It had taken just one casual remark from the Iroquois breed to fan flames in him. Around him the Snake encampment settled for the night. He watched old men at prayer, hands lifted to the red sunset. A youth played a flute next to a beautiful girl, who pretended to ignore him. Skye discovered another odd thing: a lad and a maid stood facing each other, and then the lad drew a blanket over them both. There they stood, the boy's leggins and moccasins poking out under the blanket, along with the girl's skirts and moccasins. Were they kissing under there? He had no idea. No one bothered them. Perhaps this was the accustomed way for lovers to find a moment of privacy. He stared, fascinated. Then, at dusk, the youth drew the blanket off, the girl smiled and slipped away to her family.

Maybe that girl was like his sisters, who would be married now and have children. He could be an uncle. But he would never know his nieces and nephews, not even their names.

Men gathered in groups and smoked, rotating a single pipe among them, content to sit silently in the lavender twilight. The women retreated to the river—the Malade, the sick river, Perrault had told him—to perform ablutions shielded by thick purple night with only a band of blue lingering on the high black ridge to the northwest. Youths watched the horses. Perrault had taken Skye's two out to the pasture and put them in the care of the village herders. Skye wondered whether he'd ever see his horses again; he felt distrustful and didn't know why. These people had accepted him, and yet he wasn't accepting them.

The pungence of the new-leafed sagebrush eddied through the camp on the evening breezes. The first stars emerged, as if from a veil. Young men tied their ponies close at hand and set their bows and quivers beside their robes: this village had fangs, even in the midst of tranquility. A burst of embers fled a dying fire, momentarily illumining a group of women who were whispering to each other. Someone sang a monotone melody, or was it a prayer or a chant? The high nasal voice was an old man's and it sounded like the plainsong he had heard once in the cathedral. Skye wondered what these people believed and who their demons might be, and whether their morals were the same as white men's morals—or better.

"You want a pipe, Skye?" asked Perrault, and handed Skye a lit pipe without waiting for his response.

Skye took it silently, sucked the unfamiliar smoke—he hadn't acquired the habit, lacking the pence and the opportunity until now—and coughed.

The Iroquois laughed. "You don't know nothing, sailor," he said.

"I'm learning," Skye said. He had never said anything truer about himself. In the space of a few weeks he had mastered more things than he could name. And maybe this night he would master something more. Neither his gazes nor his attention drifted for long from the two young women, who had ceased their labors and were sitting quietly, still aglow with the day.

"Damn, we gonna have fun," the old Iroquois barked. "My old Molly, she likes to rut better'n me, almost, and comes after me if I don't make her happy."

Skye could hardly imagine it. He remembered shy pale girls with ringlets, starched manners and starched frocks, keeping a stiff distance from the boys.

"Too bad you don't got some whiskey, Skye. Maybe at rendezvous you give me some whiskey, eh?"

"How far away is that?"

"Two, three weeks mebbe. Got to go down to Cache Valley, near the big Salt Lake, Bear River. Then let the good times roll, ah, ieee!"

"Isn't it a fair?"

"A fair! Why, *garçon*, it be more. No words for it. It be games and cards and makin' friends and chasing the *petites filles*. It be getting a new fusil or traps or red cloth or ribbons. It be a good brawl, too, if one likes to wrestle a bear."

"Wrestle a bear?"

"Just talkin'. Them free trappers got the hair of the bear." Perrault sucked smoke, knocked the dottle out of his pipe, and laughed. "I guess it be time to go please old Molly afore she come after me with the scalpin' knife."

Skye found himself alone and taut as a strung bow. The younger women eyed him boldly, mischief in their faces, but didn't approach. They each unrolled a pair of blankets and made a show in the tumescent dark of wriggling into them. The two weren't more than ten feet apart, maybe fifty feet from Skye's bedroll. Was one closer to him by design?

A shyness tormented Skye. Was he supposed to crawl over there? Would one come to him? Who were they? Perrault's daughters? No, they looked to be pure Shoshone, probably stepdaughters, but who could say?

No such inhibition troubled Perrault and his woman. There, in the night blackness, the grunts and pleasures of mating filtered softly outward, and the night was not so dark that Skye couldn't see a little. The sight tormented him. This wasn't what he expected: nothing private, nothing tender.

He waited for quietness, but it didn't come. Perrault and Molly whispered and laughed and made noises. What did her daughters think of this? What would an Englishwoman think of this? Skye itched to throw off his cover, but sheer fear paralyzed him. He lay in the coolness, sweating, clenching and unclenching his fists. It was up to him. That's what it came to.

And then he went to her. He didn't care what he had been or who he was or what anyone thought. He didn't care whether she found out he had never done this before. It didn't matter that this dusky savage maid wasn't the pale blue-eyed lover of his dreams. His pulse lifted until he feared his heart would burst. He crept to the nearer of the daughters, expecting anger or a shriek, and sheer embarrassment. Instead, she whispered cheerfully, tugged him to the ground, and threw herself toward him. His hands found velvety flesh, wondrous to touch, and hers ripped at his clothing, while she cheerfully rebuked him with a noisy chatter that must have awakened all the neighbors.

And after that, he discovered a whole new world filled with shining joy and inexplicable tears.

Chapter 18

In the slate gray dawn, Skye stirred with the first light, as he always did, and noted a peaceful and utterly silent village, a mood that matched his own. The young Shoshone woman, whose name he didn't even know, lay beside him, naked under her blanket.

He had slept soundly after an hour of delirium and feverish exploration. Gently he arose and dressed. No one stirred, but he saw a Shoshone on horseback among the horses, ever watchful. Skye stretched his arms upward to touch the untinted sky, and then walked down to the Malade River. He had much to think about and things to relive and remember.

Now, he supposed, he had reached manhood after his long, bitter sojourn in the belly of the navy, like Jonah in the whale. He found himself beset by various strands of feeling: pleasure, relief, peace, guilt, fear, and loss. He wondered why he felt loss and what had been taken away from him. Perhaps it was his youthful vision of romantic love. What had happened here had nothing to do with love or tenderness or commitment. Certain youthful visions lay shattered; perhaps those English and Christian things he had soaked up in the Anglican church on Sundays, or in all the instruction and example of his parents.

He knew what lust was now. This mating was bereft of spiritual communion or any sort of friendship and tenderness with a woman. He supposed this Shoshone girl was wanton, but he had no comparison.

It didn't matter. He had enjoyed a fine, mad time, and the memory enflamed him. He had known ecstasy, trembling delights, and sudden peace. He had discovered the silky joy of a woman's flesh, and had responded with an explosion of pent-up need. He had learned his desires could build again and again, and that his bedmate's desires matched his own. He would never forget that night, or the sheer happiness of the moment, when nothing else mattered. Tonight there might be more. He would while away the slow daytime hours and hope for another turn, another embrace of smooth, golden flesh.

He wondered how to conduct himself now, and feared he would offend these people. Would she smile? Pretend that nothing had happened? Want him beside her as they wended their way southward to the rendezvous of the Yanks? What was politeness among these Snake people after moments like this? Or didn't it matter? There certainly were no secrets in a village without walls, and that was different from the way Englishmen lived. In England, a liaison would be discreet, and the lovers would say nothing or give nothing away, and everything would be closeted. But not among the Snakes. One could walk through a camp like this any dark evening and know most everything about everyone.

He washed himself in the icy river water, feeling the jolt of cold as he splashed himself. When he returned, the women were just stirring, though Perrault still snored on the hard earth. Far from being shy or demure, the three women grinned boldly, celebrating a good night, and chattered at him in a tongue he couldn't fathom.

They fed him something that had shredded meat, berries, and fat in it. He wondered what it was and how he could make some; obviously it preserved well in its gut casing. It would be a good emergency food on the trail.

His Shoshone lover and her sister enjoyed themselves, glancing in his direction constantly, chattering among themselves about him, and laughing. He couldn't imagine what they were saying, and hoped it wasn't as graphic or coarse as the talk he had heard from his shipmates when they returned from shore leave. He fancied she was pretty: whatever she lacked in slenderness, she more than made up for with shining eyes. She was all aglow, as if all her feelings were sunny this fine June morning.

The sun leaped over the high eastern ridges, suddenly bathing the river bottoms in gold, but the village seemed to be in no hurry, and Skye fathomed that these people were rarely rushed. They would arrive at the rendezvous in their own good time and at their own speed. They were traversing a vast north-south valley hemmed by arid mountains with only a little scrub pine at their crests.

Last to arise, like some lord, was old Perrault. The breed stretched, made water, belched, and began joshing the women in his harsh tongue. Then at last he turned to Skye.

"She says you didn't know nothing but now you do." He wheezed cheerfully. "Haw."

"Uh, what's her name?"

"Her? It don't translate. Call her Annie." He addressed her in voluble Shoshone, and Skye caught only the name he was bestowing on her. "That other, she'll be Mariel, eh?" He laughed bawdily. "Ah, ha, good times for Skye."

"Mister Skye, sir."

Perrault wheezed and headed for the pasture where his horses were being herded. Skye elected to follow and catch his own. They weren't picketed, and he hoped he could slip hackamores over their heads and lead them back to camp.

He found the spotted horses easily enough, even amid the hundreds in the Shoshone herd, but he couldn't even approach them. They threaded their way through the restless herd, nimbly staying well ahead of Skye, who grew hotter and angrier by the minute. After this he would tie one at his camp, or hobble them both, just as he always had.

There were several herders patrolling the horses now, and a handful of villagers catching horses. The Shoshones had no trouble with theirs. The women among them often walked right up to the packhorses, caught two at a time, and led them back to camp where they could be harnessed with those drags that Perrault called travois.

At last Perrault helped him, his eyes full of mirth and perhaps contempt. The old man had a way with animals. He walked straight up to Skye's brown horse and hackamored the animal in an instant. Then he caught the other and handed both leads to Skye.

"Haw!" yelled Perrault. "You got no experience at nothing. Wimmin, horse, it's all the same."

Sullenly, Skye packed his outfit, loaded it, and waited.

Some time in the middle of the morning, the vanguard finally started south, while the rest followed when they could.

They rode while the heat built, rested a while, drifted onward under a cruel sun. But Skye saw some sort of order when he looked sharply. The young men, the well-armed warriors, rode the flanks and rear; the headmen rode at the front. Hunters and vedettes were continually riding out and vanishing ahead or to the sides. Skye realized that the village was always on guard, and its relaxed progress was deceptive.

He steered his pony close to Perrault, who rode near the rear, far behind his women, who were ahead in gossiping knots.

"You worked for Hudson's Bay, monsieur?" Skye asked.

"Ah! Dem no good bastards! Last year we quit. Yanks pay eight times more for beaver. I quit for good, bones don't like cold no more. Oh, Ogden, he mad plumb through, yellin' at us and makin' big threats like he near kill us. Say we owe HBC lots beaver. Damn! They cheat us, make us slaves so we go trade with the Yanks."

"You're not going back to Canada?"

"Non, non, *l'hiver,* too cold. My women, they take care of me. Molly, she be a widow, and dem girls, they need a good breed aroun'. I make a lodge for dem women, have me a good old age, eh?"

"I would think you'd want to go back to your own kind."

"You *Anglais,* damn, you don't know how it is. Dem Snakes, dey make you happy."

"Why do they call themselves Snakes?"

Perrault cackled. "Dem dumb Creoles, dey don't get it. The Shoshones use a wiggling finger—like dis—as their sign. It mean people dat live on curving river, like dis. But dem trappers, dey think it's snakes, and so dey call Shoshones Snakes. Call da river Snake. Eh? Whee! Pretty funny. Big joke. Snake people laugh."

"These people don't dress up. The Nez Percés wear finer clothing. Why is that?"

"Dere's another bad name. Dey don't pierce noses. Dey proud people, mean bastards, like to make war, steal Snake ponies. Mostly dey hate Snakes and Snakes hate dem. Shoshones, dey buffler people. Nez Perces, dey mostly fish-eaters but dey hunt buffalo each fall. When it get cold, dey all go over the mountains and hunt buffler and fight dem Crows and Blackfeet."

Skye absorbed all that and took his lessons seriously. Perrault was the key to understanding this country.

"What did we eat this morning?"

"Pemmican. Good trail food. Last damn near forever. Ground up chokecherries or bufflerberries, dried buffler

meat, mix her up with fat and let it cool and put it in gut.
Damn, she keeps you going. Dem women make it good.
You like Annie, eh? Maybe you got her."

"Got her?"

"Yeah, you, me, we make a lodge. You young; you trap
a little, shoot buffler, and we got three wimmin for
l'hiver, eh? You get tired of one, you take Mariel, eh?"

The idea startled Skye. "Ah, I'm heading east, Mr.
Perrault."

"Where da hell you come from? Some damn *Anglais,*
dat all I know."

Skye debated telling his story, and found no reason not
to. Swiftly, he described a young life under duress, his
escape, and progress into a new life.

"Damn. HBC come after you. Dey rule the roost. Dey
catch you. You give dem the slip—dat pretty good. Dem
roosters peck de eyes out."

"They tried at Fort Nez Perces, but didn't know what
to do with me. McTavish was too Scotch to feed me."

"Don' go east. You crazy, *Anglais?* What you do dere?"

"I want to study. Get the education I've always wanted.
Go into business."

Perrault spat and said nothing. He kicked his ancient
pony and pulled ahead of Skye, an unmistakable gesture.

Skye rode alone the rest of that golden June day wondering how he had earned Perrault's contempt. *Of course*
he would go east. And of course he would get into
college—somehow. Work his way through. And of course
he would win the life he had lost, and probably do better
because of all his bitter experience. If he had learned one
thing about this wilderness existence, it was the boredom
that permeated everything. A life like this would stupefy
him.

The cavalcade walked scarcely five miles that day,
obviously in no hurry to go anywhere, and then settled
into another camp very like the last. The hunters rode in,
some of them with deer slung over packhorses. Somehow
the meat found its way into most of the pots, along with

roots and bulbs the women had casually gathered en route. The hunters were responsible for provisioning the whole band and not just their own lodges.

Skye tried to relax but couldn't. Why didn't they hurry to the Yanks' rendezvous? He needed to talk English, not with some ignorant old French-Iroquois breed, but people born to the tongue who could supply him with information. He knew almost nothing, and needed to know everything about going east.

His thoughts turned to Annie as dusk settled, and he waited for darkness with taut anticipation. Now that he knew what was in store, his craving was worse than ever. He didn't wait for darkness; he couldn't. In the gloomy afterlight and the hush of night, he crept to the nearer bedroll. But it was Mariel this time, and she burned with need equal to his, fierce and demanding, quite different from Annie and even more gifted in fanning his flames. She exhausted him. He had never known that sort of soft weariness.

Then he drifted to sleep, his thoughts probing this new wonder in his life. Sometime in the deeps, cries awakened him. Around him people sprang up. Men swiftly gathered their weapons and vanished into the gloom. Skye hadn't the faintest idea what all that was about and waited for Perrault to tell him. But the weathered old trapper took his time, and meandered about for a while, whispering to dark figures Skye could barely make out.

The old Iroquois finally squatted beside Skye in the starlight.

"Dem damn *Pieds Noirs*," he growled. "Dey got dem horse."

Chapter 19

Skye knew something of war, even if it was marine war. He would fight. He fumbled in the starlight for some clothing and his bow and quiver. He could see little, but finally managed to pull on his britches. No one had built up the fires for fear of an arrow or shot. He needed his moccasins, and discovered them near his bedroll.

When at last he readied himself and headed for the pasture where the horses had grazed, he knew he was too late. In that darkness he could not distinguish one horse from another. He would not know until dawn whether his own horses had been stolen.

He stood guard over the remaining horses, along with old men. His effort to help had been futile and late. No moon shone, and he could barely see the bulks of the nervous animals or the other village warriors about him. He could not imagine how the Blackfeet could even see enough to take some horses, much less escape along some line of retreat. He heard no wailing, no sounds of grief, and supposed no Shoshone had been hurt.

Eventually the quarter moon rose, and then it was easier to keep an eye on the herd and watch for intruders. An hour or so into the chill new morning the weary Shoshone pursuers returned, driving numerous sweat-stained animals before them. Many of the horses had been recovered. The warriors triumphantly drove the stock through the village so their prowess at war could be observed and honored by all. Then they dismounted and walked stiffly to their lodges, their faces grave.

"Ho!" muttered the old man next to him.

The rising light soon told the story. The pursuers had recovered twenty-one horses; only a few had been lost. Skye hunted for his own and found the brown but not the lighter one. He grieved the loss, and a knot of bitterness toward the Blackfeet formed in his breast. He would remember this. He looked over his brown and concluded that it had been left in the herd; it showed no signs of heat or sweat or hard use.

Around him the Shoshones talked in their own tongue, harsh and angry sounds that didn't need much translating. Skye hackamored and led his remaining horse to his campsite, and dourly began to load it. He would have to walk now, and carry his kit on the horse. Traveling to the rendezvous wasn't going to be much fun. Still, he had walked most of the way here, so he could walk some more. And the horse would pack his gear. It wasn't so bad.

And the nights . . . He eyed the two sisters, who grinned back at him, conspirators at taking turns. He needed to think about that. His shipmates would have boasted about it, but something in it troubled him. He didn't know these women. This most intimate act had been with strangers who couldn't speak his tongue. Something was missing.

He pulled his buckskin shirt over his head, found his topper and jammed it over his unruly hair, scratched at his luxurious beard, and thought he had failed his hosts this night. He knew nothing about the warfare of the savages and knew he had better learn fast. This was not the civilized world, with constables and sheriffs. He realized he had been lucky to come two or three hundred miles without being murdered or robbed. Whatever else this night and this loss of a valuable horse had accomplished, it taught him a hard lesson.

This morning the Shoshones were in a different mood. Those who brought the horses back were honored. They paraded through the village receiving their praise, which others were eager to offer. But even though Skye couldn't understand a word, he could sense the change. No longer was this a romp toward the rendezvous, but a solemn procession, with grim-faced young men, bristling with weapons—bows, quivers, lances, clubs, hatchets, knives—flanking the women and children and elders.

Skye walked along with Perrault's women, who were quiet this morning, but then old Perrault joined him, riding beside Skye as he walked ever southward.

"Ah, damn dem *Pieds Noirs*. Dey get eleven horse—dey get away. Dey get you horse, eh? You get another. Lots of horse. Go steal one. Dey get you horse, you go take another horse from dem. We gonna get even someday, soon as we trade for powder, fusil, lots balls. Den we steal fifty horse and kill a few of dem devils. Dey got lots of Nor' West fusils, guns dey get from the *Anglais*. But we get rifles at rendezvous, eh? You come along, we go take ten horse for every one dey get."

"Are they the worst tribe?"

"Oui, *du nord*. Dey strong, much bigger den Snakes. Dey pick on us, Crows, Flatheads, Assiniboine, Gros Ventres, all dem. You kill a *Pied Noir* and six more grow in his place."

"The men are all painted up. What does that mean?"

"It means lots of things. Dem that paints is ready for war. Dey all got their private medicine, lightning, stars, like dat. Good paint, make 'em strong."

"How do they make that bright red?"

"Dat's vermilion. Dey get that from traders. The rest dey get from plants and rocks an' mix wid grease."

"If they come again, I'll fight."

"Ah, you get yourself kill. You get a good rifle at rendezvous—mountain gun like a Hawken—and den fight."

Skye didn't reply. In the right circumstances, he could do more with a belaying pin than a firearm. He couldn't afford the mountain rifle, and anyway, he was bound for the east coast and the Yankees.

"How long to the rendezvous?"

Perrault shrugged. "Maybe a few days. Who know?" He eyed Skye. "How come you walking? Go put your stuff on my woman's travois."

"Travois? My stuff?"

"Won't hurt nothing."

Skye didn't need a second invitation. He waited for the women to pull up. Perrault barked a command, and even before Skye could loosen his load, the women were pulling off Skye's packsaddle and heaping his stuff on top of their folded lodgeskins. Skye watched long enough to see that his things were securely tied down, and then put his saddle on the brown, glad to ride again.

"Now mebbe you give old Perrault a few whiskey at the rendezvous, eh?"

"If I can," Skye replied.

The days passed uneventfully, but Skye used every moment to learn what he could, often consulting with Perrault. He studied the buffalohide lodges and admired their utility. They could easily be erected in minutes, were light and portable, were designed to handle a fire within and contain its heat, and could be made comfortable any season of the year.

He had never seen a buffalo, and itched to see the awesome black herds Perrault told him about. At first Skye scoffed; there could not be so many buffalo. But when he considered the number of hides in just one small eleven-pole lodge, he reconsidered. There were thousands of hides in this village.

He discovered that virtually every part of the buffalo could be put to use: its bones became tools, ladles, kitchen implements. Its hide could become a warm winter robe, and its meat could feed a lodge for many days. Its fat and meat mixed with berries could make pemmican, and the thick breast hide of the bulls could be turned into a war shield strong enough to deflect an arrow or spear or even a musket ball. He could make good moccasin soles from bullhide, and he could dry the sinew layered along the spinal cord into usable thread or a bowstring. He could stuff buffalo hair into a pillow or saddle pad, turn the scrotum into a rattle or a purse, or tan the soft hide of an unborn calf into a pouch.

He discovered that hunting these beasts was a great enterprise and sport, and that a fast and fearless pony, trained to draw close enough so its rider could drive an arrow into the heart-lung area just behind the front legs, was a prized possession and a source of wealth and food. He absorbed Perrault's vast buffalo lore, and realized that these tribes could scarcely exist without the animal, which was why the buffalo was greatly honored among them. Not even the salmon was prized so much as the buffalo.

At first he studied the practical, lifesaving, and useful things he found among these people: he studied war clubs, flint arrowheads, the traders' iron arrowheads, the way bows were made, and the wood used in them. He watched how the Shoshone made fires, what they used for tinder, and how they preserved a live coal long enough to start the next fire. He watched two women flesh a deer hide with scrapers made of bone and a bit of iron. He studied the roots and plants the women plucked and dug and used in their stews, the yamp and sego lily and camas, and the digging tools they used to wrench bulbs from stubborn soil.

He learned something about the medicinal herbs these people used, such as dogwood and yarrow for fevers, and the various stalks and leaves that would yield a dye, such as alder and bloodroot. He pestered Perrault endlessly, until the old Iroquois breed laughed or growled at him, but Skye knew that he had to learn, and fast, to survive, and that this tribe could teach him much of what he needed to know.

All these arts and crafts came naturally to a people who planted nothing but hunted and fished and gathered nature's own bounty. He knew if he could master even the half of what these people knew, he would improve his chance to survive his long journey across the continent.

He discovered that these people had religious and spiritual traditions that conformed to their way of life, but he could grasp little of them. He saw no sign of organized religion, but he discerned that each person had his own religion—Perrault called it medicine, an odd but fitting word—his own spiritual helpers, his own protectors and mentors. Some wore small totems, or little bags suspended from the neck; others wore amulets, often a small carved turtle of wood or bone. These things interested him less than the ones that he could employ to survive in the wilds, but he was curious about them. Perrault was little help on that score, and shrugged off Skye's endless questions, sometimes turning surly when Skye pushed too hard.

"You crazy," he snarled. "Damn! You' owe me whiskey."

Perrault did tell him about one useful thing: the tribes could communicate with a hand language. Skye vowed to learn all he could; then, at least, he would have some way to communicate with these people. Maybe someone at the rendezvous could help him learn the sign language.

They emerged from the valley into a broad hazy land, with foothills rising to the east and arid drainages to the west.

"Pretty damn soon, now, Skye—ah, damn, *Mister* Skye. You be crazy."

Then one morning Skye sensed an excitement in camp. The Shoshones astonished him with their festival dress.

The women decked themselves ·in quilled or beaded buckskins or flannel; the men wore all their war honors. A barbarous beauty pervaded the whole village, along with an expectation that Skye could feel as well as see in eager, joyous faces.

They paraded that grand July day, their horses mincing and dancing, their exodus orderly and spirited. Skye felt something mad and wild clear to his bones, and rode eagerly, scarcely able to believe the transformation around him. He didn't need to be told: today they would arrive at the rendezvous.

They turned east along a sluggish river, and followed it into a wide valley with grassy plains. It seemed a barren place to Skye, almost treeless except along the river. But a haze of blue smoke hung over this place, and the rolling grasslands were dotted with horses of all descriptions and colors. Lodges clustered near the river, intermixed with brush arbors that supplied shade. Skye could see two or three white men's tents of canvas, rectangular and angular compared to the conical skin lodges. As the Shoshones approached, they began to sing and dance. The warriors strung their bows and withdrew arrows from their quivers. Was this going to be a battle? Skye watched nervously, wondering what all this was about. And then, in one wild swoop, the Shoshones dashed madly into the rendezvous, a mock attack that was met by mock resistance from other Indians, and by white men who discharged their rifles into the skies and howled right along with the Shoshones. Then the Shoshones paraded through the whole vast encampment, whooping, displaying their gauds and war honors, strutting, whirling their horses.

Skye rode among them, astonished at all this, astonished at the odd-looking white men, most of them dressed in peculiar costumes, part European but largely adapted from the tribes around them. They sported beards as luxurious as Skye's. Some wore necklaces of bone, which won Skye's curiosity.

Perrault rode beside Skye. "Dem's Crows. Dey got

here before us," he said. "Dat's de rendezvous, and now de fun start. Pretty soon dey all come sniffing around. Den dey give ribbons and looking glasses and calico and needles and knives an' stuff for my women and me. You get me jug of whiskey, and den you get one woman or the other any time." He slapped his bony knee and howled like a wolf.

Skye stared. Perrault was selling his women.

Chapter 20

Jedediah Smith dreamed of two things, adventure and wealth. A fortune would assuage the yearnings of his Calvinist soul and prove his worth before God and man. Adventure would test his mettle and make life sharp and exhilarating.

There in Cache Valley that July of 1826 he saw a way to have both. While the free trappers with Ashley and Smith's fur company began their rendezvous frolic, he was busy forming a new company to buy out General Ashley, who had at last made a fortune in beaver plews, and wanted to escape the fur trade before some new disaster laid him low.

The new partners and Ashley had been dickering all morning in their buffalo-skin lodge, but they weren't far from agreement. The lodge cover had been rolled up two or three feet, letting the playful breezes sweep in. That cooled the occupants and let them keep an eye on the glistening prairies just outside, where veteran trappers were sucking trade whiskey from Ashley's store after a year's parch, and swapping elaborate lies.

On hand also were Davey Jackson and Bill Sublette, experienced mountaineers and participants in the great Ashley-Henry venture that had probed up the Missouri River in search of a fortune in beaver pelts. There had been much to negotiate, but now an agreement was in sight, forged by Ashley and the new company of Smith, Jackson, and Sublette. The idea was simple, even if the details were complex. The new booshways, as the free trappers called them, were buying out Ashley, and would pay him with beaver pelts the following year. If they sent Ashley an express asking for more supplies, he would deliver them to this rendezvous site next July and return to the States with the pelts.

Smith knew Ashley was getting the best of the deal: the real profits in the fur trade went to its suppliers, who charged several times St. Louis prices to bring the goods a thousand dangerous miles to the Stony Mountains. But Smith didn't expect the new partnership to suffer: in Jackson and Sublette he had two masters, canny veterans who would lead trapping parties to the beaver in the fall, winter, and spring when the pelts were prime, and harvest the wealth of the wilderness. They would do, along with a handful of brilliant mountaineers, such as Bridger, Harris, and Fitzpatrick.

The partners and Ashley broke for the nooning and meandered out of the lodge into the brilliant sun. Before them lay a vast undulating prairie with enough grasses on it to keep horses fat during the entire rendezvous. The Wasatch Mountains rose to the east, their lower slopes dry and barren. Far to the southwest lay the Great Salt Lake, guarding a hostile desert beyond. Closer at hand, an emerald band of trees and brush lined the river, supplying firewood, game, and shelter to the great trapper's fair.

The event had barely begun and would last five or six weeks, until the wildmen of the mountains had squan-

dered their last plew and the booshways were organizing
and outfitting their brigades. Jed Smith—they called him
Diah—was not one of those wildmen, and had blown
nothing on trade whiskey—actually, pure grain alcohol
seasoned with tobacco and spices and diluted with river
water. He was one of them and yet he wasn't, a man apart,
a man who daily read his King James Bible and sought
the blessings of God upon his endeavors. And yet he was
a man born to lead, born to adventure, and withal, tougher
and more sagacious about wilderness than any of the others. The trappers trusted him more than any other brigade
leader, knowing he would get them through. He understood the revelries and the animal hungers that fueled
them so far from civilization, and never intervened or
criticized, although he kept apart. The trappers, in turn,
understood that about him and accepted his leadership
without cavil, a bond built on mutual respect.

Buffalo stew bubbled in an iron pot, and he helped
himself with a thick iron ladle. There had never been
many of the shaggy beasts on this side of the mountains,
and this rendezvous had doomed the last of them. But the
Cache Valley abounded in deer and elk and antelope, and
the mountaineers would wallow in fat meat.

So far, the rendezvous had been a quiet affair. When
Ashley's pack train trotted in two days earlier, the trappers lined up at Ashley's tent store and bought jugs and
cups of trade whiskey to allay a year-long thirst. The next
days were devoted to serious drinking and gambling, usually euchre or monte, using greasy old cards that had survived for years in someone's kit. But they were really
waiting for the Shoshones and Crows to arrive so they
could begin the contests, the games, the wrestling, shooting, brawling, and other revels, such as the debauchery
and whoring that took place largely at night. This was
Snake country, and these were friendly Injuns who cheerfully lent or sold their comely daughters and wives to any
trapper with a bit of foofaraw. That's when the midsummer's saturnalia would really begin.

Almost as if to answer his thoughts, Smith saw a stirring among the trappers. Someone came whooping in with news, and in minutes the word was bruited through the disorderly camp: the Snakes would be arriving in an hour or two. Bearded, buckskinned men, with visions of fair and dusky maidens dancing in their heads, laughed and howled and bayed at the sun. Tonight the party would begin.

But in his starchy way, Smith turned his thoughts elsewhere. The Shoshones would have furs to trade at Ashley's big store-tent, and Ashley would return to St. Louis with prime peltries—buffalo, elk, deer, otter, fox, as well as beaver—all handsomely tanned and valuable in the East. Next year, Ashley's store would be the Smith, Jackson, and Sublette store, and his own company would be dealing with tribesmen for those pelts, all for a fat profit. Smith reminded himself to invite the Crows and Bannacks and other tribes to come next summer and bring all the pelts they could produce. They all had furs to trade, and he intended to buy them. The Indian trade was especially profitable because they wanted so little for their furs—a little trade whiskey, a small hand mirror, a cup of sugar, a few lead balls, a few ounces of powder, some fishhooks, some calico, ribbons, and blankets.

By common consent the negotiations were adjourned that afternoon. The arrival of the Snakes was not a sight to be missed. They would be wearing their festival finery; their nubile honey-tinted maidens would be gauded out and painted; their bronze young men would be wearing their war honors, carrying their shields and lances, riding prized horses. Their ponies, many of them the spotted Appaloosa gotten from the Nez Perce, would be ribboned and painted.

Smith guessed there would be a few white men among them, probably Hudson's Bay booshways. The powerful HBC had fought the invasion of their turf by free trappers and now kept a baleful eye on the fiesty Yanks. Worse, the HBC had lost many of its trappers to the Ashley interests, and might be looking for ways to cause trouble. The Yanks paid a trapper good money for pelts instead of giving him a skimpy salary. An industrious trapper could earn several times more as a free entrepreneur than as an engagé, as the French-Canadians called them, and stay out of debt if he chose to.

"Well, Diah, now we'll see how the stick floats," said Bill Sublette.

"We'll make them welcome. Give their headmen some powder and galena. I want them to know that the partnership will be running the store next summer," Smith replied, his mind never far from business.

"I'll pass out some vermilion to cement relations," Sublette said. "I know most of their headmen."

"It'll pay off," said Davey Jackson. "I reckon we'll do better than Ashley and Henry, if only because we've got the experience under our belts. We've a notion what to do and not to do."

That was how they all reckoned it, Smith thought. He himself had gotten five thousand dollars out of his brief junior partnership with Ashley, and was plowing it all back into the new company. Where else in the United States could a man make so much in a year? A few years like that and he could return to Ohio, marry, and live in comfort the rest of his life.

The thought made him itchy. Maybe he would not enjoy life in Ohio's Western Reserve, where the westering New England Smiths had finally settled after stops in upstate New York and Pennsylvania. Return? Not after he had heard the call of the wild. The wilderness was a temptation, not only to his flesh but also his soul and his pride. It was something to pray about, this demon in him. He knew he should return to civilization and settle down and become a deacon in his church.

He discerned a great stirring on the northern horizon. Trappers whooped and ran for their mountain rifles, anticipating what would come. Gabe Bridger grinned. Tom Fitzpatrick and the rascal Jim Beckwourth slid caps onto the nipples of their rifles while Black Harris and Louis Vasquez waited patiently, a faint smile on their weathered chestnut faces.

The Shoshones raced in, their warriors kicking lathered horses straight toward the camp, lances lowered, bows drawn, the whole lot howling like wolves. It was enough to terrify a pork-eater, as pilgrims were called. But Smith watched laconically, enjoying the fun as much as anyone else. On they came, screeching blood-freezing taunts, like an army from hell. Rifles popped, the balls puncturing the sky, as the Snakes swept into the encampment.

"It's a sight," Ashley said, standing beside Smith. "Makes a man want to reach for his piece and throw up a breastwork."

Smith nodded. The Snake warriors were curvetting their ponies, counting mock coup, and showing off like military cadets on a lark. Right behind them the main body of Shoshones walked in, chiefs and shamans, squaws overseeing the ponies that dragged the lodges, all gauded in bright trade cloth, blue and red and green, with horn bonnets and fringed leggins. What a sight!

But what caught Smith's eye was the lone white man, no doubt an HBC agent spying on the opposition. Ermatinger maybe, or the legendary Peter Skene Ogden, a man as shrewd and forceful as any Yank trapper, and then some. But this one didn't seem familiar. He was an odd duck, thick as a plow horse, wearing a beaver topper and a buckskin shirt, and riding a brown palouse. The young man examined Smith and the other trappers with a gaze that had palpable force behind it, a gaze that drilled meaning out of everything he saw.

What struck Smith the most was the man's somberness. Unlike the Shoshones, he was all business. The more Smith watched, the more curious he became about the stranger. Whoever the fellow was, he had made his mark simply with his raking examination of the whole rendezvous. Well, Smith thought, he would know the man's name soon enough, and probably his business as well.

The Shoshones chose a river site east of the rendezvous for their own, and the squaws set to work raising lodges and unloading the innumerable travois. Trappers crowded about them, eyeing the maidens with hungry gazes, eager for the great July debauch to begin. This night many a trapper would squander much of his year's income, the product of long, lonely hours wading icy streams and skinning beaver and sleeping on cold ground.

Smith hiked toward the new man, who was watching silently, his gaze piercing and cautious, as if he were fleeing a past or had perceived trouble here. The man was stocky and powerful, his face dominated by an enormous nose that had probably been broken more than once. The new man squinted at this strange world from blue eyes that revealed nothing of his mood or motive. He seemed ill-equipped, and had only a bow and quiver for weapons. But it wasn't his ragged exterior that intrigued Smith. This man radiated determination and will.

The man seemed to come to some decision, dismounted, and headed for Smith and Ashley in a strange, rolling gait, leading his brown horse. "Are you Yanks?" he asked in booming voice.

"Americans, yes, and you?"

"I'm a man without a country. I've been looking for you to get some information. How far is it to Boston?"

"Boston? Boston?" Smith stared.

"Boston, mate. I'm on my way to Boston."

"Why, she's just over them hills hyar," said Bridger. "Maybe a two-day hike. Just foller the turnpike."

"I was told it was a lot farther. I'll rest my horse for a few days and then head east. Hope you can tell me a little about it. It's Boston I'm heading for, and I need to make my way. If I can be of service for a bit of food, I'd welcome it."

Trappers crowded around the man. "What's your handle, friend?" asked Black Harris.

The man hesitated. Smith knew the signs. This man was a fugitive. "Handle? Ah, a name, yes. Skye, sir. Mister Skye. Call me that. Barnaby's the Christian name."

"You from England?"

The man nodded.

"This pilgrim's looking for Boston," said Bridger to the rest. "I told him straight, it'd be two, three days if the pikes ain't muddy."

"Yes, that'd do it," said Broken Hand Fitzpatrick.

The rest nodded solemnly.

"You have to be careful of buffler in Boston," Beckwourth said. "There's a city law against making meat on the streets. Other than that, Boston's just the place."

"Skye," said Smith, "why are you going to Boston?"

"It's Mister Skye, sir. That's how I want it."

"Well, then, Mister Skye, you might enlighten us."

"There's a university in Cambridge, near Boston, and I'm going there to finish my schooling, sir. I didn't catch your name, but I take it you're in charge here."

"No one's in charge, Mister Skye. These are free trappers, not employees. But yes, I'm a partner in the fur company."

"This fellow's going to Boston," yelled Black Harris.

"You don't say," said Louis Vasquez. "Boston, is it?"

Skye nodded. "Boston, sir. It seems to be less far than I thought."

"Just head east, and before you know it, you'll be matriculating," said Davey Jackson.

"I'm much obliged to you, sir," the Englishman said. "Is there a way a man could trade some labor for some food?"

"Nope, there plumb ain't," Sublette said.

Skye looked crestfallen. "Will labor buy me a rifle, or anything at all?"

"Go eat, man," Smith urged. "They're really telling you no man starves here, and no American trapper ever turns away a hungry man in the mountains."

"I have much to learn," said Skye. "Thank you."

"You just take your fill from that kettle, and then I want to talk with you, Mister Skye."

"Show 'im how to raise Boston," Bridger said.

Chapter 21

Smith watched while the Englishman downed a helping of buffalo stew, and another. The man was hungry, and that hunger ran deep. After that, Smith nodded Skye into the cool lodge and waited for the man to settle comfortably on the ground.

An Englishman asking his way to Harvard College certainly aroused Smith's curiosity. Especially one who probably was a fugitive.

"Mister Skye, those gents were funning you. It's their way. Boston is most of a continent away. I hardly know the distance, but it must be nearly three thousand miles. You'd hike over several ranges of mountains, cross the Continental Divide, head into dry plains that run six or eight hundred miles, reach the green basin of the Mississippi, climb eastern mountains, and arrive eventually on the Atlantic Coast."

Skye nodded. "That's what Mr. Ogden told me. I'm a seaman, and don't know the land, especially here. I started from Fort Vancouver and walked for three months. I thought I'd come a long way."

"The Hudson's Bay post," Smith said, carefully.

Skye stared out upon the sunny grasslands. "Are you connected with HBC, Mr. Smith?"

"No, we're all Americans here. They're our rivals. We've lured some free trappers away from them and they don't like it. Free trappers can earn a lot more from us than salaried trappers with HBC."

Skye didn't answer for a while. "You must be wondering about me, mate," he said at last.

"We gauge a man out here by what he is, and how he fits in, and not by any other standard."

"I'll tell you my story. It's no secret."

Smith nodded. He badly wanted to hear it.

Skye squinted uneasily, choosing his words. "Seven years ago I was pressed into the Royal Navy off the streets of London. I was fourteen, on my way to my father's warehouse—he's an import-export merchant—on the banks of the Thames. I never saw my family again . . ."

Smith listened for ten minutes and nodded. He thought it might be something like that. A deserter in the eyes of the Royal Navy and HBC. If the man was telling the truth, he deserved his liberty. But men had a way of justifying their bad behavior. Perhaps there was more. "And Harvard? What about Harvard?"

"I had set my cap on a university education before I was pressed, sir. Cambridge, like my father before me. He was a disciple of Adam Smith and the Manchester school, and wanted me to take up political economy. I leaned toward literature and teaching. Well, I'm free at last. I want to start school now. Pass my entrance exam. Work my way through, somehow, some way."

"Without means?"

"A man does what he has to. I'll find a way. For all those years I plotted and schemed and waited my chance. It was hard growing up. I fought for my gruel. I faced bullies. It was harder still learning guile, but guile is what freed me. It wasn't until I stopped making trouble that they gave me a bit of liberty on deck. And that's what I needed." He gazed out upon the roistering crowd. "Am I in danger of being caught here? Will they take me back?"

"Sometimes HBC men come to rendezvous."

"They won't take me. Not alive, anyway. The earth feels good under my feet, sir. For seven years I never had earth under my feet for long."

"How'd you arrive here? What did you eat?"

"I had some fishhooks and line. Salmon, sir. I have a belaying pin and two knives, and awl, thong, and shoe leather. Also a flint and striker. I traded along the Columbia for other things. And also got help from the Nez Percés. The Royal Navy came after me, guided by some Hudson Bay men. I watched them from the cliffs. This is a big place, this America."

"You found the Shoshones."

"They found me, mate. I thought I was done for, but they were friendly."

"They're the one tribe in the whole area not beholden to HBC, Mister Skye. You were lucky. And your timing was lucky. They were on their way here for our rendezvous. This is the second."

"That's what Mr. Ogden said. He advised me to look for the Snakes."

"He told you that?"

Skye smiled for the first time. "He allowed that he doesn't care for you Yanks, sir. Now, what's a rendezvous?"

"Our free trappers trade their beaver pelts for supplies brought out from Missouri. That lets them stay here in the mountains."

"Missouri?"

"On the western edge of the United States, sir. The gateway to Indian Country. A thousand miles from here with nothing but empty plains, buffalo, and dangerous Indians in between."

Skye seemed awed. "No place a man can work for his keep along the way?"

Smith smiled. "By sheer luck, you came upon the only place." Smith wondered whether to tell Skye that he could easily sign on with Ashley and work his way to St. Louis. He could use another trapper, but he opted for honesty as was his wont. "Actually, General Ashley's returning to St. Louis in a few weeks with a hundred twenty-three packs of beaver. He could use any help he can get, and you'd be ensured of fairly safe travel. You'd never make it alone, especially a pork-eater like you."

"A what?"

"A pilgrim. A novice. An inexperienced man. It's a French-Canadian term, *mangeur du lard*. Actually, if you dodged the Royal Navy and some HBC guides, you're no pilgrim. You've got some mountain seasoning. Men are scarce here, and I'm willing to take you on. You've no trapping experience but I need camp tenders and would pay you well."

"I want only one thing: to start my life after I was robbed of it, sir. This General Ashley . . . would I be forced to enlist?"

Smith saw the drift. "He's an officer of the Missouri militia, not regular army, and this is his private business venture. No, you'd work for him by mutual agreement."

"He'll learn I'm a deserter soon enough."

"That's a risk. He'll be more inclined to wonder whether you'll be a loyal employee."

"Let me tell you something, Mr. Smith. All the while I was the King's prisoner, I never despised England or my people. I fought the King's wars against the Kaffirs in Africa—the only time I set foot on land in seven years—and on the Irrawaddy River in Burma, wars of Empire, sir, never doubting where my English loyalties lay, even if my private circumstance was unbearable. I'll want to see Ashley, and I'll tell him the whole story and let him decide."

"I'd advise waiting a while before talking to him. You

may like the free life here—especially after all those years in a ship's bilge."

"All right. I'll wait. Now, while I wait, how can I earn my keep? How can I get an outfit?"

"An outfit would cost you far more than you could earn here, Mister Skye."

The young man looked crestfallen. Then he smiled. "Guess I'll be off, mate. Long road ahead."

"No, no, that'd be fatal. You stay and enjoy the frolic. Eat at my stewpot. Meet the crowd. Give as good as you get from 'em, and they'll respect you. If you need anything from company stores, see me. Your credit's good."

"I could buy blankets?"

"That and more."

"May I ask why?"

"I could tell you that I need every man I can get, and that would be true. But you impress me, Mister Skye. You've the makings of a mountaineer."

"A mountaineer, sir?"

"It takes a breed, Mister Skye. It takes men with uncommon courage and loyalty and common sense. The mountains kill the foolish. They freeze or starve or die of thirst or get snakebit or run into Injuns and don't know how to deal with 'em. The good men survive by sticking together through thick and thin. Life depends on it, working in pairs and groups. The loners die, far from help. You wander out now and meet these gents. They aren't ordinary. They're all graduates of what we call the Rocky Mountain College—it's a school where you graduate or die."

"Graduate or die!"

"That's exactly right. But, Mister Skye, even the best go under. Friends of mine have disappeared, or died alone, not through any fault of their own. Not all their mountain skills can save them from an enraged grizzly sow, or a party of Bug's Boys—the Blackfeet—looking for white men to scalp. Let me tell you something: not in all human history has there been a breed like this, surviving in a wilderness like this. They're resourceful. You could take away all their possessions and even their clothes in a cold night, and they'd survive. I've thought about it some: there's no general rule. Some survive by their wits, others by sheer willpower or determination. Others are uncommonly resourceful and inventive. You're one of those, I reckon. You got here; other men would be nothing but white bones by now. If you want, I'll ask General Ashley to take you to Saint Louis, but I won't do it for a few days. You have things to think about and things to see here."

The young man stood, uncommonly silent, his face full of emotions that Smith couldn't read.

"You go to Ashley's tent store now. Look over the merchandise. Get what you need and tell the clerk to put it on my account. Better yet, I'll tell him."

Skye seemed at a loss for words, and finally clamped Smith's hand in his own, blinked, and retreated into the July afternoon.

What was it about that man? What a terrible story, if it was true. Smith's intuition told him that Skye had the makings. A few items out of the company store would be worth the gamble to Smith, Jackson, and Sublette. But even if Skye elected not to stay in the mountains, Smith was ready to bet his last dollar that Skye would eventually repay the debt.

Chapter 22

Throngs of wild Indians and trappers mobbed the tent store. Skye decided to wait and observe, see what could be bought, what things cost, and whether he could buy the things he needed most: blankets, a good knife, a cooking pot, and an ax. The ax he would put to immediate use. Each remaining day of this wilderness fair, Mr. Jedediah Smith would find a pile of split firewood and kindling before his lodge, courtesy of Barnaby Skye.

The proprietors had arranged the store so that all the business was transacted over a rough counter on hogsheads at the front. Clerks examined peltries, set a price, and then traded for the goods lying in barrels and boxes and shelves and packs behind them. The Shoshones in their festival dress waited patiently, many of them laden with tanned pelts of all descriptions and buffalo robes. He liked these people who had invited him to journey with them. He had come along, and they had led him to this miraculous place that made his spirits soar.

Among the crowd were scruffy-looking trappers trading pelts for odd things—hand mirrors, gaudy ribbon, brass buttons, jingle bells, yards of bright cotton calico or flannel, strings of glass beads, knives, awls, hatchets, hide-fleshing tools, cups of sugar, molasses, beans, Chinese vermilion in waxed paper cubes, even needles and thread. Women's things, mostly. The trappers were going to have a time of it tonight.

Shoshone warriors traded for bricks of du Pont powder wrapped in waxed paper, small bars of galena, as lead was called here, or a pound of precast balls, bullet moulds, flints, flintlock rifles, strikers, knives, blankets, tomahawks, lance points, traps, and awesome quantities of murky amber fluid that looked like something left by a dog on a tree, no doubt spirits, sold by the tin cup. The revels had already begun, with man and woman alike swilling the stuff, gasping, and returning to the store for more.

At last Skye took his turn. A balding young man at the counter surveyed him.

"You must be the Englishman, Skye. I'm Osgood. Diah Smith told me to put your order on account."

"It's Mister Skye, sir. I'd like a pair of those blankets, a small cooking pot, and a good ax. Also a knife—one of those big ones over there."

"Arkansas toothpick. What else?"

"That's all, sir."

"Sheetmetal pot or cast iron?"

"Whatever's cheapest."

"Sheetmetal, half-gallon." Osgood shrugged and wheeled into the storage area, dodging other clerks. He dropped thick gray blankets and an ax on the plank counter, and then added a tin pot and knife. "That do?"

"Yes."

"They come to seventeen and four bits. I'll put it on your account."

Skye had no idea how much that was, but it seemed a lot. "I'll find a way to pay it, sir."

"A dollar a plew, seventeen beaver."

Skye wondered how he could trap and skin that many beaver in a whole winter. They were making a debtor of him. Angrily, he whirled away, determined to escape these designing Yanks while he could. But the thick, heavy blankets felt good in his hand. So did the steel ax, with its keen edge, and the cooking pot and sharp knife. Now he had a way to cook food, and several weapons: the bow and arrows, the hatchet, a throwing and fighting knife, the ax, and his belaying pin, which he could use in ways these landlubbers never dreamed of. He had fought Kaffirs and pirates with no more than a belaying pin, and had fended off knives and swords with it, his hand protected behind the flare of the hickory. Let them try him now: he'd show them what a man could do with an ax and a hickory stick. He eyed his treasures and calmed down. They hadn't singled him out and weren't trying to ensnare him.

He wanted to see everything, meet everyone, explore every corner of this summer saturnalia, but he put first things first. He headed for the thick cottonwood groves in the river bottoms, looking for dead limbs. He had found a friend and protector in Jedediah Smith, and he would repay the loan as swiftly as possible. He located a fallen cottonwood limb and swiftly chopped and split an armload of wood. This he carried to Smith's lodge, and then another load.

"That's kind of you, Mister Skye," Smith said.

"It's the beginning of a repayment," Skye replied.

"You'll make friends here."

"That's my intention. Is it safe to leave my kit with your trappers? It's not much, Mr. Smith, but it's everything I have. I'm with the Shoshones now, but I'd like to meet your people."

"Bring it over and camp here. They'll leave your kit alone, 'least the trappers will. The Injuns probably will, too, but lifting a few things is a sport for them, friendly or not. Especially horses. You set up your camp here, and

I'll keep an eye on it. See those brush arbors? Those frameworks covered with boughs? Build yourself one, get out of the sun, put your loot in it. It's a home, of sorts."

Skye nodded, and chose a smooth level spot. In his months of flight, he had become an expert, learning the hard way just what a small pebble or stick or a slight slope could do to a night's sleep.

He cut still another armload of wood and carried it to one of the cookfires where any hungry man could dip a bowl and fill his belly. Within an hour he had supplied wood to all four cookfires of the mountain men, a gesture that did not go unnoticed, though the men barely acknowledged it.

Satisfied at last, he wandered aimlessly through the rendezvous, noting that these wildmen didn't wait for nightfall to imbibe spirits. Most of them had a tin cup of spirits that they attacked now and then. A few were drunk and staggering about. Two had passed into oblivion, and lay like corpses in the midst of all the revelry. People simply stepped over them.

Skye had none, and could afford none, and had rarely tasted spirits in his life, having been a stripling when he was pressed, and a prisoner ever since. But he intended to guzzle some when he had the chance.

One thing he learned in his meandering: the white men and Indians alike used this summer fair to compete with each other. He watched, fascinated, as skilled marksmen, hefting octagon-barreled mountain rifles, put balls into tiny targets—as small as a knot on a tree—at awesome distances. Elsewhere he watched men throw their hatchets—called tomahawks by some—forty or fifty feet and hit their targets. Others threw knives with just as much dexterity and deadly effect, often betting beaver pelts or a cup of spirits on the outcomes. The Shoshones enthusiastically participated in what clearly were contests of martial skills, and he learned that a few Crows were also competing.

In the course of that afternoon, Skye discovered that behind these contests was the deadly serious business of survival. Each of these mountain men and their Indian rivals could call upon these skills and often did against two- and four-footed enemies. Skye knew he would master these amazing skills, and vowed he would make himself the equal of all these trappers.

Other trappers perched on logs or stumps gambled with grubby cards, playing games called monte and euchre, their wagering done with round beaver pelts, which he gathered were worth about a dollar. Others of this bearded and buckskinned gentry simply drank and bragged. The young fellow Bridger was one of these. He lounged against a stump, sipped whiskey steadily, and told the most outlandish stories Skye had ever heard.

"I mind the time I saw this hyar bull elk, and I thought to make meat, so I lifted old Thunderbolt and let fly. But durned if the ball didn't hit glass. It just tinkled down on the ground like a busted window. That elk, he was clear t'other side of a glass mountain and I couldn't drop him nohow," Bridger said. "What was worse, that thar mountain magnified him, so I was thinking that elk was a hundred yards away when actually he was fifteen miles. Now that war nothing compared to the river I came across once that ran uphill. It came barreling through a canyon and then run uphill a mile or two, so I made me a raft and it took me clear up a mountain."

It dawned on Skye that Bridger was piling one ridiculous tale on another just for Skye's benefit, though the homely fellow never looked him in the eye or acknowledged his presence. They were testing him in ways he could barely fathom. He laughed at Bridger's nonsense and Bridger grinned in return. They asked Skye nothing about himself, and he volunteered nothing, uncertain about all this. How many of these fierce men would be as fair-minded as Smith? One thing he knew: these Yanks didn't hold to formality and status. No one was looking down his nose at Skye.

He came across none of the Hudson's Bay observers that Smith thought would be snooping around. Not a one of these mountaineers spoke with the precise tongue of an Englishman. But maybe Smith had meant Canadians, both French and English stock. Of the French there were many, most with black beards and thick accents. He heard names that suggested Scotland, names that suggested Quebec and Montreal. These were the HBC men Smith had lured away from John McLoughlin at Fort Vancouver, men who had changed sides. Skye felt safe here, but he wasn't entirely sure of it.

As dusk approached, Skye thought perhaps this assemblage would sit down to dinner, as Englishmen would have. But nothing like that materialized. Men dipped their bowls into the steaming pots. If a pot emptied, whoever felt like it sawed at the fly-specked hanging meat and started more stew. He discovered that these quartered carcasses were buffalo, and that the choicest cuts were humpmeat or rib. The mountaineers fed themselves whenever they felt like eating, roasting the best meat and stewing the worst.

But in the midst of this chaos, he discovered care and precaution. That evening trappers collected the horses that had grazed all day out on the prairies, brought them close, and hobbled them in camp. This all might be midsummer's fun, but this camp had teeth, and it could defend itself in an instant. Skye saw the lesson in it and headed out to the fields to collect his brown mare. He caught it, brought it to his camp, and hobbled and picketed it close by.

He marveled. The Royal Navy had taught discipline; these children of the wilderness had that, and initiative as well. They prepared themselves for trouble without being asked. No man in command, not Jedediah Smith or Jackson or Sublette, or General Ashley, said so much as a word to any of them, and yet this festival camp would deal ruthlessly with any emergency.

The knowledge pleased Skye, almost as much as his

keen observation of the underlying military genius in this ragtag army of trappers. He absorbed all he could of this odd gentry as he wended his solitary way through all their doings. With the advancing darkness, the trappers gathered into more intimate groups around low fires, mostly glowing coals that would silhouette no man and yet ward off the night chill. But there were gaps in the ranks. Men had vanished. He watched some of them take their leave, usually carrying their bedrolls and something else—a trinket or two, especially the round hand mirrors, or a hank of bright ribbon.

Skye felt the hot flood of his own needs, so recently awakened after the long drought in the Royal Navy. One by one the trappers slid into the night, heading for the Shoshone lodges. He chose not to try, and vaguely resented having to compete for Perrault's women, or any other women. This first night he would make friends and sample the spirits. He found a group of trappers sitting in a circle, most of them crosslegged or else simply squatting, a position they found comfortable, though it looked like torture to Skye. They were passing a jug around, and Skye knew he would have his chance for a swallow.

It was time to find out what these wild Yanks were like, and to sample some whiskey. He had rarely touched a drop of it in his cloistered life, but they wouldn't know that.

Chapter 23

Skye dreaded to open his eyes, but he knew he would have to sooner or later. His eyelids were all that protected him from the sunlight, which would lance into his throbbing head the instant he opened them and make matters worse.

Maybe if he lay quietly in his new blankets and refused to open his eyes for the entire day, the throbbing would depart from his head and the nausea from his tormented belly. He hazarded a small glimpse of the day and instantly shut his eyes again. It was as if he had been struck by lightning. He didn't want this day. He wanted to reel back time to the previous evening, before his first sip of that vile juice that swarmed down his gullet like a hundred hornets. He was feeling fine then. He doubted he would ever feel fine again. His new friends had ruined him.

He would have to get up and answer the call of nature. He couldn't escape that. Fiercely, he cast aside his new blankets and sat up, pushing down the gorge rising in his throat. Not far away, his fine friend Jim Beckwourth sat, grinning at him. Skye had made lots of friends last evening, but he couldn't remember the names of most of them. Fine old friends, the kind he had always wanted. They had passed him the jug and sat silently while he guzzled. He learned later it had been concocted just hours before from pure grain spirits, river water, a few plugs of tobacco, and some pepper for spice. Hooee!

He ignored Beckwourth and several other mountaineers who were gazing at him blankly, and crawled on all fours to some river brush, tottering like a cat with an arched back. He felt parched, and with every step he struggled to keep his belly from heaving. Last night he had taken sick, teetered from the dying campfire, and spewed out everything in his gut in one volcanic eruption. He was little better this morning. The sun crashed down on him, blinded him, and fried his brains.

He completed his ablutions, such as they were, and weaved back to his blankets, intending to collapse into them the rest of this July day. But his fine new pals would have none of that.

"Skye, if you don't get up, this child'll know you've gone beaver and we'll bury you," said Arthur Black.

"By God, Skye, if we bury you, we'll bury the biggest nose in Creation," said Beckwourth. "You have an Alps of a nose, a Stony Mountain nose. If all your appendages are the size of your nose, you're doomed to a life of pain and joy."

"It's Mister Skye, mate."

"Naw," said old Gabe Bridger, another of his fine new chums. "Man calls himself mister and the first thing ye know, ee's a booshway. What be 'ee front name?"

"Barnaby."

"No wonder 'ee got likkered up. This child never met a Barnaby thet didn't like to wet his dry with a snort or two. I known three Barnabys in my day, and you're jist like the rest."

"I thought it was Boston, Boston Skye," said Ferguson. "If it ain't, it should be."

"I knew a Boston once, but he gone under over on the Sweetwater," said Tom Virgin. "Hit's an unlucky name. It means manure in the Pawnee tongue."

They were at him again. They were at him all last night. There had been five or six passing the jug at various times, and it hadn't taken long to discover he had sat down with the wrong crowd, the elite veterans of the wilderness, and they were going to let him know it. At first they'd simply eyed him, but then they kept pushing that jug in his direction and urging him to take a good lick. He took lots of good licks.

"He's not going to make it. Let 'im be," said Virgin. "We'll put 'im in the river and float him down to the Salt Lake. That water's so briny it presarves carcasses. Skye, you get to be presarved forever in the mountains."

"No saltier than the sea, I guess," said Skye, and the men around him whickered.

"He'll be petrified salt. I seen an ol' coon turned into stone in six hour," said Bridger. "Over in the Yellerstone. He fell into one of them boiling pots, and when we got 'im out, he was solid rock from all that mineral. You think old booshway Skye'd look good as a statue?"

"Say, Boston Skye, 'ee know what day this is? The fourth day of July. You know what that means."

Skye shook his head. He hadn't the faintest idea.

"That means we catch a Brit, put 'im on a spit, and roast him to celebrate," said Beckwourth.

"Hey, that's some! We got us a live Englishman for supper," said Black. "This here's Independence Day."

Skye was getting the idea. "It's my Independence Day, too," he said quietly. "I'll join you, mates. I'm going to be an American like you. It's a country where a man can be a mister if he wants—and I want to. In England, the only misters are gentry and lords. A few months ago I made my own revolution."

"Ain't that some," said Virgin quietly. The mood changed swiftly.

Skye sat hunched and miserable, trying to ignore these fine friends and boon companions, but then Beckwourth brought him a mug of coffee, and he sipped the brew tentatively. He had rarely tasted it but he liked its aromatic, harsh flavor. They let him alone while he sipped. The coffee soon lifted his body out of its agony, and he opened his eyes again. His companions of the previous evening had mostly scattered but a few lolled about, repairing gear or whittling. Skye found an ancient pot over some coals and poured some more of the brew, feeling better as he stirred about.

Were these mountaineers like most Americans? Were Yanks mostly strange, hairy, slouchy creatures dressed in animal skins, with manners ruder than anything he'd seen among the limeys in the navy? Some, maybe, but not all. Smith wasn't like that. Tom Fitzpatrick had an Irish melody in his voice and good manners. Joe Lapointe talked a thickly accented English. Silas Gobel and Daniel Ferguson hadn't said much, unlike that blowhard Beckwourth, or that tale-teller Bridger.

Skye felt itchy and thin-skinned, and ready to show them a thing or two about a limey's bag of tricks. But they had drifted off, having wearied of their morning sport. They weren't a bad bunch but they had an edge, and they'd shown him he was a pork-eater. Skye pulled on his Creole moccasins and hunted around for a stewpot. Nothing much was cooking and he didn't feel like eating anyway so he abandoned the notion of breakfast.

The July heat boiled up and the sun was blistering the tawny earth on this July day. He needed to be alone. He jammed his topper down on his greasy locks and stalked to the riverbank, finding a trail along it that took him west onto lonely prairies where tall grasses danced in the bright winds. The more he walked, the more his legs behaved and the more energy he recovered. He slipped into a steady, long stride, the kind of stride that was the envy of any seaman confined to a teak deck. He stretched into a mile-eating gait, feeling the joyous and fertile earth under his soles. He felt a rush of dominion—he was a lord here, with no honorable sirs to stop him from walking any direction he chose to walk. Bit by bit, his body threw off the poisons of the previous night, and he felt himself again.

Then he beheld the girl. She sat on a boulder beside the river, watching him cautiously. He paused, studying this apparition. She didn't smile, nor did she reveal any emotion, neither fear nor friendship. She wore a plain buckskin dress over her slim figure. He thought she probably was no more than sixteen, if that, but how could one know? He smiled but she didn't. Perhaps he frightened her. He realized, as he stared, that she was uncommonly beautiful, with straight jet hair that shone in the white light, and delicate cheekbones and a fine, thin nose. She squinted at him, not quite suspiciously, but certainly with wariness. She wasn't Shoshone. He swiftly inventoried her dress and moccasins and face and knew she had been born to some other tribe, Crow perhaps.

Something about her stirred him. Maybe she was an Indian princess, a daughter of a chieftain, a haughty patrician among her people. She had the look, all-knowing, wise-eyed, strong-willed, swift to act and judge. He didn't know what to do, so he just stood there stupidly.

She looked so tender and young and virginal that he ached to get to know her. He wished he could just talk to this hauntingly lovely Indian girl.

He remembered a hand sign that Perrault had taught him. He would tell her that he was a friend. He lifted his right hand and held it, palm out, in front of his neck, his index and second finger pointing upward as high as his chin.

"Goddamn," she said in a dusky voice.

Skye gawked.

"You lost your tongue?"

"Ah, I was just passing by—"

"You are a Goddamn from Grandfather's Land," she said. "Across the waters. I have heard of you. You have the biggest nose ever seen. Now I have seen it. It is *big*."

"You what?"

"Sit down, old coon."

Gingerly, Skye lowered himself to the boulder and sat beside her. "You know my tongue," he said.

"The Goddamns stayed with us last winter."

"The who?"

"You hairy ones come, stay with Absaroka. We don't know your tribe until you tell us. Always, you call each other Goddamn, all the time, Goddamn, Goddamn, and then we know your tribe."

"Oh," said Skye, pondering that. "And they taught you English?"

"Taught me Goddamn. I know a little. American Goddamns, Canada Goddamns, same tongue."

"Ah, what is Absaroka?"

"Blackbird. Crow, in your words. Raven. I see you at trading store, and then some more times. I am looking for you to see the big nose."

"I don't know your name."

She squinted at him and said something he couldn't decipher. "What you call you?" she asked.

"Ah, Barnaby Skye. Mister Skye."

"Sonofabitch."

"Ah, can you translate your name? Into, ah, Goddamn?"

"Many Quill Woman."

The name seemed odd to Skye. How could he address this lissome girl as if she were a porcupine? "I think you're a princess," he said.

"What's that?"

"Daughter of a king or a prince."

"What's that?"

"Daughter of a chief."

"Ah! My mother's brother is Arapooish, chief of Kicked-in-the-Bellies."

"'Kicked-in-the-Bellies'?"

"My people."

"But you said you were Absaroka."

"Sonofabitch!" she snapped. She looked offended.

"I will give you a name," he said.

"You give me name?" She smiled. "Hokay, damn, Mister Skye."

"In my country there's a little girl who's the daughter of the chief, a princess. Her name is Victoria. I will call you Victoria."

She smiled wryly.

"How old are you, Victoria?"

She frowned, and then pointed to her fingers. "This many winters," she said, ticking off the count. It came to fifteen.

"Fifteen," he said. "I'll teach you the numbers."

"Hell, no. That's for winter. Now I sit here and make medicine. You like me?"

"Yes I do, Victoria."

"Good, Skye, pretty damn soon we have a lodge," she said. "I want a big-nose. You give ponies to my father, and we make more Kicked-in-the-Bellies, hokay?"

Chapter 24

Many Quill Woman liked the man sitting next to her beside the river, and knew exactly why. He had a certain gravity. Unlike the other pale-fleshed men, he didn't laugh much or slouch or talk too much. This one said little, but his eyes drank in everything around him. Some tragedy from his past clung to him; she knew he had endured something terrible and had emerged from it a man with strength and courage.

It frustrated her that she could say so little to him. When the American trappers had come to her village on the Elk River, which the white men called the Yellowstone, and spent the previous winter, she had learned their tongue—at least as much as she could. She didn't despise them the way the other village girls did, but tried to find out what she could. They were a strange and mysterious tribe, the Goddamns, and she doubted she would ever really fathom their ways. They came without women, and she wondered what the female Goddamns were like and why they were hidden away somewhere.

Some of them, like Ed Rose and Jim Beckwourth, were fine warriors and much esteemed by the Absaroka because they fought side by side with them in several skirmishes with the Siksika. But they told strange tales no one believed, and they wanted all the women in the village. The grandmothers enjoyed the pale men, and spent hours telling bawdy stories to them, and hearing bawdy stories from them, which made them all laugh and made the winter pass quickly. The trappers didn't conquer very many Absaroka women, though. Certainly not herself, though they tried.

The Absaroka had come to the rendezvous of the Goddamns to buy guns. Chief Arapooish had said they should, and had come himself with just a few lodges. They all bore many pelts to trade for the wondrous weapon that would help the outnumbered Absaroka keep their homeland. They lived in the most beautiful land there ever was or could be, a land of snow-tipped mountains, rushing rivers, sweet water, great plains filled with grandfather buffalo to feed and clothe and shelter them. But the Absaroka faced the cruel Siksika in the north, who were as plentiful as leaves on trees and who had gotten guns from the North West Company traders; and on the east the powerful Lakota, many times more than the Absaroka in number, threatened to overwhelm them and rob them of their rightful home in the center of the world.

So the wise Arapooish had led the People to ally themselves with the Shoshones and the pale men who had guns, and to welcome any of the trappers into their villages. And now, he and several Absaroka lodges had come over the mountains to this place where there would be traders with guns, and they had brought many ponyloads of beaver pelts, buffalo robes, deer and elk skins, ermine and otter. They had brought ponies to trade, too, because the Goddamns never seemed to have enough, and paid much for them—a pony for a gun. The Absaroka would go back to the Elk River with many guns and powder and balls, and iron arrow and lance points, and keen-edged hatchets, and flints and strikers, and awls and cloth and thread, and the Absaroka would be stronger and better fed and dressed because of these wonders.

She had seen this young man the day he arrived with the Shoshones, and something in him caught her attention. She had known from that moment that she and he would someday share a lodge; she had the inner vision that told her so. No white man had this inner vision, which is why they were inferior to the People. This man, Mister Skye, didn't see with knowing inner sight, but she would teach him how to look for the vision and see beyond what could be seen with the eyes.

She was glad he had found her there, far from the rendezvous.

"I teach you words, you teach me words," she said. If she was going to know this Goddamn better, she needed to be able to talk with him.

He nodded, but then he said, "Teach me the finger signs. I want to learn to talk with my hands."

That sounded like a good project to her, so she thought up signs to show him. She smiled, her face aglow.

She brought two fingers of her right hand to the right side of her mouth. Her fingers pointed left. Then she moved her hand leftward across her mouth. "Lies," she said.

"Lies?"

"Lies, two tongues."

He nodded and tried it. She laughed.

She clasped her hands in front of her with her left hand facing down and her right in the palm of her left. "Peace."

"That's good," he said. "Peace."

She held up all five fingers of one hand in front of her chest. "People," she said.

"Oh, that's easy," he replied. "People."

She eyed him mischievously, and crossed her wrists in front of her heart, her right hand nearer her body. She closed her hands, with their backs upward. Then she pressed her right forearm against herself and her left wrist against the right. "Love," she said solemnly, her eyes dancing.

He had trouble with that one, and she finally guided his hands until he could do it. "I'm not much good at love," he said.

She put the tips of her right fingers over her lips and inclined her head forward. "Be quiet," she said. "Now, Goddamn, this for you."

She closed her right hand and brought it to her forehead, thumb up, and then rotated her hand in a small horizontal circle, turning it up to the sun and then left. "Crazy," she said, her eyes alive with mirth again.

He imitated her. "I suppose I am," he said.

She pointed one finger of her right hand at him. "You," she said.

"That's easy." He pointed a finger at her. "You."

She touched the center of her chest with her extended thumb. "Me," she said.

"That's easy, too. Is there a sign for hunger?"

She held the little finger of her right hand alongside her stomach, and then moved the finger left and right. "Much hunger," she said solemnly.

"Show me yes and no."

She lifted her right hand in front of her to shoulder height, its fingers pointing up, her thumb on her second finger. Then she moved her hand down and left, closing her index finger over her thumb. "Yes," she said, and waited for him to do it, too. Then she extended her right hand in front of her, palm upward, and swung her hand to the right while turning it, putting her thumb up. "No," she said.

He wrestled with that a few times. "How do I say thank you, Victoria?"

She extended both of her hands outward, the backs up, and swept them outward and downward toward him. "Thank you," she said.

He did that. "I like you, Victoria. I hope you will give me many more lessons."

"Skye, you old coon, I show you how the stick floats."

He stared blankly and she laughed. Pretty soon he would have the signs, and pretty soon she would have Skye.

They strolled back to the encampment through a brassy afternoon, with the heat thick in her nostrils. She tried to teach him Absaroka words. There were so many, and she wanted him to master every one so they could talk and she could plumb his secrets.

She spotted an eagle soaring above and gave him the word, *mai shu'*. She named the wild rose, *mit ska' pa*. She named the squirrels and the ravens and the hawks. She named their clothing, and then she named their body parts, eyes, ears, nose, chest, fingers, toes. She named the earth and sky and sun and stars.

All these he repeated, but she knew he was being dutiful rather than trying to learn them. He really wasn't interested in the Absaroka words, unlike the finger signs, which he made an effort to master. The signs he could use; her tongue he could not. She sighed. Maybe her inner vision had been flawed or she had not fathomed what she had seen. Maybe he would drift away with the rest of the Goddamns when this was over.

"You don't care about Absaroka words."

He didn't deny it, but gazed at her directly in a manner very impolite. "I need the sign language," he said. "You are a good teacher. The signs will help me when I go east."

"East?"

"Yes. I will not be here long."

She absorbed that, her confidence suddenly frayed. "Where are you going?"

He tried to frame a reply and couldn't, and finally shrugged. "I don't know how to tell you. But I have a long way to go."

She squinted. "And never come back to here?"

"No. I won't be back."

"You don't like it here? You don't like Absaroka? You don't like me?"

"I like you all. But this is not what I will do with my life."

"Sonofabitch, what you gonna do?"

He seemed helpless to explain. "Go to the big villages of the Americans."

"What there?"

"Go to college if I can. Someway, somehow."

"What's that?"

"I can't explain it." But then he tried. "Did your mother teach you how to sew a dress or tan a hide? Did she teach you how to cook? A college is where I will go to learn."

"You don't need college. I teach you everything. I teach you many words and signs."

"Yes, and thank you, Victoria."

He smiled. He hadn't smiled all the way back to the encampment and his mind was drifting elsewhere, to some shores of memory where she could never walk. She wondered about him, about the sadness written on his big, creased face, and radiating from his eyes. This Skye was a sad man.

"How come you ain't happy?" she asked, a little cross.

"I am happy. I have not been so happy since I was younger than you."

"What take your happiness away?"

"I was in a boat that sailed the water, and I could not escape."

"I would be unhappy, too," she said. "We live in a good land, the center of the world. There is no better place. Chief Arapooish has said it. To the north it is too cold, and to the south too hot and dry, and to the east too wet and flat and unpleasing to the eye. But here are mountains and forests and creeks to please the eye, and everything is just right for the Absaroka people. We love our land, which is just beyond the mountains on the Elk River, and we will never let others take it from us. We will die before we will surrender it."

"I understand. I would die rather than surrender my freedom. That is because it means more to me than life."

"Ah, Mister Skye, you are a man of much medicine," she said.

"Medicine?"

"Power. You could be a holy man. You maybe have the medicine of the hawks."

Skye laughed. She stared, amazed. He had been distant all the while they strolled back, but now his gaze met hers, and fires lit between them.

Chapter 25

Skye hunted for General Ashley. The time had come to make arrangements to go to St. Louis. He intended to work his way east in whatever capacity Ashley might use him. He'd heard that this rendezvous would wind up shortly, and Ashley was eager to get back. He had a fortune in beaver pelts that he would haul to St. Louis on the packhorses that had brought out the year's provisions.

He found the general at his tent, near his trading store, sitting on a stump and bent over a ledger. The man radiated a certain august presence that impressed Skye. The man's demeanor had helped him both as a politician and as an officer in the militia. He had a noble profile, and used it to advantage, often facing sideways from whoever he was addressing.

"A word if I may, sir," Skye said, his topper in hand.

"Yes, yes, let me add up this column," the general said, a bit testily.

Skye waited until the man finished and stared up at his visitor, his gaze assessive and neutral.

"I'm looking for a position—service to you on your trip east," Skye began.

"Who are you?"

"Barnaby Skye, sir."

"Oh, the deserter Diah Smith told me about."

"Pressed seaman, sir."

"It doesn't matter what your story is. The fact is, you deserted your post, failed your superior officers, your nation, and your shipmates."

"I served Great Britain for seven years, sir."

"Not voluntarily, so it's no sign of virtue in you."

"I fought for the Crown in the Kaffir wars and once in Burma, and was blooded in Africa."

"What you say doesn't matter. You deserted your post."

"General, how much does a man owe his government?"

"Whatever it asks."

"Seven years, sir?"

"More if required."

"If your government bound you to service for seven years, with no recourse, would you serve gladly—your life disrupted?"

"That's hypothetical. Your desertion is real."

"My question, sir—"

Ashley paused, softening slightly. "I would not serve gladly and I would seek avenues of redress. But desertion? Never."

"What if there's no redress?"

"There's always redress."

"Do you know that for a fact—about the Royal Navy?"

"Britain's a great nation—"

"That's not my question, general."

"No, I don't, but I can't imagine there's any truth in your cock-and-bull story."

Skye saw the way it was heading and abandoned that tack. "I'm looking for passage east. I'll work my way there in your service. I have a horse, and that would help you."

Ashley gazed sourly at Skye. "I can always use men. I have twenty-five, and three times that many packhorses, and there's always the threat of Indians or stampedes or trouble. I never have enough horses and men. But Skye, I expect honorable conduct from men in my service. If trouble comes, will you desert?"

"I fought the bloody Kaffirs side by side with the rest, sir."

Ashley stared coldly at him. "I'll think about it, Skye. I'll be leaving within the week."

"It's Mister Skye, sir."

"Mister Skye, is it?"

"In England, it's a courtesy not given ordinary men. This is a new world. As long as we're meeting as equals and freemen, you may call me mister, and I'll call you the same, or by your title."

Ashley smiled slightly. "And what would you do in St. Louis? Patronize the grog shops?"

"I'll work my way east, sir. I wish to go to Boston."

"Ah, and become a merchant seaman. New Orleans would be easier."

"No, sir, go to college."

"College? College?" Ashley was taken aback.

"You have a good one near Boston, and I'll find a way to get in and start my life again. Before the press-gang snatched me, I was headed for Cambridge, Jesus College, like my father before me, and his father before him. He's a London merchant, sir."

Ashley snickered nasally, apparently too astonished to offer a rejoinder. Skye waited for an answer. If he should go with Ashley, it would be a long, brutal trip, not much different from his imprisonment in a royal man o' war. But it would take him east.

"Smith tells me you're a not a mountaineer," Ashley said.

"I made my way from Fort Vancouver, sir. I improved my lot the entire time, starting with little more than the clothes on my back, a flint and striker, and a few small items."

"Every bit of it Royal Navy property."

"Mostly mine. The rest back pay for seven years, sir."

"Theft."

"I never received a pence in the navy, sir."

"I don't believe you. You're a thief as well as a deserter."

"I was fined my entire pay and more, sir."

"For what?"

"Trying to secure my freedom."

"Diah says he's advanced you credit. I suppose you're going to run out on him."

"No, sir. Pay him out of service—to you, or to him, or however I can."

Ashley laughed, baring yellow teeth. "You're a rogue, Skye. You're planning to stick Smith with the debt."

"It's Mister Skye, sir. And unless you know a man's lying, you ought not to accuse. And unless you know a man's planning to steal from his benefactor, you shouldn't make that accusation either."

Ashley reddened. "I'm done with you, Skye. If I decide to take you—and I may be forced to because I'm short-handed—believe me, you'll be watched day and night."

"It's Mister Skye, sir. I'll report to you daily until you decide."

Skye left Ashley's tent in a bilious mood. He hadn't expected that sort of treatment. He had heard the man was affable, a natural politician with an eye for a profit and plenty of daring when it came to taking a risk.

He stormed over to the headquarters lodge of Smith, Jackson, and Sublette, and barged in, finding Smith and Sublette.

"How much do I owe, and what can I do to pay it?" he barked.

"Well, it's Mister Skye."

Jedediah Smith retreated into silence a moment, and

then showed those qualities that made him a leader of men. "Bill and I were just mapping out our brigades. We'll have three this year. How may I help you, Mister Skye?"

Skye felt the heat slide out of him and rotated his topper in his hands a moment while he collected himself. "I've come from an interview with General Ashley, sir. He's not inclined to employ me for—reasons of character. Very well. I have my own standards. You've fed me for several days and advanced me seventeen dollars of goods. What is the value of my horse, sir? Would that pay my debt?"

Smith eyed Skye contemplatively. "A good horse's worth a hundred to a hundred fifty in the mountains. They're so scarce it's a bargain. But I'm not inclined to put you on foot."

"I'm starting east in the morning and I'm going with a clear slate. I'll trade the horse for my debt and a good kit, including a rifle."

"You'll need your horse." He eyed Skye mildly. "I'll talk to Ashley. In the mountains these things have to be dealt with. Half his pack crew he recruited out of the grog shops of St. Louis. I don't know what's in his craw."

"Thank you, sir. I'd rather not travel with him."

Smith grinned. "Mister Skye, you've all the makings of a good free trapper, including the temperament."

"All I want, sir, is to resume my life. And I'll find the way, and do it honorably, no matter how long it takes. If that means paying you back when I get to where I'm going and find a means to survive, then I'll do it. But one way or another, sir, you'll be paid."

"You're not enjoying it here."

Skye shrugged. "There's nothing for me here. But yes, I'm enjoying it. I've never seen such sights. I have ambition, Mr. Smith, and this isn't the place for it. A university might be."

"I'll talk to Ashley. He's not being reasonable. He's

leaving in a few days, mostly hanging around for any last pelts. Some trappers are still drifting in."

"He'll find me a faithful and hard-working man, sir."

"Mister Skye, you're a lot more than that, I'd wager. You think about staying in the mountains with my company. We need men. One can be a free trapper, or a camp tender, or a clerk. Camp tenders and clerks are salaried; free trappers sell us what they catch. They're independent businessmen. Davey Jackson's leading a brigade into the Snake country. Bill here's going over the Stony Mountains to the Crow and Blackfoot country, the Three Forks area—dangerous but untrapped. Virgin beaver country, but full of Bug's Boys.

"I'm fitting out a party to find a way to Mexican California. There's a river, the Buenaventura. No one's found it, but we know it's out there, other side of the Salt Lake. I mean to find it and take it west to the California mountains. The Sierra's full of beaver. I'm a man with big ideas, Mister Skye. If Ashley won't have you, we'd be more than glad to take you on."

It was opportunity—if Skye wanted to abandon a dream.

Chapter 26

The rendezvous was drawing to a close, but Skye hadn't an inkling about his fate. General Ashley put him off each day. If worse came to worse, he intended simply to start east on his own, hazarding whatever fate had in store for a solitary traveler walking across the continent. By all accounts, he could reach St. Louis, on the western edge of the United States, before cold weather set in. After that he could work his way east.

He found himself an outsider at the rendezvous. He didn't play euchre or Spanish monte because he had nothing to wager. His one encounter with the fiery trade whiskey made him chary of sipping any more of it. Sometimes he sat quietly among the trappers, listening to that awesome braggart Beckwourth spin his tales in a patois Skye could barely fathom, or Bridger tell comic yarns that usually ended up in raucous laughter.

But Skye didn't fit in. He had an innate reserve, bred into him from childhood, unlike these wild, exuberant, cocky Yanks. His was the lexicon of the sea, and theirs the lexicon of frontiersmen cut loose from all their moorings. He came to enjoy the hairy breed who combed the mountains, but he could never imitate them. He admired their vast confidence, their fierce loyalties—but he didn't admire their inflammatory ways, with emotions seething uncontrolled just below the surface. Twice during the rendevous he had seen knife fights, men threatening each other with death.

He made friends with them all, but knew he would be leaving soon for the states and would never see them again. As the rendezvous wore on, they welcomed him to their campfires, and he put names to a hundred faces, and found them a varied lot from all over the continent, bonded only by a ferocity and courage he had rarely seen in others.

He didn't participate in the endless contests because he couldn't begin to match the skills of these mountaineers. How could he compete against men who could throw a heavy knife squarely into a knot on a distant tree trunk, or fire their heavy rifles so accurately they could split the ball on the cutting edge of a distant ax set up as a target? How could he toss a tomahawk so well that it would bury itself in a stump fifty feet away? He marveled at these things, watched endlessly, learned a lot—and quietly practiced with his knife and bow and arrows.

But then one afternoon a pair of tomahawk throwers, Jeandrois Rariet and Tom Virgin, politely invited him to try. Skye decided to grasp the nettle, and they handed him a 'hawk. He'd been watching, and tossed the hawk in a fine true arc—but it landed wrong and didn't bite the tree trunk.

"You gents have great skills," he said.

"You have to, out here," Virgin said. "Try 'er again, Mister Skye."

Skye did, as haplessly as the first time.

After that, he found himself participating gamely in all the sports. He was at his worst with the mountain rifles. The heavy weapons bucked in his grasp, ruining his aim, and he never hit a target. These men awed him, firing at the edge of playing cards, putting five shots into a fist-sized circle as far away as the eye could see, casually tossing knives or tomahawks with equal accuracy. He tried his hand, bumbled them all, took the joshing amiably, and ignored the taunts. They even bested him in the only area where he had acquired some skill—with his bow and arrows. Not a few mountaineers were splendid archers and could even compete with the Crows and Shoshones.

"I've never seen marksmen like you," Skye said to Tom Virgin.

"It's this way, old coon. Once that supply outfit pulls outa here, we got all the powder and lead we're gonna see until next year, savin' we go to some Hudson's Bay post and let 'em plunder us. So's there's none to spare. Some coons, they prefer flintlocks because there's always flint around, while other coons like caplocks because they fire when she rains. But them as has caplocks, they'd better have enough caps to last a year, or here's damp powder and no way to dry it. What it comes to is, we can't waste a shot. Naught a one."

"Why do you stay in the mountains and endure the hardship?"

Virgin spat. "'Cause it's fat times."

"You mean you make money?"

"Naw, I mean it don't get any better. You know what it's like to ride into some mountain park no white man's ever laid eyes on? What woodsmoke smells like early in a November mornin' when you're up and stretching and thinkin' breakfast? What it's like to cut into a juicy buffler hump and eat the best meat ever tasted by mortal man? What she's like to be free of everyone, everything? What it's like to have to wrestle the world every day to stay alive? To have some old coons you can count on no matter what? Naw, you wouldn't know, but you oughter think on it. A mountaineer is a king in his own kingdom."

"I haven't even seen a buffalo, but I'd sure like to sample that humpmeat."

"Buffler's shot out around here. Never was much. But over yonder, other side of the Stonies, them buffler run in bunches so thick they turn the prairie black. You'll never see the like—herds so big you can't count. Hundred thousand maybe, maybe ten times that. No man can say. Meat on the hoof. Boudins—"

"Boudins?"

"Buffler gut stuffed like sausage and cooked up real good, or just eaten up. You run dry, some time, out on the prairies, you shoot a buffler and drink what's in the boudins, and it'll get ye out alive."

Skye nodded. Another survival item to file away, something to help him cross the prairies to civilization. "Thanks for the tip, Tom. Maybe it'll help when I go east."

Virgin scratched his enormous beard and squinted. "You plumb center sartin you're going east, eh?"

"Yes."

"You've the makin's of a mountaineer, but I guess we'll never know." He smiled. "Each to his own. Me, I'd croak if I had ta live back east again. I can't even stand being around St. Louis. Get to swilling grog and makin' trouble and pretty soon, the constable's got me. Out here, you don't have to make trouble because it's always makin' itself. I'm a free trapper, and that's the only life there is."

Skye smiled. There was indeed something seductive about the mountains, and at times they tempted him. But he could hardly imagine fashioning a life out of this sort of existence. What would he achieve? If he didn't die an awful death under a scalping knife, what would he have to show for a lifetime in the mountains? He had already lost seven years.

He headed, as he usually did, to General Ashley's tent but didn't find him there. He hunted for the man and found him out among the horses, looking dour. He and his packers were studying each of the general's horses, and not liking their condition.

"Not enough rest," said Ashley's top man.

"I hoped to buy some, but all I got was half a dozen miserable beasts from the Crows. They'll have to do," Ashley said.

Skye intervened. "Have you come to a decision, sir?"

The general turned to Skye, contemplatively. "We're leaving in two days. If you want to come along, I'll not say nay. We could use your horse. I'll trade the horse for your mess."

"I owe Smith, Jackson, and Sublette about seventeen dollars, sir. Perhaps you'd employ me for that and credit their account. I'll sell the horse for the going price."

"No, I won't do that. It's enough that I'm taking you safely east."

"Very well, sir. I'll probably strike out on my own soon."

"It's certain death."

"I've been talking to gentlemen here, sir. Tom Fitzpatrick has made the journey safely more than once. Once only a short time ago."

"Tom's a veteran of the mountains, Skye."

"It's Mister Skye, sir."

Ashley looked impatient. "How about selling me your horse? I'll pay fifty for it."

"The word is that a horse is worth a hundred and fifty here in the mountains, sir."

"We don't seem to come to any agreement, Skye. You won't ever again have the opportunity I'm offering."

"I've been talking to these men, sir. It seems that I can work my way south to Mexican Santa Fe and hire on with any of the traders on the trail between there and St. Louis, and still go east this year. If you want to hire me at the wage you pay your other men, I'll sign on. If you wish to buy my horse for the going price here, we can talk about terms." He turned to leave.

"I'll think about it," Ashley said, still dour.

Skye left Ashley, convinced the general of the Missouri militia wasn't going to give him a fair shake. He really didn't want to head south to Mexico, either. He might just as easily end up in a Mexican dungeon as in a trader's caravan, or so he had heard from these mountaineers. No, the best course would be to go east alone.

He found Broken Hand Fitzpatrick at his usual spot near the Ashley tent store, and approached the genial Irishman for some advice.

"Sorry to trouble you, mate, but I'd like to learn a bit about getting across the plains. You seem to manage it regularly, and keep your hair."

"Why, bless me, Mister Skye, ye have a way of complimenting that's music to me ears. I have a little luck and a little skill and a little caution, and it's gotten me through, but with a few scrapes. Like this hand, now . . ." He held up his crippled left hand. "The things you don't expect, that's what do ye in. A rifle burst, that's what did this. Expect the unexpected."

"Could you tell me what to expect—and all the rest?"

"Ye be wantin' to go back by your lonesome, eh?"

"General Ashley doesn't look kindly on me, Mr. Fitzpatrick."

Fitzpatrick laughed. "Any bloke that stiffs the Royal Navy is a friend of the Irish," he said. "Sure, I'll tell ye what I can. The Sioux are friendly, except when they catch a man alone. The Pawnee are tribulation and death."

"I wouldn't know one from another."

"In that case, ye'll need more than luck, Mister Skye. Ye'll need a cavalry company and a few cannon. Do ye have a weapon?"

"Nez Percé bow and seven arrows left."

"De ye know the sign language?"

"I've a few words a Crow lass taught me."

"Do ye have skill as a hunter?"

"No, but each night on the trail I set a trap and often catch small things. Not good to taste but it fills the belly."

"Agh, you've the makings of a mountaineer, Mister

Skye. Do ye know the geography? Would ye know when ye reach Missoura? Do ye know how the rivers run, how the Platte runs into the Missoura near Council Bluffs? And how to find the trail that cuts that corner and gets ye to Westport, and from there to St. Louis? De ye know the tribes thataway, the Omaha, the Kansa . . ."

"You're telling me not to do it."

"Aye, I'm telling ye that, knowin' it won't do a bit o' good because ye'll do what ye have to. I never met a man so determined to get out of the mountains. You got anything against these mountains?"

"Yes, sir. They're barriers to a good life, and so are the vast plains I must cross."

"And, me English friend, what's a good life now?"

"A life of perfect freedom," said Skye without hesitation.

"And ye don't see it here?"

"No, these mountains are a prison, and the wilderness is a cage. No one here admits to the boredom, but I see it. These men have little to do. What do they achieve? Give me a great and proud city to grow in and educate myself and start a business, and the liberty to shape my life, and I'll be content."

"And all ye have to do is cross a continent," Fitzpatrick said.

Chapter 27

The rendezvous died two days later. At dawn, Ashley's men loaded one hundred twenty-three packs of beaver plus some bales of other pelts onto their horses, burdening each of them with two hundred fifty to three hundred pounds of dead weight. Everyone watched: the free trappers, the engagés of Smith, Jackson, and Sublette, the Creoles and Iroquois, the Shoshones and Crows, and Mister Skye.

A terrible silence pervaded the Cache Valley. Skye had expected the departure to be as exuberant as the arrivals, with whoops, gunfire, cheers, and catcalls. Instead, a certain gloom pervaded the great flat along the Weber River, abetted by an overcast sky that made the dawn somber. Another hard year would pass before they saw the next rendezvous, or guzzled trade whiskey, or bought the essentials and a few luxuries that would make wilderness life bearable again. By fall the coffee, tea, flour, sugar, molasses, salt, and beans would run out, and the mountain trappers would subsist once again on whatever nature provided. Friendships were being sundered, too; Ashley's contingent included a number of trappers leaving the mountains.

Skye was not among them. Ashley didn't want him. Skye had never been able to puzzle it out, but there was no point in worrying about it. Ashley had his own way of looking at things. Skye watched the general, mounted on a gaunt but well-bred charger, wave the long caravan into action, and the burdened horses walked down the Weber River, the teamsters beside them. At its confluence with the Bear, they would turn north, and then east, cross the Continental Divide at South Pass, descend the Sweetwater to the North Platte, and then east across a thousand miles of unsettled and dangerous prairie.

Skye could feel the loss and unease around him. As much as these mountaineers loved the wild life, they loved the replenishments from civilization, too, along with the news of the world. This was a moment when the men of the mountains weighed their options. They could catch up and go east if they chose. Or they could stay. It was up to each free trapper.

Skye didn't have that option. He found Smith in a pensive mood as they watched the long pack train, carrying a fortune in pelts, vanish around a river bend.

"If the general gets back safely, he'll be about seventy thousand dollars richer," Smith said. "If he doesn't, then we're in trouble, too. We'll have no resupply next summer. This business is all gamble."

"He has a strong force, well armed," said Skye.

"It's not just the Indians. Those horses might not last. They could be stolen. He doesn't have enough spares. Disease, cold weather, rain and mud—there's more things to go wrong than you can imagine, Skye."

"Ah, sir, I prefer to be addressed—"

"Yes, yes. I know."

"Sir, why was he so hostile?"

"The deserter business. He takes his generalship seriously, even if it's the militia."

"It didn't matter that I was pressed in?"

"Not with him."

"Mr. Smith, I'm told that half of Ashley's crew are thieves and murderers recruited out of the grog shops of St. Louis. He hired them willingly enough. Does he really think I'm worse than that lot?"

"It's in him to feel that way."

"Because he's a general of the militia?"

Smith shrugged. "Apparently so."

"I come from a nation where we're subjects of the Crown. Subjects—human fodder to be employed as the Crown chooses, with few rights and no heed paid to a man's dreams and hopes. I thought your Constitution and Declaration of Independence proposed a different—"

Smith laughed suddenly. "You don't need to make your case with me. I don't share Ashley's views." He surveyed Skye expectantly. "Well, Mister Skye, have you come to a decision?"

"Yes, sir. I'll be heading east on my own in a day or two. I'll get there somehow."

"Without a rifle, without knowing sign language, without hard experience. It's suicide."

"That's what Tom Fitzpatrick said. If I die, I die. I intend to get on with my life. If that means risks, then I'll take risks. I've taken risks from the moment I slid into the Columbia at Fort Vancouver. I'll take more."

"If I can't employ you, then I'd suggest you work your way south to the Mexican settlements. Taos, especially, and go with the next trading company. That's not safe, either: you'll run into Utes, Cheyenne, Comanches, and maybe some Lipan Apache. But it's probably better than going alone down the Platte."

"What'll happen here, now?"

"Most of us'll be moving out in a week or two. Shoshones and Crows'll drift off. Their trading's over."

"But you have trade goods, don't you?"

"Lots of them. We use them all year to barter for pelts or keep the peace or resupply ourselves. But by next summer, we'll be out of everything again."

"What are you going to do next, Mr. Smith?"

Jedediah Smith gazed westward, and Skye sensed the man was seeing virgin land, untracked wastes, surprise water holes, hidden trails. He smiled. "There's a river that runs across that desert somewhere, an arrow pointed at California. Ogden's been looking for it. I tried last year. It's not north of the Salt Lake, so it must be south. That's where I'm going."

"But what about trapping? Not many beaver in the desert."

"The Sierra Nevada, Mister Skye, the mightiest range of all, lies out there—somewhere."

Skye had the sense that Smith was more explorer than businessman, and wondered about it. A fur outfit needed pelts, not adventurers.

Smith returned from whatever uplands of the mind he had been visiting. "Davey Jackson's taking a brigade into the Snake country. He wants to push Hudson's Bay out. Bill Sublette's taking a brigade into the headwaters of the Missouri, Three Forks, Crow, and Blackfoot country. Much the most dangerous of the brigades, but it's virgin country—never trapped. All he has to do is keep Bug's Boys at bay."

Skye knew the term. Blackfeet. "Tell me about them."

"The Blackfeet are proud, brilliant, numerous, and brutal. They'll torture you slowly—or rather, their squaws will—just to hear you scream. They've plenty of horses, skills at war, and rich country full of game. They're never hungry, never poor. They're well armed with trade fusils—smoothbore flintlocks they got from the old North West Company. But Mister Skye, a man can get rich there. Really rich. That's prime beaver country. That's a land that'll yield a young fortune to the trapper who gets there first. That's our ace. If Davey's outfit finds the British have gotten there ahead of him, and I run into trouble with the Mexicans, Sublette's our hole card. He's taking the toughest, bravest men he can find, men with mountain savvy, and they'll need their wits if they intend to keep their hair."

Smith was grinning at Skye, a question in his face.

"What could a man earn in good beaver country?"

"Enough to take him east and put him through a year, two years, of college. Maybe more. Of course, you'll need some items, especially a mountain rifle that fires plumb center, some caps, powder, lead, a horn, and several other things, including at least half a dozen traps. About a hundred dollars of goods, advanced against your harvest. It's a rich land for a man with the heart and soul to take what's there for him. Set a man up for years, maybe. A few free trappers are getting rich, depositing money in St. Louis."

Skye didn't take the bait. He smiled at Smith—the offer acknowledged with that smile—and drifted away. The morning was still young. He would have a few days to think about it. He wandered across the forlorn flat, over trampled grass and abandoned bowers, their leaves dry and brittle. The place had changed. A certain spirit, a breath of life and excitement, had flown away on the wings of Ashley's pack train.

The mountaineers didn't compete or gamble that morning, but sat about talking quietly, the boast gone from their voices, their thoughts on the fall hunt. There'd be little drinking tonight. Those who had a jug of precious whiskey would save it for some future time, maybe a winter bacchanal, guarding it jealously because it could not be replaced. But he knew most of the free trappers had squandered everything, saved back nothing, and were poorer than when they arrived two or three weeks earlier, even in debt to the company. It wasn't in them to hold back.

He found old Perrault and his women packing up.

"Ah! Skye, damn good rendezvous, *oui?* I got plenty drunk. Eleven times I get drunk, and don' spend a pence."

"It was good."

"You get drunk?"

"Once."

"Ah! You stay, you learn. You staying, eh?"

"No, I'm going east in a day or two."

Perrault made a motion that looked like a scalping knife rotating around his head, and leered. *"Au revoir,* Royal Navy," he said. "Dis ain't the sea, dis is de wilds, and you gonna find out how wild soon."

The women looked prosperous and grinned at him. They were festooned with bold ribbons, combs, bracelets, beads, necklaces, rings, and bright clothing swiftly crafted from tradecloth. They were packing new knives, tin cups, jugs of molasses, jingle bobs, arrow points, and a lot more things they had wrested from the trappers during their rowdy sojourn. The younger sister had smeared vermilion over her cheeks. Her eyes still shone, and Skye smiled back at her, remembering his nights with her, his exploration of all the mysteries of love that she and her sister had provided just for the pleasure of it.

"What'd you get?" Perrault asked. "Everybody get something at rendezvous. Shoshone all got stuff. Lots powder and ball, guns to fight Blackfeet."

"I have a cook pot, ax, knife, and a pair of blankets," Skye said. "And a debt to pay."

"Ah, forget it. Dey don' expect repay."

"I expect to repay. It's how I am."

"Well, we go now. Maybe not see you again. Damn, never see you again. You go get yo'sel' kill."

Skye nodded. "I don't expect to be back," he said.

Chapter 28

The gifts touched Skye. He had not received a gift since he had been pressed into the Royal Navy, and now he could barely cope with the flood of feeling racing through him.

He tried on the moccasins that Many Quill Woman had fashioned for him and found they fit him perfectly. Somehow, she had gotten the measure of his feet. These had been cut and stitched from elkskin as soft as velvet, and felt as if he had worn them for years.

She looked at him expectantly, her gaze sharp as a hawk's, to ascertain his pleasure.

"These are beautiful, Victoria," he said softly, rubbing the supple leather with his hands. "I don't know how you knew my size."

She smiled. "I measure your feet. Do you like the beads?"

He admired the red-and-black geometric design she had patiently sewn into the leather, using trader's beads she had acquired at the rendezvous.

"Yes. These are beautiful."

"The design is a prayer to the four winds to take you where you will go."

She smiled, her brown eyes liquid with pleasure. He admired her lithe, taut figure, her sharp, angular features, and her hawkish gaze that seemed to penetrate into his soul and read his every thought. She had some way of fathoming everything around her with those remarkable eyes that saw through material things to the spirit that lay at the essence.

"I have more," she said proudly, and handed him another gift even more precious. Ten arrows.

"Victoria—" He couldn't speak. So she had seen his quiver, counted the seven remaining arrows, and knew he needed more. These were handsome arrows, long, with iron trade points bound by sinew over the haft, and three gray feathers anchored also by sinew to the rear. Each arrow was dyed with stripes of color around its shaft.

"The blue—it is for sky. The yellow is for sun. The four black lines—for you. I do not make these. The arrow maker make these. Big medicine. Now you have Absaroka medicine. Eiee!"

He slid fingers along the smooth surface, admiring the way a shoot of wood or reed had been scraped and planed into a straight shaft that would fly true.

"Absaroka make best arrows," she said proudly. "Now you eat, or go kill Siksika."

"Maybe these will save my life," he said.

She turned solemn. "Maybe so."

He felt bad because he had nothing to give her. He had subsisted as a pauper all through the rendezvous, living upon the charity of others. But the need raced through him and he knew what he would do. He plucked up one of his new blankets and handed it to her. It was gray, with black bands at the ends, thick and well carded, of English manufacture and phenomenally warm. These blankets came in pairs, and he would spare one for this lithe young Crow woman who had taken a fancy to him.

"I want you to have this. It is warm and well made," he said.

She took it, fondled it, her eyes alive with joy and delight. She wrapped it around herself, turning it into a robe or a capote even as she drew it tight under her crossed arms.

"See, Mister Skye? You make me happy."

She did look happy. He felt bathed in it. Something in her reached out to him, touching his core. She radiated a quality that seemed mysterious to him, as if she had magical powers.

"It will keep you warm when it is cold," he said.

"You make me warm," she replied, her face alive with delight. "Why do you go away? Is this not the best place, the center of the world?"

She knew his answer; they had rehearsed his reasons several times on their walks, or in their quiet moments beside the Weber River. She wasn't really asking; she was begging him to stay.

"I must go. It is my destiny." He felt uncomfortable. She had seen something in him and wanted him for a mate. She had made that plain. But he couldn't imagine himself tied to this dusky savage the rest of his life. He wanted a fair-skinned, blue-eyed English girl, or if not that, an American girl much like those across the Atlantic. She would be gracious and thoughtful and well schooled. She would be full of merriment and feeling and passion. She would become his wife gladly, and gladly she and he would raise a family. No . . . not this sharp-boned Crow woman, even if she seemed a cathedral in her own right.

He had tried to tell her about schooling, but without much success because the idea of formal education was outside of her ken. He had tried to tell her of his family, his father's business importing Chinese tea, silk, bamboo, rattan, copra, and ginseng while exporting British manufactured goods; of commissioning vessels to carry his cargoes halfway around the world; of a race of island geniuses who were dominating the sciences and arts.

His explanations had largely sailed past Many Quill Woman, and often her face darkened and softened when he spoke of it.

"We know nothing of these things," she had replied quietly once, and he sensed she was feeling defeat.

Now that surrender was in her face again.

"I will not be coming back," he said, not wanting it to sound so harsh, but not wanting her to have false hopes either. "But wherever I am, I will remember you, Victoria— do you like that name? Perhaps I shouldn't call you that."

"A name is a gift, Mister Skye. I like the gift. If I am Victoria to you, then it pleases me." She paused, squinting at him sternly. "You have eyes for your own kind. I see this. I have never seen a white woman. They must be big and strong, not small like me. I know about this. I have eyes for a good Absaroka man sometimes. A warrior with many honors. That would be good. Then I would be proud. My man would give to the People. Many scalps, many buffalo, many horses. He would feed the old and hungry. I have eyes for a man like that. But I have eyes for you, more than that."

"I would like to visit your village someday."

"Ah! The Kicked-in-the-Bellies. We have a strong village, and we have many Siksika scalps on our lances. You see only a few of us here. Many did not come. Just the ones with skins to trade for powder and guns and blankets and pots. We have many, and many children too. You will meet them."

"I hope I do—someday."

"Soon, Mister Skye. I have the inner eye. My spirit helper the magpie gives me the eye when I cry to see. I saw you with my inner eye. You go away and come back. The magpies are all around you, bringing you back. You have bear medicine, and someday you will wear the claws of the great bear—you call him grizzly—as your medicine. You will see. This I saw with my inner eye, so it will be."

Skye didn't protest. Let the savage girl have her fancies. He had told her plainly what his future would be and what he expected from his life. He only hoped she would find some good Crow warrior and find happiness. But he doubted it. He didn't know much about these American Indians but he sensed that Many Quill Woman was not a typical young woman on the brink of marriage. Something set her apart. Her destiny would take her in some strange direction.

"When are you leaving?" he asked.

"Arapooish say in the morning if the medicine seers tell him this is the right time to go back to Absaroka."

"I will see you off. And I will remember you because of the arrows and moccasins. How did you know my size?"

"You left a print in the dust. I make good moccasins. My father's wife makes good moccasins and I learn from her. You will take those moccasins into any Absaroka village and they will tell you what lodge they came from."

"And who made the arrows?"

"My father's brother Sees the Wind is an arrow maker. A holy man. He goes to the river to look for the right stalks. He catches the hawk for feathers. He goes to the distant cliffs for dyes. He blesses each arrow to make it strong and true. But I must tell you something. Do not shoot at the bear; the bear is your friend and helper. Send your arrows into elk and deer and antelope. Pray to each four-legged that gave up life so you could eat. Thank each one—this is what you must do when you kill. You will not have much chance to kill a buffalo, except maybe an old bull waiting for the wolves. But that is poor meat."

"I will remember."

She smiled suddenly, threw her new blanket over them both, and laughed. He started to pull it off, but she stayed him. "No, no, this is how Absaroka boy and girl whisper to each other."

Skye stood, astonished, half-embarrassed, under the small canopy of the blanket, while Victoria pressed close to him, their small world hidden from others, and yet all the more visible for being in plain sight of the whole encampment.

"There, Skye, this is how we do it."

She hugged him. He crushed her close, absorbing her sweetness and tartness all at once, something heady and private, as fragrant as roses in their privacy. She laughed and then ran a gentle hand through his matted beard. "Hairy man," she said. "We ain't got hair. You got more hair than a woman. Are all white men so hairy?"

Skye didn't quite know how to answer. The Crow warriors he had seen—for that matter, all the Indians he had seen—had little chest hair, and not much of a beard. "We're hairy people."

"Are your women hairy all over, too?"

Skye laughed uncertainly.

"You don't know. You are in that damn boat too long. Damn, Skye, you need a woman."

Under the blanket, the talk had taken a more intimate turn, and Skye was half enjoying it, half wondering how many dozen mountaineers were gathering silently around them, ready to hooraw him the moment the blanket came off.

"Good-bye, Mister Skye. You remember Victoria." She squeezed him hard and pulled the blanket away. Just as he suspected, a solemn conclave, including that rascal Beckwourth, Gabe Bridger, Tom Fitzpatrick, Bill Sublette, Davey Jackson, and even Jedediah Smith, stood in a circle and broke into applause.

Victoria squealed, glared at the impoliteness of these white barbarians, and ran toward her people.

"Them Snakes call me Blanket Jim," Bridger said. "Looks like I'll have to defend the title."

"Not for nothing did the Crows make me a chief among them," said Beckwourth. "Last winter I multiplied their population by fifty."

"Very touching, Mister Skye," said Tom Virgin. "We allus knew you had the makin's of a mountaineer."

Chapter 29

The rendezvous broke up under a heavy overcast that matched the mood of the seventy-odd mountaineers. Something joyous had fled, and now the trappers and the engagés of Smith, Jackson, and Sublette repaired their gear, looked over their horses, and waited for the command of their bourgeois, or brigade leader.

Their life had emptied suddenly, and even though it was high summer they were thinking of icy streams, shivering through unbearable cold, starvin' times and rough encounters with Indians. Skye sensed the change of mood and was glad he wasn't a part of all this. They might be as free as meadowlarks, but their lives were hollow, too, and filled with long stretches of sheer boredom. They might master the subtleties of nature, or learn the tongues of the tribes, but this was hardly the place to find progressive ideas or commerce or the arts, all of which Skye fully intended to pursue. Tempting as the life was, he could never be a mountaineer.

It was time to be off. He had waited to the last to see what sort of opportunity might arise, but none had. He would go east alone and almost unarmed. He had come this far from Fort Vancouver; he could find his way down the Platte if he had to, thanks to Fitzpatrick's careful description of the route. He found Jedediah Smith packing his camp gear into parfleches and making ready to leave.

"Mr. Smith, I'll be heading for St. Louis now," Skye said tentatively. "When I get there I'll find employment and repay what's owed—over seventeen dollars, I believe. You have an account with General Ashley and I'll deposit it there."

Smith smiled mildly. "The mountains aren't for you, eh?"

"No, sir."

"You don't have the itch to see what lies in the next valley, or what a coon must do to get from here to there, or see some amazing sight never before witnessed by a white man?"

"Those are all absorbing things, sir. But I have other plans. It's a dream that sustained me for days and weeks and months in ships' brigs, a dream that kept me going when I holystoned the decks, or climbed the rigging, or gazed at a distant shore where I would not touch foot."

Smith nodded. "I have strong business instincts myself. Hope to leave the mountains in comfortable circumstances in a few years." He smiled. "But those aren't my only hopes. Here in America, Mister Skye, Yanks have a westering instinct. We settled the east and then pushed ever westward across an unknown land, always itchy to see what lay beyond the horizon. It's bred into us."

Skye sighed. "I lack the instinct. But I'll never forget this, and the fine men I've met here. You're friends."

"I won't try to dissuade you. But we're putting three brigades out and you could join one. We can outfit you and you could spend a year and come out ahead."

"I've thought on it, and I'll just take my chances. I'd be grateful for some directions."

"I'll draw a map."

Smith extracted a sheet of paper—a precious item in the mountains—and a lead ball intended for his rifle, and began to draw with it, much to Skye's surprise. The lead left a clear mark on the paper.

Swiftly Smith drew rivers and mountain ranges, his hand replicating some vast map in his mind. Skye marveled that this quiet young man knew such a large part of a continent.

"We're here in Cache Valley. You need to get to the Platte, which'll take you to the Missouri, which'll take you to St. Louis and the Mississippi. You have several options. You can go over to Bear Lake, and then cut east to the Seedskedee, and cross a wasteland to South Pass, then to the headwaters of the Sweetwater, and down to the North Platte, like this."

Smith sketched in a trail with dotted lines. Skye knew that sticking to it would be much harder.

"It'll be easy to find your way because you'll be following Ashley. You can't miss the passage of so many horses and men. It's also the fastest route east. But I'd suggest you go with Bill Sublette's brigade up to the Snake. He'll be cutting north at Henry's Fork, heading for the Three Forks of the Missouri, but he'll show you where to leave the Snake—at a place called the Hoback. You'll end up on the Seedskedee, and from there you'll go over South Pass—the Continental Divide, but you'll hardly know it. The Wind Rivers are just to the north, a majestic range, and you'll be passing around their feet. This'd take you out of your way—you'd lose maybe ten days—but you'd profit by traveling with experienced mountaineers and learning their ways, which I strongly advise. And of course, you'd be safer while you're with them."

"I'll do that, then."

Smith peered at Skye solemnly. "I'm sorry you're not staying, but I understand. Let's go talk to Bill."

Skye followed Smith out of the lodge and over to the partner's half-shelter. "Mister Skye's going east, Bill, and I suggested he go with you a piece to learn what he can. Head him for the Hoback."

Sublette grinned. "Maybe we'll make a trapper of ye afore we get shut of ye. I'm planning on winterin' with the Crow—with the Kicked-in-the-Bellies. You want to spend more time under that blanket, you just stick with old William."

Skye nodded. He shook hands with Smith, liking this man who had swiftly made himself a legend among those who knew him.

"Thank you. I'm in your debt. If you come east, look me up."

"Not likely, Mister Skye. East makes me itch and sweat."

Smith's brigade was the first to pull out, heading straight south toward unknown arid country. Smith intended to strike the old Spanish Trail between Santa Fe and California, but no one knew just where it was or how it ran.

Davey Jackson pulled out next, with a large group of free trappers and several women, a colorful outfit with lean, bearded men in gaudy buckskins, tough looking and sharp eyed. Every man had a mountain rifle and the skill to use it murderously. They were heading into the Snake country, looking for areas not trapped out by Hudson's Bay, intending to be a Yank presence in disputed land.

Then, midday, Bill Sublette's brigade abandoned the forlorn flat, with Skye riding along. His rested horse danced under him, and he had to relearn the horsemanship he had taught himself. He carried his warbag on his lap, but it didn't trouble him. He was on his way again, and that sent his spirits soaring.

Twenty-four veterans of the mountains rode beside him, including Bridger and Beckwourth. They rode without military discipline, each man in his own style, and yet these Yanks were fanged and strong, and could give better than they got from any passing band of Indians. They would have to be: they were penetrating Blackfoot country for the first time, and death rode with them. Some or all of these men would not return to the next rendezvous, and yet each had elected to head into the prime beaver country of the north, as yet untouched because the ferocious Piegans, or Siksika, or Bloods, barred the way.

Skye thought that the casualness of this caravan might not appeal to the lord generals or captains of the British army, who would have organized the company into formation and put vedettes out on the flanks. Perhaps Sublette would do that when they reached dangerous country, but Skye would be long gone. They would show him the path and send him on his way.

Thirty-one men; that was the strength of this brigade. There were enough, they said, to hold off a whole village of Blackfeet. Those mountain rifles, accurately fired, would keep even a massed enemy at bay. There were no women in this brigade; Sublette had forbidden it.

No one spoke. They had talked themselves hoarse in the rendezvous. That was the social time. This was the time to head leisurely north through shortening days and chill nights, mapping out beaver-rich creeks and rivers to trap later when the fur was prime. This was the time to enjoy summer warmth while it lasted in these northern climes, time to have fun, make buffalo meat and jerky, harvest strawberries and chokecherries and other wild fruit. Time to gird up for winter, fatten the horses, braid rawhide horse tack, tell tall stories. Skye had heard more than a few yarns, and realized that storytelling was one of the ways these men made time pass in a land without diversions or outside news. Adventure and utter boredom appeared equally in the lives of these mountaineers.

For several days they wandered north until they struck the Snake, and then turned upstream, traversing a flat country but never out of sight of towering distant ranges.

Sublette often rode with Skye, gradually extracting from him the whole of his life in the Royal Navy and much about his childhood as well.

"I reckon an old coon like you'd think twice about returning to civilization, seeing as how you treasure your liberty," Sublette said.

"I treasure it. And I'm counting on your Yank government to protect it. But life is more than liberty. A man needs purpose and a dream, and my dream is to finish what I started and enter commerce."

Sublette didn't say anything, and Skye knew that his own preferences didn't sit well with these children of the wilds. The balmy days fled by one after another, hot midday, cool in the evenings, uneventful.

The river hooked around to the east again, and then one evening Sublette told Skye that they had come to the parting.

"Tomorrah we'll take Henry's Fork north and you'll stay on the Snake a while more, but not as far as Davey Jackson's Hole."

He stooped on bare earth and scraped a map with a stick. Skye had to find the route that had been traversed by the Astorians early in the century. If he found the right one, it would take him over a pass and down to the Seedskedee. And then he'd face a long stretch of waterless wasteland until he hit a small creek at the western foot of South Pass . . .

Skye memorized the map in his head, knowing how hard it would be to translate to the real world what Sublette was scraping in the clay.

That evening, while feasting on a buck mule deer that Emanuel Lazarus brought in, the talk turned distinctly odd.

"Mr. Bridger," said Beckwourth, "do you think Mr. Sublette'd give us a week off?"

"No, Mr. Beckwourth, Mr. Ranne, and Mr. Fitzpatrick proposed it, while Mr. Reed, and Mr. Daw objected because they want to make the beaver come."

"A pity," said Beckwourth. "How about you, Mister Skye?"

"I'll be taking my leave tomorrow, mates."

"Mates? Mates? What sort of word is that? Call us mister."

Skye smiled.

"Time we elevated the manners around hyar," Bridger said. "Now, you ain't never to call me Gabe agin, though I'll accept Blanket Jim at rendezvous. From now on it's mister. High-toned, like Mister Skye hyar. Mr. Bridger, that's me."

With that, they all pronounced themselves misters and said the brigade was mightily elevated by the courtesy.

"Tell us again why y'ar Mister Skye," Isaac Galbraith asked.

"Because this is a new world," Skye said, simply.

"Yep, it's that all right," Beckwourth opined. "But mister ain't enough. Call me chief. Call me headman. Call me Lord Beckwourth, or baron or viscount or duke."

Skye smiled.

"Now, Mister Skye, old coon, onct ye get onto that Astorian patch, ye got to watch for the petryfied forest. Everything in her's turned to rock," said Mr. Bridger. "I saw me an elk turned solid rock there not long ago. And there's a marble grizzly rearin' up at the east end."

"And beyond the petryfied forest is the Amazons," said Mr. Beckwourth. "Two hundred seventy beauteous Injun women who won't let you pass until you pleasure 'em."

They managed all this until the fire died and the stars blanketed the sky, and Skye knew he had friends, and they were feeling loss at his departure. And he knew as well that he would feel a similar loss for these wild Yanks.

The next morning, one with a chill on it, they rode an hour to the confluence of Henry's Fork and the Snake, and there they parted. In the northeastern haze loomed a range topped by three spiky peaks.

"Them's the Tetons," Sublette said. "Snake runs right

under 'em on the east side, but you won't go that far. All right, Mister Skye, keep your topknot on."

It was the mountaineers' blessing.

"Thank you, gentlemen. Keep your topknots on."

He rode away from them, a lone man in a wild, lonely land, with tears in his eyes.

Chapter 30

The Snake River divided itself around countless sandy islands and sparkled merrily through lush meadows or sudden patches of pine. It harbored along its banks more wildlife than Skye had ever seen, and in its transparent waters trout leapt and darted.

He found himself riding through an Eden that would have been the envy of Adam and Eve. He had little trouble filling his demanding belly now that July was fading into August and every bush brimmed with red, black, and silvery berries. He scared up deer and martins and elk, and once a yawning brown bear. He watched bald eagles circle above him and redtailed hawks dive for their dinner. Sunlight glinted off the cold complex waters, dazzling his eye. The screech of meadowlarks, kildeer, and red-winged blackbirds gladdened his spirit and told him that all was well.

The cheerful river ushered him across a golden plain and into somber mountains. Now the river pulsed through an intimate valley hemmed by vaulting pine-clad slopes, and Skye knew he must look for the vaguely described turnoff, Hoback River, that had been the route of John Jacob Astor's party heading for the Pacific coast in 1811.

He missed his companions, but the river had become his bosom friend, endlessly delightful to eye and soul. He was glad he had traveled a piece with Sublette's brigade, not only because it had cemented friendships but also because he had absorbed the ways of the mountaineers, an eager acolyte in the liturgy of survival. Skye had absorbed their innate, unspoken caution. Even though they might be talking to each other or seeming to pay no attention to the terrain, in fact they were constantly scanning horizons, studying dark blank woods, places of trouble and surprise. Without a word being spoken by Sublette or anyone else, they paused at defiles or river passages or at any place hemmed by brush or forest, and one or another would circle around for a hard-eyed look. These children of the wilds would not be surprised if they could help it.

He mastered their camp techniques, too. They grazed their animals until dusk and then hobbled and staked them close at hand. They built their small fires in hidden places, preferably under some branches that would dissipate the smoke. They scanned the heavens with knowing eyes, and prepared for a wet night if the omens told them to. They could thatch an effective shelter in a hurry, knew how to keep their spare clothing dry, and knew how to find dry tinder and build a fire where a drizzle wouldn't snuff it. Whenever they had spare meat, they hung it high and away from their camp, or jerked it if they had time. Occasionally they heard wolves, and constantly enjoyed the night-gossip of the coyotes, and sometimes counted their silences more important than the night-talk.

The wilderness and its omnipresent dangers had driven these men together; out in the wilds they were boon companions in a way that could not be replicated in the sullen cities. Skye had blotted up all of this during his brief sojourn with Sublette's men. He missed them so much it surprised him, and to counter his bouts of loneliness he focused on his future, examining his dream, over and over.

Boston was the great American seaport; there would be import and export businesses, very like his father's. He would apply at once, knowing he could be useful. Those matters had been bred into his bones and he had heard his father's talk at many a meal. He would clerk, and save his pence, and apply at the college. He would study political economy as his father had done, and English literature, as he wanted to do. Then, someday, with a bachelor degree in hand—albeit at a late age—he would start his own business, win a wife, start the Skye family, and settle into an abundant life.

All these things he rehearsed and rehashed as he rode up the Snake, almost to prevent the bewitching river and the golden wilderness from seducing him. The Snake took him deeper into the mountains, and now he experienced sharply cooler weather, especially at dawn. Summer still reigned, but the higher he climbed the closer he peered into the future. He would have to hurry east. Sublette told him it would take three months to make St. Louis, and by then the nights would be cold.

He almost missed the Hoback River, taking it for an inconsequential creek, but he spotted a prominent blaze in a tree. The mountaineers had left their own road map. He turned his lively horse eastward and rode through an intimate canyon that made him uneasy because he felt hemmed in, almost like being in a ship's brig. He saw no sign of recent passage, though plenty of evidence that man and beast had come this way.

He topped a somber alpine pass one day, and began descending into what he understood would be the drainage of the Seedskedee—he wondered about the origins of that name. Once he struck that clear, cold river he was to descend it until he reached arid plains. With a little luck he would find a trail that would take him across a waterless flat to Big Sandy Creek.

He descended into an alpine valley where a river whirled through swampy flats. It wasn't a welcoming land, and he hurried through it, wanting a dryer and more comfortable climate. Nature was fickle, joyous one moment and sullen the next. This was a valley choked with brush, a place where he could easily be surprised, and that made him itchy. He urged his reluctant horse across numerous creeks, around mocking bogs, and along the edge of fearsome dark pine forests. Moose lived there, and he saw one after another standing in bogs, eating what grew close to water. This was country where winter came early and stayed long, a land locked by snow most of the year.

But the rushing Seedskedee gradually descended, often in a formidable canyon that made him feel imprisoned. One eve, just before the sun dropped below the western ridges, he located a good campsite on the river, a flat with tender grass, deadwood for fire, and some protection from the chafing winds. He slid off his brown horse and set his warbag and gear on the grass. He needed to stretch legs that had been imprisoned in the Nez Perce pad saddle too long. He wondered if he would ever get used to riding long distances.

They materialized out of the brush and woods, silent brown forms, a dozen, fifteen, all mounted, some wearing vermilion streaked across their cheekbones, others painted with subtler earth-hues garnered from nature. His heart sank. He lacked even his bow and quiver. Every one of them wielded a weapon, mostly drawn bows, but two brandished flintlocks. One had a war hatchet while another carried an iron-tipped lance.

Skye hunted his memory for the sign: *friend.*

Right hand. Palm outward. Index and second finger pointing up.

They stared. He tried *peace.*

Clasped hands. Back of left hand down . . .

Nothing. They eyed his horse, noted the gear on the ground, including Skye's bow and quiver. They talked to

each other. Skye hadn't the faintest idea who they were
or what might happen. A mountaineer might know, but
not a British seaman. But then, suddenly, he had his
answer: these warriors wore moccasins of smoked
leather, almost black, something he had never seen
before. *Pieds Noirs*, Blackfeet. His pulse raced. He
sensed he was in mortal danger, maybe even moments
from death. Six or eight nocked arrows pointed at him.

One of the warriors, apparently their leader, grunted
something to the rest. That one bore a terrible scar across
his left cheek and the edge of his mouth and two other
jagged scars on his powerful torso. He had seen war. Skye
knew the signs.

Two of them slid nimbly off their horses and walked
straight toward Skye. But they didn't touch him. Instead,
one grabbed Skye's horse. The other plucked up his
warbag and quiver and bow.

"Stop!" bellowed Skye.

A fraction of a heartbeat later, he stared at an arrow driven into the soft earth between his legs. They were itch-
ing to kill him. He forced himself to calm down a little,
but now his heart pounded crazily. Had he come all the
way from the H.M.S. *Jaguar* to end up here, dying a
lonely death in an empty land?

"I want my goods back. Leave that horse. I've done
you no harm, but I'll fight if you want." Bluster. He had
learned to defend himself in the Royal Navy with bluster.
If he hadn't taken on the bullies, he would have starved to
death or suffered abuse from his shipmates.

He thrust a finger at the headman. "I'll settle it with
you," he said. "Get off that horse and we'll settle it." He
had brawled enough in the navy; he'd brawl here if he
must.

Something shifted in the brush behind him, a passing
animal. The warriors stared into the thickets, seeing nothing. Skye ignored that, and walked furiously toward the
headman, who sat his horse quietly, a deadly war ax in
hand. One blow could cleave Skye's skull. Skye pointed

at the man and at the ground, inviting the headman to get down and fight. The man stared back with expressionless black eyes, a faint triumphant glitter finally rising in them. He spoke low, the sibilants hissing from his lips.

Two of the warriors walked cautiously toward the red willow brush, and then one froze and barked something. In that moment, Skye was forgotten and a strange guttural grunt drifted from the brush. Skye stared, electrified by something he couldn't quite name. Then he saw it: a huge humped brown bear, erect on its hind paws, its nose silvery with age, eight, nine feet high, a monster, its small eyes focusing here and there, its wet nostrils flared. Skye had the sense that this monster could land on all fours and murder half these warriors—or himself—before they could run ten yards.

No one loosed an arrow, and Skye grasped why. An arrow might be little more than an irritant, something to turn this bear berserk. They all stood frozen, the warriors on foot and the rest on crazed horses that were becoming impossible to manage. Skye's horse fought the line, shaking her head violently.

In that frightful moment Skye did something he knew was terrible even to think about. He walked toward the bear, driving his limbs forward. The bear loomed higher and higher, awesome in height, its breath fouling the air, and Skye expected his life to end with a single swipe of a paw. Skye walked past the warriors on foot, closer and closer, his gaze and the grizzly's gaze locked. He came within twenty feet, then ten, his vector taking him past, rather than toward, the monster. He could not say why he was throwing his life away, only that he saw it as a small, frightful chance to escape. But these warriors were Blackfeet who preyed on isolated white men, and he had no other choice. They watched, mesmerized.

The bear snorted, the hairs at the nape of its neck erect. It snuffled and growled but stood as Skye walked past, its attention divided between Skye and the host of enemies before him. And then, suddenly, it shrieked. Skye had never heard a sound like it, and it drove shivers through him. The bear sprang, but not at Skye. It snarled toward the massed warriors, and Skye heard howling, the screech of horses, the thump of arrows finding their mark, and shouts of terror.

He ran until his wind vanished from his lungs, and ran some more, and stumbled along the trail he had recently negotiated, never looking back. And then, a half-mile distant—at least he thought it was that much—he did stare back, finding nothing. No bear, no Blackfeet. But that didn't mean anything. In terror, he raced further up the Seedskedee, splashing through tributary creeks, running until he dropped and the night cloaked him.

Chapter 31

Bear medicine.

The little Crow, Many Quill Woman, had discerned something Skye could barely fathom. The bear was his brother, his guide, his friend, his protector. She called it medicine. He tried to dismiss the savage superstition, but he couldn't. He had walked right by that enraged grizzly and survived.

The dawn chill numbed him. Gray mist blanketed the land, filtering the first light and rendering it pale and shadowless. He rose from moist ground, his body aching, yearning for a fire, warmth, food. But he had nothing.

He tried to fathom where he was. Pines loomed in the mist. He was somewhere on the upper Seedskedee. He had run until he dropped, and didn't know how far. A mile, maybe two. He stood, rubbed his aching legs and arms, and swung his arms to make heat in his body. He was ravenous. He had only the clothes on his back, his worn moccasins, and a sheathed knife at his waist. With that he must live—or die.

He started down the river again, needing to search the place of ambush for his gear. Perhaps it was still there. The bear may have driven off the Blackfeet. He needed flint and steel, bow and quiver, ax and hatchet, his blanket, and his sailcloth poncho. But anything, anything at all, would help.

The mist cleared as he hiked, but the relentless chill lingered. This was August and this was high country. Everything looked different in the morning light and he wondered if he would even recognize his campsite, which he had seen only in twilight. Wilderness was tricky and a man was hard put to say whether or not he had passed by.

At last the river entered an intimate defile and he knew he was drawing close. He had set up his camp in such a place, out of the wind and hidden from view. He passed through the red willow brush and came upon the campsite so swiftly that he had not been cautious. But the Blackfeet had departed. A horse lay on bloody soil, brutally clawed and half-eaten. These were bloody grounds. The stink of terror reached his nostrils.

His hair prickled, and he squinted hard into the shadowed brush, fearing the wounded bear or even the Blackfeet. He saw nothing and heard only the beat of his racing heart. He began a systematic search, in wider and wider arcs, hunting for something, anything, he might use. But the gory site yielded nothing. He tried to fathom what had happened. As far as he could tell, they had not killed the bear. There was no carcass or entrails. But had the bear killed any of them? He found no evidence of it, but wished he could read sign as easily as the mountaineers.

He widened his search and came up with a broken arrow with a bloody metal point. He kept it. The sheet-metal point would make a tool. He studied the arrow, noting its fletching and the dyes that marked it. This was a Blackfoot arrow and he wanted to identify it, sear its markings into his mind. He found what appeared to be the bear's trail through broken willow brush, and the sight made him prickle. The beast was leaking blood when it retreated. He hoped his bear brother would heal. How odd and savage it was to call the murderous grizzly his brother.

He widened his search until he knew for certain that the Blackfoot war party had left him nothing. Despair seeped through him. He could no longer build a fire, sleep warm, trap animals, fish, drive an arrow into game, escape the rain or sun, repair his moccasins, or ride to safety on his horse. He choked back desperation, knowing that despair wouldn't help him. What would someone like Bridger or Fitzpatrick do? He gently probed the ashes of the fire, hoping to find a live ember, but he found only cold black disappointment.

Flies swarmed the carcass of the horse. Skye realized suddenly that he had a mountain of meat before him—if he had the courage to eat it raw. He wondered if he could slice it thin and jerk it in the sun a day or two. Wolves or coyotes or something else had gnawed out its belly and demolished a haunch. Feeling queasy, he set to work with his knife, slowly ripping and cutting hide back from a forequarter until he could saw at the flesh. This would be a long, miserable task. His new knife had already dulled, making the work all the harder. He squinted about nervously, worrying that the Blackfeet might return, or the maddened bear, but he discerned only the quiet of an August morning.

All that afternoon he sawed at the carcass, eating tiny, digestible slivers of raw horse meat. He could barely chew bite-sized pieces, but he managed to down thin wafers of flesh, and gradually his hunger eased. Green-bellied flies swarmed, making his task miserable. Once he found himself staring at a pair of coyotes. He rose, roared, and they fled.

Then he discovered the Blackfeet had left something after all: his belaying pin. They probably could see no use for it. He hefted the smooth hickory shaft and knew he had an effective club. It gladdened him. He returned to his butchering, determined to make enough meat to sustain him until—what? Until he got help? Until he was ready to go east again? He dreaded the answer. Late in the afternoon, he realized he couldn't stay at this place of carnage all night, fighting off wolves and bears, skunks, raccoons, mountain lions, badgers, and whatever else would compete for the flesh of the horse.

He eyed his fly-specked pile of meat dourly, wondering how to carry it with him. Then he knew. Horsehair. He examined the long tail of the horse, discovering three-foot strands of durable hair. For once he was glad he had been a seaman. Swiftly he sawed off a mass of hair and knotted the strands into a web. He worked furiously, unhappy with the crudity of his efforts but glad to see something useful take shape. An hour later he completed a horsehair web that would carry the meat and might be useful in the future. He loaded his meat into it and stood.

He was ready to leave—but where?

He had come to the most paralyzing juncture of his life.

East across the plains with only a butcher knife and his wits? Or retreat back to the Snake and hunt down Sublette's brigade? Or try to find the Kicked-in-the-Bellies, his little Victoria, and some sort of succor?

He started east. Boston. That was his objective, after all. But fifty yards down river he halted. There would be no help—but constant menace—for a *thousand miles*. He stood miserably, unsure of his course. And then he knew why he could not go east: even if he managed to find food, his moccasins would wear out. He would be forced to hike barefoot across merciless ground bristling with cactus, rock, sticks, debris. He needed a horse, weapon, spare leather, an awl, and thong to survive.

He retreated to the campsite and watched two ravens and a hawk flap away from the carcass. Had his dreams died here? No. He would go east when he could. For the moment, he needed the help of the mountaineers. He needed an outfit and that meant working for the brigade.

Another year would slide by before he could pick up shattered dreams.

Reluctantly, hating every step, he headed upstream. Fate had decreed that he would not reach civilization this year. He had to find Sublette's brigade before he starved and before his sturdy Creole moccasins gave out. He hiked through dusk, retracing his route, splashing through icy rills and creeks because he could no longer ride a horse across them. In the last light he hunted for a place that might offer warmth, and found a spot. He settled at last against a south-facing rock that had absorbed the day's sunlight and now radiated it.

He cut tiny slivers of raw horse meat, chewed and swallowed them one by one, until he could no longer see. He unlaced his moccasins, hoping to dry them out, and settled down to wait for dawn. But a wind rose, whipping icy air through his buckskins, numbing his toes. And a light rain fell for a while, making him all the more miserable. If he didn't find shelter he'd die. He endured the stopped-clock night, working his arms and legs to drive away the numbness. Sleep eluded him. He was much too miserable. He heard the soft rustle of animals approaching and swiftly tied his net of horse meat high in a pine tree. Then he waited, his belaying pin in hand. But nothing happened.

Then, some time later, the cloud cover vanished and he beheld a sepulchral world lit by a pale moon. He would walk. Nothing else would do. He started up the gloomy river, stumbling through copses of pine and aspen, dropping into unexpected bogs, and sometimes pausing when a cloud bank obscured the pronged moon. A thousand desolating thoughts crowded his mind, but he furiously drove them back. He had not won his freedom only to surrender.

An odd purplish light tinted the land with the coming of dawn. Skye had no idea how far he had come. As the daylight intensified, rosing distant ridges and then painting them gold, he found himself in unfamiliar country.

The Seedskedee meandered ever upward into bold mountains, golden in the low dawn sun. But he was lost. He studied the ground, looking for sign of his own passage. At some point yesterday he had descended a drainage, a lively creek, down to the Seedskedee, but he had crossed dozens of those and may have gone past his turnoff that would take him over the pass and down the Hoback to the Snake.

He studied the riverside trail carefully, finding no mark of passage, but he continued to ascend the river. The wilderness played tricks, making short distances seem endless. But now a deepening dread filled him. He did not know this country. The mountaineers understood it, but he had never set foot in it and didn't know the way out. He hiked up the river until he judged the sun was at its apex. He found some cattails, pulled them up, washed the starchy roots, mashed them with a rock, and gnawed on the tan pulp.

But he was lost. Everything seemed alike: pine forests, swamps, the burbling river, bogs, aspen groves, the scent of sagebrush in the air mixed sometimes with the heady scent of pines. Sudden drafts of cold air eddied past him, and occasionally he stepped into warm pockets, where he lingered to let his cold limbs warm, and his wet leathers dry.

But the stark truth was, he didn't know where he was, or where he was going, or what he should do. He was lost in all the ways a mortal can be lost.

Chapter 32

Skye knew he had come to one of those momentous crises that shape a mortal life. This journey had been filled with portentous events, things that would mould him for the rest of his days on earth. He was lost, tired, hungry, lonely, and without counsel. He had been robbed of sleep and his body felt leaden, dragging his spirits downward.

Despair was the enemy. Discouragement, defeat, surrender haunted him. He sensed he would never escape. He would die a terrible death here in a cruel wilderness. It had all come down to this, he thought bitterly. Was there no justice in the universe? Would those wigged and powdered lord admirals whose press-gangs had stolen life and liberty from him enjoy long and pampered lives while his bones moldered in a wild place?

He found a boulder heated by the early sun and sat against it, letting the wan warmth comfort his body. He closed his eyes, trying to summon courage. He had never felt so alone. And yet, as he sat there, he knew he was neither helpless nor alone. In all the years of his captivity he had never let his faith die: he had believed the God of Creation watched over him and would free him from his sea jail in His own good time. Now Skye was free—but where was God now?

He focused on that. He talked to God, told Him about the miracle of the grizzly that let him pass by, of food and succor that appeared when he needed it, of gratitude for being freed and alive and the master of his destiny. He didn't know if his babbling was prayer, exactly— certainly not the sort that was recited in the Anglican masses he had attended—but it was a conversation with his Lord, and he felt peace steal through him.

When he opened his eyes he beheld the wilderness, golden in the early sun, not enemy but friend. Some crows cawed mightily. He watched iridescent black and white magpies terrorize lesser birds. He remembered that Victoria had called the magpie her medicine-helper. He felt the first zephyrs of the morning eddy past him, redolent of sage and pine and the mysteries beyond the next ridge. The bright sun pummeled his leather shirt, warming it and him. Its rays caught his thick beard, fondling his face, and his hurts ebbed.

This was Creation, undisturbed by man, and the sight of it moved him. He hadn't expected that. This was not a dark and hostile Creation, but one that might serve him, nurture him, empower him, even as it empowered the many tribes who lived comfortably in the midst of it. Long before white traders showed up here, these tribes had drawn everything they needed, food and shelter, clothing, tools, meat, medicines, vegetables, seasonings, dyes, weapons, and more from this wilderness. The wilderness was his friend, his nourishment, his spiritual succor, his delight, his shelter, his fortress.

The day vibrated. Nothing felt quite as glorious as a late summer day in the high country. The heavens ached with joy. Skye stood, stretched, letting his new courage permeate his entire body. He knew he had come up the

Seedskedee much too far and now he would retreat until he found the way to the Snake River. He sliced the last of his horse meat and chewed on it, finding the raw flesh foul. He spit it out. It had sustained him for a while but now he would need other foods.

He hiked downriver much of that morning and then found the turnoff. It showed signs of passage he had missed in the moonlight: his mare's hoofprints. He climbed the trail all that day, past grassy parks dancing in sunlight, past burbling rills and creeks, past aspen glades where every leaf quaked. He passed beaver dams and ponds, thickets of chokecherry laden with ripe berries. These he plucked and gnawed, sustaining himself even though the well-named fruit had a vicious taste that puckered his mouth.

He topped the divide and knew he was once again in the drainage of the Snake. As he traveled he came across campsites, and he paused to examine each one for discards, lost tools, anything helpful. And they did yield a small harvest. At one he found a bone awl. At another a pair of worn-out moccasins, too small for his feet but with some usable leather. At another place he found what he supposed was a flint hide flesher. He plucked it up. Flint was precious. A piece of steel might give him fire, cooked food, warmth. He thought of trying the back of his knife on the flint, but hesitated. If he broke his knife, he'd be in even worse trouble.

His left moccasin wore through and he cobbled a patch on it, knowing it wouldn't last long. And yet he kept on, sleeping under rock overhangs, dodging mountain rains, acquiring some cunning about wind and rain and cold. He survived on what he could harvest, which was little even in the season of fruits. But on the Snake River drainage he found camas again and kept himself alive by pulverizing its starchy bulbs. The camas were so abundant that his desperate hunger eased and life brightened.

A few days later he found himself back at the confluence of Henry's Fork and the Snake. He arrived there on a hot August afternoon and searched the river bank, seeking signs of passage. But rain had obscured any sign. Now he faced decisions again. He could chase after Sublette's brigade, plunging into new country, and quite possibly never contacting the elusive trappers. Or he could retreat to the Shoshone or Nez Perce settlements, places he knew and could reach. He headed north to join the brigade and win an outfit. Henry's Fork took him across a vast tree-dotted plain with the three arrogant spikes of the Tetons looming far to the east.

His trousers had worn to rags so he employed his bone awl upon the rotting fabric, piecing them together. His moccasins were failing, too, and even his leather shirt had been pulling apart at the seams. The wilderness might be his friend but it wasn't keeping him provisioned, and he worried about the future in his mind, desperate for alternatives. He had grown weary and listless, too, and ascribed the weakness to a lack of meat.

One early morning he spotted a group of riders so he hid in a thicket of red willows. Some southbound warriors passed him by. Or maybe they were hunters. He didn't know. They weren't painted. They had two horses apiece, and from the little Skye knew about such things, he supposed they were buffalo hunters, saving their fresh horses for the chase. They didn't see him or suspect his presence, and soon they were gone. The sun had been up only a short time; maybe he could find their camp.

He followed the fresh trail northward for an hour or so, and discovered the camping place beside the river. Smoke coiled from a dying fire. A gutted yearling elk hung from a heavy limb. They had eaten what they could and abandoned the rest. Joyously, Skye added twigs to the embers, blew gently, mumbled magic, and evoked a fire. Then he scrounged for deadwood, having to search wide and far because he lacked the means to hack it from the surrounding cottonwoods, alders, and willows. He butchered great, dripping slabs of red meat from a haunch and skewered them with a green twig, his stomach rumbling with anticipation.

While the meat roasted, he cut more elk meat into thin strips he intended to smoke into some sort of jerky, no matter that he might spend two or three days at it. He had not eaten like this for weeks and he intended to make the most of his bonanza. Thus did he spend that sunny day— eating, gathering firewood, cutting haunch and neck and rib, smoking, and drying meat. He peeled the hide farther and farther back as he worked, and finally he spent an hour at twilight cutting most of the hide free of the hanging carcass. He found his fleshing tool and began to scrape the inside of the hide, doing it awkwardly until he staked the hide to the ground so he could get some purchase. It was slow, hard, unpleasant work, interrupted by trips to feed the precious fire. By the time that darkness engulfed him, he had cleaned much of the hide.

He foraged for firewood again, afraid that he would lose the fire in the night, and eventually rounded up enough to keep it going. He would sleep warm that night for a change. He pushed ash over some live coals, built up the fire, and settled down, feeling content at last. One war party had taken everything away from him, another had left him these gifts. Even here in these wilds, his fate had been decided more by other mortals than by nature. It was something to think about.

That night he slept on his new elkhide, welcoming whatever small relief it offered from the hard earth. He smoked meat all that night, rising instinctively when the fire needed tending. In the morning he roasted camas bulbs, pushing them as close to the flame as possible while he continued to smoke meat. He ate ravenously, his appetite whetted by the previous feast. Then he devoted the entire day to his tasks—preserving every scrap of meat that he could, scraping and softening the elk hide, collecting firewood, roasting camas bulbs until he had a formidable larder. He spent a second night at that fire, reluctant to surrender it but knowing he had to push ahead. Somewhere in this vast wilderness was a brigade of trappers who would welcome him into their ranks. And somewhere—he was hazy about the place—a slim girl living among the Kicked-in-the-Bellies of the Absaroka people would welcome him to her lodge, and perhaps to her arms.

He left at dawn, saddened to abandon the fire. His horsehair net was burdened now with smoked and dried elk meat, roasted camas bulbs, the discarded moccasins, the scraping tool, his belaying pin, and the stiff, rolled-up elkhide. The weight of all this was surprising, but it gladdened him: now he was a man of substance.

The overcast sky that morning reminded him that soon the season would change. Even now, in this high plateau, he felt the sharp night chill, which would soon deepen and last longer and longer as the sun fled south. He hurried north, sometimes intersecting tracks he thought might be Sublette's, but he didn't really know. Most of the trappers' horses were unshod, and most of the men wore moccasins, which made their passage little different from the passage of the tribes.

His Creole moccasins finally gave out, and he painfully fashioned new soles out of his elkskin, and anchored them to the worn soles with his bone awl and some thong. It took half a day, but he was not barefoot, and that was a miracle.

He ascended Henry's Fork, passing through a gorge into alpine parks laced with lodgepole, swamps, and broad grassy vistas. He saw abundant game but he had no means to shoot any, and was constantly reminded of how helpless he really was. He spotted buffalos one afternoon, a small group that included a bull and several calves, and he marveled at them. The monsters got wind of him and raced away at surprising speed. Skye knew he would not be feasting on humpmeat soon, not unless another miracle happened.

At the northern end of this plain he encountered austere

pine-clad mountains, and after crossing a low divide he found himself staring at a gloomy lake. It took the better part of the afternoon to walk around to its outlet, and there he found the water flowing north. This water wasn't flowing toward the Snake; it probably was draining toward the mighty Missouri and Mississippi if he understood the geography. If he had passed into the Missouri drainage, then he had put the Snake country behind him, and he had entered the hunting lands of the Blackfeet Indians with only a belaying pin to defend himself.

Chapter 33

Hidden in a dense thicket of juniper well up a slope, Skye watched the Indian village parade by a half mile below. He had no notion what tribe this was—how could a British seaman know?—but he knew he was safest well hidden and far from the river.

For once he was grateful he didn't have a horse. The vedettes flanking the great migration would have spotted him instantly, or followed his fresh hoofprints. He supposed he was safe enough, although the sight of several hundred Indians, countless dogs, and endless numbers of horses, some dragging travois, shot fear through him.

By all accounts, these were not the same sort of Indian as those who inhabited the fishing villages along the Columbia, and even the friendlier tribes in this area—his mountaineer friends had listed the Crow, Flathead, Shoshone, and Sioux in that category, along with the Bannacks if their mood was right—could pose trouble for a lone traveler.

This village was migrating up the Madison River, away

from the Three Forks country where Skye hoped to find
the Sublette brigade. The last of the day's sun caught the
clouds of dust raised by the passage of so many horses,
and painted the very air gold as the village slowly wound
past. But then the column slowly came to a halt at a riverside flat below Skye.

Swiftly, the herders moved the horses onto grass away
from the glinting river, while nimble squaws unhooked
travois and unloaded packhorses. The village would stay
there for the night. Skye sucked air into his lungs and
exhaled slowly. He was trapped, at least until dark, and
maybe after that if there were sentries patrolling the herd,
as surely there would be. Between the sentries and the
dogs he would have a devilish time sneaking away.
Suddenly the half mile between him and this crowd
seemed like no distance at all. He studied the legs and
feet of those antlike mortals so far away, hoping to discern whether these Indians wore the dark moccasins of
the Blackfeet, but he could not say. Much too much
space, and failing light, kept him from ascertaining that
crucial fact.

He was thirsty but he couldn't simply walk down to the
water's edge and sip that fine, clear snowmelt. Hunger bit
at him, too. He had gone through his smoked elk and
camas bulbs and had been finding precious little to eat
along the Madison River.

There was nothing to do but lie patiently in the sun-
warmed juniper, enjoy its resinous scent, and wait until
darkness liberated him. Fires flared along the riverbank,
one by one, miraculously blooming to life and radiating
orange light into the purple twilight. Below, the herders
were driving a multicolored mass of horses out on the
flats. Wary brown warriors in breechclouts hobbled or
picketed their horses close to the campsite. Lodges rose
here and there, first a cone of poles and suddenly an
entire Indian home. He eyed the skies anxiously, looking
for signs of bad weather, and found some. Towering gray
thunderclouds loomed behind him, and more black-

bellied clouds were gathering muscle off to the south. So the lodges were going up this night.

From his haven, he began to enjoy this spectacle. Something powerful radiated from this village. These people looked after themselves, each to his own comforts and lodging, without direction. The warrior society that had been appointed to guard this village was posting its men around the area, all of them on this side of the wide river, making a safe cocoon for the women, children, and old people within. Once in a while, the eddying winds brought him the smell of meat cooking, which maddened him and tempted him to stand, walk downslope to the village, and surrender to his fate among friends—or foes.

Thus did he struggle with himself for a half hour or so, until something shocked him out of his reveries. He heard voices, so close that the low exchange lifted the hair on the nape of his neck. Not thirty yards away, in an adjacent juniper thicket, lurked four dusky savages, wearing only breechclouts and moccasins—smoked black.

Blackfeet.

He flattened himself to the earth, grateful for his worn leather shirt, his dark hair and beard, his begrimed trousers. If he could scratch his way deeper into the earth he would have. His pulse catapulted. He felt sweat blossom from every pore in his body, and in moments he had drenched himself with it. He lay motionless, waiting for the crackle of brush that would signal his doom. Here would he die. Here would the scalping knife circle his forehead. Here would be his last memory—perhaps of the violent pop as his hair yanked free of his skull.

But after the first rush of terror, he peered about him, slowly surveying his lot. Four Blackfeet. Maybe others were somewhere upslope, horseholders over the ridge. This would be a horse-stealing party. Sometime in the night they would pad down the sagebrush-choked slope, slip past or kill the night herders, and drive away as many animals as possible, probably fleeing toward the Blackfoot stronghold to the north.

So the village below was probably Shoshone or Crow. Maybe he could find a haven there, slipping into the village after dark. Maybe he could warn them—if he could make himself understood. But what sort of reception would he meet? Likely killed on the spot, an intruder rising out of the night. And how could he escape the alert Blackfeet hidden barely thirty yards away? No. He could not move, not yet.

Skye lay motionless, grateful for the ebbing light that gradually cloaked him in blessed darkness. Only once in his life had he been so close to death, and that time a wandering bear saved him. It took sheer willpower to lie motionless, calm his body, steady his pulse, stop his rank sweating, and prepare himself. He had only his belaying pin and his new knife. The belaying pin would help him; the knife would not.

He had some serious thinking to do. Somewhere above him there would be youths holding the ponies while the warriors worked down to the village herd on foot. He wanted a horse. The Blackfeet owed him a horse, and he'd like two or three more for good measure. A few horses would solve most of his troubles, and if worse came to worse, his transportation was edible.

He ached to grab those horses. He wanted a bow and quiver, too. He could either slip away in the darkness and hope not to get caught in the maneuvering when it all blew up—or he could hunt the hunters. He swallowed, trying to draw moisture to his parched throat, knowing what he was going to do, and marveling at his folly.

The night deepened, save for a blue band of last light riding the western ridges. The stars emerged as if the night sky were shedding veils. He listened closely, hoping to discern whether other Blackfeet occupied other thickets. But he heard nothing save for the occasional gutturals of the warriors nearby. Slowly he rolled until he could stare upslope—snapping a twig as he did. But nothing happened. In the shadowy light he studied the black slope, wondering where the rest of the raiders lay waiting, and whether they could be taken unawares. His only advantage was that they wouldn't be expecting him; they would expect one of their own.

He strained his eyes and ears, trying to make sense of what lay around him, but couldn't. The darkness had deepened to pitch, and no moon illumined the night. Would these sharp-eyed savages strike in blackness so close they could not see their own hands? He would know, eventually.

His thirst became an agony, but he ruthlessly choked back the temptation to sneak away for a drink. This was his sole chance for a horse, for a weapon, for food and shelter, and he would take it. He had taken chances from the beginning, driven by his vision of liberty, a sunny uplands of owning his own destiny. He had slid into the icy Columbia from the H.M.S. *Jaguar,* walked into Indian villages, wrestled the wilderness and its wild inhabitants, walked past a grizzly that could have butchered him with one swipe of a paw, all for his freedom. Now he would risk his life again.

Blackness lay thick upon the land. The stars vanished under the giant storm clouds he had seen at dusk. Distant thunderheads flashed staccato white and purple, and sharp cold breezes nipped through his sanctuary, running icy fingers over his neck. He became aware, in the midst of all this, of a gradual increase in light. The gibbous moon had risen, shooting its glow in and around the storm clouds, rendering visible the murky flat far below.

Sure enough, the Blackfeet stirred. He heard them talk softly, and then creak out of their shelter, their movement veiled by wind and the distant rumble of thunder riding high peaks. There were six. Startled, he watched the enigmatic figures spread out and stalk downslope. Each carried a hackamore and reins of some sort.

He watched them descend, melding themselves into the tall sagebrush. He glanced sharply upslope, left and right, and then eased out of his thicket, his senses keen and sharp and clean. Off to the northeast, perhaps a quarter of a mile, was a saddle, probably a watercourse. The Blackfeet had come from there because it was the only place they could come from. He hurried upslope, angling north, taking advantage of the thick juniper as much as he could, wondering whether he was being observed from above. If so, he couldn't help it and would deal with it as best he could.

He paused occasionally to check on the progress of the horse thieves, but could no longer see them. The storms blotted up light again. He hurried upslope, his heart racing, pushing against sharp cold air. Then commotion rendered the night. Far below, a giant hand swept the herd into a gallop. Skye had no idea which way it was running, only that the thunder of many hooves ruptured the peace. He edged over the ridge and found dense aspen beyond.

And through the leaves, he discerned two Blackfeet and several horses.

Chapter 34

The tricky light gave Skye pause. Were there two or three? Did one hold a bow with a nocked arrow? Did the other hold the horses? He waited for the shifting clouds to reveal more, but time was running out. Down on the Madison River the rumble of hooves and the howls of Indians at war shattered the peace. Were the raiders coming here? Skye crouched deeper into the shade of the aspens, sorting it out.

A moment of moonlight gave him a glimpse of the valley before him. Both of the horse holders were mounted now, ready to flee along with the rest of the Blackfoot raiders. And the stolen herd was thundering closer, driven this way by the raiders. In a moment they would flood over the rim and through here. He waited witlessly, not knowing how to deal with this. If the raiders were coming this way, so would the village warriors in hot pursuit. Skye studied the terrain, looking for escape, but naked slopes hemmed this valley. He had best stick to the aspens. The raiders would drive their stolen herd up the valley and into the next drainage.

The first of the horses boiled over the saddle and he instantly flattened himself among the aspens, hoping the night would conceal him. A dozen horses, then another, twenty, thirty. He couldn't say. And herding them were the raiders, riding stolen animals they had bridled. The herd halted abruptly at the sight of the horse holders and their excited mounts, then milled and circled. The raiders shouted something, and the horse holders turned their mounts and led the herd down the long valley. Skye watched the Blackfeet race by and then waited for the village warriors to follow.

He almost missed the black horse, hovering in the darkness. Was it lame? Why didn't it run with the others? It whinnied sharply, and a moment later a wraith appeared at its flanks—a foal, born that spring. The mare nudged the foal furiously, wanting to catch up with the herd, but the foal didn't budge. Skye watched, mesmerized with possibility. The foal was limping. The mare wouldn't leave it. Maybe there was a chance.

Nervously, Skye eyed the skyline, expecting the village warriors to burst into view. The clouds obscured the moon again, plunging the whole tableau into murk. Maybe that was his chance. But what would he catch the mare with, and how would he hold it and ride it? He had only his belt. That would have to do. He eased toward the mare, which watched him alertly but didn't run because her foal couldn't. He talked softly, aware of the howls of war just over the saddle. He closed slowly, talking in a low voice, and then looped the belt over her neck, catching her even as the frightened foal limped away from him.

He was out in the open when the first of the defenders topped the saddle. He saw them, and then he didn't as the fickle light vanished again. He stood stock still; there was nothing else to do. The village warriors raced through one by one, their focus on the lost herd ahead and not upon

Skye and a black mare off to one side, as inert as the trees and rocks.

Then no more came over the ridge and a quietness returned to the little mountain plateau. Slowly, Skye led the mare toward the aspen grove. The foal complained, but followed slowly, limping heavily. Skye drew the horses deep into the grove and quietly ran his hand over the mare, soothing the nervous animal. The mare pressed her nostrils into Skye and inhaled, gathering her own form of knowledge, and then nudged him.

Skye rejoiced, but he also puzzled over his dilemma. When would the foal be able to walk again? Was the mare broken to saddle or packsaddle? Without a hackamore or bridle or halter, how could he handle the mare or picket it at night? Would the pursuers return this way, or would they find another way back to their village?

He couldn't know.

He ransacked his memories of the Shoshone and Nez Percé he had seen. Some of them used the simplest imaginable means of steering or controlling their ponies. He recollected that many a child had looped a line over the nose of the horse, knotted it under the jaw, and used the two ends of the line for reins. That was all. He could do that. He could cut his remaining elkhide into strips and braid them into a crude bridle.

He ached to leave, but couldn't. He might have to suffer many more thirsty hours in this aspen grove before the village moved and before the injured foal was ready to travel, but the prize was worth it.

He had a horse—if he could keep it, and keep his hair.

One by one, he yanked the long fringes off the hem of his buckskin shirt and tied them into a short line that he anchored to the loop of belt around the mare's neck. And then he sat down to await events, holding her on a gossamer leather thread she could easy break. But she was content and let the foal suckle, and did not test his line. He sat through sharp cold, a few drops of rain, and deep silences. The riders did not return. The mare stood quietly.

With the first light, Skye studied the meadow and saw nothing at all but mist and grass and trees. He tied the mare to an aspen and slipped up to the saddle, where he beheld the village down on the Madison River. Guards circled the remaining horses. No one was packing: the village was awaiting the return of the pursuers. He returned to his own alpine meadow and discovered a nearby rill, where he drank greedily.

He thought of slaughtering the lame foal, and resisted the idea. He hunted the bottoms for something edible, finally settling on some miserable chokecherries. He plucked what he could, half afraid he would be spotted by returning riders, but no one came. He retreated to his aspens and gnawed at the bitter, mouthpuckering berries, barely able to endure them. They didn't alleviate his howling hunger. He bided his time by cutting elkhide thong and then braiding a three-strand line two yards long, and then tying it to the belt around the mare's neck. He had a stout lead rope, and a potential bridle.

At midmorning the mare seemed restless, so he cautiously led it out to graze. The foal barely limped now, and Skye hoped he could travel soon. He took the mare down to the rill, fearful of discovery. The mare drank, grazed, and stood quietly while the foal nudged her bag and drank his breakfast.

All that long day he lingered in the aspen grove, occasionally letting the mare foray to grass. Late in the afternoon he climbed to the saddle and discovered the village had left and was nowhere in sight. Joyously, he led his mare down to the campsite, looking for castoffs, lost items, food. He could almost feel the presence of the villagers there. Only a few hours earlier this place had been a nomadic home, filled with grandparents, children, men and women, chiefs, seers, revered oldsters, dogs, ponies. Now it was a naked flat.

He systematically scoured the whole area, finding one

treasure after another, the losses of war. He found a hack-amore and then another, a broken hobble, several broken rawhide lines, snapped apart when the stampeding began. He also found goods that had been deliberately aban-doned, probably because there were no longer the horses to transport them. A good parfleche lay on the ground, and in it some pemmican. A rawhide packsaddle. Various moccasins and leggins. A red bandanna, which he imme-diately folded into a headband to corral his unruly mane. None of the moccasins fit him but he thought he could use the leather for patching. He found a hatchet in a pas-ture and rejoiced, running his thick thumb over its dull edge. He would sharpen it somehow. But the prize was a beaded fire-starter bag, handsomely fringed, lying in grass before a circle of rocks that had pinned down a lodge cover. Within he discovered a flint and steel and a nest of powdery tinder. Fire! That was like capturing the sun. Joyously he loaded all the loot he could manage onto the packsaddle and lowered it gently on the mare. She didn't mind. But the fire-starter bag he carried at his waist. Never again would he be without the means to kin-dle a flame.

He wolfed some of the pemmican and then started north, walking well back from the Madison River for fear of encountering more trouble. He was tempted to start for the East once again, but common sense overruled that. Given a rifle to kill buffalo or deer, a pair of blankets or a poncho against the weather, he might have endured the great plains. But autumn was tucked in the breeze and he had only the clothes on his back. He had learned enough about wilderness to know that his best bet was to join the brigade and let the future tend to itself.

He took the northbound journey in easy stages, letting the foal rest frequently. But the little rascal recovered much faster than Skye anticipated, and soon was dancing along beside his mother. It was a gray, skinny and proud and full of new life. A soft whicker from its mother brought it to her side whenever it pranced too far away.

And as for the mare, it seemed docile and at peace as Skye led her northward. The mare was ugly, with a roman nose and crooked legs, but he loved her.

Skye felt rich. Never had he enjoyed life so much. The grasses had turned to tan, and the heavens were mostly clear and bold blue. Every thicket burst with berries, many of them unknown to him. He tried them all, cautiously at first, and then eagerly. He had lost track of the days, but knew this was September, a time when the whole of creation glowed and fruit burdened every limb.

He felt at one with the world around him, having at last arrived at his own accommodation with wilderness. This mountainous world seemed friendly, rife with possibility, alive with birds, small and large animals, fish, clear creeks, stately pines, grand ridges, towering clouds, whispering breezes that sometimes foretold him of the winter that would swiftly descend.

Almost every night the wolves howled from ridge to ridge, and sometimes just beyond his campfire. He feared them. They seemed bloodthirsty and vicious, and endangered his horse colt. One night when they lurked just beyond his camp, he sprang up with a roar and ran at them. A long while later they mourned from a distant ridge. His colt didn't make wolf-bait that night.

He worried more and more about finding Sublette's brigade. He had seen no sign of it, although he studied the trails along the river for the prints of shod hooves or white men's boots. He was deep in Blackfoot country now, and walked cautiously, well away from the trails when he could, even though it meant climbing slopes and fighting through groves of pine and aspen. A man without a weapon was risking his life in this country.

The swift river drove through canyons, crossed broad flats, dominated huge valleys only to plunge into ravines that forced him to detour. And then he grew aware that he had reached a huge basin set in the midst of distant mountains. Grassy hills dominated the basin, but the white-peaked mountain ranges lay thirty, forty, fifty miles distant. It was mountain-girt, actually, with cottonwoods, aspen, and pine along the creeks. He spotted buffalo sign everywhere, and soon saw bunches of them, massed black against the golden fields of grass. He knew what this place was: Sublette had described it and drawn it into the clay as he made his map. This was the Three Forks country, the headwaters of a great river called the Missouri—and a favorite hunting area of the murderous Blackfeet.

The Sublette brigade would be here—if it was still alive. The whole area was overrun with beaver. Skye passed dam after dam along each creek. Whoever had the nerve to trap here could harvest thousands of pelts in short order. But perhaps it was still too early. Skye knew that these trappers didn't begin their fall hunt until the pelts were prime. Sublette wouldn't be here—not yet. He would be in some safe place, waiting for the cold.

But where was he? How could Skye find about thirty men in an endless wilderness? His life depended on it.

Chapter 35

Lakota! News of disaster raced through the village, and now the Kicked-in-the-Bellies gathered silently around the returning hunters. Some bore wounds, their bandages bloodred in the autumnal light. Some rode double because they could not sit their ponies without help. Another, Coyote Waits they said, lay in a travois near death. All that was terrible enough, but not so terrible as the four ponies that bore the dead, who hung over the saddles, the bare skulls of their scalped heads dangling toward Mother Earth.

Many Quill Woman watched bitterly, hating the Lakota dogs who had ambushed the Absaroka hunters. Never in her memory had the Kicked-in-the-Bellies suffered such a disaster, and she thirsted for revenge. Soon the howling Absaroka warriors would race out upon the plains to hunt down the Lakota and put an end to their victory dances.

Many Quill Woman knew every one of the dead. They were all of her Otter Clan. That made it all the worse, a terrible dishonor upon her clan, and also on the Lumpwood Society, whose young warriors these were. Their medicine had gone bad, and she ached with the shame of it. Someone among them had violated his sacred power, or betrayed his trust, or had touched what he must not touch and had not told the rest.

They were camped, this Moon of the Turning Leaves, near the confluence of the Yellowstone River, which her people knew as the Elk, and the Big Horn River, in the heart of the buffalo country. The buffalo brothers and sisters could almost always be found here, and indeed with each sun the hunters killed more and more, keeping the women very busy. This was the season to make pemmican and jerky against the winter, to scrape and clean hides that would become lodgeskins or winter moccasins or leggins, to feast on good humpmeat and tongue and bone marrow, and to store away plenty of salty backfat against the time when the Cold Maker ruled the earth. Later, when it grew cold, and the buffalo had grown their winter hair, there would be another hunt for humpmeat and bone marrow and backfat, livers and hearts, as well as warm buffalo robes to sleep in and for hides to trade to the white men for weapons and pots and knives.

But Many Quill Woman didn't want to think of that. Among the dead was Barking Coyote, who had eyes for her. She had spent many moments with Barking Coyote, sometimes in the bushes away from the village, liking him even if he was skinny and awkward. He was going to ask for her soon. Any day he would stake two ponies before her father's lodge, and leave a gift of tobacco and maybe a good pipe, and wait to see whether the gifts were accepted. But he wanted more honor first.

Now he hung lifeless from his pony, his eyes seeing nothing. An arrow driven into his chest had killed him. She stared at his naked skull and shuddered. He would wander the spirit world without a home, looking for his lost hair, the mark of selfhood, never content and never at peace. Barking Coyote's mother began to wail, and Many Quill Woman turned away. It was hard to bear death and loss without wailing. She had her own way of grieving, just by seething silently, angry because of loss and helplessness.

But many of the women wailed, and soon the widows would cut their hair on one side or chop off a finger at the first joint, making themselves ugly to show the world their true feelings. Two widows this time. The rest of the young men had not taken a woman.

These hunters brought back not a single trophy. No scalp dangled from their lances. They had counted no coup and had no proud stories of bravery to recite before the elders. The Lakota had won a total, brutal victory that would shame her village for years when the story was remembered around the council fires of the Absaroka. She felt mortified as she followed the mob toward the big lodge of Arapooish, Rotten Belly, the greatest of all the Absaroka. But even as they gathered before his lodge, he emerged with his face painted white in mourning. Nothing was said. The whole story lay upon those horses and the empty lances. This hunting band had gone out to kill buffalo, and ended up being surprised and killed by Lakota devils hiding nearby. That was a common enough event, but older warriors and hunters would have been better prepared for it.

The big-bellied, hook-nosed chief stared at the empty lances, devoid of any Lakota scalps, nodded and retreated to his lodge. That was all. They had given him the news. The families of the dead reclaimed the bodies and led away the ponies while all the village watched and the women wailed. Soon they would be building scaffolds and laying the dead upon them, wrapped in a robe, face to the sun, along with their bows and quivers for their spirit journey. The ponies would be slaughtered so that the departed would have a steed to ride on the trail to the stars.

Many Quill Woman watched until there was nothing more to see, and then retreated to her father's lodge. She beheld her stepmother, Digs the Roots, fleshing a new buffalohide staked to the earth. This one would replace a well-smoked hide high in the lodge cover, which in turn would make fine, soft, brown moccasins capable of turning water because of all the grease embedded in the leather.

"Ah, daughter, the one who was playing the flute for you is gone," her stepmother said as she scraped. She had carefully avoided naming the dead, for it was improper to say the name or even think it.

Many Quill Woman nodded. "He was brave. His family will be proud," she replied. "He died a warrior and gave to the People."

"But he is gone to the ancestors. You will miss him, Many Quill Woman."

"It would have come to nothing," she said.

"Ah! I thought so. You have not been the same since the summer. You should not think about the Goddamns. They are a hairy, dirty race."

"One is different," she said. "I think about him."

She had been of two minds about the one who had died. The dead one was truly a good Absaroka from a prominent family with many honors in battle and two medicine-bundle keepers among them. He had seventeen winters and was just coming into his manhood. He had been a warrior for three years and had won honors. He had counted coup twice, and had won the right to wear a notched eagle feather in his jet hair. She had been honored by his attentions and the soft whisper of his willow love flute outside her lodge.

But ever since the summer rendezvous, she had been restless, and had moments when she wished the one who was dead would abandon her. She kept finding fault with the young man and knew she shouldn't. The one who interested her, Mister Skye, would be long gone now, off to his own strange world, but he seemed big in her mind, a relentless presence who filled her soul in the night. She didn't believe any of his story. Big ships with twenty sails on the Great Waters, villages so big it took hours to walk from one end to the other, guns so big they could shoot an iron ball too heavy for one man to lift, homes of fired clay so big many lodges would fit into one, streets paved of stone. She knew he had invented these things to entertain her. Nothing under the sun could be like that and she took it as his whimsy, not as anything real.

But he was different from the other pale men, more serious, more direct and truthful, more tender and honest. He didn't laugh much; she had barely seen his hairy face break into a smile. It was as if some terrible burden lay upon him that he could never set down. She didn't really know why she was drawn to him, only that he set her heart afire and she wanted to be his woman. She smiled. Maybe it was his nose. He had the chief of all noses, a nose to be proud of, a nose that made him a giant among all people.

She cut a snippet of black hair from the left side of her face to express her mourning for the one who had gone, but she did not cut half her hair the way a widow would. She walked to the pond where she could see her reflection, and saw how plain she looked. That was good. The cut hair would warn suitors off, and that was what she wanted.

Maybe Mister Skye wouldn't come. She had seen him walking over mountains after she had cried for a vision one moon earlier, and she placed great stock in that. But she didn't really know whether he would come back, and she knew all about false visions, the work of Coyote the Trickster. Even if Skye came with the trappers to winter with the Kicked-in-the-Bellies, and even if she met Mister Skye again, her parents would not approve. He would have nothing to give her father; he would also be a man without honors among the Goddamns, and her father would disapprove.

But enough of this! She put such things aside and hiked through the rustling grasslands to a distant hill where she went to be alone with the Spirits and to bring Magpie, her spirit counselor, to her. These days were bursting with glory, and she exulted in the golden warmth, the brown grasses humming in the fresh breezes, and the dome of the cloudless sky. Off to the southwest rose the snowy Big Horn Mountains, but other directions offered prairie and hills dotted with the sacred juniper and stunted jack pine. It was the most beautiful place on earth, a place to think about the First Maker, and his children Sun and Earth.

When she reached the crest she settled into the rustling grass, letting the breeze whip through her hair and eddy into her dress and over her slender body. She needed guidance, and felt something large but as yet undefined just beyond her knowing. She implored Magpie to show her what was there, just beyond. She begged her spirit counselor for the inner eye that would enable her to see past the visible world. Something large, something important and urgent was stirring her, and she desperately sought to know what it was.

She saw the familiar rakish bird fly by, a flash of white and black with iridescent blue tones. Magpie alighted some distance away, danced on one foot and the other, and broke into the sky, raucous and arrogant. Magpie was like Many Quill Woman, harsh and rowdy and not a bit sweet.

"Blessed is my counselor," she said. "You have come to share your wisdom with your daughter."

She felt her power, her destiny, too. She would not be like other Absaroka women, for she would teach herself the ways of war. She might be small and light and fragile, but she would be deadly. She thought at first that she would make war for the People like the great warrior woman Pine Leaf, because the People had lost so many young men to the Siksika and Lakota. Yes, she would learn the ways of war for her tribe and village, but she would learn war for other, mistier reasons as yet unclear.

She stayed an afternoon more, trying to sort out what could not be described in words, and then trotted back to her lodge and sought out her father.

"I wish to have a bow and arrows, and I wish to be taught," she said.

"You?"

"Yes, I have seen it. I must know how to fight."

"If you have seen it, and if you know it is a true vision, we will do it."

"I have seen it."

"You will war for the People, because we have lost so many."

She nodded.

"No woman may touch my bow or arrows or quiver or their war powers will wither. But I will get you a bow. The family of the one who was killed will give you one of his bows and will be pleased with your vision."

"I must tell you there was more to the vision. Yes, I must learn the warrior skills, but it won't always be for the People."

Her father eyed her sharply.

"For another Absaroka village?"

"No."

"For another People?"

"No, for myself and the one who becomes my man."

Her father stared a long while and nodded. "It is a good thing," he said uncertainly.

"Yes. This one will need me," she said.

Chapter 36

At first Skye saw nothing. He was examining the great mountain-girt basin from the top of a noble hill, looking for the Sublette brigade—and signs of danger. Puffball clouds plowed shadows across the giant land while zephyrs made the whole world vibrate and the late summer light shiver.

He knew he did not have keen eyes, or maybe he simply wasn't seeing what experienced trappers saw. During his brief sojourn with Sublette's men, he came to realize they read nature in ways he couldn't fathom. They saw meaning in the flight of birds or the way antelope fled. Silences meant a lot. The sudden cessation of birdsong could mean trouble. The scents on the wind told stories to them that Skye didn't grasp.

He lay in the shivering brown grass studying a panorama so vast he knew he could fathom only this small southwestern corner of it. But what he saw seemed a hunter's and trapper's paradise. Creeks and rivers laced this land. Broad meadows supported buffalo and elk and deer and antelope. Moose browsed the bogs. Willow brush and chokecherry thickets and copses of aspen or cottonwood gave shelter and food, and were the home of the beaver.

He waited patiently to make sense of all he saw as he squinted north and east. At last he spotted movement, small and dark and uncertain. But as he studied the faint motion, it came to him he was seeing a herd of running buffalo, maybe a hundred or so, and they seemed to be coming his way, although the distances made him uncertain. Yes, buffalo, black beasts over a mile distant, and more. Mounted riders among them, drawing alongside one. Sometimes a giant animal would stumble and fall, and the riders would leave it and race after another.

Indian hunters. Blackfeet.

The realization shot terror through him. The stampeding buffalo were heading in his direction, along with the hunters. He watched, mesmerized, not knowing what to do. He was in open country, grassy hills, without cover. Just behind him, his mare and foal stood in plain sight. He had been a fool to come here, throwing caution to the winds.

Sublette wouldn't be here in the heart of the Blackfoot hunting grounds—not yet. Not until the beaver were prime. They had explained it to him. Not until November, when the beaver had grown their winter pelts, were they worth taking. He was alone among hunters and warriors famous for casual butchery of any white man they encountered—sometimes with ritual torture to prolong the agony.

The herd grew closer and larger, and he was amazed by its speed. These big, clumsy beasts could run as fast as the fastest horse. He was trapped. All he could do was slip back below the ridge line along with his horses, and wait events. He retreated until he was out of sight of the herd, and clung tightly to the lead line of his excited mare.

He could hear the thunder of the herd just over the

ridge, and once in a while he thought he heard the ululating howls of the hunters. They passed by. The herd had veered up the broad valley rather than boil over his ridge. He felt drained. Sweat soaked his leather tunic. He was not yet out of trouble and could not know whether a horseman would suddenly top the ridge and spot him.

Now Bug's Boys, as the trappers called them, were ahead and behind him, and his life wasn't worth a pence. He could think of nothing to do but wait for dark, which was a long time away. He didn't know which direction to go. He could run into the savages in any direction, at any time. He surveyed his situation, which wasn't bad, actually. He was simply high up the slope of a long grassy hill. Below, a creek ran somewhere. But he saw no cover other than a little scrub juniper. Well, that would have to do. He cautiously led his horses to a likely dark patch covering an acre and waited there. The mare grazed contently, no longer quivering with the sound of a stampede in her alert ears.

In the relative safety of the juniper, calm returned to him. For several months he had been transforming himself into a mountaineer. He had learned steadily, and now he would employ what he knew. He acknowledged he was afraid, and couldn't help the rush of fear every time he thought of the Blackfeet. And yet, the trappers dealt with that same fear day after day. They went about their daily toil with that fear never far from them. How did they do it? Skye marveled at their courage, and hoped to discover within himself the same fatalistic acceptance of danger along with their sharp, tough confidence that they could weather trouble.

He waited for several more hours and then, upon seeing no sign of danger, quietly walked eastward past giant foothills that guarded the towering peaks to the south. He knew from the crude maps drawn by Jedediah Smith and William Sublette that off to the east somewhere, over a high pass, lay the land of the Crow Indians and the Yellowstone River, the greatest tributary of the Missouri.

There he might find safety, and maybe even Sublette. It would be the logical place for the brigade to wait for cold weather.

Two uneventful days later he reached what seemed to be the southeast corner of this giant basin, and beheld a sharp notch in the mountains, cut by a small creek. Signs of passage suggested the trail was heavily traveled, which worried him.

He turned into it, followed the creek beneath gloomy gray ramparts of limestone, and eventually topped the pass. At its crest he saw off to the southeast the most majestic mountains he had ever seen, jagged ramparts capped with new snow. He descended a long grassy valley and found himself a few days later on the bank of a large river he believed was the Yellowstone. It curved here, turning from its northward direction to an easterly one.

If he was right, this was Crow country, and while that didn't preclude the arrival of other tribes, including the Blackfeet, he began to feel less fearful. The river flowed at low ebb, and he found he could ride the mare through belly-deep water to a long semiwooded island that would offer him some concealment and protection.

He found a hollow near its eastern end where he could build a small fire that could not be seen from either bank, and settled down for the night, plagued by mosquitos. He rejoiced to be in Crow country. His thoughts turned to the girl he had renamed Victoria. Suddenly she was present in his mind. He wasn't going to Boston, at least not until next summer, and her image danced before him, slim and fierce and tender. He wondered if he could find her, and if her family would welcome him when the cold set in.

His larder was reduced to cattail roots again, and he spent an hour collecting the miserable food. He kept smelling roasting meat on the wind, and ascribed it to his all-too-familiar hunger, which often excited fantasies of banquets.

"Well, dammit old coon, if you're goin' to come all this way and not jine us, then the devil with ye."

The voice behind Skye raised the hair on his neck. He whirled and peered into the dusk, discovering slope-shouldered Jim Bridger, old Gabe himself.

Skye roared. Bridger howled like a wolf. Trappers materialized out of the gloom and hugged Skye. The mare, picketed on grass nearby, reared back and broke her tether. Someone caught her. Skye fought back tears that welled unbidden.

"Why, old Mister Skye's a daddy, looks like," said one, observing the horse colt.

They escorted Skye to the other end of the island, taking his horses and gear with them. There Skye discovered Sublette and the whole brigade, much to his relief and joy.

And meat. Buffalo roasted over two fires. These mountaineers weren't concealing their presence, and the fires threw light on the far shores.

"He looks poor bull, don't he?" said Beckwourth. "I guess we got to put some tallow on him."

"He's been cavorting with Blackfeet women," said Black Harris. "That'll thin down a coon in a week."

Skye didn't argue. This outfit understood. Eat first and then talk. He ate. Succulent, dripping buffalo meat melted in his mouth. He wolfed down one cut, and another, eating with his fingers, juices running down his jaw and off his fingers. He had his fill and he kept on eating until he couldn't stuff another morsel into his mouth. Two additional quarters of a buffalo cow hung from thick limbs. He would soon tackle another pink, hot, dripping slab of the best meat he had ever tasted. But now he felt satiated, and that was an odd sensation.

They studied his plunder, what little there was of it, his mare and foal, his crudely patched moccasins, his mended tack.

"Hard doin's, eh, Mister Skye?" asked Sublette when Skye paused.

"I got here," Skye said, pride welling in him. "Pretty good for a limey sailor."

"Ye come over that pass?" Bridger asked.

Skye nodded.

"I don't suppose ye saw any Bug's Boys. Just limey luck."

Skye wiped his mouth with his buckskin sleeve. "I saw them but they didn't see me."

"Hull country's swarming with 'em. We come through at night, so damned many of 'em."

Skye nodded. Apparently he had done something even more daring than he realized. At ease for the first time in days, he settled back into a tree trunk and told them his story, beginning with his departure from the rendezvous, his loss of everything to the Blackfeet, the bear that saved him, his indecision and fear and despair when he was lost, his desperate quest for food, his wild moment on the Madison River when he was caught between a village he couldn't identify and raiders who came within a few yards of him.

"Poor doin's. Probably Shoshones, maybe Bannacks," someone volunteered. "Best not to tangle with Bannacks. Miracle you didn't get your ha'r raised."

They questioned him at length, and he asked them about their journey, which had been uneventful until they reached the Three Forks and found Blackfeet everywhere. After that they had slipped over to Crow country, the great bend of the Yellowstone, and had been here a fortnight waiting for the weather to cool, feasting on buffalo.

Sublette raised the question on all their minds. "What are your plans, Mister Skye?"

"To enter your service, sir."

"I thought so. We can use every man we can get. You'll need an outfit. We carry two or three spares; every year someone or other loses his plunder—traps, rifle, flint, and steel. We can outfit you."

"How will all that earn out, sir?"

"Camp tenders earn two hundred a year. Your outfit'll cost about a hundred. That means you'll have a mountain rifle, pound of powder and a horn, lead balls, thirty-two to a pound, half a dozen traps, a good skinning knife, blankets, and some odds and ends including a few yards of flannel."

"You'd make me a camp tender?"

"It's an apprenticeship, Mister Skye. Free trappers earn more, but you'll need to learn some things first. Beavers don't just come to you and offer themselves up. We try to have one camp tender for every two trappers but we're short. You'll skin and dress the pelts, dry 'em out, cook, keep the fires going, and herd the company horses and mules. It's hard work and these old coons'll give you all the grief they can. Next season, or maybe sooner if you're up and the beaver's coming, you can go out and trap and make a good living. You ever shot a rifle?"

"No, sir, except a few times at the rendezvous."

"Not even in the Royal Navy?"

"I wasn't a marine, sir. I was a powder monkey mostly and then a seaman."

"Well, you'll be getting some lessons in the mornin'. You'll learn the whole drill, from keeping your piece clean and dry to making meat. We'll burn a little du Pont. Old Fitzpatrick here, he's gonna turn you into a mountaineer. Let me tell you something, Mister Skye. Learn how to use that rifle. How to load fast and shoot slow and never waste a shot. A red man can pump six or seven arrows at you in the time it takes you to reload. So every shot counts. Believe me, before we're done with the Three Forks, you'll be put to the test."

Chapter 37

When the grass gave out, Sublette took the brigade off the island and into a broad valley of the Yellowstone that was hemmed by majestic mountains.

Skye marveled at its beauty. Never had he seen such a place.

"Up ahead a piece is Colter's Hell," Bridger told him. "With biling springs, hot water that shoots out of the ground, and the smell of sulphur. It's the doorway to Hades. We all been there and peered in and saw the old horned rascal hi'self grinnin' up at us."

Skye smiled. He was onto old Gabe.

"You don't believe me, eh? Well, we'll go have us a sample." He turned to Beckwourth and Tom Fitzpatrick. "Old Barnaby hyar don't believe in Colter's Hell. I reckon we'd better go show him where a man can get a whiff of sulphur and brimstone."

"Skye, you don't believe in hell? We found it and we'll show it to you," Beckwourth said. "We'll show you where you can roast your pale white hide. This is where Old Bug himself lives."

"It's Mister Skye, mate."

"Well, you'd better tell that to old Satan," said Fitzpatrick. "The devil should address a man proper."

Skye smiled. This had been going on ever since he arrived. For days he had devoured good cow—the mountaineers made sure he knew good cow from poor bull—and sometimes elk or mule deer. For days he had slept warm under two thick blankets spun and carded in England. For days he had learned wilderness arts, fire tending, hide dressing, and how to shoot his heavy, octagonal-barreled rifle.

They had disabused him of various notions, such as that he should stand up to shoot. Instead, they told him to lie down or get behind a tree or log or rock, and make no target at all. He should steady the barrel on anything solid and squeeze the trigger sweet and true. They didn't have much powder or lead to spare, but a man who could shoot true could make the difference in a scrape, so they instructed him anyway. They taught him how to load fast, even how to load without measuring powder in an emergency; how to drive a patched ball home with the hickory rod clipped under the barrel, how to pour a little powder in the pan, how to scrape out damp powder after a rain because if he didn't he wouldn't be armed.

He progressed from clumsiness to some skill, occasionally hitting a distant target, and they pronounced themselves satisfied that he could make meat or send a few red devils to the spirit world. He wondered about that. He had fired cannon in war, and brawled in bloody mayhem, but coolly aiming at and killing a mortal bothered him.

Skye, Bridger, Fitzpatrick, and Beckwourth set off on horseback that golden October noon for the gates of hell, and told Sublette they'd be back the next day. Skye kept his counsel, expecting that all this was an elaborate prank on a pork-eater. But it would be fun, and he'd had little enough fun in his constricted life. They rode south along the Yellowstone, scaring up flocks of Canada geese and ducks and alarming a few snorty cow moose and calves.

Beckwourth was at his gaudiest—to impress the ladies certain to be dipping their toes in the boiling waters, he said—with elaborately quilled buckskins he had talked some Crow maidens—or matrons—into making for him. The fringes of both his tunic and leggins were extra long. He wore a great floppy felt hat that concealed his dusky face, and his untrammeled dark hair stretched far down his back, making him rakish. The man had style, Skye thought, and never more so than in his bawdy recollections of nearly the entire distaff side of the Crow Nation.

"Why," Beckwourth was saying, "I was so smitten by Bad Bear's buxom virgin daughter Raccoon, the Teton Queen I called her in honor of her assets, that I went to the chief and made him a proposition. 'Ol' Bear,' sez I, 'I want Raccoon for my very own, and in return I'll be in your service, come war and come peace.' Well, Bear, he smiles, and sez he'd be honored, and he sent Raccoon over and I indoctrinated her in all the arts of amour for a fortnight, spending a pleasant January last winter. My reputation grew—deservedly of course—and next thing I knew, Bear's wife and three other daughters came into my lodge for their own initiation, and that's how I spent a pleasant February except that I was plumb exhausted and out of sorts by March."

Well, they were all marvelous liars: Beckwourth, that son of a white man and slave woman, most of all, and if that was what wilderness did, Skye supposed he would turn into a gaudy liar himself.

Bridger was steering them toward a conical peak to the southeast, and then into its foothills. Skye couldn't imagine a less likely place for brimstone and sulphur, and waited patiently to see how this great prank would end.

"We're getting close now, Skye. You can smell the sulphur. Wherever Bug is, there's the smell of burning sulphur," said Fitzpatrick. "This is just a sample, sort of an outlier. Hell's real front gate's another fifty miles south of here up on a steaming plateau where boiling water erupts and sulphur stinks up the air. I've seen old Bug hisself, and so has Bridger, but Beckwourth's so saintly Bug leaves him alone."

They were progressing up a bleak gulch with a small creek in it. The creek steamed in the crisp October air, which puzzled Skye. His husky colt poked a nose into the water and jerked back. They finally arrived at a place where water boiled out of a steep hillside and into pools, one below the next. Steam billowed into the chill air, and Skye realized the water actually was hot.

"Well, ha'r we are. I'll go pay Bug the admission," Bridger said, vanishing into brush. The rest were picketing their horses on the grassy slope and peeling off their duds. Skye watched, uncertain, wary of a prank. They'd get him down to the buff and then ride off. Yes, that was it. The whole elaborate business would teach him a lesson.

"Couldn't find the Divil," said Bridger. "Guess we go in for free this time." He began tugging on his moccasins. "I left him a message that ol' Skye was hyar, sampling the Divil's wares."

Next thing Skye knew, his comrades were poking toes into the pools, sampling them for heat, and then lowering themselves into the water with many a happy sigh. Where was the prank?

"Well, Skye?" Fitzpatrick, in waist-high water, addressed him. "Are you a shy fellow?"

"It's Mister Skye, mate."

"Well, this pool will boil off your cooties, and the next one up will boil you. Go down two pools and you can sit for an hour without getting lobstered."

Skye needed no more invitation. He dropped his grimy duds, stepped into the pool, and found himself immersed in just-bearable heat, which swiftly opened every pore and swept away every ache. He celebrated. Rarely in his brief life had he experienced a hot bath. He marveled at the water and wondered where it came from and what subterranean fires heated it. The water exuded a certain mineral odor, and Skye sensed that it had leached chemicals out of the bowels of the earth somewhere under this hot-bellied mountain. This was probably volcanic country.

That evening, they feasted on cow elk after Skye had collected wood and built a small fire for them.

"Actually, Skye," said Beckwourth, "we was elected to bring you hyar. The vote was unanimous."

Skye waited.

"You got the smelliest feet in Creation, and we was commanded to bring you here to clean your toes so you didn't foul up the whole camp."

Skye hardly knew what to say.

Bridger hiccuped and snickered.

Skye got the drift. "It's Mister Skye, gents. When you introduce me to the Devil, remember it."

"Bug wouldn't let 'im into hell, not with them feet," said Bridger.

They were making him one of them, but not without some initiation rites. Skye sensed how he stood with them. From their standpoint, he was an odd duck who talked with an accent and used sailor words and harbored a vision of going back to the civilized east. But he knew he had done something they admired, something that might have sunk even the most experienced of them. He had survived two encounters with the Blackfeet, picked up a horse and food and gear along the way, and somehow made it to the brigade through a wilderness he didn't know. They were going to put him through some more of this, but all the while they were teaching him everything they knew about staying alive in a land without roofs and constables and butchers and bakers. Skye glowed within. These were friends as well as mentors.

Leisurely they rode back to Sublette's encampment. The aspens had bloomed yellow and withered to nakedness, but the cottonwoods were just reaching a burnished gold radiance, somehow joyous and sad. The air had changed, and each breeze carried tiny knives in it. In camp, the pace quickened. Skye found himself jerking meat, packing "Indian butter," which he learned was the soft tallow that accumulated along the back of the buffalo—a delicacy that mountaineers as well as the tribes cherished and ate raw. It preserved well, and Skye filled leather sacks with it.

They trapped a few beaver just to have a look at the pelts, and pronounced them not yet prime but getting there fast. Skye learned to roast beaver tail and to flesh each pelt and dry it on a willow hoop. Sublette kept him busy but he still found moments he could call his own, and these he used to master the arts of war as it was fought here.

They showed him an Indian-made bullhide shield so tough it could deflect arrows and even a rifle ball that hit it askance. They taught him to throw a knife and a hatchet, and he, in turn, showed them the sailor's weapon, the belaying pin with its flared cusp that protected the hand from lance and knife. He surprised them in several mock fights, deftly deflecting a wooden mock knife and a mock lance fashioned from a stick, and thumping his adversaries in the ribs, or neck, or knees, which set them to howling. He knew little about shooting arrows or bullets, but when it came to close quarters, he won their respect in a hurry.

"That Royal Navy's tougher'n I thought," said Fitzpatrick. "It can fight with a damned stick."

"It fights with cannon and mortar and sword mostly, mate. But the seamen brawl with a marlinspike or cutlass, and they're handy if we're about to be boarded. Mostly the lads just pound on each other. Those sticks are everywhere on deck; the rigging's wrapped around them. All those lines off the masts end up wrapped over belaying pins."

They weren't grasping much of that, but they were

learning fast how to fight with a hardwood stick that protected the hand that held it.

Then one day the wind shifted and blew a cold gale that kept them from cooking because they couldn't keep a fire under anything. That night the temperatures dropped and it snowed sleety wet flakes. Skye hadn't thought much about winter camping, but now he did. He shivered under his blankets through a brutal night, wondering how he would survive that sort of ferocity. By morning he was numb and discouraged, soaked with snow, and colder than he had ever been.

The mountaineers joked about it, but he knew he'd die of the catarrh if he was subjected to much of it. Then he listened closer. They weren't really joking. They had a way of making their misery light by ridiculing it.

"Two months of hard cold work," said Beckwourth, "and after that, paradise."

"He's talking about them lustful and willing Crow women," Blanket Jim Bridger explained. "And them warm lodges with a hot little fire right in the middle, and thick buffler robes to lie in. Beats a dugout or tent or brush hut any time."

Sublette gathered them around the breakfast fire. "We'll head for the Three Forks," he said. "Beaver's prime now, and maybe Bug's Boys'll be in their lodges. But keep your powder dry. Pull those loads; I want fresh powder under every lock."

The lark was over.

Chapter 38

Cold was the enemy. It numbed and shocked Skye. He had been cold many times at sea, in unheated seamen's quarters, fighting North Atlantic gales, soaked with icy seawater. But on a ship there was usually refuge. In the wilderness refuges were few and took a long time to build.

November had barely started and yet it snowed daily, sharp blizzards that drove ice down a man's spine and numbed his fingers. He wondered how the trappers functioned at all, standing in icy creeks while they set their traps, going out each day to toil in bone-chilling cold, their hands too numb to set a trap or hold a rifle or pull a trigger.

Skye's leather shirt didn't serve him in this weather, and he yearned for the pea jacket and woolen skull cap he had traded long before. A few trappers had buffalo coats to warm them. The Creoles had blanket capotes, practical hooded affairs sewn from a trade blanket. Skye knew he would need such gear fast or go under, so he ransomed his future to buy an old blanket capote from Broussard, a giant Canadian, and good gloves from Adams, one of the free trappers. Not even that was enough, because his feet froze. Many of the men had woolen or fur leggins, and so Skye bargained for a pair of these as well, and then rabbit-fur liners for his moccasins. By the time he was properly outfitted, he owed seventy dollars on top of his two debts to the company—one for the equipment he drew at the rendezvous, and the other for the outfit provided him by Sublette. Next summer, when debts and wages were squared, he would still be in the hole.

If this was November in the northern mountains, he wondered what January would be like. But by then the brigade would be holed up in Crow lodges, awaiting the return of spring and the second bout of trapping. His days were filled with hard work, which never ceased, although some brief interludes of warm weather made life easier. Sublette had led them over the pass into the Three Forks basin, and had set up camp close to the pass—an avenue of escape if they ran into Bug's Boys. This was Gallatin River country, and beaver flourished on every tributary, offering Sublette an incredible harvest.

Sublette made Skye the camp tender for Bridger and Fitzpatrick, and thereafter Skye was responsible for the horses of both men as well as his own, plus cooking, shelter, fire, and fleshing and drying the pelts. Skye felt lucky to work for two of the wiliest veterans in the mountains. He cut deadwood and kept fires going, fleshed and dried the thick pelts on willow hoops. He tended the horses, keeping an eye on them night and day, keeping them picketed and hobbled and on good grass. Once, when the snow rose higher than they could paw through, Bridger showed him something: he cut green cottonwood limbs and let the horses gnaw on the soft bark.

"They'll make a living on it," Bridger said. "We call it mountain hay. Had me two plugs that got so fat on it I had ta prop up their bellies on a cart."

Skye laughed. Old Gabe Bridger could never impart information without putting a twist on it.

Skye suspected his own mare was pregnant, which suited him fine. In his spare moments he haltered his rambunctious horse colt and began training it to lead and carry a small load. Occasionally he was given some free time, and then he hunted buffalo, which were plentiful in that vast basin. Bridger showed him how to creep in on them from downwind, and kill one with a single shot aimed just behind the forelegs. Thus did he contribute juicy humpmeat, tongue, and flank steaks to the brigade's cook pots. He also accumulated a few winter-thick hides, which he learned to stake to the ground and flesh and then soften and brain-tan into robes. He intended to sell them or trade them—anything to get out of debt and go east next summer.

It took days of miserable toil to flesh a buffalohide, and days more to rub brains into it and then soften it. But now he slept comfortably with good robes above and below him. He had a product the free trappers wanted and they bought his robes on tick. Skye discovered that a few buffalo robes draped over a framework of limbs could shelter storm-harassed trappers. And he turned one damaged robe into a wooly greatcoat, patiently lacing the parts together with thong.

Then, in December, the days turned warm again, even though the sun vanished in midafternoon. The weather amazed Skye. Just when he thought this country would be brutal it turned as mild as early autumn, and the whole brigade pulled off layers of clothing and stretched in the balmy air.

But William Sublette wasn't pleased. He called them together and issued a stern warning. "Bug's Boys'll roam for a week or two. I want the horses in camp every night. The camp tenders'll build a brush corral. I want the trappers to go out in parties of four, two armed and watching while the other two work. Maybe that'll bring less beaver; but it'll save lives. No man leaves camp alone, and no man goes unarmed."

Skye listened soberly. His buffalo-hunting forays were at an end for the moment and his work redoubled with all the extra horse handling. That's how it went for a while until the day they found Polite Robiseau dead and scalped. He had left his colleagues a moment to use the bushes—and that was how they found him an hour later, his leggins down, his skullbone bare in the weak winter sun, an arrow protruding from his back.

His Creole trapping friends brought him to camp over the back of a horse, and they buried him under a cutbank because the ground remained frozen. No one said much of anything. The mountaineers' silence howled louder than words. His partners quietly divided his traps and gear, their faces inscrutable behind their thick beards, their eyes leaking grief.

But as soon as that was completed, Sublette and his veteran trappers wordlessly saddled their shaggy-haired horses, armed themselves, and rode out. Skye wasn't surprised. This platoon would strike back and hard if it could. He watched Bridger, Fitzpatrick, and the rest ride away, their heavy rifles in their laps, held in mittened hands. If it was war, they would take war to the Blackfeet.

In camp, Skye and the other tenders raised log and dirt and rock breastworks while they waited, and cleared away nearby brush that might conceal a warrior. No one spoke. The eight camp tenders had no leader, but every one of them was aware that menace lurked just beyond, perhaps in the pine forests, or high on the ridges. The Blackfeet were famous for their audacity. They were bold, daring, courageous, and skilled at surprise. Skye had heard plenty about them even in his short time with the brigade.

Skye eyed the camp tenders dourly. Four were Creole boys—Bouleau, Lapointe, Le Clerc, and Baptiste— perhaps fourteen or fifteen, new to the wilds. Then there was Scott, a sandy-haired ne'er-do-well, lazy and sullen, a runaway. He sat with his rifle in hand, doing little. Louis Pombert was an experienced Creole mountaineer who simply preferred camp duties, a good man who was building a log breastwork that would defend one flank. And also Manuel Estevan, a Mexican, good with horses, swiftly herding the animals into the camp and picketing them.

Skye did what he could, arranging the bales of beaver as a breastwork and adding saddles and gear—anything that would protect a man from an arrow. He'd been in battle, but he sensed the others hadn't. They toiled through the midmorning and then waited in a stretching silence for Sublette's force to return. The sight of the scalped Robiseau was heavy on his mind, the yellow skull bone and sliced flesh shocking to see.

The low December sun briefly topped the ridges and warmed the camp for a spell, making Skye sleepy. It seemed preternaturally quiet. A crow catapulted into the air and flapped away swiftly, electrifying Skye.

"They're on us, mates," he said. "Over there." He pointed across an innocuous expanse of snow-patched meadow.

"Who says?" asked Scott.

Skye didn't reply. He crept into the stronghold made of logs and beaver pelts and laid the heavy black barrel of his mountain rifle across it.

The Blackfeet came silently and in a rush, all on foot, about six or seven.

"Hey!" yelled Scott, diving for cover. Skye glanced at the fellow, who lay flat on the ground behind a log, his rifle useless unless he overcame his terror.

The rest of the men positioned themselves, rifles ready. "Watch our backs," Skye yelled to Pombert. They were protected by a wide creek, but not much.

The first arrows struck from the rear, thudding close. Skye whirled. The ones out on the meadow were feinting; the main body of the Blackfeet lurked in the woods across the creek, well protected by trunk and limb and log. Still, any Blackfoot firing an arrow had to rise, aim, draw the bow, and shoot. There would be targets. Two

arrows seared close, thudding into the pelts with sicken-
ing force that made Skye wince. He heard a rifle boom
and saw a puff of smoke. Pombert, experienced mountaineer, was showing mettle.

Skye sighted down the barrel at a shadowy place he
knew concealed a savage, and waited. A moment later he
saw a flash of movement; the warrior rose and loosed an
arrow. Skye caught him in his buckhorn sight and
squeezed. Flint hit frizzen, the rifle whoomed, driving the
butt into his shoulder. The Blackfoot cried and collapsed.

Skye ducked, poured powder, patched a ball, and
jammed it home, and then poured powder into the pan
and cocked his weapon, his heart wild in his chest.
Around him he heard more booms, and more howls from
the naked woods beyond the creek. The feinting warriors
regrouped and howled from their side. Skye whirled.
Someone had to keep them at bay or the camp would be
overrun. They made a small target a hundred yards away,
but Skye wanted to keep them far away. He settled his
rifle on a bale of plews, picking a shadowy distant form,
taking his time. An arrow thumped into the furs just
beside him. He swallowed.

His shot sent another Blackfoot tumbling, and immediately the rest of the ones out on the meadow drew back.
Skye found himself sweating, even in the December air.
Sourly he measured a charge and poured it down the
muzzle, drove a ball after it, picked at the fire-hole which
had been fouled, and looked for another target. He heard
five shots explode like firecrackers, and knew that the
ones in the woods were rushing the camp and that at least
five of seven rifles were empty. He whirled again, finding
a dozen of the devils at the creek and more pouring up to
it. Pombert shot a Blackfoot, but that didn't slow their
wading through the icy creek. Skye waited a moment
more, until the first reached midstream, and then he shot.
The warrior dropped into the river and stained it red. The
Blackfeet around him howled but didn't stop. Scott burrowed deeper behind his log. Enraged, Skye dashed over

there, grabbed the loaded rifle, and shot a warrior who was running into camp with hatchet raised.

"Fight!" roared Skye.

Scott whined.

A horse took an arrow, screeched and bucked. Blood gouted from a wound in its ribs.

A volley from the Creole boys slowed the charge through the creek, but it was too late.

Chapter 39

Blackfeet were everywhere. Most of them went for the horses, which were hobbled and picketed.

Three came at Skye. He dropped his empty rifle, picked up his belaying pin, and bulled straight at them. He knew what to do at close quarters. Murderously he whacked aside a lance, smacked the forearm of a man drawing a bow, jabbed at another lunging at him with a tomahawk. Skye whirled, braining a warrior behind him. Something seared his arm, shooting wild pain into his skull.

He spun and dodged, never a static target, inflicting mayhem with his hickory club. He saw Pombert fighting for his life, swinging his rifle against a big warrior armed with a lance. Skye ran to Pombert's help, with his own assailants hot on his heels. He jammed his belaying pin into the giant warrior, toppling him, and spun to face his assailants again. But others were swarming in from the meadow and the creek. It would be over soon.

He heard a volley. A warrior staggered. Others howled,

clasped flesh wounds. Then Skye got caught up in the infighting again. A knife sliced his ribs. Another volley, and the Blackfeet suddenly retreated, gathering their dead and wounded. Sublette and his veteran mountaineers rushed into camp and out the other side, chasing the Blackfeet into the creek. The mountaineers urged their horses through the creek and kept after the retreating Blackfeet. Skye heard howls and shots from the woods, but the wall of timber concealed those events from him. He was bleeding from half a dozen places that stung wickedly.

Scott stood up and grinned, unscathed.

Pombert was all right. The Creole boys forted up behind packsaddles and supplies were alive but several leaked blood. Skye armed his rifle, then pulled off his bloody leather shirt and began stanching blood with a rag. He had no bandaging. Vicious hurts tortured him.

"Monsieur Skye, let me do dat," said Pombert. The veteran Creole swiftly cleaned and bandaged Skye's arm and then washed Skye's rib and shoulder wounds. "I will sew dis," he said. "You hold rag tight."

Pombert deftly threaded a needle from his kit and sewed Skye's rib wound together while Skye groaned at every prick. His side sheeted red, but the bleeding stopped when Pombert finished up. Skye's pulse slowly settled back to normal but he felt sick and feverish. He could barely breathe. One stocky young Blackfoot lay dead nearby, a hole in his bare brown chest, his sightless eyes malevolent. Skye had shot that one with Scott's rifle. The raiders had taken their wounded with them but Skye thought they had lost two dead and four or five injured, some of them gravely. That was a heavy loss for so small a party.

Scott loaded his rifle and grinned, as if to celebrate a victory. Skye stared blankly at the man and said nothing. Scott had been useless, and Skye made note of it without condemning. Some seamen in the Royal Navy ran rather than fought when it came to close-quarters fighting. Skye felt no moral outrage, only a sense that Scott would not be a man to partner with when it came to trapping.

Sublette's riders drifted back one by one. They splashed across the creek into camp and noted Skye lying shirtless in the cold with red-stained bandaging wrapped around his middle and his arm. Sublette dismounted and came to Skye.

"You all right old coon?"

"I will be."

"Anyone else hurt?"

"Go ask them. Pombert is all right."

"They steal any horses?"

"I don't know. Some of those devils went for the horses, but they were hobbled and picketed. Couldn't be stampeded."

"We'll count. I don't think we lost any, except the one that took an arrow. I saw your mare and the colt. They're fine."

"Good. What happened in the woods?"

"We chased 'em hard. They headed for the pass and we chased 'em up a way until they set up a defense up there. We know you did some damage. They were carrying three, four wounded, dead—who knows?"

"You got here just in time. Two minutes more and we'd have gone under."

"I heard different, Skye. You were licking 'em."

"It's Mister Skye, sir."

"Yes, it's *Mister* Skye, old coon. And it'll never be anything else as long as free trappers are in the mountains."

Sublette patted Skye's shoulder and hastened to discover what else was amiss in camp. Skye heard him talking to Pombert, Estevan, and the Creole youths, and then drifted into oblivion. Sublette helped him to shelter and threw a thick buffalo robe over him, which he welcomed.

He woke at dawn to fever, his forehead burning even as his limbs froze. He felt weak as a newborn and wondered how he would manage his camp duties. But he didn't have to. At first light Sublette was hunched over him. "You rest, Mister Skye. We're moving tomorrow."

"I could use it, mate. Pretty sick."

Sublette nodded and Skye burrowed deeper into his robe. But then Bridger was squatting beside him. "You'll be fine, old coon. Meat doesn't spile in the mountains."

Skye hurt too much to laugh.

"I mind the time when I had an arrer in my arm, and I got Greenwood to pull her out. He had to dig out the point. It didn't infect because we were over six thousand feet. Below six thousand, everything mortifies."

"We're below that here."

Gabe Bridger whooped, stood, and vanished, only to be replaced by Fitzpatrick, who was running his hands over the belaying pin.

"Your club's ruined," Tom said. "Lookit this."

Skye squinted at the pin. Several deep gashes marred the hickory. A hatchet had chipped out a piece.

"That's probably how it was when I jumped ship."

"No, it was plumb virgin until now. I'd never seen one and I looked it over back at rendezvous. These scars were made today. When you're up, I want a lesson with it."

"Nothing to learn. They come at you, you hit and thrust and deflect. I didn't do it well or I'd not be sewed together now."

Fitzpatrick grunted, patted Skye on the shoulder, and wandered off.

Skye healed swiftly. Even the next day, when Sublette moved camp twelve miles to the Gallatin River, Skye managed to load his gear and ride. But no one would let him work. The camp tenders refused to let him build a fire, collect wood, cook, or butcher the buffalo that Bridger shot along the way.

Things changed subtly. They didn't forget to call him mister anymore. They were deferential, which bothered him. He had done nothing more than fight for his life in a tight corner, but now they were acting as if he'd won a war. And now they simply ignored the surly Scott, plunging the youth into deep isolation. Scott wasn't much, but a trapping outfit needed every man, and this outfit needed Scott to help keep camp. The young man exuded anger, envy, and a lot of other things Skye could only guess at, and spent a lot of time out of camp by himself. No one said a word about him, but every man in camp was monitoring Scott.

Beaver were plentiful, and for a few days the trappers brought back all they could carry. Then the weather changed. The wind rotated north, bringing gloomy overcast with it, and the temperature plummeted. Gray ice formed along the banks of the creeks. Skye dreaded and hated mountain winter. He could barely sleep at night, with every breath freezing in his beard and his body numb even under blankets and buffalo robes. As soon as he was able, he began building a real shelter, walling off an undercut rock cliff and laying up a rock fireplace that would resist the wind and throw heat into his refuge. Some of the veterans laughed at him and said they'd be moving about the time he finished—but they were the first to settle against the fire-warmed rock of the cliff when their daily toil was over.

At least it didn't snow much, though an inch or two fell now and then, and the horses had to paw down to grass more and more. No Blackfeet showed up but Sublette never let down his guard. This was their prized hunting ground; they would be back in force to revenge themselves for their wounds and deaths and dishonor. Bug's Boys never gave up. The free trappers went out in fours each day, armed and ready, but the deceptive quiet continued deep into the short days of December when the wan sun came late and fled in the middle of the afternoon, plunging the river canyon into a cold blue gloom.

Skye ate more beaver tail in those weeks than he wanted, and wished for some good buffalo hump. But the free trappers had turned industrious. This was the prime season, and from well before dawn to deep into the long nights they devoted themselves to trapping. They baited their traps with castoreum, the musk that drew beavers to the jaws of the traps, staked them in the icy water of half-frozen creeks, ran their trap lines, pulled beaver after beaver out of their ponds, and staggered back to camp with a heavy load of dead animals, too tired to say a word. Skye tried to keep up, to flesh each day's take and dry the pelts on willow hoops, but the hides froze and never did clean properly. He sensed that when the next warm spell and sunlight came, he would have to dress a lot of pelts over again.

All this was hard, dull, numbing work that lowered spirits and set men to dreaming of a hearth and comfort. Tom Fitzpatrick spent a week jabbering about bread. All he wanted was a taste of fresh, hot, yeasty bread. The Creoles dreamed of cognac or beer or women. Arthur Black wept for a lost love in St. Louis. Skye didn't dream of anything. He toiled through the wintry days, fought cold, suffered every time the wind blew or snow fell, and kept quiet. Somehow, next summer, he would go to the eastern seaboard. No sane man would stay in these empty, lonely, miserable mountains if he could escape.

One day Scott disappeared. Sublette and a strong party followed his tracks for several miles and found him near the pass, heading for the Crow villages, carrying a pack with some company sugar and the last of the coffee in it. Sublette brought him back and confiscated the sugar and coffee, which they were saving for Christmas. They would not have another sip of coffee until rendezvous— if then.

"I should have let him go," Sublette said to Skye. "He wasn't pulling his weight here, and we don't need him."

But Skye sensed that Sublette's anger cut much deeper, and that Josiah Scott's future in the brigade would not be pleasant.

In the middle of December, the gloomiest time in the

mountains, Beckwourth began to talk about the famously available Crow women. He didn't boast. He simply raised the topic, mornings and evenings.

"Ah, Marse Sublette, think on it. Warm bufflerhide lodges, thick buffler robes, soft sleeping pads, hot little fires with hot little ladies, stewpots fulla buffler, full bellies, jokes you wouldn't hear no tight-lipped white woman tell. Ah, Marse William, it be time to make it over the pass before we're snowed in hyar. What a pity it'd be if the pass got snowed up and all your faithful old coons, excepting myself of course, took to blamin' you for their dire misfortunes."

Sublette smiled. "We're making the beaver come," he said.

And then it stormed.

Chapter 40

William Sublette knew he had tarried too long in the Three Forks country and would probably pay a price. The beaver pelts were piling up and he had stayed on, hoping to beat the weather. But now the weather was beating him.

Dan Ferguson and Peter Ranne hadn't returned. Their traplines were the farthest away, and the blizzard caught them. They were probably holed up safely enough, but Sublette didn't know, and when you don't know, you find out. But right now, the snow was deluging down, so furious and thick a man couldn't see much or walk a hundred yards without getting lost. He had no choice except to wait.

Sublette tried to remember what Ferguson and Ranne took with them, whether they had enough gear to hole up safely, build a shelter, climb into their buffalo robes, and wait it out. At least it wasn't brutally cold. That would come when the clouds cleared away. The trappers would have beaver tail for food—if they could build and keep a fire in such a swirl of snow. Both men were veterans of the mountains, and he shouldn't worry.

But he did. He was responsible for them, and every man in the brigade knew that he would employ the entire resources of the brigade to help any of them in trouble. From time to time they eyed him, waiting to see how far Smith, Jackson, and Sublette would go for its free trappers. He would show them, not to prove something but because every mountaineer owed that to every other mountaineer. That was the unwritten law of survival.

He stared irritably at the swirling snow. A foot and a half lay on the ground, enough to make travel hard work for man and horse. He was angry with himself. He knew he should have crossed the pass and holed up with the Crows long since. But the beaver harvest had been incredible, riches piling up each day, plew after plew out of streams that had never been trapped. He had thirty-two packs, and each pack was worth about three hundred when delivered to General Ashley at the rendezvous. Almost ten thousand dollars against the company's sixteen thousand debt.

He should have pulled out. They could be snug and happy in a Crow village by now, whiling away the days when the rivers and creeks were frozen over and the beavers were snug in their lodges. This storm would seal the pass over to the Yellowstone country, and it was unlikely they could get to the Crow villages until spring. The brigade faced a grim, cold stretch trying to survive in huts.

He heard the sound of an ax, and knew Skye was out cutting green cottonwood limbs for the horses to gnaw on. They could no longer paw through to grass, and the soft underbark was the alternative. Cottonwoods were the trappers' hay. But it took constant effort to feed fifty horses with cottonwood.

Skye worked at it constantly without being asked. He took care of his mare and horse colt, but he didn't stop cutting until the whole herd could gnaw at the lifesaving bark. Some sort of demon drove him. When the rest of the brigade was hunched around the fires, gabbing, playing euchre with ancient decks, that ol' coon Skye was out doing the work of three. He'd make a finer mountaineer—if he stayed in the mountains. Sublette squinted through the swirl at the distant man, doubting that the Englishman would. They would see the last of him at rendezvous.

He turned to Bouleau and Scott. "Go help Skye," he said.

"It won't do any good," said Scott. "We should wait until after the storm when we can work easier."

"You heard me."

Sullenly, Scott gathered an ax and followed the Creole out to the cottonwood groves. Sublette watched him go, his belly roiling. His brigade would never again include Scott. He had dealt with all sorts of men, including escaped criminals and loners and men ditching wives, and they had mostly turned themselves into mountaineers and trappers. But Scott was a shoddier sort of man, evading work, dodging responsibility—and a coward. He had heard all about Scott's conduct during the set-to with the Blackfeet. Skye hadn't said a word, but the rest of the camp tenders did.

Some of the Creoles materialized out of the white whirl, dragging firewood. He had put all the Creole camp tenders on that task, and warned them not to get out of sight. The whirling snow veiled the camp even at fifty yards, and filled footprints in minutes. There were plenty of things to worry about, such as running out of meat. Buffalo were plentiful around Three Forks, but getting to them in deep snows or blizzard conditions was another matter. It fell upon his shoulders to feed thirty men. Usually beaver tail sufficed. The trappers brought back the meaty, muscular tail of every beaver they trapped. But when they couldn't trap—such as now—starvin' times crept up fast.

"You worryin' again?" asked Beckwourth. "No good in

it. After this blow is over, I'll just wade over and rescue them pork-eaters."

It was braggadocio. Jim Beckwourth knew perfectly well what it would take to reach the missing men.

"All right. I'll send you alone," Sublette retorted. "Your prowess is all you need. You have eyes that see through whiteouts, legs that never falter in drifts—"

"And a way with women that never fails," Beckwourth said.

"What's that got to do—"

But Beckwourth was laughing softly.

The cloud cover cleared off about dusk, revealing a fat moon that lit the snow-bleached land. The temperature was dropping fast and the horses' muzzles were rimed with frost. Sublette made his decision right then.

He found his veteran trappers crowded into one of the shelters.

"Let's go," he said.

They nodded. No one needed an explanation. They began bundling up, pulling on spare gloves, donning thick leggins they tied over their moccasins, pushing homemade beaver hats down over their long hair. Fitzpatrick cut kindling with his hatchet, until he had a bundle of it—enough for a brief fire, enough to start over if snow should douse a blaze.

His trappers and mountaineers would go with Sublette, twenty in all. And each would lead two horses. If that veteran outfit didn't find Ranne and Ferguson, the pair couldn't be found. The trappers loaded packs onto some hairy horses; other horses carried nothing for the time being and would be used to break trail through soft, treacherous, hock-high snow and even higher drifts. Skye dragged a fresh cottonwood limb to the herd and paused, watching the veterans load up.

"Mister Skye, I'm putting you in charge here. We're going after 'em. Don't know how long."

"Yes, sir. I hope you bring back good news."

The night glowed white. Overhead, stars pricked a jet

sky, cold and distant. Sublette judged that they had five hours of moonlight and then would have to hole up until dawn, which would come late this time of year, days from the winter solstice.

He turned to Gabe. "You know what creeks?"

"Not exactly, but them coons were beyond us, and we were beyond the rest—up the Gallatin."

"All right. We'll rotate the lead. About a hundred yards for each man and horse, and then go to the rear."

They stumbled resolutely through the snow for hours, breaking trail, resting briefly, plunging through drifts, dropping into hollows unknown and unseen beneath the thick blanket. The moon quit them at a place without shelter, so they huddled in their robes, numb with cold and surrounded by blackness. Sublette knew his cheeks and ears and nose would be frostbitten, but there was no help for it. The night was thick and black and bitter, bad enough to make a man wonder why he had come to the mountains. But after a moment he knew why: not to get rich, but to test himself. He had seen something evolve in all his mountaineer friends—those who survived. It wasn't just confidence or resourcefulness, but something else. It was—how could he phrase it?—a fullness of manhood. The mountains spawned a race of giants.

The horses crowded close to each other for warmth, disconsolate under their loads, occasionally coughing. They were in good shape, largely because Skye had wanted them to be. Now and then a man stood, stretched, made his limbs work, cursed softly, groaned, and slouched into his robes again, pummeled by bone-chilling cold so bad that every slight eddy of air was a torment.

Long before dawn, they were off again, using the smallest hint of the coming day to navigate through the Gallatin River flats. When the sun did burst over the mountain ridges, the snow blinded them, and they squinted against the murderous brightness and pulled their hats low. In minutes his eyelids hurt, and every muscle around his eyes ached. The frost-covered horses walked wearily now, having gone long without food and water. Horses drank more water in the winter than in the summer, and wouldn't eat snow to allay their thirst. The Gallatin River had largely frozen over in the night.

The mountaineers let their horses drink at an open tributary creek and then dismounted and broke trail again.

"Are we close?" Sublette asked Bridger.

"This child don't think so. We got a piece to go."

"I've a mind to make camp, rest the horses for an hour, try to get something hot in us."

Bridger nodded and led them to a good spot, largely free of snow, where a fire could be built against a cliff that would throw the heat back at them. They cooked frozen beaver tail, fed the horses some cottonwood, warmed themselves, and then started out, knowing they could go only two more hours until darkness settled again. But the moon was already up, so they could continue deep into the night.

About dusk Bridger consulted with Fitzpatrick, and reported to Sublette. "This hyar's our creek. Ferguson and Ranne're over in the next drainage. But beyond hyar, I don't know."

"We're close, then. They'll be holed up around here."

They broke trail through unknown country that rose steadily. The horses had to be pulled and tugged now. Sublette's face ached, and he knew his fingers, cheeks, nose, and toes would be frostbitten a second time. Around him men cursed, slapped the offended flesh to drive life into it, and continued. They came to a large creek tending west, and decided that was the turnoff.

Sublette pulled his Hawken from its soft leather sheath, checked the priming, and fired into the quiet night. The roar shocked his ears. He reloaded, having trouble making his fingers work. They waited. No answering shot drifted to them. He tried again, and only silence replied.

"We'll go up this creek and fire every little while,"

Sublette said. The creek ran through woods, and the party stumbled over hidden logs and fought spidery branches the moonlight didn't reveal to them.

Then they heard the wolves, howling mournfully into the night, back and forth, one bunch to the south, another to the north. Sublette had the itch to murder the first one he spotted. They were nature's killing machines. Half of his men wore wolfhide hoods or hats because of the warm fur, and that was the only use for a wolf as far as he was concerned.

They fought their way up the drainage another two miles before the moon quit them, and made camp in an elk yard cleaned of snow. That night they built a bonfire and warmed themselves half at a time, frontside and backside. But no one slept. No one had answered their periodic shots, and in that fire-breached darkness each was wondering how Ferguson and Ranne went under.

Chapter 41

The rescue party did not return. Two bitter days rose and fell without news. The sun barely crawled above the nearby mountains and then plummeted into another endless December night.

Skye scanned the trails restlessly, his eyes watering and hurting from the blinding light of the snow, but saw nothing. A vast silence permeated the mountains. He longed for the call of a bird.

All the firewood and green cottonwood was exhausted, and the camp itself was in peril. Meat was running low; they needed a couple of buffalo and fast. Skye studied the country farther down the tributary creek they were on, tiring himself as he pushed through thick ridges of snow. He came to a like place with plenty of cottonwood, a little grass swept clean by wind, and open water. He would move there even if it was windier than the present camp.

When he came back he gathered the reluctant camp tenders, who hated being exposed to bitter cold, and told them they would move camp that day.

"Four or five hundred yards downriver. Not too hard, mates. Horses'll tramp a path for us. There's plenty of wood and feed, and we'll be that much closer to some buffalo."

"What gives you the right to boss us around?" asked Scott.

The man had been sour toward Skye ever since the battle with the Blackfeet, and now he sounded truculent. Every camp tender knew the answer; Sublette had put Skye in charge.

"Let's get moving," said Skye, not answering. "We've a lot to do."

"I said what gives you the right?"

"Mr. Scott, I'd like you to pick out six or seven horses, drive them ahead of us, make a trail. Follow my prints along the creek."

"I don't feel like it. That's too much work for this kind of cold. We should wait for Sublette."

Skye stared at Scott a moment, wondering whether to confront him, and then turned to Pombert and the Creoles. "We can be set up and warm before dark."

Pombert smiled and nodded. The Creoles drifted into their huts and emerged better dressed against the cold. They had all moved camp many times and hardly needed instruction.

"What do we do with the trappers' outfits?" asked Bouleau.

"Move them. We're each tending camp for certain trappers. Their outfits are your responsibility."

"I'm staying," said Scott.

Skye turned to the man. "Then stay," he said.

The rest started to dismantle the huts, pack gear, gather the miserable horses. Moving camp was a formidable business, especially on a day with a bitter wind to add to the misery. It would take hours to build new huts and throw the buffalo hides over them and start fires again.

Scott stared sullenly as the others began to work. But when Estevan and Lapointe began dismantling Scott's lodge, he howled. "Leave that there," he bawled. Scott loomed a foot over Estevan.

Skye's patience was running thin. Life in a wilderness camp in weather well below zero on Fahrenheit's scale was precarious. It was impossible to stay, but moving would be hard, cruel work. Scott stood six inches higher than Skye, and didn't lack brute strength, but if the matter had to be forced, Skye decided to force it.

"All right, Scott," Skye said, waiting.

"Think you can whip me, Skye?"

"It's Mister Skye, mate."

"Think you know what to do? You've been in the mountains a long time and know what to do?"

Skye didn't reply. He stepped closer. He would hurt Scott, but he didn't want to. He had learned a few things in the Royal Navy.

"Well, aren't you the tough one, throwing weight around," Scott said.

That was good. Scott was using words rather than fists. Skye stepped closer. "Get to work, or try me if you want."

"I never take orders from a stinking Englishman."

Skye stepped closer until he was almost chest to chest. "Show me," said Skye softly. His breath plumed the air. He stood ready, waiting for Scott's move.

"I quit," said Scott, whirling away. "Tell Sublette."

Skye watched the man retreat. Scott had nowhere to go and would be back in an hour. Skye nodded at the rest and they began the miserable exodus. They toiled through the brief day, dragging gear, driving horses, cleaning snow away from the sites of the new huts, trying to start fires when the sparks off their flints died before they nested in tinder. Skye finally sent Pombert back for some live coals because none of them could start a fire with flint and steel.

Scott packed his horse, pulled his thick robe around him, and smiled.

"I'm going to the Shoshones," he said. "Tell Sublette he owes me and I'll collect at rendezvous."

"If you make it."

Scott glowered. "You think I can't."

"It's a long way."

They all watched his back until he vanished. Skye didn't like it. Sublette would blame him for provoking the trouble and losing a man. But the camp had to be moved, and Skye thought he had waited a day too long at that.

They still weren't settled when the early dusk overtook them. Skye grimly chopped firewood first—that was the critical need and the key to surviving the next fierce night. They picketed the horses on the cleared grass, worked at building buffalo-robe huts with numb fingers and frozen ears, and finally crawled into their new huts, frozen, exhausted, and hungry.

Scott didn't return. Skye wished he would, not because the man would help out but because the man would kill himself through his own misjudgment.

The next day dawned clear and breathtakingly cold. None of them dared venture beyond their three-sided huts, built to trap the heat of the fires before them. Skye had never seen a winter's day like this; blinding bright, cruel, and murderous. Sublette didn't show up all day. In an odd way that comforted Skye. The booshway wouldn't quit until he had given Ferguson and Ranne every chance.

Then, at dusk, the trappers quietly rode in, frost-rimed men on silver-patched horses, hunched deep in saddles, buffalo robes over their laps and legs. Skye watched anxiously as they drifted in one by one. Sublette studied the new camp, nodded, and tried to dismount, falling into the snow because his limbs didn't work.

The other trappers tumbled off, unable to stand or function. Skye helped them down and to the fires. Pombert and the Creoles rushed into the cold to help. Sublette warmed himself at the nearest blaze without saying anything. The result of the search was obvious to all.

Skye dreaded the questioning he would receive once the trappers were settled. But what happened couldn't be helped.

"This is a good place," Sublette said. "Where's Scott?"

"He quit. Headed for the Shoshones."

"Why?"

Skye sighed, wondering what to say. "Wouldn't move."

"Did he test you?"

"Yes."

Sublette nodded. Skye waited for more, but there wasn't any. He supposed it was a rebuke. A better man could have talked sense to Scott. Now the company had lost a man.

Chastened, Skye returned to his camp tending. The trappers looked half-frozen, too tired to eat, and miserable. They had brought a frozen elk haunch with them, so the camp tenders set to work roasting it. Later, when they all had feasted and warmed before the roaring fires, Sublette told his story.

"We checked three drainages and never saw sign of those ol' coons," he said. "We plumb froze to death, fought drifts, weathered hard nights, but we kept looking. Covered a lot of land. None of us was keen on giving up. They're dead or alive—we don't know. Probably gone under. We're feeling lower'n a snake's belly. They were good men. I'd trade a thousand Scotts for each of 'em," Sublette said. "They made the beaver come."

"Your men look bad," Skye said.

"Frostbite mostly. I got some flesh going black. I hope it doesn't mortify. Every one of us has some frostbit flesh."

"It don't spile in the mountains," said Bridger. "If our flesh falls offen us, we'll freeze it and keep it for poor doin's and eat it when we need it."

No one laughed.

Skye found himself wanting some encouragement. He had moved the camp and now man and animal were better off. He didn't hear it from Sublette or the trappers. But neither did they complain. Maybe they expected him to do it. Maybe that was why Sublette put him in charge. Skye pondered that in the orange firelight, wondering why the esteem of these men meant so much to him. He would abandon them next summer, but here he was, nursing every sign of approval. Maybe it was just that no one had ever approved of him. Maybe it was because these mountaineers were taciturn, especially in weather like this that put a man on edge. Or maybe their minds were simply occupied with Ranne and Ferguson, each of them wondering what had become of their veteran friends. If death could overwhelm two of the wiliest men in the brigade, it could overwhelm any of them.

The next days were among the worst in Skye's young life. If anything, the cold was worse. It didn't matter how many fires a man surrounded himself with; he was always on the brink of freezing solid. Nothing in a fo'c'sle, or high in the rigging on a bitter day at sea matched this cold and misery. Ranne and Ferguson didn't come in, but no one expected them to. Man or horse couldn't travel without frostbiting their lungs. They couldn't hunt, either, and Sublette put them on short rations. If they couldn't make meat soon, they would be eating one of the horses. Beyond the physical misery, gloom overtook them. The sun scarcely appeared. Men were too cold to talk, and sunk into their icy robes.

Skye kept himself occupied just by dreaming of his return to civilization. Wilderness had nothing to offer him, except a few seductive weeks in early summer when the sheer joy of the warm season lifted him. But all he really had gotten out of this was boredom, toil, fear, and anger.

Christmas came and went, but no one celebrated it, and half of those in camp weren't aware of it. Then one day, in the space of an hour, it warmed. Skye marveled. One minute he had lain in his robes, waiting for life to begin, a while later he threw off his robes, felt delicious warm air eddy through his buckskins, felt a wild liberty build in him, the freedom of a man emerging from prison, and stepped into a mild afternoon.

"Chinook," said Bridger. "I mind the time we were

plumb froze to death, and down to stewing shoe leather for soup, when the Divil comes up outa them geysers on the Yellerstone and heats up the country almost to biling. So hot in January we was drenched in sweat. I had me a bath and went courtin' Injun wimmen."

"How long do these chinooks last?" Skye asked.

"Maybe long enough to get us to a Crow village," said Sublette. "Let's go."

"You mind if I leave some shelter and fixings behind for Ferguson and Ranne?" Skye asked.

Sublette shook his head. "They've gone under, Mister Skye."

"I'd like to leave a shelter up, and hang some pemmican from a limb. I'd like to leave some kindling, and I'll leave my flint and steel."

"Don't ever be without flint and steel. If they're alive and have their rifles, they won't need flint and steel. Any man with a rifle has both."

Skye considered it a revelation. He had never thought of a flintlock and some gunpowder as a means of starting a fire. He still had much to learn.

"Sure, ol' coon, you leave a camp for them," Sublette said. "Half shelter, dry firewood, some beaver meat hung high up. If they're alive, they'll know where to find us—with the Crows. And if they aren't alive, we'll donate the camp to the Blackfeet."

"I just have a feeling," said Skye, wondering why he thought they were alive and holed up in a place he could almost envision.

"You're a mountaineer, Mister Skye," Sublette said. It was the compliment that Skye had craved for days.

Chapter 42

The brigade fought its way over the pass to the Yellow-stone country, and it was like arriving in the promised land. The chinook winds were even warmer on the east slope and had eaten away most of the snow.

But man and beast needed a rest after wrestling with soggy six-foot drifts, so they camped on the great bend of the Yellowstone again. They were in dire need of meat, so Sublette sent every hunter out while the rest made camp. One by one they drifted back around twi-light, all of them emptyhanded. The game had vanished. Deer and antelope would be herded up for the winter—somewhere. Buffalo would also herd into groups—somewhere. Anything else that might make meat was hibernating or had fled south.

They ate the last of their emergency pemmican, scarcely two mouthfuls apiece for the twenty-seven men left in the brigade, and settled down for the night with empty bellies and a sense of foreboding. The horses fared better on brown bunchgrass that grew abundantly north of the river.

Skye knew from bitter experience what life was going to be like without food, and set out in the twilight to remedy the situation. He hiked along the riverbank until he found what he wanted, an inlet covered with dead, brown cattails, their stalks decaying on the ground. He cut through the frosty soil and examined the roots. Yes, they were edible—smaller and harder than when they pumped life to the fronds above, but they would make a food of sorts. He dug several pounds of the roots, washed them in the bitter-cold river, and got back to camp just before dark.

He lacked the means to turn roots into flour, the way the Indians did, but he found some smooth river rocks and a flat rock surface, and began mashing the roots into pulp. Then he boiled them in the company cookpot, drained off the water, and ended up with a tan mush that tasted bad but was thick and starchy. Some of the others watched him disconsolately, scarcely aware that he was producing food. They were meat eaters.

When the mush had cooled he ate some of it, enough to satisfy his hungers, and set some aside for breakfast and lunch. The only man among them to pay attention was Tom Fitzpatrick, who watched, tasted, and smiled.

"I'm always looking for ways to get along," he said. "This is one I didn't know about, ol' coon."

"They kept me alive when I had nothing. I mashed them when I couldn't boil them. I had no fire for weeks."

"All the better to learn about," Fitzpatrick said. "We could feed this camp if we had to."

"Don't know that most of 'em'll touch it," Skye replied. "Not my favorite taste."

Fitzpatrick smiled. "We call it the Rocky Mountain College. Some learn their lessons—and the rest go under."

Fitzpatrick helped himself to another finger-load, and settled down beside Skye for some serious eating.

"What do you think happened to Scott?" Skye asked.

"He would've headed for the Shoshones. Probably made it because of the chinook."

"What do you think happened to Ranne and Ferguson?"

"I'd guess they're denned up with a b'ar."

"Alive?"

"I think so. B'ar would be warm. They couldn't hear our shots from in there."

"What if the bear woke up?"

"They do all winter. But they're not full of fight. Couple ol' coons could go in there for a snooze, long as they were quiet about it."

"Are you whistling in the dark, mate, or do you put stock in it?"

Fitzpatrick grinned and shrugged. "The wild world isn't what we think. I've gone alone from the mountains to Saint Louis. A man who's resourceful can make it."

"Why're you here, mate?"

"It's a calling. Maybe I'd have been a priest. This is religion."

"Religion?"

"This is holy, Skye. Don't you feel it?"

"No. It's mostly boredom, fear, pain, discomfort—and starvation. What's wrong with a roof over your head? Pretty women?"

"Rules, Skye, rules."

"It's Mister Skye, mate."

Fitzpatrick laughed and helped himself to more mush. "That's a rule I could do without. But as long as it's rooted in a sentiment that would please any son of Ireland, I'll accept it."

"I'm going east next summer. What advice have you?"

"Don't count Indians friends when they're friendly, and don't count them enemies when they threaten you. Avoid them unless you can't help a meeting. Every encounter means trouble. The friendly ones want every item in your kit, the rifle especially, but they'll settle for your horses or a kettle or all your knives. Take some twists of tobacca with you. Tobacca's a peace offering, and it binds them if they accept it. But don't count on it. Don't count on anything. This evening I was counting on an empty belly and now I'm full. I'm indebted."

That night the wolves howled. Skye had never heard such wild yelps, eerie screams, yapping sounds. Maybe he could shoot one in the morning. He didn't relish eating dog but he relished an empty belly less.

Sublette and the hunters saddled up before dawn, intending to ride straight toward the northeast where the wolf chorus had erupted and kept on all night.

Skye wished he could go. His duties locked him to the camp.

"Start the cookfires, Mister Skye," said Sublette. "That yapping last night was buffalo talk."

"How would you know that?"

"You'll learn it if you stay in the mountains."

Skye watched every free trapper and hunter in the outfit throw saddles over shaggy horses, which looked fat inside their hairy coats. Skye knew better. His mare was ribby under that matted hair, and his colt was worse. The horses wouldn't have much energy in them this time of year.

That afternoon they rode in—without meat, looking dour. Seventeen had left, but ten returned. The others were still out prowling, and might stay out overnight.

Skye waited patiently for Sublette to unsaddle and picket his horse.

"The wolves downed an old bull so poor there wasn't much to begin with. Naught but a skeleton and half-eaten hide now. Loner bulls like that, they leave the herd to die. Or the young bulls drive 'em out. Fitzpatrick says you made some paste out of roots. Got some?"

Skye dug into his pot and handed Sublette some of the mush.

"Gawdawfulest stuff I ever put between lips," the

booshway said. "You damn Brits don't know what food's supposed to taste like. Line up the camp tenders and go harvest a pile of it."

Skye laughed.

He dragooned the camp tenders and set them to work along the banks of the Yellowstone, digging up roots out of half-frozen bog areas. They didn't get much, and grumbled the whole time, but ere long they had reason to be grateful. The hunters returned with nothing, mad and cussing and ready to chew out anyone who complained.

That night the whole brigade dined on a few mouthfuls of cattail root, duly pulverized and boiled and seasoned with a little salt. They didn't say much, and the ridicule that Skye was expecting never erupted.

"Poor doin's." That was all anyone said. But Skye sensed respect. He had conjured up a meal of sorts, and the English pork-eater had shown the mountaineers a thing or two.

The next day the wind shifted north and they knew they had better hurry to the Crow villages before the next blast of arctic air. They packed without breakfast. They were plumb out of everything now, and full of self-pity, gnawing hunger, and rage. The hunters set off; they would rejoin the brigade down the Yellowstone a day's journey.

They rode with the wind, the slivers of icy air on their backs, numbing their necks, bullying the weary horses. At the nooning Skye boiled water and served it. The brigade groused but drank the hot water.

"I always knowed that when it comes to cooking, Skye, you're some," said Bridger. "This hyar's the best concoction ye ever did serve us."

An hour later the mountain veterans taught Skye a thing or two. A ravine choked with buffaloberry had survived the predations of birds, and the company set to work collecting the remaining silvery fruit. But it came to mouthful apiece. Skye was growing faint.

They halted at a place where the river plunged through a narrows hemmed by grassy slopes. The hunters and trappers found them there, and had nothing to offer.

"The trouble with winter is that the game herds up, and you got to know where they yard," Beckwourth said.

That observation didn't feed anyone. Skye had one more idea. He borrowed a fishhook and line from Tom Fitzpatrick and wondered how to manufacture a fly. The Yellowstone was running low and transparent, and he thought it would yield some trout. He found a bit of frayed leather, odd threads dangling off it, and worked his hook through it. It didn't look like an insect. It didn't look like anything.

Behind him the camp tenders built fires close to the limestone cliff and put up half-shelters because it looked like the weather would turn in the night. Mare's tails had corrugated the heavens all day. The brigade was in a surly mood, and demanding that Sublette send an express rider to the Crows. Food for some foofaraws, powder, and lead.

Skye hardly knew one freshwater fish from another and no one had ever described their habits to him. But he thought a mouthful of trout would help, so he rigged a pole, dropped his bizarre thing into the Yellowstone, wiggled it gently while there was daylight enough to attract the denizens of the deeps.

And felt a hard yank.

A minute later he beached a fat trout.

"You damn Brits don't know what good food is," said Sublette, eyeing the three-pound silvery fish. Skye grunted, freed his hook, thrust the flopping fish at Sublette, who held it as if it were a hot potato, and dropped his line into the river again.

In the space of an hour he caught four more, and then the light faded. That came to only a few mouthfuls per man, but they all were fed after a fashion. And the Yanks weren't making fun of him this time, although they cussed the fishbones and opined that there were good reasons most tribes hated fish.

"Thank you, Mister Skye," said William Sublette. "This is the miracle of the loaves and fishes, Royal Navy style. I am coming to admire the British pallet. But you forgot the sauce."

"Get out the traps," said Skye, "and put the fishheads in them, well away from camp. It was something I learned to do on the Columbia."

Sublette stared, nodded, and gave the command. Skye thought they might catch breakfast.

Chapter 43

The fish-baited traps yielded an otter, raccoon, and fox. William Sublette watched the camp tenders swiftly gut and clean the animals and salvage the meat. There wasn't enough to feed twenty-seven starving men much, but each man would have a few mouthfuls of gray meat—if he could overcome his queasiness about eating it.

The cold had returned, but it wasn't as severe as the spell they had endured in the Three Forks country. A nippy northwind probed at Sublette's clothing, finding ways to chill his neck and ears and ankles. He ached for summertime, when the mountains glowed and a man had few worries. The hot fires in each of the four messes warmed frontsides but not backsides, and the men were in a foul mood.

The camp tenders set the meat to roasting over the fierce fires after carefully setting aside the offal, which would be used tonight to bait traps again—if the hunters failed once more. Sublette sometimes thought this brigade was cursed with grief. It had lost too many men, endured too much hardship. And it would have been much worse off without Skye. The Englishman had found ways to feed them more than once. Miserable food, things the free trappers despised—but things that kept them alive. Skye was showing every sign of being a natural mountaineer and a leader.

Beckwourth was having his usual good time. "I don't think I'll eat otter," he said to Skye. "I prefer roasted camp tender."

The men had been bantering with Skye these past weeks, a sure sign that the Englishman had become one of them. Sublette watched Skye work, admiring the man's industry and resourcefulness.

Every man got a few bites of meat that morning. Some whined about it but no one refused it. The mean wind sliced into them all—this upper Yellowstone country was famous for its winter winds—and Sublette was eager to get going, put the wind to their backs, and hasten to the Crow villages.

Once again the brigade packed and loaded their horses. The hunters fanned out, more determined than ever to make meat and lots of it. Their senses and instincts, always keen, had been sharpened this morning by deep hunger that verged on starvation. Sublette thought they would succeed this hard day.

He waited for Skye to load his gear on his mare and start east once again under a weak winter sun that promised more heat than it gave. He fell in beside Skye, choosing to walk rather than ride, so he could talk with the Englishman.

"Mister Skye, what are your plans?"

"The same as always."

"You know, you'd have a future with the company if you would stay in the mountains."

"I'm sorry to disappoint you, Mr. Sublette."

"You're a natural. You found food when a brigade full of veteran mountaineers couldn't find any. You wisely moved camp when you had to, in spite of the serious grousing of a misfit."

"I did what I had to. We were out of firewood and feed."

"They tell me you dealt with Scott very well—patiently at first, giving him a chance to cool down, and then firmly. Faced with a fight, he caved in."

"I lost a man."

"No, good riddance. You did what you had to. A good leader does just that. Scott resented you ever since he proved himself a coward in the fight. They all saw it, and they all saw you. After that he was just looking for ways to cause you grief. I was expecting something like that when I put you in charge."

"It seems a man's every act is watched and reported to you."

"A brigade is a close-knit outfit, Mister Skye. Reported isn't quite the word. I have never asked or expected men to report about the conduct of other men in the company. But because this is wilderness, and we're never far from trouble—starvation, sickness, Indians, thirst, thunderstorms, hail, freezing to death, drowning—these things are chewed over, and rehashed, and chewed over again. It can't be helped."

"It's the navy all over, mate. When you fight beside men, they look you over and you look them over."

Sublette nodded. They hiked along the north bank of the Yellowstone after detouring around a canyon, and now passed through a forest of bare cottonwoods. Rugged white-tipped mountains rose in the north, separate from the great spine of the Stony Mountains that lay south of the river. This was the raw, noble, harsh country the Crows called home, glorious in the summer, vicious in the winter.

"You may have surmised that I'm leading up to something, Mister Skye. You've proven yourself even in the brief time you've been with us. Next summer, at rendezvous, I'm going to propose to my partners that you become a brigade leader. There would be a base wage of eight hundred dollars and bonuses based on the number of pelts your brigade brings in. With your skills, you would probably be rich in three or four years."

Skye squinted at the distant mountains, which were dazzling in the morning light. His blue eyes, nested in hollows of reddened and weather-chafed flesh, seemed to seek visions in the thin winter air, and concealed from Sublette the thoughts that were crawling through Skye's mind. "I'll think about it, sir," he said at last.

Sublette wouldn't be deterred. "Mister Skye, I well know your lifelong vision of educating yourself and going into business. It nursed you through years of grief. And nothing I'm proposing now would keep you from it if you eventually want to pursue it. But you've a chance here to establish yourself for the rest of your life. Will you at least think it over?"

"Yes, of course."

Gunshot drifted on the wind, faint but unmistakable. The sound gladdened Sublette. It didn't signify war or trouble; it signified game. "Hear that?" he asked Skye. "That's meat."

Skye smiled.

An hour later they came to a noble stand of cottonwoods beside the river, and found the hunters waiting there, fires already going. It was only midmorning, but the brigade was about to feast.

"Fat cow," said Bridger, who had been out with the hunters. "In fact, three fat cows and one calf, and as many as we want. Two, three miles yonder." He pointed north.

Fat cow! Word whipped through the brigade. Fat cow!

Sublette swiftly dispatched half a dozen camp tenders to help butcher and haul the meat. They would take it all and the hides, too, good gifts for the Crows. Butchering and transporting four buffalo was a major undertaking. They had come only a few miles this day, but so what? Starving men would have fat cow, and the horses could use a rest.

"Mister Skye, you stay. Unload and picket the horses on whatever grass you can find. We'll stay the night. This hyar campsite even has a name. Big Timber, named after those noble cottonwoods yonder by Lewis and Clark—actually Clark, coming down the Yellowstone with Sacajewea and a few men, heading east to meet Lewis at the confluence of the Missouri."

Skye knew nothing of that, but he nodded and set to work, unloading the horses and picketing them one by one on brown grass where they could make a living. A vicious wind wailed through the naked branches of the cottonwoods, shooting ice into Sublette's flesh, but he didn't mind.

Fat cow!

Sublette stepped off his horse, unloaded and picketed it, and then cut deadwood from some nearby cottonwoods. It would burn hot and fast. Cottonwood smoke was foul compared to the resinous smoke from pine wood, but it made a good fire. He kept his Hawken rifle at his side, as always. Just when you thought you might be safe from the red devils, that's when they surprised you. But he had little fear of them now, in the dead of winter, when they would be telling stories in their lodges.

He noticed that Skye wasn't armed, and thought to tell the man. There were things Skye needed to learn.

"Mister Skye, where's your rifle?"

"With my gear, sir."

"Have it with you. Someday that practice will save your life. And no matter what you're doing, eye the horizons constantly."

Skye nodded, collected his rifle, checked the charge of powder in the pan, and set it close to him while he picketed horses.

By the time the first of the meat arrived—several huge chunks of haunch laced to the saddle—Skye and Sublette had a camp set up.

"Shall I start roasting it, sir?" Skye asked.

Sublette shook his head. "It ain't hump. Set it aside."

Skye looked disappointed but said nothing.

Together, they pulled the red meat off the packhorse

and set it aside. Sublette felt his belly rumble. He and Skye could be cooking this meat right now; he and Skye could be feasting, filling their empty bellies at last while the rest were butchering. But the thought of humpmeat, fatty and tender and laced with flavor, stayed him. Even starving men should wait a while for humpmeat. Or tongue. That was another feast. There was a lesson Skye would learn soon enough.

Another burdened horse arrived, bearing a green hide with a huge chunk of meat and bone within, along with a tongue. Sublette opened the parcel and eyed the meat happily.

"Mister Skye, that's hump. Run a cooking rod through it and start it roasting over a low fire. You'll see that it's worth the wait. And then start the tongue cooking."

"My stomach doesn't agree, sir."

Sublette laughed. "Damned English don't know fat cow from poor bull," he said. "You see how that meat arrived special—all wrapped in a hide? There's a mountain message in it."

Sublette helped Skye rig up the fire and block the wind that was whipping the flame. "I've camped here at Big Timber half a dozen times and every time the wind pretty near drove me out," he grumbled.

No meat arrived for a long time, and then the whole brigade arrived at once, packhorses loaded, crude travois dragging huge hulks of buffalo.

"We been samplin'," said Bridger, whose cheeks were bloodstained. "Best lights I ever bit into."

Skye looked appalled.

"Raw buffler liver, Mister Skye—it's a mountain man's sweet. This child'll show ye next time. And maybe we'll roast some boudins, too, as long as you're a pork-eater."

"You actually eat raw meat?" Skye asked.

"Mister Skye, we got vices ye never heard of. We'll teach ye the whole lot of 'em, one by one," Bridger said. "Now whar's that hump we expressed down hyar? I'm plumb sick of yore vittles—raccoon and swamp roots. This child don't eat coons and roots, you hear me?"

But Skye was grinning. He pulled the dripping hump-meat off the fire and began sawing down to the bone, sending aromas into the wind that drove Sublette half mad. The meat, blackened on the outside, remained pink at the center and dripped juices. Solemnly, the brigade gathered around the cookfire to observe all this.

"Ye don't get any, Mister Skye," said Bridger. "Ye got to cook the next hump, yonder, and then ye can have our leavings. That's what ye desarve for feeding us dead fox and marsh roots."

"That's right," said Tom Fitzpatrick solemnly. "We've all decided that you don't get any. You can stick with your dainty British cookery."

Sublette watched Skye redden and then relax, and then bellow. "Mr. Bridger, Mr. Fitzpatrick," he roared, "cook your own bloody meat."

Old Gabe Bridger—who was scarcely older than Skye, actually—cocked an eyebrow, grimaced, looked exceedingly pained, and then hoorawed.

No pork-eater was Skye, Sublette thought. He was a mountaineer now.

Chapter 44

"The pale men are coming!"

Many Quill Woman heard the village crier, Buffalo Hoof, chant his message among the lodges of the Kicked-in-the-Bellies. Swiftly she drew a thick buffalo robe about her and slipped through the low lodge door into a wintry day.

She saw no trappers, but that was as it should be. Even in winter, the village wolf soldiers had detected the pale men far away, and reported the news to the chief, Arapooish, and the elders and seers. By the time the pale men entered, the village elders would be gathered before the chief's lodge to receive them.

Tonight there would be feasts and merriment. The People of the Raven had little to do in winter but tell stories and have good times around the lodge fires.

She waited impatiently, giving place to the warriors and elders as a young single woman should. Had he come? She would know soon. But she already knew, having seen with inner vision. Even though Skye had talked of going far to the east and the big waters there, he would come. She smiled. Magpie had known more of his future than he himself had. Magpie was a true counselor who saw all things and led Many Quill Woman to her understandings. Magpie didn't go south in the winter the way other birds did, but stayed right there, making a living even in the cold season.

Swiftly the lodges emptied themselves as the people dressed against the icy wind and gathered in the harsh sunlight to witness this event. Maybe the liar Beckwourth would be with them again. Beckwourth called himself an Absaroka chief, which amused her people. But he was a brave warrior and had fought beside her brothers in wars against the Siksika, so they would honor Beckwourth and supply him with women. Beckwourth never had enough of them. Many Quill Woman hoped that her father entertained no such notions about her. Let Beckwourth winter with Pine Leaf again. They were made for each other. The thought made her smile. Pine Leaf, the revered warrior woman of her people, didn't really like Beckwourth either but Beckwourth didn't know that.

How handsome was her village this year. They were fat because they had made a fine fall hunt, and had many robes and parfleches full of pemmican and frozen buffalo quarters hanging high above the snapping jaws of dogs. They had traded many beaver pelts at the rendezvous and now the warriors were decked out in crimson or blue, and women were wrapped in thick blankets with black stripes at either end, and had tied their straight hair with ribbons gotten from the traders. Oh, how she loved her village, with smoke curling from its many lodges, and fat horses gathered nearby, safe from the Siksika dogs. Here were great men and seers, the proudest of the Absaroka people, choosing to live in the village of the great Arapooish, vanquisher of the Siksika, terror of the Lakota, and the only chief in many years who blessed his people with good times.

She saw the pale men enter the village, and as always

they excited curiosity. Where were their women? Why did these men come to the mountains without their wives and children? This thing had baffled her people and none of the elders or seers could explain it. Somewhere, these trappers had hidden their women. Most of the Absaroka had never seen a pale woman. Many Quill Woman had never seen one, and she suspected they must be ugly and mean, so the pale men were ashamed of them. It was said that the pale women were kept in a hot land far to the east because they could not take cold weather, and there the pale men repaired now and then to add to their families. What a strange custom.

The Goddamns made a great show, riding in procession into the village, escorted by the Kit Fox Society, the young warriors doing the policing of the village this winter. The Goddamns did not sit proudly on their ponies, with backs straight, like any Absaroka man or woman. These pale men slouched, and spat—a terrible insult— and even looked directly at the Absaroka instead of averting their gazes as politeness required. Still, they made a great spectacle, and Many Quill Woman thrilled at the sight of these barbarous men, so empty of manners and so lax in their conduct that they scandalized her people.

Their terrible beards plumed their faces until one could scarcely see the face hidden by them, as if the beards were masks to conceal these men from the eyes of the seers, who plumbed the depths of all mortals. They wore magnificent hats and headdresses, all of their own design, obviously their secret medicine. Some were made of fox or beaver or otter, some made of buffalo or the material they called felt. They carried their heavy rifles in saddle sheaths, usually fringed and decorated. But not one of them dressed like another, and each was so different that she could hardly say that they were all of one tribe.

She watched eagerly, awaiting the sight of the one she ached to see, and wondering if she would recognize him behind his beard. She would. She would know his blue eyes and his big nose. She spotted Beckwourth—ah, how he was smiling, his brown eyes dancing with delight. And she spotted others she knew from previous visits, all bristling with beards. Many passed, strange men, and then she saw him near the rear, just as he saw her.

Her heart soared. "Mister Skye!"

"Victoria!"

He had come. Her inner vision had told her he would, but she had doubted and now was ashamed. His gaze bored into her, searching her, noting everything about her, and she flushed with warmth, even in the biting cold. But he had stopped the procession and he knew suddenly that he must move on. There were welcomings to be completed before she could greet him.

She raced toward the great lodge of Arapooish, twenty-two poles, big enough for six wives. There would these pale men be welcomed. She felt aglow. She could not say why she felt so happy. Skye was not a great man among them, and he was near the rear, giving place to the leaders of the brigade. Why did she care? Maybe a witch had cast a spell, or even an evil spirit from under the waters, swimming among the fish in the places of the dead.

The leaders of the pale men dismounted before Arapooish and the elders, leaving their horses to the lesser ones like Skye who stood back, a man without status among them.

Beckwourth did the honors. He could speak the tongue of the People.

"My esteemed chief, Arapooish, Rotten Belly, we have come to offer you gifts," he said, enjoying himself. But Beckwourth always enjoyed himself, even when he shouldn't. "Here, behold the tobacco," he said, handing her chief a twist. That was ceremony. The gift of tobacco signified many things, but most of all peace and friendship. Her chief nodded, and his son, Arrow, accepted.

"And here, behold the blankets," he said. The one called Sublette, leader of the brigade and a trader, handed the chief two beautiful green blankets with black stripes at their ends. Rotten Belly handed these treasures to his son.

"And these are for the beautiful wives and daughters of Arapooish," Beckwourth said. The trader chief handed hanks of bright ribbon—bold blue, yellow, red, green, orange—to Arrow.

"And behold this, great chief of the Absaroka."

This time Sublette brought forth a heavy rifle from his pack, along with a horn of powder and a bar of the soft metal.

"Ah!" The Absaroka warriors crowded close. This was a noble offering from the pale men. "Aieee!"

This gift the chief accepted with his own strong hands. He hefted the shooting stick, cocked it, examined its beauty, and smiled.

"My friend Beckwourth, we welcome you to our happy village. We are as brothers to you, and you have sealed our friendship with your splendid offerings. Together in battle we are a match for Siksika or Lakota even though they are many more than we are. May you enjoy your time with us, and may our lodges shelter you from the fury of the Cold Maker. The women will erect our council lodge for you, and it will hold many Goddamns. The rest of the pale men will stay with their old friends and share our lodges. But tell me, Beckwourth. When will the pale men bring their wives so we may see them and try them?"

Beckwourth smiled. "Maybe soon, Rotten Belly. We are far from them, and must bring them a long way."

"Well, we await them. We are eager to see them, and often we wonder about them. I want one or two, and will give many robes for one. Come now, escort your headmen into my lodge, and we will smoke the pipe and counsel for a while." He eyed the crowd. "You women who are hospitable and of good heart toward the pale men, put up the council lodge, that these friends of the Absaroka may find warmth. The Cold Maker roars."

She watched the chief's lodge swallow the Goddamn headmen. Fitzpatrick, Sublette, Bridger, Beckwourth. She knew every one of them from other times. Arapooish's wives sought shelter in other lodges while the great ceremony of the pipe proceeded. Many women rushed to put up the poles of the council lodge, pull the massive buffalohide cover up the cone of poles, and pin its sides together with willow pins.

Now she was free. The sacred ceremony of the pipe might continue within the chief's lodge but all who were witnesses to the arrival were released. She sought Skye and found him beside a mare. He had cared for her, and she was fat, and so was the spirited little gray stallion at her side.

"Goddamn Skye sonofabitch," she said joyously.

He gaped at her as if he were buffalo-witted.

"Don't you know me?"

"Victoria. Of course."

"You come. I tell you so."

Skye smiled wryly. "You knew better than I did."

"You get many beaver?"

"No, I am a camp tender—I don't trap. Not yet. But how are you? Are you a warrior's woman now?"

The Goddamns were so ignorant. Anyone could tell from the way she wore her hair loose that she wasn't. The women who had men braided their hair. Couldn't he see that? "No damn good," she said. "We talk. I like my name, Victoria. I will take it. Come."

She beckoned him to her lodge and he followed, leading his horses. "Come, come, come," she said, irritably.

Then she presented him to her stern father, Walks Alone, and stepmother, Digs the Roots, who waited before the lodge huddled in their robes. They had met him at the rendezvous and had steered her away from him—and all pale men.

"This is the Goddamn for whom I waited," she told them in her tongue. "Magpie gave me the inner eye to see the man within the face-hair. He is from another tribe of

Goddamns, across the Big Water. Skye is his name, like the heaven above us. What a great name, for the whole home of stars and sun and moon. He will be great among them in a winter or two."

They nodded, reserved and curious. Then her father urged caution. "He is not great among them. He came near the end of the procession, one of the last and least. This is not good. We will ask Red Turkey Comb to see what must be seen, and I will make him a gift of a pony for it."

Victoria pushed back her annoyance and responded dutifully, as befit her station. "Yes, that would be good. We will learn about Mister Skye. Nothing escapes Red Turkey Comb."

Her father nodded, ushered Skye into the lodge, and performed the ceremony of the pipe with the man, while she and her stepmother, or little mother as one was called, and sister and brother observed silently.

Her father was welcoming Skye, but she knew that it was a formality. He had higher hopes for his oldest daughter.

Chapter 45

Skye marveled at the beauty of the Crow village. It nestled under sandstone bluffs, within an arc of a laughing creek, protected from the bitter winds that whistled across the rolling prairie above it. Each lodge was shielded by willow and chokecherry brush that further subdued the winds. The blackened peaks of the golden lodges leaked lazy smoke into a stark white, gray, and tan world.

Wherever Skye turned, he found the genius of these people making life bearable and comfortable. They had chosen a perfect site to winter. Cottonwood and willow forests offered plentiful firewood to feed the hearths of the lodges, while tawny bottomlands supported the village horse herd, and the sandstone escarpments on both sides of the creek corralled the horses.

They had put him and the other camp tenders and clerks in a sixteen-pole lodge made of twenty-seven buffalo hides sewn tightly together. It had taken a dozen women to raise the heavy lodge cover after they had erected the tripod and laid the other lodgepoles into its apex. After that they had spread buffalo robes on the ground within, layers of them until the icy earth no longer bit those who lay upon it.

Skye swiftly learned how to manipulate the leather ears of the lodge to harness the breezes and draw out the smoke of the small lodgefire. The women had hung an additional shoulder-high dew cloth from the lodgepoles within, which made the lodge so warm that a man could sleep without burying himself in robes. He had never seen a European tent half as comfortable.

Those first days he explored the village, examining lodge after lodge, admiring the artistry that brightened the lodges with figures of animals or geometric designs, or what he supposed were medicine symbols, household gods blessing those within. The veteran trappers had wintered with these Kicked-in-the-Bellies for several years, and had found berths in many lodges. Some had even been adopted by families or into the tribe.

He counted forty-one lodges, and using the mountaineer formula of eight to a lodge, calculated that something like three hundred and twenty or thirty persons inhabited this village. He felt its power and comfort and protection, felt its ancient knowledge of all the ways to find meat, or preserve food for emergencies. He felt the power in the bows and quivers of its warriors, and in the warrior societies that vied with each other for honor. He walked freely among these people, exchanging smiles because he couldn't talk with them.

He did not escape work here. As a camp tender he was responsible for cutting copious amounts of deadwood from the cottonwood groves, for the fires never ceased consuming fuel. He was also responsible for several horses as well as his own, and looked after them each morning.

Within a day or two after he arrived he felt a euphoria such as he had not experienced since boyhood. He could not explain this exultation, only that it coursed through every fiber of his being. Instead of cowering before a brutal northern winter and suffering its numbing cold, he found himself enjoying each bright day. The long nights bloomed into yarning and storytelling parties around hot lodgefires of the hospitable Crow. Most days, the sun warmed the intimate valley for a while, brightening the world of these cheerful people before vanishing midafternoon behind the western bluffs. But the winter didn't seem hard.

How could a man be melancholic in paradise? Yes, it was that, in its own magical fashion. He slept warm on three buffalo robes, and not even the presence of a dozen others disturbed his slumbers. He could not remember a happier time.

Each misty dawn, when the sun was rosing the bluffs, the village hunters, along with the trappers and mountaineers, saddled their winter-shaggy horses and rode out to make meat. It took constant effort to feed so many mouths.

In some ways, hunting was easier in the winter, except when the weather turned foul or bitter. The animals herded up, the mule deer and antelope forming into bands for mutual warmth and protection. The buffalo gathered into small herds in valleys where they could escape some of the wind. In heavy snow the buffalo could be driven into snowbanks, mired and surrounded, but these days, without much snow on the prairie, the hunting was harder and required more cunning.

The guns of the mountaineers contributed mightily to the village's larder that January of 1827, and that made them all the more welcome among the Absaroka. Massive quarters of buffalo hung from stout limbs, along with the carcasses of deer and antelope. Only elk were scarce this winter.

Skye heard about it all but was not free to hunt. Not yet. As the juniormost member of the brigade, he had the most work, and William Sublette did not neglect to keep him busy chopping wood for the brigade's hosts as well as the big lodge that housed the camp tenders. Even so, Skye had more free time than he had ever known. Time to explore, learn the ways of these brown people, master their arts and crafts and weaponry, and try to make friends even without the employment of words.

One twilight he pulled a buffalo robe around him and slipped outside for a breath of fresh air. Stars winked in the slate sky. He realized he was happy. He had never known what it was like to enjoy life.

He heard the wolves patrol the ridges. He often did. They boldly probed the camp most nights, the smell of meat drawing them in, but the frozen carcasses hung well above their snapping jaws.

"Goddamn Skye, I have waited for you to come, but you do not," said a low sweet voice beside him. He whirled. She was there, wrapped in the black-banded gray blanket she had been wearing about the village, the one he had given her.

He had been avoiding her, and she knew it.

"Victoria—"

"You have given me a good name. I have told the seers that this is my name now."

Somehow he felt snared by an invisible web that was spinning about him, and it troubled him. He had other plans, dreams spun in a ship's brig to keep him alive when he had no reason to live. He could not let this slim savage demolish them.

She studied him—one could take it as a glare, so intense was her gaze—from brown eyes that radiated irritability and love in strange harness. Jet hair framed her sharp features. The hair vanished under her blanket, along with the rest of her lithe figure. He had never thought of beauty in these terms—only in pale, blue-eyed English terms—and found her all the more intoxicating because she awakened something unforeseen in him.

It wasn't just Victoria that was intoxicating him. This wild sweet liberty, this coming to manhood in the mountains, this strange sovereignty over his own life and destiny, far from organized society—all these things had stirred something so profound that he was having doubts about everything he believed in.

She waited patiently for him to speak, but he could muster no answer. How could he tell her that he didn't want her attentions?

"Sonofabitch, Skye, I go now." She turned to leave.

"No—Victoria—"

"I am cold. I came to invite you to the lodge of Red Turkey Comb. He is a seer and a man with great power and will help you find vision. Then you will know what you must do and what powers have been given you. He will see you if you offer him a gift. Have you something to give?"

Skye didn't. He could scarcely be poorer. "No . . ."

"Yes you do. He is old, and his fires need wood."

"Wood?" Skye veered toward the council lodge and plucked up an armload of cottonwood limbs he had cut that day. He wasn't at all sure why she was taking him to a shaman, and it would probably offend his own beliefs, but he was curious. What could a savage mystic do?

She smiled and led him toward a humble lodge set apart from the rest of the village. There she scratched gently on the door flap, and they heard a muffled voice from within, which she answered in her own tongue. Then she gestured him in. He pulled aside the flap and penetrated into a dark lodge with only embers in its firepit. The shaman sat beyond the coals, silent and barely visible.

Skye set the wood down while she said something to the old man. He nodded, beckoned Skye to sit on his right. She settled herself across from the old man in the place of least honor according to custom, and loosened her blanket. She wore a white doeskin dress, brightly quilled in geometric patterns. She fed some of Skye's wood into the embers. In a moment they blazed and swiftly warmed the lodge, the flickering light playing off her brown face and glinting in her hair.

"Red Turkey Comb is pleased with the wood. He had none this night, and now he will be warm."

Skye realized how much a simple gift could mean, and knew that he would leave an armload for the old man each day. As the light bloomed, he took the measure of the shaman. This one was not at all ascetic in appearance, but a heavy man with sagging flesh and a measuring gaze.

The shaman listened quietly to Victoria for a while.

"I tell him about you. I tell him you confused and don't know what to be. He think he help you be."

That confounded Skye but he kept quiet. She would have to do the talking. He could understand some Absaroka words, but he couldn't describe his life or his hopes to this old man.

Time passed and the evening deepened, but the shaman didn't hurry. The old man touched Skye's hand and closed his eyes. Then he tamped tobacco in a short clay pipe, plucked up an ember with a leaf, lit the tobacco, and smoked.

Then Red Turkey Comb closed his eyes and chanted something that sounded like a supplication.

"He is asking the grandfathers and The One Who Made All Things to give you vision," she said. "You must prepare yourself with your own pleading. Talk to the grandfathers."

Skye nodded. He didn't know where his life was taking him, and perhaps this wattled old shaman might give him answers.

Now and then the old man eyed Skye contemplatively, his gaze searching and direct. Skye felt he had no secrets left, for the old man had fathomed all there was to know of him.

Then, for a long while, Red Turkey Comb closed his eyes and sat so still that Skye wondered whether he had fallen asleep, as old people do. But then he returned from wherever he had been, and began talking softly to Victoria.

"He is honored to have such a man as Mister Skye visit him and seek to know the medicine that flows out of him," she translated. "He sometimes has little to offer, but this time it all came to him clearly, as bright as summer sunlight . . . Mister Skye is a friend of the People, and with his mighty arm will help the People against the Siksika and Lakota. He will be honored by all the Absaroka, and welcome in any village of the People."

She smiled. This was good news to her, even if it excited wild doubts in him.

"Mister Skye will become a name known to all the People of the grasslands. He will be a name known to his own tribe. He will fight many times, sometimes to save himself, but more often to help his own tribe, or the Absaroka, or—his women."

"Women?"

She nodded. "That was what was spoken."

"A wife and daughters."

She smiled and said nothing.

"But I'm planning to go east."

She translated that to Red Turkey Comb, and then translated his voluble reply.

"The past is a broken bowl and cannot hold broth again. The dream that sustained you was a good dream because it gave you life and hope each day on the big waters. But it is gone, and a new destiny is yours. You will be honored. Even the Siksika and Lakota will speak your name with fear. Even the grizzly bear, your brother, will honor you."

Skye stirred restlessly, not liking that.

"Goddamn Skye, you got big medicine!"

Skye nodded skeptically, unsure of what to do next. But the old man stayed him with a wave of the hand, and dug through a parfleche behind him. Then he handed Skye a necklace made of giant grizzly claws, each arched and lethal-looking, and five or six inches long. They were strung on a thong and separated by blue-enameled wooden trade beads. Victoria gasped and then translated.

"Wear this. It will tell the People of your powers," she said.

He handed it to her, and she knotted it behind his neck.

"There is no greater sign," she said.

Red Turkey Comb stood, a signal that this interview was over, and Skye and Victoria bundled themselves and pierced into bitter cold. Skye knew, in the dark, that something had changed.

Chapter 46

Something portentous had happened to Skye in the lodge of the shaman, Red Turkey Comb, but he couldn't fathom what it was. He knew little of Indian belief, and distrusted even that. He tried to make light of the prophetic vision about him, but couldn't. Somewhere, floating just back of his thoughts, was the understanding that his life had changed so his future would, too.

He wore his bearclaw necklace uneasily, feeling odd emanations from it, powers he ascribed to savage superstition that he would soon put behind him. Living in a Crow village could do that to a man. Sometimes he pulled the necklace over his head to examine it and run his fingers over the dark, lethal grizzly claws. Whoever had fashioned this necklace knew the power of those claws. The root of each had been encased in blue tradecloth, and a small hole had been bored in each to take the thong of the necklace. The lustrous blue beads separating the claws added to the beauty of this insignia of power.

But more than beauty stirred him as he ran his blunt

fingers over the necklace. He felt stirrings of things he couldn't put a name to. He remembered walking past the towering grizzly on the trail, past claws just like these that could have shredded his vulnerable flesh, and yet the bear had let him pass, a friend and brother. Now these claws were a bond. He and all the bears of the world were brothers. He had somehow taken into himself the powers of the bear, its strength and resourcefulness, its lordship over all the other creatures that walked.

Was he now a bear? No, he was Barnaby Skye, but a man infused with something new and transforming. He saw it at once in his daily contact with the Absaroka people. Word of his visit to Red Turkey Comb, and the old shaman's seeing, swiftly spread through the Kicked-in-the-Bellies, the news on the lips of the village crier and the source of gossip everywhere. Skye sensed it. The young men, once indifferent or hostile because Skye had spent so much time with one of the most desirable maidens of the village, now stopped and exchanged greetings, and paused to admire his necklace.

Somehow the bearclaw necklace invested Skye with power and prestige and made him an important man among these people. Even Victoria's family was treating him differently, the father less solemn and distant, her brother less imperious. Skye had done nothing to merit this attention, and supposed it was merely pagan superstition at work. In any case, he would be leaving the mountains in a few months. The necklace would be an entertaining curio to show his classmates someday.

He supposed his trapping friends would swiftly put the new camp tender in his place, but it didn't happen. Beckwourth, for instance—the one veteran he thought would make light of the necklace with his usual barbed wit—examined the necklace solemnly and told Skye to live up to what was given him. Sublette studied the necklace, smiled, and added his own mysterious prophecy: "Guess you won't be going east after all, ol' coon. That's good. We need you."

Skye started to protest but fell silent. He wasn't so sure he wanted to go east. He had been thinking about what the shaman had told him. The bowl had been broken and it would no longer hold his old life in it. Who was he now? He worried that in his mind as he went about his tasks, cutting firewood each day, cooking, checking the horses. Who was he? Or rather, what did he want now?

Once, exasperated with himself, he borrowed a small round mirror, a favorite trade item, and studied himself in it, trying to find himself in his own image. He examined his giant nose, long and thick like a hogback ridge, and he found his blue eyes and angular features. But he no longer saw the London boy, and even the sailor was barely a memory. He could no longer conjure up his seaman's life, his tiny bunk, his sullen obedience—most of the time—to imperious officers, his wild, birdlike joy when he had climbed high in the rigging and could see a world that extended beyond the wooden hull of his ship.

Gone now.

In his looking glass he beheld a hardened man with a knowing face, a man ripped from civilization and unlikely to return. An ugly, bearded man in fringed buckskins, who wore his hair loose, or anchored with a red bandanna. A man whose chest bore an ensign that made him a king or a prince in these Absaroka lands. He recognized a new man, and he knew he had been transformed.

Another arctic blast drove them all into their lodges, but now he found himself a frequent guest at the lodge-fires of these people, sometimes with Victoria, often not. The Crows came to him as he cut wood, invited him with gestures or a few words of fractured English or a few Crow words, and then he would spend an evening with one or another clan, often accompanied by veteran trappers. There, in the intimacy of the lodges, he would devour buffalo rib roast with a dozen others and then listen to stories. How these people loved to spin stories! He swiftly gathered there was more to it than entertainment.

These tales conveyed tribal history, taught lessons, explained spiritual mysteries, reaffirmed the power of First Maker and all their other Above Ones, and told of the beginning of the world and the creation of the People.

Then, sometime late in the evening, it befell the grandmothers to tell their own stories, and Skye at first could barely believe what he was hearing, and thought his limited knowledge of the Crow tongue was deceiving him. The old women, some toothless but always grinning, eagerly began wildly bawdy stories, swiftly convulsing their audiences with their humor. How could this be? Skye listened uneasily, glancing at the assorted wives and daughters who were enjoying these unabashed tales about mating, the size of genitals, getting caught with someone, sexual prowess, boastfulness about things that Skye had never heard discussed in mixed company.

And there was Victoria at some of these parties, laughing wickedly at these tales spun by grandmothers. She wasn't like a British girl, either innocent of such things or feigning ignorance. She had always stirred him, and ever since he had first gazed upon her at the rendezvous he had wanted her. But in those summer days, when he knew he would be leaving the mountains, he had set aside those feelings because she was different from the Shoshone girls he had dallied with. He couldn't explain it. Now, in the confines of the lodges, and with a new future being born in him, those feelings flooded back. But of course it was not love, he told himself. How could he love a savage?

But he could. The more he and Victoria learned how to talk to each other, often in a patois of Crow and English words enriched with gestures, the more entranced he was with her sharp-etched humor, her swift tenderness, her many ways of nurturing him, and the promise of delights unimaginable that brimmed from her eyes. He had been a lone man too long. He thought of sharing a lodge with her in the winter's cold and in the high days of summer. He thought of her smooth brown body beside him, her yearnings and his joining in the night, a life together, a family—

How startling it was to think of children. His and Victoria's children! All his days, he had thought of himself as a son, not a father. The realization that he was a grown man, free, no longer just a son, no longer tied to England, astounded him. In all the years in the Royal Navy he had perceived of himself as a youth, but now that frozen image was melting away in the rush of events. At age twenty-one, he was capable of siring his own family, sons and daughters, slim and dark like their mother, blue-eyed like himself. He was a man.

The cold spell dissolved one February day in a rush of warm west winds, and he ventured out again, along with the rest of the Absaroka people. The sun was returning, bit by bit, and the high plains glowed in the afternoons, the brown grasses absorbing the warmth. The air remained chill but was sweet and dry. Soon now William Sublette would tell his brigade that the spring hunt would begin; the ice was melting in the creeks and the beaver would be swimming out of their log homes. The realization made Skye restless. He didn't want to leave this paradise where winter had been tamed and the Absaroka told and retold their stories and he had made many friends.

He did not want to leave Victoria. With the milder weather, they spent more time away from the village, and the sight of her in her gray blanket always melted his heart. They had touched a little—some innate delicacy had made this bonding different from the ones he had experienced with the Shoshone women—but now he ached for her and he was flooded with visions of her with him in the thick, warm buffalo robes. He wanted to hug her and never let go, and he knew she felt the same hungers.

But of course the Absarokas were never alone. Each lodge housed grandparents, a man and his women, children, brothers, sisters. The act of love was done in company, and that was how those things were well known to all. A lodge was black at night, without windows, but the soft noises of love told their own tales to all. How could he endure that? Would he find it intimidating to love her only a few feet from her parents—even if they were married Absaroka fashion? He could not say, but he desperately wanted a lodge of his own, and a sweet privacy with her.

One day William Sublette told his brigade they would leave for the Three Forks country early in March, and trap until the beaver were no longer prime. That was only days away, and the news tore through Skye's soul, wrenching him.

Skye thought about Victoria, and how they had come to each other from such different worlds, but also how they had weathered into each other, spending golden moments, experimenting with words, sometimes saying nothing at all in contented silence. He had to act now or he would lose her. Victoria's parents could give her to any Absaroka warrior at any time. There were many who would gladly leave ponies before the lodge and had eyed Skye as a rival. It was now or never. He wasn't sure it would be a good match—the differences were real. But he loved her. He had never loved anyone before, but he knew he wanted her, would always want her, and would be desolated if he lost her.

He walked out to the herd, which was up the creek a mile or so, and found his mare and yearling colt among them, shaggy, thin, but not in bad shape, all things considered. She shied away from him, but he persisted in walking her down, and eventually he caught and haltered her. The colt came along.

He looked the yearling colt over, finding it big, well-developed, dark and cocky. It had scarcely been handled. But after a while it let Skye touch him, rub its ears, run a hand along its neck under the mane, scratch its jaw. Then Skye slipped a loop over its neck and held tight when it yanked back. The colt stopped resisting sooner than Skye had thought, and let itself be haltered, as it had been the previous summer. He led the colt, tugging firmly when it resisted the pull of the lead rope, breaking it to halter.

He lacked a comb to curry the colt, but perhaps it didn't matter. He had a fine, strong yearling with a friendly eye and a good way of moving. He hoped it would be enough. He led the colt away from its whickering mother, led it back toward the village, led it through the village lanes, now teeming with people who were scraping hides, smoking, fletching arrows or enjoying the mild weather—to the lodge of Victoria's family. And there he tied the pony to a picket, his heart riding on the work of his fingers.

Chapter 47

One memorable afternoon Daniel Ferguson and Peter Ranne walked into the village leading their burdened packhorses. Word raced through the lodges, drawing trappers and the Crows.

Skye heard the news and ran toward the newcomers, not believing it. But there they were, in good flesh, showing no sign of unusual hardship. Even their horses looked pretty decent, though their thick hair could be deceptive.

The trappers whooped and hollered and carried on in a way that Skye, with his British reserve, would never quite get used to. A crowd of Crows gathered, just as curious as the brigade. They had heard the story of Ferguson and Ranne's disappearance and probable death during the bitterest days of December.

"Knew we'd find ye hyar," Daniel Ferguson said. "Only the pass kept us from coming over. Fifty-foot drifts or ye can call me a liar."

"Maybe ten-foot drifts, ol' coon," said Sublette quietly, cheer radiating from him.

"No, fifty footers. No child could get through, so me and Peter, we made snowshoes."

"How'd ye get the horses over?"

"I made snowshoes for mine. Peter made skis for his hosses, and they were some, except his nags couldn't stop on a downslope."

Beckwourth guffawed. Bridger grinned. Skye could see that Bridger was thinking up something equally outlandish, but for the moment Ferguson had him buffaloed.

"What happened, Daniel?" Sublette asked, an edge sharpening his voice. "We went looking. It went hard. We near froze before we gave up."

Daniel Ferguson peered innocently about him, enjoying the crowd. He lifted his beaver cap and took his time, knowing he was the cynosure of their attention.

"You got some tobacco? I could use a smoke," he said.

"Not until rendezvous."

Ferguson looked disappointed. "That was all this child lacked, was a good smoke. We plum had everything else any ol' coon would ever want. We was having fat times, excepting that we lacked a pipeful. That sure was a sore point."

Skye listened skeptically, amused and impatient. This old trapper was going to drag out his story for an hour.

"I had every trapper out looking for you," Sublette said, pointedly. The booshway wasn't going to stand for this much longer.

Ferguson leaned upon his mountain rifle, surveyed his audience again, and apparently judged that it wasn't going to get any larger. "Well, sir, it be like this. Me and Peter, we seen that old storm a-brewing and black-bellied clouds a-comin', so Peter, he says to me, 'Let's git.' So we lit out because that was a mean storm and we were a piece from camp. We didn't git far before it was snowing and blowing, but we pushed along, slipping and sliding, leading our nags and hauling beaver. We got down out of the drainage all right, and got out to the flat country all right, but the snow was coming and I was feeling testy. So

I said to Peter, I says, 'I know a place to go. I saw her once when I come through hyar a few winters ago by my lonesome, dodging Bug's Boys.' "

He paused, letting it be understood that he knew the Three Forks country better than the rest of them.

"Instead of comin' back to camp, we just hightailed on down the Gallatin until I see what I'm lookin' for, a big billow of steam right in the middle of all that falling snow, snow coming down in buckets so we can hardly see a trail.

"So I says to Peter, 'Ol' coon, we've arrived in the middle of summer.' He looks at me like I've gone beaver, but he leads his nags, following me, and pretty soon the steam gets so thick a man can't hardly see, and I says, 'Peter, we're at the gates of July.' "

All this took translating. Skye had never quite fathomed the argot of the trappers, but as near as he could tell, Daniel Ferguson was saying the pair had not only abandoned the area they were trapping, but had hiked far down the Gallatin River instead of heading for camp.

"Hot springs!" bellowed Ranne. "He taken me to hot springs, biling up outa the ground, letting off steam so thick a man couldn't see his own hand. This child stood on the banks of a pool with green grass growing around it, and the horses soon took to it. Snow falling all over, steam rising, snow vanishing into the steam, and heat coming at me.

"Well, old Daniel and me, we unloaded them hoss, unloaded our gear, unloaded our plews, stripped buck naked, and tippytoed into that thar pool until we was plumb up to our noses in hot water. That water, she felt so good it was better'n rendezvous. Pretty soon I'm so warm I've gotta go down to the cooler end of this hyar pool. It's snowing, and a few flakes land on my hair, but no matter. It's like walking through the pearly gates. I had me a soak, and old Daniel had him a soak, and pretty soon we got to thinkin' we should head back to camp—but we can't. We can't get out. It's too cold out. The snow, she quits, and a breeze comes up so sharp and cold that I'da freezed up solid if I stepped out.

"I look around, and it's plain this place is known to somebody; there's a few shelters around, an old lodge standing, some buffler hides over frames—things like that. A Blackfeet resort, that's what I'm thinking, and I'm glad it's January and all them Bug's Boys are hiding in their lodges. So I says to old Daniel, 'Old boy, it's getting too late and too dark and too cold. I guess we'd just better suffer all this misery and go back to camp in the morning. Them horses is fine—they got all the green grass they can swaller, growing along the banks where it stays warm.' "

Ferguson nodded. "I reckoned we'd fetch pneumonia if we climbed out and tried to go through all that snow back to camp. So we stayed the night. Next morning, it was clear and so cold a man'd freeze just trying to put his duds on, so we just hunkered in that hot water. I was getting a little wrinkled, like a raisin, but it didn't matter. I was getting so hongry my belly was a-howling, but we couldn't get out. I thought, old boy, this hyar's how ye'll go under, starvin' to death in a hot pool ye can't get outa."

Ranne broke in. "Them elk is what kept us a-going. They come for the heat. They see us and don't care. They come just to stand in that pool up to their bellies, and stay warm on the coldest day of the year. Steam's billowing up, but we see elk all over, keeping their toes warm. So, Daniel, he swims over to the bank to get old Jezebel, his rifle, and he kills us a cow elk. We got eats—if only we can get out and gut it and carve on it and build us a fire— but we're plumb stuck in the water. It's so cold we can't even think about cooking elk over a fire, and we're thinking maybe we could bile some elk in our pool, but it's not that hot. So we just stay up to our noses, and feel our skin wrinkle and cook, and starve."

The booshway interrupted. "We were looking for you. It frostbit every man," he said, tautly. "We searched every drainage, fired shots and got no answer, looked for a message—and finally left, every man among us thinking you'd gone under."

"I know, I know. But we couldn't get out of that pool," Ferguson said.

"And besides," said Ranne, "we got us some company."

Skye could see the few Crows who knew some English try to explain all this to the crowd of Kicked-in-the-Bellies solemnly taking in the palaver.

"Company?" asked Beckwourth. "Probably Bug's Boys."

"Bug's Girls," said Peter Ranne.

That sure got attention.

"Twelve of 'em," said Daniel Ferguson.

"Beeeuties," said Ranne. "All about seventeen, eighteen, and fairer specimens of the Wilderness Tribes no coon ever set sight upon."

Some of the Crows growled.

"Ahhh, got to the meat of the story," said Beckwourth.

"They didn't see us old boys at first on account of the steam, so they set up their two lodges, all the time jabbering and carrying on, and pretty soon they doff their blankets and capotes. And then they doff all the rest, and stand there plumb beauteous in the mist, the fairest damsels we ever did see . . ."

"And then this old coon sneezed," Ferguson said.

"And they seen us," Ranne said. "They squeal, and then look us over, and then they decide we ain't takin' scalps and come on in. Well . . . it be some party. I don't reckon I ever been to a nicer party. Men and wimmin get along better in hot spas."

"We got to know 'em all. They's Piegans, they say, off for a lark. They was sociable, and they invited us to share our elk in their lodges after the plunge, and so Daniel, he gets one lodge and six beauties, and me, I get the other lodge and six beauties, and that's how come we never did get back to camp."

Skye listened, rapt, and couldn't quite imagine why the trappers were laughing and hooting and making light of the story. Unless it wasn't true . . . was this a mountaineer joke? The part about the hot springs seemed true enough—but what about the Blackfeet women? Had they arrived in a blizzard? Had they invited the trappers into their lodges after a plunge?

Skye watched Beckwourth and Bridger slap the missing trappers on the back and make sly jokes. Those Yank mountaineers had their odd ways. Skye could not say why bawdiness made him uneasy. Maybe it was simply that he had spent so much of his young life in a ship's brig that he never learned much about women. All he knew was that for him, these things were serious and sacred, and he hoped Victoria would feel the same way. Maybe he alone in the world thought that a man and a woman should form a union of hearts before they formed a union of bodies. Maybe the world would laugh at him. He knew the Crow people would. Maybe Victoria would, too. Wasn't she born to them?

The Crow, still translating, all broke into broad smiles, for this was a story tailored to delight these bawdy people. Skye realized that it didn't matter whether the tale was true; there was so much fun in the telling and the imagining.

Only William Sublette didn't laugh, and then he finally surrendered, too, the torment of the search forgotten in the joy of seeing two boon companions alive and well after several brutal months of winter.

It turned out that the wayward trappers spent those months at the hot springs, minus their fantasy women, feasting on the animals that came there to escape the bitter cold, trapping beaver in nearby flowages, and generally having a grand time until they could make it over the winter-bound pass to the Crow country.

Skye searched the crowd for Victoria, wanting to know what she thought of all this. But he didn't see her. He wandered back through the village to the lodge of her parents, his thoughts far from the two returned trappers and their alleged bacchanal. The yearling was gone; it had been accepted by her father and mother.

Chapter 48

In one dazzling moment Skye knew his life had forever changed. He peered at the lodge, somnolent in the winter sun, and at the place where his colt had been tied, and wondered. No one came to greet him. Perhaps no one was within.

He thought of Victoria, his promised one. He ached to sweep her into his arms and crush her to him. He ached to talk with her, feel her sharp voice in his ears, rejoice in her wild humor. Now he wanted to hear her whispers in the night.

"Victoria!" he cried, but the lodge did not reply.

"I love you!" he cried, but the busy Crow village ignored him.

What did it all mean? What would happen? He looked about, seeing the ordinary life of a winter-bound village. Smoke drifting from lodges. Curs meandering from lodge to lodge, sniffing cookfires, looking for bits to eat. He saw old men wrapped in blankets shuffling from one place to another. Was this the life he had committed himself to? Had he made a desperate mistake?

A worm of regret crawled through his belly. What had he done? Had he tossed aside a life of achievement just because some hot desire boiled in his loins?

He sighed. The bowl had been broken and no longer held his life within it. Whatever he had been—English youth, seaman, prisoner, merchant's son—all that was gone. There was only the present and the future. Only Victoria. Only the mountains. Only the trapping, the rendezvous, the life of a wilderness vagabond.

A grandmother shuffled by, paused, grinned toothlessly, and touched his bearclaw necklace. Then she patted him on the arm. The necklace meant something to them all. Or rather, Red Turkey Comb's perception of his power and destiny meant something to these people. Surely it had meant something to Victoria's father, who had accepted his single colt. A beautiful maid like Victoria might have won a bride price of many horses and a stack of other gifts from an eager suitor.

He had bear medicine, but what was that? Did it mean only that he was strong? He couldn't answer that, but maybe in time he would know. The grizzly was king of beasts. Skye knew he was no king of beasts, and no match even for the warriors of this village, or the hard mountaineers in his brigade.

He drifted through the village, looking for Beckwourth, who would know what all this meant. No one among them knew the Crows better. Beckwourth would probably be in the small lodge inhabited by Pine Leaf, the warrior woman of the Absaroka, who had been Beckwourth's lover for years. According to the legend, Pine Leaf had vowed never to marry and to become a warrior for the Crow nation until she had revenged the tribe for past losses. She wasn't large but she was nimble, a fine archer and horsewoman and lancer, and had fought brilliantly beside the male warriors, often rallying them when all seemed lost, and becoming a famous woman among all the plains tribes. A maiden she might be, but no virgin, and she had welcomed the rogue Beckwourth into her arms, something that Beckwourth bragged about amidst all his other bragging. Skye wondered if a tenth of what Beckwourth said about himself was true.

Skye found the lodge next to a grove of giant cottonwoods, and scratched gently on the door flap, as was the custom. Beckwourth himself pulled the flap aside.

"Mister Skye," he said. "Come in."

Skye entered and waited while his eyes adjusted to the darkness. He beheld Pine Leaf sitting crosslegged, wearing a simple doeskin shift. She motioned Skye to sit at her right, the traditional place of honor. Beckwourth, lean, mottled brown, and mocking, settled down on the other side of her.

"Do you know the beauteous Pine Leaf?" Beckwourth asked.

"We have met."

"Ah, behold a woman known across the Plains. She has counted coup more times than most warriors in the village. She has turned routs into victories. She has bestowed her favors on Beckwourth and no other. Beckwourth treads where no Crow chief or warrior treads." Beckwourth laughed softly.

"I am honored to be in the presence of such a great one," Skye replied slyly.

Pine Leaf obviously understood all this, and smiled. Scars laced her lean, hawkish face and bare arms, giving credence to her reputation as a warrior.

They bantered a while more, and then Skye turned to the issue that had brought him. "My colt has been accepted by Victoria's father. What happens next?" he asked.

"Accepted, eh? Why, you do what comes naturally." Beckwourth grinned, his even white teeth gleaming in his dusky face.

"I need serious advice, sir."

"If you don't know how to do it, you shouldn't get married."

Skye stared at the lodge door. Beckwourth wasn't going to help him. The rogue would make a joke of it, turn something sacred into carnal humor.

But Pine Leaf intervened, and began talking quietly in the Absaroka tongue to Beckwourth. Skye could understand just enough to catch the drift.

"She says it's time to teach you about the customs of the Absaroka, so I'm delegated. She says Many Quill Woman's a mighty big catch because she's so pretty and has good medicine; half the young men in the village'd give every pony in their herds for her, but the other half think she's got a sharp tongue and don't want nothing to do with her. She's plumb mean to 'em. That mouth of hers is some."

Skye laughed. Victoria's sharp tongue was one of the things he loved about her. She could gut a braggart faster than she could gut a deer, and one of her targets had been Gentleman Jim Beckwourth himself.

"Now, here's the way the stick floats. Many Quill Woman's gonna disappear until the big day. You won't lay eyes on her until then. Her daddy'll send word to you to fetch her at an appointed time—likely, sundown, day after tomorrah. And there she'll be, all dolled up in finery."

"What do I do then?"

"Skye, is your brain solid wood?"

"It's Mister Skye, sir."

Beckwourth grinned malevolently. "You haul her off to your lodge and honeymoon."

"But what of the marriage ceremony?"

Beckwourth chortled. "It isn't like that. You get Many Quill Woman, you take up with her."

"No ceremony?"

Beckwourth shook his head. "Oh, her pap'll have the town crier announce it and they'll have them a parade.

And when you wander over to the lodge, he'll give you a few things—the family's gifts to the new couple."

"Such as?"

"Well, it's traditional to give a small lodge, and some ponies to haul it, and the furnishings, along with the bride."

"A lodge? Ponies? I just gave them my colt."

"A bride's family don't stint to set her up, Skye."

"Will there be a feast? Any formalities?"

"Mebbe so. They'll show her off to the whole village. Mebbe ride her through the village, her brothers leading her horse. Let all the village see her in her finery. And they'll show the whole village what they're gonna give you—the lodge, the ponies, and stuff. Mebbe stop at Arapooish's lodge for a little showing off."

"I haven't anything but the clothing on my back. I'd hate to come to my own wedding looking like this."

"Mebbe you should talk to Sublette. You should be looking your best."

"Do I bring her parents a gift?"

"You already have. That little stud colt told 'em you want their daughter. Now, Skye, there's a custom you should know about. From now on, never speak to your mother-in-law, Digs the Roots, and she'll never speak to you. If you see her, look away. If you need to talk to her, send the message through someone else. Mothers-in-law got nothing to do with sons-in-law. Not ever. Except me, of course. I talk to Pine Leaf's maw all the time. These Absaroka let me do whatever I want because I'm a chief. Me and Pine Leaf, we run the wars around heah."

"But you're not married."

Beckwourth laughed gently. "You're bright sometimes, Mister Skye. When it comes to mothers-in-law, these Absaroka are a lot smarter than you white plantation owners."

Skye shrugged. He knew nothing of that. In England he had been too young to consider such things, but he remembered his grandparents, and all the love they had bestowed upon his parents and himself and his sisters until his grandmother had died in her early fifties.

Skye visited a while more with the rogue, and then retreated into the cold twilight, enjoying its peace and the quiet of another winter's night. The earliest stars had punctured the veil of the heavens and glittered above. This aching, mysterious wilderness had become his world, and he was more familiar with the barking of a wolf than he was with the rumble of a passing hansom cab. The starkness of the land appealed to something wolfish in him, something lonely and uncivilized, something that could not be broken to harness. He hadn't known, when he slid into the Columbia long before, that he was saying good-bye not just to the Royal Navy, but to civilization. He grew aware of the necklace on his breast, a device imbued with mysterious power that made him a man among the Crow people. He touched the claws, feeling their sharp length, the violence in them, the sheer animal force they conveyed to him.

He thought of Victoria, as fierce as the land and as wild, the ferocity of her love and loyalty so bright and bold that it had blistered his pallid British ideals. She was a savage woman to match the savageness of his heart. Now she would be his mate. Once he would have chosen some oatmealy English girl, now he would be bored by any woman who hadn't lived close to death and starvation and war and the wild beasts of the fields and forests.

Skye looked into the darkening skies and saw Victoria. He peered into the shadowed cottonwoods and found her there. He studied the ridges where the wolves and coyotes and painters prowled, and saw her spirit striding beside them. He saw her in the icy haze, in the glowing lodges emitting sour cottonwood smoke from their nestled poles. He saw her in the sweetness of the village, in the umber faces around the lodgefires at night, in the exquisite quill-work on a bodice, in the rabbit-fur calf-high moccasins these people wore through their winters. He saw her in the ancients shuffling through their night errands, and in the children scurrying to their homes at the end of a day.

He did not know what would happen next, or when he might be permitted to carry her away with him, off to some private place, where he could hold her in ways sweet and sacred. But he would know soon.

Chapter 49

Skye found himself in a whirl of activity he little understood. Victoria simply vanished, and he wondered which of the many lodges hid her and why he could not see her. February petered out and March rushed in on cold winds and bold blue skies.

The old women of the village smiled at him now, and the children gawked as he passed by. Beckwourth told him that Victoria's family was prominent; her father was an important subchief who had counted many coups and was a leader of the Lumpwood Warrior Society.

Skye learned that Victoria's own mother, Kills the Deer, had died two winters earlier, that Victoria had a brother and two sisters, that Victoria belonged to the Otter Clan, and that her family was the caretaker of one of the village's most sacred medicine bundles, which was opened each spring at the first thunder.

He wondered why the family had accepted his single pony and not the lavish offerings of so many of the village's young men eager to win a beautiful maiden from an important family. He couldn't entirely ascribe it to the word of the shaman, Red Turkey Comb. There had to be more to it than that. Skye did not know and supposed he never would know. There would always be a gulf between the Absarokas and himself.

One afternoon he found William Sublette and sought the brigade leader's counsel.

"She'll be the only woman with the brigade, sir. Does that bother you?"

"Bother me? She'll make the work lighter, Mister Skye. And keep you in the mountains where you belong. She'll do what I couldn't do: give you a reason to be a mountaineer. Davey Jackson's brigade has a dozen Metis women in it. We put the Creole trappers with wives in his brigade because it would face less trouble over there among the Shoshone and Nez Perce. We're in dangerous country here, Skye. You and your bride know that."

Skye grinned. "What we're getting is another warrior, sir. She's a good hand with a bow, and I aim to teach her how to shoot—after I learn."

Sublette smiled. "I'm counting on it. Now, Skye, there's something all the old boys want to give you. Come along."

Dutifully, Skye followed the brigade leaders to the council lodge that housed so many of the engagés. There they had all assembled, grinning mischievously as they lounged around the lodgefire, and Skye feared he'd get a hazing of the sort reserved for bridegrooms.

But they sat about awkwardly, even shyly, tongue-tied for once. Even the veterans, like Tom Fitzpatrick, suddenly looked awkward.

Finally Peter Ranne cleared his throat, looking like he was being led to the gallows.

"The coons reckoned a man should have himself some fancy duds for his wedding," he began. "So, the outfit, we got you some skins sewn up by the women hyar. Weddin' skins, that's how we call 'em."

They unfolded a fringed elkskin shirt, tanned to a soft

gold, with quillwork across the chest. The shirt was wondrously crafted, and decorated with bear paw insignia.

"Put her on," yelled someone.

Skye did, marveling at the fit and the gentleness of the leather. They gave him fringed leggins, too, matching the golden shirt, and then a pair of high moccasins with bullhide soles.

Suddenly Barnaby Skye was overwhelmed. These were friends. They had dug deep to offer him a treasure like this. These were the best friends he had ever known.

"I—thank you," he said, hoarsely. He could not say more.

"You're a straight shooter, plumb center," said Bridger. "You got a maiden a man'd die for. Hyar now, wear these skins—at least until ye get to your little honeymoon bower and take 'em off."

Men laughed, and Skye sensed a yearning among them. Certain Crow women they could have for a bit of foofaraw. Love, marriage, ties to the tribe were something else, something large and tender and misty in their hearts. These mountaineers had opened their purses and wrought a miracle. He marveled that the village women could have sewn and quilled the shirt and leggins so swiftly.

"I've talked to Arapooish," Sublette said. "Tomorrah, Mister Skye, you'll be married. The next day, we're off. Sorry to cut short your honeymoon, but the streams are thawing and there's beaver to trap."

"It won't stop our honeymoon," Skye said.

"Ye'll be plumb tuckered out," volunteered Black Harris. "Tending Victoria and tending camp."

Men laughed. One by one they stood, stretched, slapped Skye on the back or shook his hand. He had expected a rough and raucous hazing from these ruffians of the mountains, but they had celebrated his happiness tenderly and shyly, with a wistfulness in their manner.

"Well, old child, ye come a long way," said Bridger.

Skye nodded. Could the man about to take a bride be

the same man who had slipped into the icy waters of the Columbia, determined to escape slavery or die?

He wandered the village itchily that afternoon, trying to fathom its mysterious ways, sometimes lonely, sometimes angry that he couldn't find Victoria, sometimes feeling left out because no one told him anything, or what he should do, or where he should be, and when. Couldn't these Absarokas even tell him what to expect?

But then, in·his restless wanderings, he discovered a small new lodge apart from the village, erected in a park surrounded by cottonwoods. The lodgepoles had been newly hewn and debarked. The lodge, of fine buffalohide, bore the track of the bear, brown prints around its lower perimeter. Skye knew, suddenly, that this was a gift, his new home. Tears welled up unbidden, and he was glad no one saw them.

He slept in fits that night, doubts crawling through him like worms. It wasn't too late to stop this. He could back out. He could finish up his time with the brigade and go east. He could hew to his ancient dream. What business had he with a savage woman and savage people? The dangerous wilderness would only murder him in time—or bore him, or leave him an outcast, forever cut off from his own kind.

But then in the deeps of the night, he knew he would not stop this wedding. The seaman, the deserter, the old Barnaby Skye, never had a life, and he was abandoning nothing important. The new Barnaby Skye would have everything a man could ever want.

That bracing morning, marred only by overcast, he washed in the bitter-cold creek, shuddering while he cleansed himself, and dressed in his new buckskins. He marveled at their golden beauty and warmth. Carefully, he lowered his bearclaw medicine necklace over his head and straightened it on his chest. The cruel claws fanned outward, emblematic of something that Red Turkey Comb, and all these Crows, had discerned in him. That something was what had won Victoria. The necklace seemed a heavy burden to him in a way, binding him to these people even as it required that he live up to the message embedded in those claws.

The men around him watched silently, somehow pleased by the sight of their new comrade Skye decked out in mountain finery and ready for his bride.

The morning ticked by and nothing much happened, although Skye discerned swift furtive activity in the village. He paced through the herd, checking up on his mare, walked the creek, and then returned to his lodge. A wan sun drove off the overcast, and by noon a bright warmth had settled on the village of the Kicked-in-the-Bellies. Then, midafternoon, the village crier, an old man with great bellows, rode among the lodges, bawling his message for all to hear. Skye stood before the council lodge, still uncertain. But even as he waited along with his mountaineering friends, who had all gauded themselves with red bandannas and ribbons for this occasion, Skye beheld a parade. At least it seemed like one. Victoria's father, Walks Alone, and brother in all their ceremonial regalia slowly rode by. Their groomed horses shone in the winter sun and danced proudly.

Skye's new father-in-law radiated power from his stocky frame. He wore a buffalo-horn headdress and carried a lance wrapped in red tradecloth. A small medicine bundle hung from his neck. His son, Victoria's brother, wore two eagle feathers downward, ensigns of war prowess, and passed by proudly. He was older than Victoria but her sisters were younger.

Behind them rode Victoria, looking so beautiful that Skye's heart lurched. She was regal. Her small, spare frame radiated pride and joy this nuptial day. Her black hair glinted in the coy sunlight, two braids falling over her breast, each braid tied with a bright blue ribbon. A streak of vermilion divided her forehead. For this occasion she wore a loose dress of whited doeskin, so full in the skirt that she could ride astride her glistening dappled horse. Intricate green quillwork decorated the bodice, and the pattern was repeated along the fringed hem that fell over high bead-decorated moccasins. She was fragile, proud, joyous, and commanding all at once, and something tender radiated from her.

Skye saw her and loved her. She pretended not to see him at first, but then she gazed at him. That glance, so direct and searching, shot a flood of love and eagerness between them. He ached to reach out and help her off her lively mount. A boy followed, leading three horses, each of them laden with buffalo robes. Others of her clan followed, each in dazzling ceremonial dress.

The villagers crowded close, exclaiming at the lavish parade, studying Victoria, eyeing Skye, whispering and smiling. Others walked by, men and women dressed in dazzling finery, one after another. The Crows were a handsome people, he thought. And in their own fashion they were clad in their form of military dress uniforms and ballgowns, artfully fashioned from tradecloth, beads, quills, leather, feathers, and dyes. He loved them; his heart sang out to each of these relatives as the parade wound by.

It did not stop before his lodge but continued toward the great lodge of Arapooish, who waited there along with his many wives and children. The parade didn't stop there either, but continued to the small lodge of Red Turkey Comb, where the old shaman greeted them with a simple nod, and then around the village, four times in all, for that was the sacred number. Then, at last, Victoria's father drew up his horse before Skye.

A great crowd had collected. All the village, it seemed. Skye didn't know what he should do and hoped they would prompt him. But it turned out that he didn't need to do anything.

They helped Victoria dismount and brought her to him. He had never seen a woman so beautiful or radiant. Her golden flesh glowed. Her bright dark eyes saw only Skye and held him in her vision. He saw love. He beheld her slim figure in the soft, delicate white doeskin, and then he reached out to her, clasping her small hands in his big ones. She smiled. Her hands felt right and good in his. He gazed upon her until the world fell away and he saw only her, and saw her joy, and knew that what he was experiencing was sacred.

Then the youths who had followed her in the procession presented Victoria and Skye with three fat horses, two of them dragging travois laden with wedding gifts: robes and horse tack, a willow flute and drum, moccasins, parfleches, gourd rattles, a reed backrest, the tawny pelt of a mountain lion, half a dozen snowy ermine, elkskin gloves, and several pairs of moccasins. Villagers exclaimed. Victoria smiled. She said nothing, as if for once she was required to hold her sharp tongue in abeyance.

Skye didn't know what to do or say, but he had been around the tribes enough to know that he could add his own ceremony to theirs, and they would honor him for it, and enjoy his contribution. He raised a hand.

"My friends, my brothers, my sisters, my parents, my children: with this union I have become one of the People and you are in my heart even as Many Quill Woman has entered my heart. To her I pledge my love, my life, and all that I am and will be. She is my love, now and forever. And you are my clan and my family."

"Sonofabitch!" said Victoria.

The trappers laughed. The crowd smiled.

A few Absarokas began to drift away, and Skye sensed that they were unhappy the pale man from across the sea had taken the belle of the village from them. But others lingered on, especially the old women, wreathed in smiles and filled with blessings. Skye couldn't understand their words, but he certainly grasped their messages.

His mountaineer friends awkwardly shook hands or clapped him on the back or permitted themselves a bawdy comment that set Victoria grinning. And then they, too, drifted away in the late afternoon quiet. The wedding festival was over. It had been a parade, a way of making the event public. Stops at the lodges of the chiefs and criers and shamans. A display of a family and a clan's glory. Some gifts for the couple.

He and Victoria gazed at each other in the gathering silence, and she smiled.

"Well, Mister Skye?"

He could not speak. He drew her to him, and she responded.

"Let's go to the lodge," he said.

"We got horses."

"They can wait."

She laughed bawdily, but she plucked up the halter lines and tugged the horses along the way to the little lodge in a quiet corner of the woods. "Somebody gotta have sense," she said to Skye. "We picket the horses, and then you show me what a goddamn grizzly bear you are. Eiieee!"

She laughed until she doubled over, and Skye couldn't understand why it was all so funny, but he roared.

Chapter 50

Many Quill Woman slid out from the warm robes, wrapped a fine red blanket around her nakedness, and stepped into the cold dawn to welcome the day. She loved the first light, the sacred moment when the Sun Father caressed the breast of the Earth Mother.

She loved the quiet, the mists of night, the grayness that slowly yellowed and rosed into color. She peered sharply at the slumbering camp, her senses seeking anything amiss. She saw and heard nothing. The horses dozed. The trappers slept, all but one. But this was always the most dangerous moment, the time when the Siksika dogs howled down upon the unwitting to murder and steal. William Sublette knew it, too, and habitually arose before first light to watch and wait. He was a good chief.

He stood before his hut, absorbing the rhythms of the new day there at the Three Forks, the beaver-rich wetlands where the streams joined to form the Big River, which the pale men called the Missouri. He nodded. She hurried to the leafless brush, braced for the cold water that would drive the langorous night from her lithe body, and performed her ablutions.

Numbed, she hurried back to her small lodge, dropped her blanket, and dove into the thick robes, nestling against her hairy man. White man had so much more hair all over than her people, and it amused her. She had married a hairy bear. He stirred and drew her to him until her small breasts pressed against him. They would not mate now; they would draw strength and love from each other to nurture them through the day.

His big paws traced the lumps of her spine, his rough hands pleasuring her smooth flesh. She caressed his cheeks, toyed with his growing beard, and played with his shoulders.

"Victoria," he said, and she was gladdened. She loved her new name. He had said it was the name of an English princess who would someday be queen of his people across the Big Water. She marveled at that. The Absaroka had never had a woman chief.

"No goddamn Siksika this day," she said.

"Someday they'll come. It's still too cold."

"I'll kill some."

He hugged her tight. "You're good with your bow. We'll do some more shooting, and soon you'll be better than I am with a rifle."

That pleased her. He was teaching her to shoot and she was very good as long as she could rest the heavy barrel on something solid. Someday she would be a warrior woman, like Pine Leaf, and help her man in times of trouble.

She nestled her head into the hollow of his shoulder, content. These two moons had not been easy, and she hadn't anticipated the strange, bewildering world she had entered when she and Skye had become mates. The very morning following their marriage the big chief Sublette had marched his trappers westward into Siksika lands, and she had barely found time to say good-bye to her people. It had torn her heart to leave her Kicked-in-the-

Bellies behind and head away with these pale Goddamns into a fate and life she couldn't even fathom.

That tormented dawn after their wedding, following a sweet and merry night in which she made Skye groan and laugh and cry, they had heard the call of the chief, Sublette, outside the lodge. Muttering darkly, her bearman had dressed, and she had thrown on an old calico dress, grabbed a blanket, and then had swiftly dismantled the new lodge, storing the seven lodgepoles travois-fashion on one pony, and the lodge cover and their few possessions on another travois. Around her, bearded trappers, breathing frosty plumes in the icy air, wrestled packs onto mules, saddled, damned the First Maker—that was the thing that always amazed her—and departed when the sun was well up and the sleepy Absaroka village could observe their passage.

Ah, those first days were hard! Even now, she hated to remember them. There had been so much she hadn't thought about. She was the sole woman in a brigade of the pale men. And she found herself responsible for the sole lodge and household among them. The rest of these hardy wild men slept under blankets in the frosty night, or built half-shelters of canvas, or erected crude huts. They were crazy. She and her man would enjoy the comfort of a tiny lodge with a fire in its belly to warm them.

She had no one to talk to except Skye. Maybe a word sometimes with Beckwourth, who mangled her language and privately laughed at her people. But no other woman. She ached to chatter with Absaroka women. That was how the chores vanished and the work was made light. But there was only Skye, and often he was so busy cutting wood, or skinning and stretching beaver pelts, or cooking, that she couldn't even talk to him. She had wandered disconsolately through the camp each day, waiting for the nights, desolated with her loneliness, an alien among these wild men.

They had treated her well enough but they didn't understand her and she didn't understand them. And Sublette eyed her, or the lodge, as if waiting for the chance to condemn, or to tell Skye he was delaying the brigade, or that Skye and his woman were burdening the whole outfit. She knew that, and it chilled her, so she wrestled ferociously with her chores, the horses, the erecting and dismantling of their little lodge. She would not bring shame upon her man.

Nor was that the end of the trouble. They had eyed her hungrily, and studied Skye enviously, their thoughts filling their bearded faces. The all wanted a warm lodge and a woman, but there was Skye, the least among them, with both and it made them bitter. She saw it, even though they spoke another tongue. Some of them made Skye suffer. He was camp tender, and they made him work all the harder and found fault with all he did. She knew enough of the Goddamn tongue to know they were shooting word-arrows into him. But he smiled and said little. Only when they crossed a certain line, saying things about her, or how Skye and Victoria spent their nights, did her bearman rear up and make them back away.

She liked that. Skye had been slow to anger and endured all sorts of demeaning things—if they were made in jest. But he was brother of the grizzly, and sometimes he became a bear, and the trappers learned that Skye had his limits and could roar if they pressed him too hard.

They brought in many beaver—this untrapped country was thick with them—and Skye worked until he dropped, fleshing and stretching, cooking beaver tail, cutting wood, cleaning camp. She assuaged her loneliness by helping him, taking over much of the cooking, making moccasins for the trappers, chopping cottonwood limbs, and sometimes hunting in her free moments, using her bow and arrows expertly to bring down an occasional doe or buck.

After a while she had been rewarded with a different sort of look from the chief, Sublette, and then smiles, and then affectionate greetings. The men changed, too. Now

Bridger or Fitzpatrick would pause at her fire and exchange insults with her. She discovered they loved insults, and she had hoarded up an armory of bad words to cuss them with. The Absaroka didn't have any bad words, but the Goddamns did, and it tickled her to loose them like thunderbolts whenever they came around her.

As the old moon passed, and the new one came, she knew she had won them. She was still lonely. Her heart cried for her people. She ached to hear her own tongue instead of this awful English she despised. But things were better, and the trappers were happy because they were making beaver and hoarding up some money to squander at rendezvous on spirits and women and shirts and blankets and shining new traps and rifles. She ached for the rendezvous herself—because then she could be with her own people. All she wanted was friends.

She drew tight against Skye, and he responded.

"You know, Victoria, marrying you was the best thing I ever did," he said. "You've given me a new life—and it's better than the one that filled my dreams so long."

And then she wasn't lonely, at least for the moment. And because he was happy, she was, too.

"Mister Skye," she said. "There's you and me, you and me. You got bear medicine. I got the magpie. Sonofabitch!"

Author's Notes

This novel inaugurates a new Skye's West series in which Barnaby Skye is a young mountain man in the Rockies. The new series will cover the period from 1826, when he arrived in North America, to the time he became a guide in the late 1840s. The first eight Skye's West novels were set in the 1850s and 1860s, when Skye was a guide and a western legend.

Jedediah Smith, who appears in this story, was not only a giant of the fur trade, but one of the preeminent explorers of the unknown American West. After the 1826 rendezvous he embarked on a long, perilous journey in which he sought a route to Mexican California. He found one, but at great cost. By the time he returned to the 1828 rendezvous, he had lost nearly all his men, first to Indians in the Mohave desert, and then to Indians in what is now Oregon. While his men were more or less under arrest in California, he made a perilous trip to the 1827 rendezvous to report to his partners, nearly losing his life and those of his two companions en route. He himself died a few years later on the Santa Fe Trail, the probable victim of Comanches.

I have depicted legendary mountain men such as Tom Fitzpatrick and Jim Bridger fictionally here, but have attempted to portray their well-known traits accurately.

—Richard S. Wheeler
August, 1996